NAPOLÉON'S REVENGE!

A PSYCHOLOGICAL THRILLER

BY

D.K. Beyer

PublishAmerica
Baltimore

ISBN: 1-60441-605-X
PUBLISHED BY PUBLISHAMERICA, LLLP
www.publishamerica.com
Baltimore

Printed in the United States of America

"Never interrupt your enemy when he is making a mistake."
Napoleon Bonaparte

I would like to thank good friend Joe Alger for his support, and encouragement; he believed in me more than I did. Thanks, Joe.

Chapter 1—Day One
THE DOUBLE PHONE CALL

Arthur Wellington Wellesley or Wellsy as most called call him was a nervous wreck and it wasn't even ten o'clock, yet. He had been a jumble of nerves for the past two hours. He looked again at his gold-plated Movado Luno watch for the seventh time in six minutes. The minute hand could not move fast enough for him as he waited for her call. She said—promised—she'd call at exactly ten with her answer. She promised no games, too. Her answer would be either a straight up yes, or no; nothing in-between. He tried looking at the clock on the wall. It read the same as his Movado Luno, 9:52. "Alexandria," he mumbled, "will you please call?" Then, fear swept over him, again. *She could; she might just say no.* And just like that, he didn't want the phone to ring. A *yes* and he was in heaven, on top of the world; a *no* and he was in torment, hell.

Twenty-eight year old, Alex sat on the loveseat next to the yellow telephone. She looked up at the clock. She was sure of her answer, but how should she tell him. *Just blurt it out!* No, that was too ordinary; Alexandria Mae Southerland was far too sophisticated for that response. She tingled as she thought about the situation. She decided to dial and let it just go as it was meant to be. She picked up the receiver and dialed four of the seven numbers, and quickly hung up, again, for the second time. "Grrrr," she said, as she thought about his *job!* "Why can't you just quit," she stated rather than asked to the open air of her apartment. She loved him so! Nevertheless, she hated his all encompassing job! That was the conflict; he would never give it up. He was already married, married to that badge of honor.

It took all the courage Wellsy had to not answer on the first ring. But, before the second ring, his cell phone chimed in as well. He grabbed the phone beside the chair. "Hello, Alex, is that you?" She gushed '*yes*,' back at him. "Hold on, my cell is blasting away. It's the Captain." *Grrr*, Alex thought. She was taken aback, but she knew he was on call. He was always on call, twenty-four seven. Just give me a second Alex!" She grudgingly understood. She hated it. She loved him, and hated his job with the same intense passion; opposite ends of the spectrum, naturally! The fact was she admired his quick advancement in the department. He was brighter than bright. He was able to solve any crime. His mind was intoxicatingly bright. He could outthink anyone, and that was a great asset, but...

Wellesley took the Captain's call. It was short, only 32 seconds, long enough. Too long for her! He hung up the cell and snatched up the home phone, again. He explained he had to roll. "Homicide," she asked? He responded in the affirmative. She gave an expletive back and rang off. Thirty-two year old Lieutenant Wellesley's response to his hopeful engagement to Alex would have to wait. He was already a ball of nerves, yet he had to put that aside. Alexandria, after ringing off, sat and sobbed, thinking, *maybe I shouldn't*, after all.

Wellesley jumped into his 2008 beryl green Jeep and shot north up 337, Hampton Boulevard headed toward the Old Dominion University campus, which stretched from the Elizabeth River to the Lafayette River in Norfolk, Virginia. Although the college is situated in a metropolitan setting, the land offers a small-college look and feel, with tree-lined walkways offering plenty of room for someone to find quick hideaway and, or, a quick escape; if, when needed.

Once on campus, Lieutenant Wellesley headed toward Barksdale Field, near the location of Landrum Hall. Landrum—an all female Hall dormitory—lay in central location of the campus, making it an easy walk to nearly anything on campus. The dorm is situated directly between the old and newer part of the campus. While Landrum was the perfect location for campus living, it was also the perfect location for the perpetrator, if he was working, alone!

It wasn't hard to find his way. The former Dominion graduate got off on West 43rd Street to and proceeded towards Elkhorn. From there he could already see the blue, red and yellow lights flashing against the dark clouds from law enforcement vehicles over a half mile away. *How can there be so many lights*, he pondered.

Upon arrival, three campus police units, and several other department vehicles lay before his eyes: two units from the Detective Division, one from ViCAP (Violent Crimes Against Persons) and another from Sexual Assault and Family Violence. There was also a FBI unit present from ViCAP as well. The Norfolk police and the FBI had an agreement to coordinate, collect, analyze, and disseminate all information relating to violent crimes within the City of

Norfolk. Such information is usually forwarded to the FBI's ViCAP for the purpose of identifying patterns or similarities amongst violent crimes nationwide that may have been committed by the same offender.

Wellesley thought it strange that the FBI unit was already at the crime site, unless, somehow they had already made a connection—a link—with another state, or other homicides that had patterns or similarities to this one, nationwide. In other words, the astute Wellesley thought that this crime site might already be linked to a known or unknown offender from another state or states. This had to be total speculation, or so he thought, anyway. He proceeded forward; maybe they knew something, already, though it didn't seem likely. Just past the FBI's unit was the bright yellow Hummer of Captain Ernst Herrington from the Strategic Management.

Just up the hill, and parked on the grass was the car of Ted Castle—Forensic—and except for two additional ambulances; the last car he saw was his own Captains', Henry D. Rodgers from the First Patrol Division, Blue Sector. Rodgers was the Commanding Officer on the Scene. Rodgers' Sector Lieutenant, Wellesley had just pulled on to the lawn in front of Landrum Hall.

At the same time the Sector Lieutenant pulled up to his Captains car, Hank Blister arrived from the Police Operations Center. He parked just behind Herrington's unofficial Hummer. *Gad, this had to be bigger than big* the young Lieutenant realized. Wellesley looked around for the Mayors' car; after all, everyone else seemed to be attending. The Mayor's car wasn't in sight! *Maybe he's just late,* Wellesley thought as he grinned within.

As he slid out of his jeep his thoughts slipped back for a couple of seconds to his own days as a student at this beloved campus just a little over a decade ago when he received his Masters degree in Police Science. His college, his campus—as he called it—was originally founded in 1930 as the Norfolk Division of William and Mary. His campus had grown over the years and stood before him—today—as an emblematic historical monument to colleges across the United States. This gorgeous classic campus in darkness still offered two colonial revival-style buildings that he had spent so much time in, and his recollection stood before him of the beautifully manicured Williamsburg lawns that were dotted with stately oak trees offering a glimpse into Old Dominion's earliest days. His thought was quickly swept away by the booming voice of Blister, "God awful, isn't it Lieutenant?" Neither man had a clue as to how bad it would be once they stepped inside. "I understand you are heading up this case, Lieutenant."

"Don't know about that. All I know is the Captain called me here, pronto."

"Trust me, Wellsy," Blister boomed back. "It's your baby, totally! It's your type of crime!" *How would he know*, Wellsy, pondered? *What did Blister know?* He put the thought aside and walked toward the central dormitory on campus.

The Lieutenant looked about the premises as they walked toward the dorm. Standing about forty yards away was—as he estimated—about two hundred people, most probably students dotted the dark moon skyline. In front of the assemblage, four campus patrols milled about. The Lieutenant sauntered over to college rent-a-cops and suggested they find a comfortable way to disperse the crowd, indicating that there wouldn't be anything for them to see, anyway.

The guards balked at his command, but began the process, anyway. Some of the crowd left, dispersed. Others merely repositioned themselves. It was mid-October, an engaging fun filled night, except for the slaughter that waited inside. As Arthur turned and watched Blister enter the building, an uncontrolled shiver went through him, and then—just as quickly—Alexandria slipped back into his mind. He zeroed into thoughts of her, until he walked but two feet into the dormitory.

For the next seven hours, there was only one glimmer of thought about the woman he adored more than life, itself! Nevertheless, she would have to wait; love was going to have to linger, if it could! He knew she would never understand! Neither would he!

Wellsy was about to meet a new brand of serial killer.

At first glance, his thought was; *this is personal*! Indirectly; he was correct; Wellesley just didn't know it, yet! Over time, it would become way too personal to him, too! It would become personal to her, too, Ms. Alexandria Mae Southerland.

It was deeply, endingly too personal to the three girls, inside, two of them dead, and the third who just might as well be.

It was personal to the Perp, too. Yes, it was very personal to Nabulio; he left behind a massacre with very specific clues; clues that were hidden—masked— by nearly 200 years of personal circumstances; circumstances that would accumulate over the next one hundred days.

How could those two-hundred year clues be discovered, let, alone, solved once exposed? Lieutenant Wellsy was the answer; or was he?

Chapter 2—Day One
AFTER THE EVENT

Nabulio had driven two miles an hour over the speed limit, intentionally; after all, Norfolk's finest never pulled anyone over for traveling merely two miles an hour over the posted speed limit. Thirty-nine year old, Nabulio wanted to blend in and he certainly did. He drove quietly listening to Ludwig van Beethoven's Symphony number nine, while thumping his right palm on the bottom of the steering wheel keeping to the beat of the music. It filled him. Relaxed him. Released him. He needed it, and would continue to need it.

He headed north up St. Paul's Boulevard. At Princess Ann Road, he turned the hard right and traveled in a southwest direction toward home. Eighteen minutes later he clicked the button, turned into his driveway, slowed, waited eight seconds for the garage door to fully open and eased his silver 2006 Chrysler PT Cruiser into it's place. He clicked the button, again, and stayed in the car until the garage door found the cement pavement. The plastic raingear crinkled and snapped as he eased out of the Cruiser. He carefully removed the lining he'd been sitting on. He laid it on the garage floor. Next, he opened the trunk and removed the garbage bag and it's contents. He placed the batch on top of lining, and then folded it all together. He then carried it to the entrance of the house from the garage.

His gloved hand opened the door that lead into the alcove. He turned to the right, opened the door and descended to the basement. He opened the furnace's iron-trap door, and stuffed the bag into the opening. Next, he took off his gloves and tossed them in, and then he disrobed, and every stitch of clothing went into the orifice. He closed the iron cover, and locked it home, and then he turned on the blast of fire, which burned and eventually disintegrated his belongings. He moved to the north side of the basement, collected the gas can and returned to the furnace. He poured about a cup and a half of gas on to the floor; moved the contents around with his hand, making a circle of gasoline that covered the spot he had place the bag. He crossed to the west side of the basement and washed his hands in the sink, not bothering to dry them. He then withdrew the matches from the shelf above the sink and crossed back to the pool of gas. He ignited the match, and then the gasoline on the floor. He watched the bluish, yellow, and orange flame engulf the irregular circle. He watched until it burned itself and any evidence it contained, out.

He scampered upstairs to his bedroom and showered in very hot water for nearly twenty minutes. Half way though he stepped back, spread his legs for balance and leaned forward pressing the palms of his outstretched arms and hands against the front of the shower. He leaned in, putting his head down and allowing the spray of water to drench the back of his neck. The hot water felt good, cleansing; as well, it should!

* * * * *

He closed his eyes and saw Carolyn Ann Nowicki staring up at him. Her eyes were wide and wild, unbelieving. The soundless word *WHY* kept streaming from her mouth at Nabulio. Silence, again and again came shouting back at her. Finally, it was audible; her attacker heard it. He bent over her, placed his mouth to her ear and whispered *your sacrifice brings forth my blessings*.

From that point forward, death could not come fast enough for Carolyn. She begged for it, but the screams of pain were muffled by the duct tape he had placed over her mouth to keep the seven cotton balls in her mouth, and at the same time, stifle the ensuing screams. He had driven sixteen-penny nails into the floor, and then secured her hand to the nails with heavy elastic strips. The elastic wraps about her wrists were the closest she had to clothing; he had stripped her earlier; ogled, but did not touch.

Next, he spread her legs just a little farther than they could normally go, and then did the same securing process with her ankles. He then drove four more nails near her side, one on either side of her bare breasts, and two more, one on either side of her hips. He secured her torso with elastic wrap to the four nails.

Carolyn knew she was about to be raped.

It looked as if her body was cemented to the floor by bands of tape; she was. There was little room for wiggle. Yet, though the excruciating pain, she wreathed, lifting her trunk up off the floor, several times. Each time, he yelled at her to *shut up*, as if she had such accommodating control.

Downstairs, Jessica could only wonder. She tried desperately to undo the duct tape that bound her to the stair's newel post. Tears streamed down her face.

Her heart pounded. Would she be next? Was he killing Carolyn? She heard another blood curdling muffled scream. It caused her to wet herself.

He withdrew a three and a half inch pocketknife that had been tapped to the thigh of his rubber suit. He opened the knife and commenced to carve on her abdomen through her muffled screams of fear and pain. When done, he admired his bloody handy work. He had carved it in French of all languages—a kind of twisted humor his progenitor would eventually appreciate, or would he—would the idiot W even have a guess, a clue? No, probably not! But, on the other hand, to think him an idiot could result in severe consequences. Nevertheless, notwithstanding his foe, he admired his artistry and craft. He whisked away the blood and admired his handiwork.

le plus dangereux
le moment vient
avec la victoire!
#1

With that that task accomplished, he left Carolyn wreathing, suffocating with pain! He raced back down the stairs. Jessica June Andersen was still securely duct tapped to the banister at the floor of the stairway. He passed her by, and ran around the banister across the room and through the archway and examined, the crumpled body on the floor, April. She was still out cold. Her jaw had already turned a purplish black, and her lip needed a few stitches. *She'll be fine*, he figured. He didn't care as long as she was alive. Nevertheless, he took all her clothing off. He placed her bra and panties under her body, and snatched her jeans and blouse and put them securely under his arm.

He raced back to the stair's banister. He looked at Jessica; her eyes were wild with anticipation. She had heard the hammering, and the gut curdling muffled screams. He cut her loose of the stairs and flung her 133-pounds over his shoulder and pranced up the stairs, taking two steps at a time. Jessie, as her roommates called her, eyes went wild as she saw her roommate's nude body spread-eagle on the floor bleeding which seemed to be, bleeding from everywhere. It looked as though she had been gutted. Jessica needed a closer view, but that wasn't going to happen. She did, however see, that Carolyn Ann's life was running out of her in blood. She wanted to help, but her own fear crowded out any hope or willingness. She threw up all over his shoulder. He didn't care; he was in his rubber suit. It would just offer more evidence for W to figure out; the idiot!

Nabulio tossed Jessica to the floor, and forced her on her backside. She sat. He told her to lie down. She muffled *no* through the tape over her mouth. He took the heel of his knife and jammed it to her jaw, cracking it. She offered a scream though the tape. The pain was enormous. She heard her jaw crack or break, it didn't matter which. She was so scared she barely felt the pain throbbing within her. He pushed her down hard. Her head hit the floor with such force she nearly lost consciousness. He then ripped at and sliced at her clothing. Several times in the process of working faster than he needed to, he sliced her here and there with the knife just as he did with Carolyn. Each time she screamed through the duct tape; just like Carolyn.

In his angst and fury, he would slice her seven times in all with two of the slices penetrating over an inch and a half deep. Those piercing and slicing hacks were just one less slice than what Carolyn had received when she went through the same process. He didn't care. He didn't even know he did it. Finally, she was completely nude.

Blood flew everywhere, while he was focused on his task. Next, he spread her legs like that of her dying roommate. She tried to bring them back together. In anger, he forced them open again, and then sat on her left knee, and put his feet on her right leg, one foot in the middle of her thigh and the second foot was place just below her knee. He pushed her legs apart as far out as the distance of his legs would reach. She felt something rip; tear in her groin area, and in her upper thigh. The pain was excruciating. Something had ruptured. Somehow she managed to think, *just rape me and leave it at that.*

He then stood up. Her legs automatically closed some, and as they did, a piercing pain shutter through her from the damage. He straddled Carolyn's body such that he was facing her feet. He leaned over and grabbed Jessica's right ankle by the heel and pulled her hard toward him, jamming her foot hard into the private section of her roommate. He pulled with such force that the ankle dislocated. Carolyn's seemingly lifeless body awakened to a new pain in her groin. Both women's muffled screams were unnoticed by the their perpetrator. He spread her and fastened her to the floor the same as he had Carolyn. He looked at the four legs, outstretched. Two perfect V's signified, clearly, his VICTORY! After admiring his work, he then deeply carved her, but, before he used the knife, he ripped the duct tape from her mouth, tearing off a good two-thirds of an inch of skin from her lower lip. He then stuffed seven cotton balls into her mouth and then duct taped to her mouth closes, again. He couldn't afford her to be too noisy. Then, he carved, again, in French:

le secret de guerre
mensonges dans le
communications!
#2

Finished, Nabulio ran to the bathroom and took the bath towel off the bar, rushed back to the girls and wiped the still flowing blood off their abdomens, several times. Neither wreathed with pain, they were past that, and in deep shock. He then took the corner of the towel, and dabbed up the coagulated blood and went to the wall and smudged-wrote with the blood rag:

LA VICTOIRE APPARTIENT au plus perseverant!

It took him five trips back and forth from the two bodies and the wall to accumulate enough blood to write his entire message. At last, it was finished. He stepped back and viewed his work: the two co-eds on the floor; the perfect inscription on their abdomen; their innocent nude bodies, open, welcoming future visitors, and offering symbolized, VICTORY. He was most pleased of his handy craft

He reached down and took the tape off the inside of his suit. He removed the paper and the cigarette and a single match. He read the paper carefully, making sure he had not missed a step. Satisfied, he ate the note. His first step of revenge had been successfully completed. Well, all but the last couple of intentional events, but they would wait until he traced the house for evidence. He moved toward the stairwell.

The telephone rang. A message was left for Carolyn. Some guy named Seth was wondering if she wanted to go to the bar for a drink around midnight. He said if he didn't hear from her, he'd stop by, maybe.

Nabulio decided to alter his plan. It was risky but worthwhile. He traced his steps back to April. He had enough nails and tape. She was staked out as the other two. He tucked her underclothing under her head, for comfort. The tape was badly placed on her body, to be sure she could get out, herself, and escape to freedom. The process would buy him a little more time, though he knew he wouldn't need it. He made six trips back and forth, up and down the stairs to collect enough blood to fingerprint a message on April's stomach: Not part of the battle, W. He wrote it in English so W would understand; understand if he were bright enough. Nabulio knew W was more than bright, enough. He had history, a general's history.

He checked out the rest of the house for unwanted tells that might give him away. He found none. He went to the kitchen and took a saucer from the cupboard. He placed it on the newel post of the stairs. He lighted the cigarette, but didn't smoke it. He hated smoking. He made sure that some of the upper part of the cigarette got some blood on it. When the cig was about half burned, he put it out. He smiled, something for them to think about! He loved war, he loved the individual battles, more, and, the loved the dance of war!

He walked into the bedroom. Carolyn was looking straight at him. He spoke. "Thanks for your participation. You were the first, but not the last." She wanted to ask why, but the tape wouldn't allow it. He leaned over and kissed her forehead, then slit her throat to the bone with his knife. Jessica was wiggling; she knew. He looked at her, and offered his thanks to her as well. Before he slit her throat he said, "You have very nice breasts. I promise I will not touch them."

He knew W would think him a serial killer. That was W's problem; he'd learn, otherwise. This was the new beginning of the completion of an old war. Nabulio knew it, and Nabulio knew W would figure it out, too, but, by then, it would be too late, much too late.

He turned out all the lights in the house, one by one. As he walked out, the telephone rang, again. He listened to the recording, and waited for the caller to leave a message. He/she didn't bother. *No matter*, he thought.

Step one was over with added perfection.

He zigzagged from tree to tree until he got to his destination, his ride. He opened the door and slid onto the plastic sheet that waited his bloody return. He then headed home listening to Ludwig van Beethoven on the way. Once he twisted the rear-view-mirror; even in the dark he saw the spattered blood on his face. He smiled, *evidence of battle.*

* * * * *

He came to his senses. He was clean enough. He stepped out of the shower and toweled off. He turned, looked into the vanity mirror; the spots of war were gone, down the drain, and the rest, incinerated, except for the evidence in his desk drawer; the plan, the photos, school records, their history that he wiped out, tonight. *Should I keep all this?* Does a General keep his divine plans for his legacy? He needed to give that some thought, no rush! W didn't have a clue. He'd tend to it later.

Dang it, he remembered! He shot upright, ran to the basement, got the rag, doused it with the flammable liquid, and raced to the garage. First, he wiped the door knob inside the house, and then the door knob that lead into the house, and then the door handle of the car, then the steering wheel, and then the area of the trunk were the key hole was. *How could I have been so foolish to forget?* He then opened the glove compartment box and read the note he'd left for himself. He read them, twice. He had covered it all, now it was done except for the last two items. First, he ate the note, and then went to the incinerator and burnt the rag. *Sometimes you are a dumb ass, Nabulio!*

Twenty minutes later, naked, in his den, he planned the second battle. He saw their bodies one more time, beautiful, innocent, but, victims of war, nevertheless! He was so tempted to touch, but he was above that. For now, anyway! After all; he was a man, and a man can only well, you know; can't help to look, if not touch!

CHAPTER 3—DAY ONE
THE DOUBLE V'S

At first glance, he thought the house looked normal. At second glance, Wellesley froze. He didn't move another inch. As he was slipping on his elastic covers over his shoes, he asked the patrolman at the door, "Where's the Chief?"

Officer Stanton pointed through the opening to the left of the staircase, and across the room and then fingered, indicating through the second opening. "He's in there." The Lieutenant stepped in uneven steps, avoiding stepping in or on any blood. That's what he saw on second glance. There were smudges of blood all over the place. It looked as if someone had stepped into puddles of blood, and then ran around leaving prints and smudges, everywhere indiscriminately, but purposely. He, also noted, or at least it looked like there were too many *other* shoes that had inadvertently stepped on or over the smudges already; he was pissed. He took one step through the second opening, and saw the Captain. "Chief, who is in charge here, you?"

Captain Rodgers looked up into the piercing green eyes of the red faced Lieutenant; he pointed at him and said, "I was until now. Now it's your baby, totally, Lieutenant; I'm here to help, assist in any way you want, it's a mess, Lieutenant, we'll be here all night." Wellesley knew what that really meant. It meant that *he* would be here all night. That thought caused him to think about her, Alex. She would be expecting his call; a call that would never be made, tonight, and he knew it! *Damn it!* Unfortunately, Alexandria knew it too, and that might just be the last straw. He didn't have any more time to give to that personal situation, now! *Just plain shit*, he thought, and then he went to work.

He ordered, "Then remove all unessential people out of here post hast, Captain. Please, Captain, do this for me; there are just two damn many people here to suite me." Wellsy looked around, and offered characteristically; "This isn't a damned zoo, and I've already counted seven smudged different blood-

18

shoe prints just in walking in here, alone; let's get them the hell out of here, pronto!"

Rodger's responded; "We've already photographed down here, Lieutenant. It's all, okay."

Wellesley shot back, "Photos or no photos," he paused, "regardless of what you say, I can tell, the damn place is already contaminated, and with all these smudges, how in the dickens am I going to reconstruct what happened."

"Point taken, Lieutenant, I'm on it!"

"Thank you, Captain." Wellsy quickly paused, again and then added, "Who found this mess anyway? I want to talk to him." Rodgers used his thumb and pointed to the Campus Security Guard to his left. She looked pale and weak. She straddled two over turned kitchen chairs. Her right hand was embracing the top edge of a third chair. Her lips and nose were inside the small opening of the brown lunch-bag held by her right hand. She was taking deep breaths, or trying too, anyway. He took one more look at her, and then looked to the Captain and said, "Her first, right?"

The Captain retorted, "It's worse than that, Wellsy, it's not only her first homicide, it's still her first week on the job, four days total." An awkward moment passed, and then Rodgers added, "In case you are wondering, the two of us are in here so she can regroup. She's been though a lot; you get my point?" Wellsy nodded. The Captain continued; "And for the smudges, they've all been photographed down here, nothing's tainted, Lieutenant, but you are right about reconstruction. I'll take that responsibility." He then, added, "We have a print of the perp's shoe, or we think so, anyway as we can't figure out whose shoe it could be, if not the Perps!"

"A shoe print?"

"Yes, well not exactly. It's a print, indeed, but it maybe of a shoe covering of some kind. We don't know yet." He sighed, "They'll tell us when they know.

"Like the ones I have on, and you don't Captain."

"Let's not push this too far, *Lieutenant*!

Wellsy got his point! "Ok, Captain, but please; again I request, get all unessential out of here, *now*; he forcefully offered, and continued, "I'm sure the place is tainted, already, despite your thinking; no offense, Captain." The Captain tossed him a very displeasing glance.

"Offense taken, Lieutenant," the Captain fired back."

"Sir, they're just too many people here for me. Please do that for me, Captain; I'm talking about doing that right now, this very second. I'm going to take a quick look around. How many, dead?" He looked up, and over his shoulder. "What have we got here?"

Rodgers tried to calm himself, offering; "First of all, Lieutenant, we've got all professionals here, there isn't any tainting," he reiterated, for the third time, and then continued, "this isn't the Los Angles police department, you know, and secondly, the bodies are upstairs in their bedroom, same room. Walk up to the right, stay to the right on the stairway, so you don't *contaminate, anything, Lieutenant*" he said, as he smirked, and then offered; "There isn't anyway to get up and into the bedrooms without stepping on blood, somewhere. "The blood down here, came, we believe, from the perp coming back and forth up and down the stairs several times. It is a blood bath down here and more than you can believe, upstairs, Lieutenant." The Captain, paused for a second, scratched his head, and continued, "Both women have been butchered up." He continued, "But, we believe that they were dragged up stairs by their hair, but we're not sure. Forensic will let us know that, too for sure. Hair follicles should tell us that, but you know all that." He briefly paused, made a guttural sound and offered, "I would guess—obviously—that the girls were kicking and screaming and maybe bleeding, and flinging blood around and about the stairs, but we know that they were definitely alive at that point. We think the perp gagged them first thing to keep their voice level low, Lieutenant, there was a party to the north making all kinds of racket, too. We doubt anyone heard anything, but we're checking; campus security is helping out with that aspect."

Rodgers picked up the blow horn and blasted a message for all unessential personal to get out, immediately. He added, "If you're not sure if you are essential, then you aren't, so leave! Lieutenant Wellesley is here, now, and it's his case, and he wants you out, so go, now!"

Wellesley asked who his assigned Detective was and what was he doing! Rodgers offered that Detective Strange was currently with forensics somewhere in the house, probably upstairs. Wellsy, asked the Captain to call him down; the Captain obliged.

Detective Strange came downstairs two steps at a time, hugging the wall. The Lieutenant was pleased to see Strange had on elastic slippers; it eased his mind that contamination might not be as bad as her first thought. Wellsy put the Detective at the door, instructing him to interview everyone who left. The Detective was to find out what each investigator saw, what they knew, when they arrived, and what they did or what they were currently doing; now. Strange was also to have each person write down everything they saw, and everything they did. Each was to leave what they wrote with Strange. The Detective—tomorrow—would make two copies of each report, and then return the originals to each person by tomorrow, noon. The second copy would go to his

Lieutenant. Each person was to call the Detective if they remember anything they'd forgotten previously. This procedure was the thoroughness of Lieutenant Wellsy; no stone was left unturned, ever!

Wellsy watched six people come down stairs as Rodgers offered up the Campus Security Guard's name, Jessica House. Wellsy walked back into the small room where the petite female Guard was now sitting. He told her to just sit tight and Detective Strange would get her full statement within a few minutes, but she was to also write it all up, before she left. "No matter how long that takes, you got that?" She nodded. "I don't want a nod, I want a, yes." She nodded, again and said, 'yeah, sure.' He told her that he understood that this was hard for her. He touched her shoulder in recognition. He thanked her and assured her that she did a fine job; thoroughness!

With that accomplished, Wellsy crossed though the two archways and turned to his left toward the stairway. He had to wait, as three more people came down the stairs. He pointed at the Detective and told the trio what he wanted them to give Detective Strange their report. Wellsy then took his first step up toward the bedrooms. Captain Rodgers stopped him. "Wait, Lieutenant, there's one down here; she's with Captain Herrington." Wellsy offered a quizzical look squirreling up his confused face. Rodgers added "You know, Ernst Herrington, Strategic Management Division."

"What, there's another body down here? She never got dragged upstairs?"

"No, she's a witness!"

"WHAT," Wellsy exclaimed half yelling? "There's a witness to all of this and I'm just now hearing about it, Captain? What the hell is going on here?"

Rodgers simply offered back more information, "She was here. She heard. She saw!"

"She heard, and saw, saw what, Captain?" The Lieutenant took a quick breath and asked, "What kind of witness is she, anyway?"

"Like I said, she was here," the Captain, bellowed, "he beat her with his fists, but didn't cut her, he just knocked her out after asking her what her name was."

"Did she tell him?"

"She lied, and she says that she told him her name was April Pinkerton. The bastard just waited around for her to come back to life, and then according to her, he cuffed her, backhanded across her face, cutting her lip, and breaking a tooth. Again, he demanded to know her real name…"

"Wait a minute, Captain, you said he backhanded her, cutting her lip and a tooth was broken; he did that with his hand?"

"Yes! Why?"

"Well, damn, I'd think that that would have done some damage of his hand." Wellsy scribbled on his note pad.

"Yeah, that makes sense, Lieutenant. Anyway, this time she told him the truth about her last name; Foster, and then, according to Foster, she thinks he took the butt of his knife and cracked her face. As best we know, she was out for nearly an hour or so, we don't really know how long she was out, and neither does she."

"I doubt it was that long," Wellsy offered. He stopped; thought for a couple of seconds, and then started to ask, but Rodgers beat him to the draw; he asked, "When she got her senses back, she noticed that she had been stripped naked. The bastard had nailed her to the floor, over there," he pointed to the location of the telephone. "She had been spread eagle. She hasn't been examined, yet, but it doesn't look like he sexually assaulted her."

Wellsy noticed that six nails had been pounded into the floor, and that short strips of tape and been wadded up and discarded. Some of the tape still clung to the nails. "Anyway," the Captain, continued, "somehow, she got herself out of the bonds that held her and ran outside. She said she didn't know where to run too, so she came back inside, only then did she actually realize she was naked." The Captain, paused, thought, and then continued. "It gets a little disjointed here, Lieutenant, but she says that she then touched herself, looking for evidence of semen, I guess. Then, for some reason or other, and she's not sure about this, nor does she understand, but she ran back in and found her under clothing, panties and bra, put them on and then dialed 911 and then she believes that she fainted, passed out, I guess." He thought for a second, "That's about it for her. I guess."

"Good, Lord, why didn't we get her to the hospital, immediately? Damn, get her there now, Captain, and do it under armed guard, and I want a team outside her room if she has to stay at the hospital, and if she's going home, then I want a patrol outside her address," Wellsy echoed as he walked toward the room where Foster was in with Herrington. The Lieutenant abruptly stopped; turned back, and asked, "Why did she run outside and then return?"

"Like I said, we don't know, nor does she." Rodgers continued, "The conjecture is that she was afraid that he was still in the house. Why she came back in, we don't know either; nor does the girl; we believe she just wasn't thinking; shock is my guess. Anyway, she came in and called 911 as I've already, stated." Wellsy turned toward the captain to speak, but the Captain was first, "Lieutenant, this is her home, her dormitory; she lives here with the others."

"Well, get her to the hospital, anyway" he interrupted, "and find out where she can stay the night. Get a female cop on her, immediately. Do we have any females here, now? If not then get one with her, now, and get Herrington away from her." He then yelled across the room to Strange, "Detective, I want to know absolutely everything that Captain Herrington knows everything. I want him grilled, and don't become intimidated with his rank." The Detective nodded, back. He turned back to Rodgers, "Where is she, the Foster girl?" Rodgers grunted and motioned his hand that she was around the corner to his left in a small room.

Wellsy slowly, softly opened the door to the room. Herrington was whispering to her; Wellsy interrupted, stating; "Excuse me, Ms. Foster, April, but I need to talk to you for just a minute or two. I'm in charge of this case, I'm Sector Lieutenant Wellesley, the officer in charge of this case." He said that for the girl's sake and especially for Herrington as well. He looked to Herrington, "Captain, I need the room."

"And, you are!"

"I just said who I am, I'm Sector Lieutenant, Wellington or Wellsy's the name I use. This is my case, Captain, and you won't be needed until we're all get together and develop *my* plan; though I seek your input, naturally. That is your job. That is your specialty. You are vital to that, and that will come soon, enough."

The Captain indicated that he'd like the *Sector* Lieutenant to step outside for a moment with him. "No, Captain, I know what you have to say and you are way out of line. This *is* my case, if you have a problem with that; my boss, Captain Rodgers is just outside this room. Take it up with him. Now, thank you but I need to talk with Ms. Foster. You are dismissed, Captain." Herrington mumble some words like, well like sour grapes. Anyway, he begrudgingly left, offering Wellesley a sneer.

April was still in her panties and bra, shivering. Wellsy left, secured a blanked for her to wrap herself in, and quickly, returned. She was still sobbing. Unknown to April, her face was splattered with blood, her roommates—somehow—but not her own. Wellesley briefly excused, himself—again—and went into the hall and asked Detective Strange to get the female Security Guard in the room with him, immediately. As soon as Jessica House arrived, Wellsy asked her if she knew where April's clothing was. She knew; she went to get them. Wellsy yelled after her, "Don't taint anything, and watch were you walk." He stood in the doorway until she returned. He briefly left them alone until April was fully dressed. He told House to stay with April until a female officer arrived, then House, along with the officers were to see that April was to be taken to Sentara Norfolk General Hospital, pronto.

That settled; it was time to view the case before him. Before walking to the stairs, he made a quick note that he was to meet with April first thing in the morning with Detective Strange. He climbed up the stairs, taking two steps at a time. He noticed the tape on the newel post, and the spattered blood on the railing, and the walls. He saw someone's smudged blood on the wall. It was Jessica's blood he would later learn. It happened when her head hit the banister, and then the wall when being dragged or carried upstairs by the perp.

Wellsy looked into the bedroom on the right. It was dark; no light had been turned on. From the doorway he looked about with his flashlight. It was clean—evidence wise—nothing out of the ordinary. It was obviously a woman's room. It was messy. Clothing was tossed indiscriminately, everywhere. College textbooks were on one of the two beds and on the floor beside the other bed. One bed was made, the other disheveled. He yelled out, "Has the light switch in this room been dusted?" He heard a 'yes,' back. He flipped on the light. Above the messy bed, a handwritten sign made from poster board stated:

APRIL'S ROOM, ENTER BY APPOINTMENT, ONLY!
NO MEN ALLOWED, EXCEPT BY INVITATION!

Below the second line, April had—obviously—put a heavy dose of dark-red lipstick on her lips and kissed the poster board. Under the lipstick kiss she wrote, 'There's more where that came from, big guy.' He gave the room one last look, for tonight, anyway.

Wellsy walked out of the room and turned to his right. He passed by the stairs and stopped to the doorway to his right. On the right side of the door entrance there was a few strands of red hair, and a smudge of blood. Later it would be noted as belonging to Carolyn. A minor insult from her twisting and turning while the animal carried her into her bedroom. Ted Castle—Forensic—and his crew of two others were inside the room, examining, dusting, photographing, and the works; doing their job most efficiently.

The co-eds were fully exposed. After all these years, and after all he had seen, Wellsy wanted to vomit. Both girls, stone cold dead with lifeless eyes, wide open looked to the ceiling, perhaps searching to God for help. Both—throats slit—nearly severed to the spinal cord in Jessica's case. Then, he noticed, and the fact that he noticed witnessed his intelligence. He saw it clearly, without question, he knew, he understood from just one look, the double V for victory. "I assume they have been photographed?"

Ted Castle didn't even look to the Lieutenant. "Certainly. Of course!"

"I want a photo that you didn't take."

"Trust me, Lieutenant, we took them all."

"No, I want one more. I want a picture, actually two of them, one from each angle. I want photos from the vagina of one woman to the vagina of the second. In other words, I want from toes to vagina in one picture of both girls, and a second picture from the other girl to the other."

"What do you see, Wellsy."

"I see a double victory sign, Theodore, that's what I see. And, I want it photographed, because we are going to see it, again, I fear."

Ted looked at the bodies one more time, but looked through the eyes of the Lieutenants eyes. *Damn*, he thought, he just might be right. Earl Watson, one of Ted's assistance took a quick peek. "You sure you don't want a private picture for yourself, Lieutenant?" Wellesley gave Watson a glare that put the man back to work with total silence for the rest of the time they shared the room.

"Were they sexually molested, Ted?"

"Nope. Don't think the perp touched them at all that way."

"I didn't think so."

"What do you make of the bodies, the carving, Lieutenant? It's French, I think, or looks like it to me!"

Wellesley walked closer to the bodies. He didn't answer Ted, right away. He studied the girls up close. He looked deep into their blank eyes. "Talk to me," he whispered. He looked at the disgraced hammer the perp had used to drive the nails. He looked at their faces, closely. He looked at every inch of them, and then looked to Castle. What have they said to you, Castle?"

"Nothing yet, except fear, but I know you mean scientifically. I don't have that yet. I've looked at them as you are now. Like I say, nothing yet. I'll work throughout the night. Give me till noon tomorrow, maybe after two, okay!" Wellesley merely nodded in disappointed agreement.

"I'm pretty sure I know why they were tied down, though."

"Yup, me too. They had to be carved;" the Lieutenant, tossed, back!

"I agree, but why not kill them first. Was it to inflict more pain?" Wellesley didn't answer, but he didn't think so. He kept thinking about the double V's. He kept thinking, victory, but victory over whom? *Perhaps the police*, he thought, or *the women, themselves*. But, then, there were the inscriptions on the bodies. The V's were definitely a message, well, obviously, so, but so were the French phrases. He read them aloud with near perfect accent: "le plus dangereux le moment vient avec la victoire!"

Ted looked over at him. Wellesley then restated the phrase back in English, for Ted's sake. "The most dangerous moment comes with victory! Number one."

Castle started to speak. He was waved off. Wellsy then read the second French phrase, "le secret de guerre mensonges dans le communications!" He turned and looked at Ted looking at him and translated, "the secret of war lies in the communications! Number two." He put his fingers to his jaw, and responded, "Damn, Ted, these are clues, they have to be, just as the legs are. He's toying with us?"

"And the wall," Castle inquired.

Wellsy didn't respond right away. He ran the two carvings in his head, computing, thinking, why French? Who were the messages for, directly, the cops in general? His captain? Himself? Who, or whom, or what, he pondered? He didn't even look up. After he saw the hair strands and the blood on the outer door, he had taken in the words on the wall, and translated them into English, "VICTORY BELONGS TO THE MOST PERSEVERING." He wondered if the perp meant to write MÉRITE, or DESERVING, instead of PERSÉVÉRANCE, or PERSEVERING. That would certainly make more sense. So, did he use the wrong word, or was he using the exact word he wanted? Did he speak French, and English, or just French, or just English. There was a lot to sort out, here.

"Lieutenant," Ted, asked?"

"Oh, sorry, Ted, the wall says, 'Victory belongs to the most persevering."

"Then, Lieutenant, that's you. You are the most persevering man I've even meant."

"Oh, shit, Arthur spat back, "So is he!" The cop thought for a second and turned to Castle, stating; "He's not done. He has a point to make and he'll keep spouting it, and doing it until we get it!"

"Huh, what are you saying, Lieutenant?"

Arthur Wellesley didn't address Ted's question. He kept running the three thoughts—the three messages, together—over and over: 'the most dangerous moment comes with victory! Number one.' He couldn't figure out the 'Number one,' aspect, so he left that part out for the time being. 'The secret of war lies in the communications! Number two'. Again, he dismissed the 'Number two,' part, and considered the first. Finally, 'Victory belongs to the most persevering.'

After three minutes, suddenly, sudden enlightenment came. Wellsy had it all figured out, or so he thought. The bad guy got past his 'dangerous moment'— the escape—with a clean getaway; he was free. *Yes, free to kill again, but* Wellsy thought—no—*not to kill again, but to communicate, again.* Yes, he would kill, again, but only for the purpose of communicating. The cop made a new notation to his notes. He looked at his watch. He thought of her; *No,* he screamed inside his head; adding, *not now!*

This wasn't an act of just killing. There was a lot more to it, behind it. He was having some kind of killing *war*, and these killings were merely a *means to an end*. It was the killer's way of beating the cops, or maybe, just beating one cop, the lead cop—me—Wellsy, thought. He realized that last part was silly, as, he, himself, didn't know he was going to head up the case until he arrived at the house of death.

Finally, the big note on the wall, the killer did mean specifically 'persevering,' because victory belongs to the most persevering. He was telling us, perhaps—me—that he knew we, or I—Wellsy—would persevere, but so too, would he—the killer—and to him that preservers the strongest, wins. It's mind over matter to win! It was war, all right; but why?

Arthur thought more about numbers one and two. He then spent some time trying to decide the significance of the numbers. At length, he decided that the carvings on the women's bodies worked together, but the message on the wall stood alone, otherwise the perp would have put a number three next to the wall message, but he didn't. Perhaps—the Lieutenant thought—it was the order in which they were killed.

For the time being, all of it had to be left unsettled. He was pretty sure of his assessment, however. But in no way was he going to communicate his theory to anyone, it was, after all, a rather strange take on the whole of it. He decided to keep it personal. He would strongly suggest that this guy wasn't done! He would save his V philosophy, and study those double V's for some time. He told Ted, that the V theory stayed between the two of them, for now!

He turned his attention to the small details of his two victims. After another hour and a half in the key bedroom, he went down stairs and worked out a scenario of how it all took place. He decided that Ted—forensic and group—would have to do that. There were just too many possibilities to fathom!

He looked at his watch. It was seven minutes after seven; a.m. He told Strange that he was going home for four hours sleep, and suggested the Detective do the same. He suggested they meet at the precinct at noon.

Strange agreed, and then said, "He's not done, is he?"

"This is but the first battle of many, Detective, just one of many." They walked in silence to their respective cars.

Standing along side of his car, Strange, offered, "Hey, Lieutenant, there's something, I don't get."

"There is a lot I don't get, Detective. Give it to me, anyways!"

"Well, the numbers one and two on the bodies, I was just wondering, do you think he gave us the order in which he killed them? Is that what the one and two are for?" Before Wellsy could respond, Strange added, "Because otherwise, I'd think he would have numbered the writing on the wall, also!" Strange received an unexpected answer!

"That's why you are part of the team, Detective, to fill in the obvious to those of us who cannot." With that, the said, "Thanks! I believe you are right on target." He got in his car and took off to ponder all of it, but especially what the Detective had just suggested! Strange decided sleep could wait. He went to the station and did his report; instead!

Then, the Lieutenant went home, and fell asleep for two hours and twenty-seven minutes. He shower and shaved, and placed a call to Alex. She looked at her phone, and saw the incoming callers I.D. She let it ring. She let the voice-mail tell him that she wasn't home. He didn't believe the voice-mail. She knew he wouldn't! She did what she had to do. So did he; he was off to headquarters, thinking the whole way there, about the killings, and about his… He wanted to say fiancée.

Chapter 4—Nearly Five Years Before Day One
THE BLUE HIPPO

November 24, 2000, Alexandria Mae Southerland walked out the Classic Village Resort in the heart of the Green Mountain Inn, Stowe, Vermont. Though the walkway had been recently shoveled, and basically absent of snow, her lift foot slipped about two inches forward, and that was enough, as both feet slid forward and the rest of her went backwards. She fell right in the arms of the tall muscular Arthur Wellington Wellesley. He made a great grab, catching her under her armpit, and immediately they tumbled to the ground, together, her backside ending up on top of his thighs and knees. Neither was hurt. Both were embarrassed, she for falling into him, and he for accidentally cupping her breast when they went down. Both were apologetic.

Alexandria was glad he caught her, though embarrassed. He was glad she fell into him; she was beautiful. After her fourth apology in less than forty-five seconds, she agreed to pay him back by allowing him to buy her lunch, as long as her girlfriend could join them. They decided on noon inside the lodge.

At 12:31 p.m. Arthur was about to leave; he'd been stood up, again; first by his would be male companion for the weekend, Chuck Irving. Irving's boss wasn't going to let Irving make the trip, either. His boss made the reckless decision for him all because a client decided to invest $300,000 in their mutual funds, and he assigned Chuck to handle the investor. Arthur left three dollars on the table and got up to leave, just as the beautiful woman showed up minus one girlfriend. The girlfriend, Alison Reynolds was snowbound in New York City. It didn't look good for the entire trip, which was to be just the weekend to begin with. It was Friday, and she was canceling.

It wasn't love at first sight, but it went way beyond like. The oddest thing of all was when they found out that they actually lived only six miles apart in Norfolk, Virginia. Alex, as he learned to call her was a senior at Old Dominion, and was scheduled to graduate in the ensuing spring. Wellsy, as she learned to call him had just finished his Masters a semester before and was now working on the police force. She didn't like the idea that he was a cop, but she liked him well enough, and the fact that he had recently received a promotion was a good thing, a good sign. She thought that he was upward and mobile, that showed good quality.

The couple skied, tobogganed, and then made a snowman, together. It was only on Sunday morning that they had their first kiss, just before she got into the taxi to go back to the airport. They agreed to meet a week or so later. That week was but three days old and they went to a movie and watched *The Transfusion of Life*. It was a waste of money; movie-wise.

After the movie, they had a wonderful, an exquisite dinner date at The Blue Hippo Restaurant in downtown, Norfolk! It was a remarkable movie and dinner date, but it was at The Blue Hippo that they truly found their match in life. It was the beginnings of what would become, deep love. It was one of hundreds of dates they would have, but the first date at the Hippo is where the magic happened. She went home tingling as a girl in love might do. She had found love; nothing else in the universe mattered.

Arthur made his mind up that she, Alex; she was the one, the only one for him. He told himself that one day when they were old and gray, perhaps on his sixty-fifth birthday he would bring her to their little love spot, the Blue Hippo Restaurant where it all began. He laughed at himself, realizing that she would probably dump him in a month.

She tried to go to sleep. She tossed. She turned. She missed him, already. He took her breath, away. At 1:15 a.m. she couldn't stand it any longer. She called Alison Reynolds and told her everything. At the end of the call she told Alison, "I'm sorry I woke you up."

Alison merely replied, "Don't worry about it. Love is like that! Alison, after all, knew all about love. She was just a fortnight away from marriage.

Their relationship was as wonderful as anything either of them had previously had. They became more than lovers, they were best friends, companions; deep rooted friends. They learned everything about each other. For instance, she learned that he had had amnesia when he was fourteen. It only lasted five days, but it was a scary time for him and his family; he had been playing football in the back yard and as he went out for a pass he ran headlong into a tree. How stupid is that. Anyway, he fully recovered.

She also learned that he had a clever quick mind. His thinking process seemed to soar above others. He could just flat outthink anyone; except her; of course. She learned that he had a blind spot, too, her. When he told her that, she giggled. She had total control over him. She learned that he liked strawberries with milk, cold pizza and beer, women in silky underwear, and that he was in the Order of DeMolay as a young boy and became the president, or Master Counselor of the origination, or something like that he told her.

He learned that she was an avid reader. She pretty much read a book a week, or at most a week and a half. She was a history fanatic. She read everything from Sherlock Holmes to how the Three Stooges came to be. She read serious history, and silly history, but she retained most of what she read. He wished that he had that wonderful ability; he did, he just didn't realize it. She knew the life of Benjamin Franklin, Thomas E. Edison, Walt Disney, Ronald Reagan, and Muhammad Ali: the boxer and the man. She also knew Napoleon Bonaparte, Mickey Mantel, Truman Capote, The Kingston Trio, and the list went on and on. She had read scores of books. She said, "Yup, I have all this needless information in my head, and somehow I can recall most all of it, but, it's all just useless information." He promised her that a time would come when some of that useless information would be a help to someone. He replied, "Well, love, you never know when it might come in handy." They laughed together.

They loved knowing everything about everything about each other. There weren't any secrets, either. They also shared a common personality trait in a backwards way—if you can call it that—as well. He had this super keen electric mind, and she loved to solve puzzles of all kinds; not picture puzzles, however, but mind teasers, or word or letter games. For him, either he solved it quickly, immediately or he went on to something else. He didn't have any stay tentativeness. On the other hand, she could waste a zillion hours on figuring out rhythms, or formulas, or possibility traits or structures that lead probably tendencies. Time didn't matter when she was involved with this kind of game. She was a bulldog to the end.

He, on the other hand, he had this super quick mind, meaning he would think of things faster than most. It was a blessing and a curse, as he would become easily bored if everyone was trying to figure something out and he had already solved in his head. He would become ill at ease waiting for them, and while waiting, his mind would meander. So, they shared a kind of bond in their unique abilities to cipher though stuff just at different speeds.

Their bond of love was so strong that nothing on earth could separate them, one from the other. No, nothing, nothing except for his work that is. Alexandria had a great deal of trouble playing second fiddle to a job that basically put Wellsy always on call; at any hour, any minute, or second for that matter. And then, of course, there was always the danger aspect. How does one ever get over that? She couldn't! Other than that, and that was gigantic; there was little that stopped them from marriage, children and life ever after. But, that, that was a big but.

After Alexandria finished her student teaching, she got a job almost immediately at Young Park Elementary School, in Norfolk teaching third graders; she loved it. It became her passion. She learned from that, and began to understand how Wellsy could love his work so much, but still, the time requirement and the danger of his job was always there.

The couple moved in together for four months in October, but he said he couldn't continue in this manner; he couldn't live like husband and wife and not have that cemented in actual marriage. Actually, she agreed, so she moved out and took an apartment closer to her job. They found the new relationship strained. They both needed more, so, in their sixth year of dating, he bought a ring, took her to the Blue Hippo and asked her to marry him.

Never, had she ever wanted to say the word yes, with greater joy. Never! But! But there was the job, his job. She wanted to be his wife, and the mother of his children, at least 2 if not 3 of them. But…

He told her to think about it while they ate. She could think of nothing else. At dinner's end, they went for a drive, heading west for about fifteen miles. They stopped near Norfolk's Ocean View Beach. It was a lovely area that stretched unbroken for nearly eight miles along the Chesapeake Bay. They parked. They talked. She looked at the ring, the symbol for what it represented. They were quiet, listening to the water, smelling the air. It was romantic. They kissed, caressed, and whisper the dance of love to one another. They belonged together, forever, eternally, if possible. She wanted this man to love her, protect her, and be the husband of her children so deeply.

"I can't she said."

"He was shocked, "You're saying no!" He wanted to die!

"No, I'm not saying no. I'm saying I can't decide tonight. Give me two days, Arthur.

"Good grief, this is serious," he laughed, trying to ease the tension, "you're calling me Arthur. You haven't called me that since the night we saw that stupid movie."

"Please don't make fun of me, this is really hard."

"How much time do you need."

"Look, you know I'm going to my mothers for a few days. The kids are out of school and I've not been home in a long time. Give me until Friday night, please. I promise, I will call promptly at ten and you give you my answer." He couldn't do much more than agree, so, he did.

On Friday night he sat by the telephone with the greatest anticipation of his entire life, and that is when the two telephones rang at the same time, his home phone and his cell phone. That is when all hell broke out at Old Dominion. That is when then, the unknown Nabulio, reached in and did his best to destroy their lives, together, forever. All the concerns Alexandria had about his job would scream at them both that their marriage could never happen. It appeared that Wellsy would become married to Nabulio, by possession. There would be little time in his life for anything, else! Alexandria was put on hold.

* * * * *

Wellesley looked at his watch. He had a meeting at noon with the entire team. He gathered his facts, his assessment. He was ready. But, would the team accept his theory. This was no regular serial killer, if there was such a thing as a regular serial killer, but Wellesley was sure that this monster was using young women's deaths for some other greater goal than just killing them. He was the only one that might suggest serial killer, as—of yet—there wasn't any reason t think that, unless you happen to be Arthur!

But, what evidence did he have? None really! Except for one thing, if this ogre were truly a serial killer, he would not have allowed one of the three young women to live. On the other hand, by allowing one of them to live, he showed his power; he could kill whom he wanted to; total control. Why April? How could Wellsy get the team to see this odd killer as he really was? If he told them the truth of what he believed, they might just think him a lunatic, too. Would anyone on his team agree? Dare he take this bold step? He would!

As he left his office, and walked toward the conference center, his thoughts switched to Alexandria. Why didn't she answer when he called? There was only one reason. Her answer was, no! At a time when he needed all his faculties to muster support from his team, he felt deeply alone. He loved her so. Could he just up and walk away. Surely he could find other work. It was true. He was in love. He loved her. He loved his job. Which would he have to give up? Or, had she already decided for him?

Chapter 5—Day Two
THE MEETING

The twelve o'clock was delayed until one fifteen, as Captain Rodgers was in an unscheduled meeting with the City's prosecutor Alison Walworth on a shooting matter that took the lives of three gang members. Rodgers told Wellsy to go on with the meeting without him that he'd be able to catch up. Everyone on the team knew better. If the Sector Chief wasn't there, there wouldn't be a meeting or the whole process would get bogged down once he arrived. Most on the team had all been though this kind of thing before. Rodgers would come into the room, late and ask to be updated. He would then interrupt every two or three minutes with a question. That was his style. Wellsy decided to wait so the meeting—as a whole—would be shorter, not longer in the long run of things.

The table was large, oval; it could comfortably seat up to twelve. At the head of the table Arthur Wellington Wellesley, the Unit's Sector Lieutenant and the bright man in charge of the entire homicide investigation sat nervously. To his right was seated the tallest and widest man in the room, Detective Earnest Lance Strange. He often went by his middle name. Captain Ernst Herrington from Strategic Management Division was seated next to Strange. Next to Herrington was the smallest person in the room, Hank Blister from the Operations Center. The next seat was unoccupied, and at the end of the table belonged to Henry D. Rodgers, Wellsy's Captain, and First Patrol Division, Blue Sector, and Commanding Officer would sit when his unscheduled meeting was over.

Sweeping back around the table and next to Rodger's empty chair was Detective Ted Castle, Forensic. Campus Security Guard, Jessica House— scared to death—was next to Castle.

House was an invited guest to the meeting, which she thought would be way over her head. She was not scheduled to give a detailed report, but was expected to note her involvement, as she was the first on the scene—outside of the perp and the three women—of course. She was mostly there to answer any question that might be pertinent to the investigation and her involvement. Honestly, she felt like she was more in trouble then actually there to assist. Her keen insight would, however, become clearly noted before the meeting was over.

Joshua Caruthers from Crimes Against Persons Unit, Homicide Section sat stoically next to House, followed by FBI Agent Harriet Flister from ViCAP (Violent Criminal Apprehension Program). Captain Ernst Herrington from the Strategic Management Division sat angrily next to Harriet. Ernst was still upset that the Lieutenant had summarily dismissed him at the crime scene; though he squarely knew that the Lieutenant had the power and jurisdiction to admonish him as he did. Herrington had specifically made an appointment with Rodgers to discuss this very topic. He wanted disciplinary action taken against the Lieutenant, but the Captain's unscheduled meeting with prosecutor Walworth had superseded his meeting with the Rodgers. Herrington sat fuming, looking for the first chance to embarrass the kid, Wellsy!

The kid looked at his watch, and stood. "Ladies and gentlemen, I'm truly sorry for this long delay. Captain Rodgers told me he wouldn't be more than ten minutes late. Let's take a ten-minute break and reassemble." Everyone except Wellsy, Herrington, and Jessica House left the conference room. Understanding her anxiety, Arthur asked if he could get her anything. She said no, but then asked where the ladies room was. Herrington arose, walked her to the door and motioned. He then closed the door and glared at Wellsy. "Can I do something for you, Captain," Wellsy prodded with a wry grin?

Herrington jumped at the chance, "I'll have your job before this day is over, buster. Mark my word. You've insulted this Captain last night, and you'll never verbally attack me, again. I have a witness. That pretty young thing that just left here heard your, every word you uttered last night, you buffoon, and I'll have her testify against you. So don't even think of starting this meeting. You got that, buster? Because, Lieutenant Wellesley, you're through!" With that, he opened the door up, and exited. Wellsy just smiled, or would it be better to say he actually, smirked! *What an ass and he has the nerve to talk about House as 'that pretty young thing.'*

Herrington took less than four steps outside of the Conference Room and walked smack into Captain Rodgers. "Ah, Captain," Rodgers said, "I just saw everyone leave. Is the meeting over, or just taking a little break?"

Herrington didn't give the Captain a response to his question. Instead, he said, "Come with me for a moment, Captain, if you don't mind, I'd like to talk to you!" Things could not have worked out better for Herrington; he very willing followed the chief to the office of Rodger's secretary's office, June McCormack. The Sector Chief asked June if he might use her space for a moment. McCormack rose and slipped out of the room. Their meeting took less than three minutes.

The meeting was brief, Herrington walked out of the office wanting to go home. He had been tongue lashed for his conduct of superseding the actions of a junior officer in charge of an investigation. Regardless, the fact that Herrington out ranked the Lieutenant, the Lieutenant was in charge of the investigation and therefore such behavior as that of Herrington's was totally unacceptable to the Sector Captain. Rodgers made it clear that Herrington had no business interviewing April at the crime scene to begin with, and that he stepped far beyond his position of duty, and furthermore, he had no business at the crime scene, anyway. "That is not your job, nor your place, Captain Herrington."

Herrington tried to say that—as Captain of the Strategic Management Division—he could go where he damn well wished. Rodgers snapped back, telling Herrington to keep his mouth shut, that he was to be one hundred percent professional and make an apology to the Lieutenant before the meeting began, or—if he preferred—he could hand in his resignation, immediately. "Either is acceptable to me, Captain." Rodgers sneered.

Herrington said, "But…

"There aren't any buts, Captain. You have your choices. Make one of them now, but I warn you, if you don't apologize to the Lieutenant before this meeting starts; you are gone! Am I clear, *Captain*, or would you prefer to be a *Lieutenant*, again?"

Herrington stood his ground. "Sir, I have a grievance against the Lieutenant. I…"

"Fine, you have made your choice. Leave!"

"What? I will not leave!"

Captain Rodgers opened the door and stepped outside. He saw Patrolman David Atwater at the water cooler. "Officer, would you step in the office for a second."

The young patrolman said "Sure, Captain," and entered the office.

The Section Chief turned to Atwater, "Would you escort Captain out of this building?"

"Sir" Atwater, replied?

Herrington's countenance fell. He let out a deep sigh and responded, "The officer can leave, Chief."

Rodgers said, "Thank you Officer Atwater that will be enough. You've been a great help, thanks officer." Atwater walked out of the office scratching his head. *What was that all about?* With Atwater gone, the Captain then repeated his comment of less than two minutes, earlier, "You have your choices, Captain."

"Okay, but we're not finished with this, Captain. Mark my word."

"So noted, now scat! You have an apology to make, now! Don't you?"

By the time Herrington arrived back to the conference room, several had returned. He walked up to Wellsy and said, "Could we step outside for a moment?"

Wellesley was about to put this whole discussion on the line. He didn't care who was in the room, or listening. He wasn't going to listen to this anymore. He looked up, and over the shoulder of the Captain, he saw Sector Chief. Rodgers winked at him. *Whew!* Wellesley took a deep cleansing breath; his Captain put him at ease. "Look, Captain, Herrington, there really isn't anything to say. We were in the troughs of a tuff investigation. Why don't we both take the high road here and just let it be, okay with you?"

Herrington wanted to do just that and be done with it, but he was under orders. "Well, Lieutenant, Rodgers says I have to…"

"No need to, Captain. You don't need to say a word, I heard what you were thinking, and whatever it was, I accept! Okay?"

Maybe this Lieutenant wasn't so bad, after all. They shook hands. Herrington couldn't let such honor go unfinished. "Arthur, you're okay, really. Thanks! No offence intended."

"None, taken, Captain!" He paused, "Come on, we have an investigation to work through together. Let's get it underway."

Everyone took his or her seat for the Strategy meeting. Wellsy decided to further cement the working relationship by beginning with a far-outreaching statement, "Folks," he began, "we are fortunate to have one of the great strategists at the table, today, Captain Ernst Herrington from the Strategic Management Division. I look forward to his ideas as this meeting, and subsequent meetings that will surely take place." Rodgers gave Wellsy another wink. *The boy was bright.* "I'd also like to mention, by way of introduction, Jessica House of ODU Campus Security. Officer House was first on the crime scene." The Campus Guard nervously nodded in unwanted and unneeded recognition.

Everyone at the table was then asked to introduce him or herself, though most knew one another. After the introductions the Sector Lieutenant held up a handful of papers. "I've put together and open ended agenda, to keep us on track. It's open because we can add items, as they become apparent or necessary, and, people, we can jump from topic by topic if we must, but we'll use the agenda so we don't forget to cover certain items." He passed the papers around the table.

Each at the table looked, and read.

Agenda, Double Homicide of

Carolyn Ann Nowicki and Jessica June Anderson

Introductions

FBI Agent Harriet Flister from ViCAP (Violent Criminal Apprehension Program).

Impressions by Lieutenant Wellesley

Summary of note on the Crime Scene by Detective Strange

Forensic Report

Continued Impressions by Wellington with regard to Forensic

Break Lunch, catered in.

Assessment by Captain Rodgers

Insights and or Comments from Operations Center, Hank Blister

Crimes Against Persons Unit, Joshua Caruthers

Captain Ernst Herrington from the Strategic Management Division, Assessment

Other Business, or Additional Comments

Assignments

Next Scheduled meeting!

Charge to the Group, There will be more! Lieutenant Wellesley

The business of introduction was—at best—silly, as everyone knew one another except for Jessica House, so it was for her sake and to calm her nervousness a bit. The Lieutenant then turned the time over to FBI Agent Harriet Flister from ViCAP. Agent Flister's report was short and concrete, "There doesn't seem to be any connection with any other crime or crimes in the US or Worldwide as far as the FBI is concerned that link the Co-eds killings with any other US incident." With that, and if there weren't any questions, she asked if she could be excused. She left, after thanking the group for their notification to the Bureau. It was appreciated. Captain Rodgers thanked her for her patience. She snapped back, "All in a days work."

The agenda jumped from item three and then to ten when Joshua Caruthers from Crimes Against Persons Unit, Homicide Section felt what with the FBI no longer on the scene, that perhaps his involvement might well be served later in the investigation. The Lieutenant, agreed. He too was excused.

"Well, back to the agenda" Wellsy offered, "let me suggest where we are." He went over what they knew from the notes collected from Detective Strange, plus the Detective's follow up discussions with everyone who attended the Landrum crime scene. There weren't many wholes to fill in, even though Herrington had not cooperated with Strange at first. Strange, Wellesley and Herrington knew that would change, immediately. So, everyone was pretty much on the same page at this juncture, anyway.

The Detective then went over the statements of April Foster that he and Detective Strange gathered. "She had little to offer," he told the group. "The trauma of the event seems to have served a huge blank in her mind. Let me put it this way, "She is so distraught and scared that it took her well over three minutes to think of her own first name. She will—most likely—need therapy for some time. I hope to God that she at least recovers." Wellsy and Detective Strange would follow up with her, later. It would not be fruitful.

Wellsy offered, "Thanks, Detective." He let out a gush of air and continued, "Let me assure each of you that the things I'm thinking at this juncture are purely speculative, but very plausible, and credible. I begin with something that might startle all of you. I do not believe these senseless killings are that of a regular Serial Killer, if there was such a thing as a regular Serial Killer." He looked about the room, making eye contact with everyone, individually. "This monster, I believe was using these young women's deaths for some other greater goal than just killing them because he is a crazed lunatic, or because his mother hated him, or his dad beat him, or a dozen other common occurrences that make up the make up of a true Serial Killer! I don't believe he is such, at all." There was a mumble throughout the room.

"Don't get me wrong," he continued, "we've not, yet actually, acknowledged him as having that title, after all, there has been but one double homicide at this point, and, yes, it could be nothing more than a love triangle, but I don't think so." Captain Rodgers started to interrupt. "Please, Captain, let me finish. I have a bit more to say on this critical matter."

"I'll wait then."

"Very good. Thank you, Captain." He took a breath. "I know what all you are thinking, so just hold on and hear me out, please. Yes, we do have what we might call the seeds of a Serial Killer, but I don't believe that he sees himself that way at all. Of that I am about ninety percent sure!" He paused for affect. "Look, and I know I am repeating myself, but we don't even have but one double homicide. Yet—and I don't think I am wrong. Will everyone at this table yield to the notion that we do—in fact—have a Serial Killer here, right now, just for the sake of argument?" There wasn't a negative respond, so he said, "Right!"

His eyes searched the table. He gave anyone who disagreed with his theory another opportunity to speak up. He waited. There weren't any remarks. "So, we're on the same page on that, but perhaps for different reasons."

He cleared his throat, "Now, think for a moment, what do we have in the way of evidence? None really! We have two dead bodies that were diced, sliced, carved after being nailed to the floor. We have no true motive, or one we can put our finger on as of yet, and we don't know if these two women were friends or strangers of their assailant." He, again, paused to let that sink in!

"Additionally, if this ogre were truly a serial killer, he would—most likely—not have allowed one of the three young women to live. On the other hand, he showed his power that he could kill whom he wanted to, total control. But, folks, let me ask, why not April Foster? You have to ask yourself, why is she still alive? The perp didn't even attempt to kill her; scare the living hell out of her, yes, but he *wanted* to let her go, intentionally. He didn't even actually tape her to the floor, Ted will affirm that much."

Several looked to Ted Castle; he merely nodded in total agreement. "Yeah," Wellsy offered "the Perp made sure she could get away; it was intentional. He let her live so that he could make that statement." Wellsy sighed, and added, "Look, this is all speculation; it's just conjecture. I am not saying he is a serial killer at all. As a matter of fact, I don't think he is. But; then there's his statement written in blood: '*I kill whom I want to kill.*'" Wellsy took a few seconds to think. *How do I get this team to see how odd this killer really is? If I tell them the truth of what I believe they might think me a lunatic, too. Dare I take the next bold step?* He did. Mustering all the courage he had, he let it fly. "All of you have seen the bodies as have I. I have studied them, much more than I would have liked to." He let out a deep sigh. "Let me pass out a copy of one of the photos that was taken before I even saw the bodies." He passed around several copies of the two women tapped to the floor. "Does anyone see anything of importance?" Ted began to raise his hand. The Lieutenant waved him off. Ted had already had this part of the conversation with Wellsy at the crime scene.

After giving everyone about a minute, he continued, "Here is another photo that I specifically asked Ted to take. He passed out the close up of the double V's.

"Guys, focus in on the total picture, and no I'm not asking you to look closely at any specific part of their anatomy." He was pleased that no one chucked at that. On the other hand, he was displeased that none volunteered, anything, hopeful.

"Ok, he said, "here are the prints of the three messages the perp left, each brutally carved—while they were yet, alive, I'm afraid—on their abdomens and on the wall." He passed out the photographs of the three notes; three separate photos. "I know you are all familiar with them by now, but do not only look at them, but also listen to them as I read, them. Concentrate on the detailed wording. These were planned, I tell you. They did not happen by happenstance; they were clearly thought out! Wellsy stepped to the chalkboard, and flipped it around. He had previously written them out, both in French and in English. The first says,' he read in French first, and then in English, "'the most dangerous moment comes with victory! #1'" He paused. "Now read it a few times."

He waited, giving the group more study time. He then continued. "The second carving says," again, he read it in both languages "'the secret of war lies in the communications! #2.'" Think about that." He was quiet again, for nearly a full minute. "Finally," he said, "Look that what he wrote on the wall in large letters, capitals." He read it slowly, and succinctly, "'VICTORY BELONGS TO THE MOST PERSEVERING!'" This time, he gave them three full minutes to contemplate all of it. He then asked, "Anyone?"

They were all dumfounded, except Ted—the Forensic guy—he knew, but then he knew because Wellington had told him, therefore, he remained, silent. *Wellesley is one smart guy*, Ted, still thought. After, yet, another minute, he offered, "Go back to the close-up photos of the two women." He was silent for another moment.

"I got it," House, offered, "I've got it!" Suddenly she was silent. She figured she wasn't actually a part of this team and had no business speaking. She then offered, anyway, "Give them another clue, Lieutenant. Give them the picture of the nails that are still in the floor of where April was tied up, too." *Wow*, he thought, *she really did get it*. She was far smarter than he had given her credit. Rodgers was duly impressed as well.

Wellsy, then passed out the close up of the nail configuration of that of April Pinkerton as well. It was obvious, she, too had been placed in a spread-legged eagle position. At that, he asked them all, again if they noticed anything, key!

Still, not one of them got it. Jessica House couldn't wait any longer. "May, I," she asked. Wellsy allowed her, her moment of *victory*! He was proud of her. Her life was coming back together. She spoke, "He—this guy—has an ego the size of Jupiter. Five times he said, or better, yet, taunted victory."

"Victory?" Captain Rodger's ballyhooed, "indeed, victory!"

"Okay, wait a minute, we have that written twice, but what other three times," Herrington, asked. "Where do they come from?"

House looked back at him and smiled. She put two fingers up in the air, her index and middle finger. She put them up in the shape of a V. "V, she said, V for victory.

Herrington and everyone else looked at the two photos, and the two vaginas, plus they could see by the nail layout that held the tape and forced the shape of April, into a third vagina or a third V. It was proof positive. Herrington spoke, "He's pushing his victory in our face, the words he used, the double V's their legs make, and also that of April's V. Not only that, they are all nude. Is he saying he owns them because he owned their vaginas? He owns women."

"Yes, I agree, but may be not the owning of women; I'm not sold on that part, yet." Wesley added, though he thought it was crudely worded. You've got it, Captain Herrington, but he tried his best to make a tough game out of it?"

"What, with the nail pattern as well," Herrington challenged

Wellsy, responded, "Not exactly, Captain, but close enough. But, in a way you are right. He was totally in control of them, all three of them. They were his victories. Yes, maybe he did own them, after all. He could do anything with them that he wanted too, and he did, indeed, shove our faces into it, but he assumed we would focus in on the exposed vaginas, and not the shape in which he staked them out!"

"There is more to it than that, Lieutenant," House, offered.

Rodger asked her to go on. She said she didn't know but something else was bothering her, but she couldn't put her finger on it." During the whole process of the investigation, she never would figure it out, but another female would, Alexandria.

Captain Rodgers noted that the words were equal to his gloating. "He wrote, 'the most dangerous moment comes with victory #1'" The Sector leader paused for just a few seconds and continued: "Lieutenant, he wanted us, you Lieutenant to know that he was victorious, and the possibility of getting caught was the most dangerous because he had hung around so long—spent the extra time—to do this nasty work, the carving and the wall writing." He paused, and swallowed, hard. "It was very, very dangerous to spend that added time." Wellesley wanted to interrupt the Captain, but decided to wait. He allowed his superior to continue. "Everyone," the Captain took a breath and went on: "He had total control, over them—the women—and over us—the law and the order people, and perhaps, particularly over you. Lieutenant."

Wellsy waited while they all read and looked at the photos, again. He offered, "People, look at the second carving of his work; the second carving says, 'the secret of war lies in the communications! #2.' Think about that." He was quiet again. "Finally," he said, "look that what he wrote on the wall in large letters, all capitals." He read, "'*VICTORY BELONGS TO THE MOST PERSEVER-ING!*'"

Lieutenant Wellsy offered; "That is exactly my point, he *didn't* hang around extra time to do the torture, and to do the tying, and to do the spreading, and to do the carving, and to do the writing on the wall. No Captain that is why he went there in the first place. He went there to do those things, specifically, all of them. He wanted to show us his victory, but not over them—the two or three women—but over us!" He paused, "Perhaps, as you suggest, Captain, me, and me alone." Wellsy took a breath. "You see, not only did he show us his victory over them and us, but he let us know that he had to persevere to accomplish that." The Lieutenant then stopped and looked around the room while he continued, "If we are to catch this methodic lunatic, we must persevere beyond his own callas behavior. We must be better than him."

"So, how do we catch him?" House asked.

"We outthink him. We have to realized, that he only murdered these hapless women to offer an opportunity to talk to us!"

"Who are we?" Ted asked.

"I'm not sure we know, yet, only subsequent killings will answer that, unfortunately!" The Lieutenant, offered.

House was really getting into this whole thing. Wellsy had new respect for this woman.

"Well, Ms. House," Rodgers, asked, "Will he tell us how to catch him, or doesn't he want us to catch him?" Herrington asked. Sadly, house didn't have the answer to that, she shrugged her shoulders and looked to the Lieutenant for help.

"Wellsy smiled at her, and he then chimed in, "No, Captain, I believe he wants to catch us!"

All stared at the morose Lieutenant. Jessica House spoke up, "I think he will be one sly fox, but, indeed, he wants us to chase him until he catches us." Wellsy smiled. The rest of the group looked at the wisdom in the room, a young security cop from Old Dominion and a very young Lieutenant were coming up with gems.

"So," House said, "we either catch him, or eventually, he kills us." She paused, and then added, "That would be his true victory! He will lie in wait for us, and perhaps one at a time. To be honest, I believe he would like to capture one of us and torture that person to offer revenge to the rest of us!

"What does that mean." Herrington, asked.

The Lieutenant, answered, "Study the clues, and if you don't get it, yet, be patient, he will leave more and more clues with more and more dead women, and/or men. So wait for more clues and watch more women, or men, or both, die, but we must understand fully the clues we have now. They are all we have now so study them. I will tell you one more time; he is not a Serial Killer by definition. He is a serial avenger. He's getting back at someone, or something. He will kill, and kill, and kill, again!"

"What does that mean, Lieutenant?" Detective Earnest L. Strange, asked.

"Well, I told you all earlier, that you might think me off the wall, but here it is." He took a breath. "There is something to these notes and to his words, and carvings. It's all about victory in the end, or retribution, or vengeances that I think will all tie to a greater something. I don't have that yet, but I believe he wants to end with some special killing; the rest is foreplay up to that point." He sighed, "To catch him, we must find his true target." He then added for affect, "Foreplay for him, and death for others. It's his means to justifies his end, or vengeance of some kind." With that, the Lieutenant asked, "Any question?"

There weren't any; all were spellbound. Lieutenant Wellesley then gave them a charge to work harder and faster, for many more killings would appear with messages, to boot. "No," he said. "He is not a Serial Killer by definition, but the results are the same! He is looking for his next victim, or victims, as we speak, unless, of course, he has the entire operation already all planned out. It's all part of his game; perhaps a war and this is but one battle of that war. God help us!" Wellsy turned to Captain Ernst Herrington from Strategic Management Division. "Captain, the floor is yours."

"Let me think on this, Lieutenant, let me think! But I do have a question if you will take it?"

"Ask away!"

"What are the one and two about as numbered on the bodies, about?"

He didn't need to pause or to think, he let it fly; "I think in part you have answered it with your question, sir. We know he killed them nearly at the same time. Which first, we cannot tell, but my guess, he killed them in order, one and two."

"Meaning that he killed Jessica, first and Carolyn second." Herrington, added."

"Your guess is as good as mine, but study the clues. The answers are surely there. See how many ways you can calculate his comments." Wellsy paused. "Any other comments or questions?" He waited. "No! Then we are adjourned." He added; "If you come up with anything, contact Detective Strange or me, either way." He then asked if the Captains had anything?

"None, appearing, the meeting is adjourned," he offered, and then added, "Thank you all for coming," and then he added, "and if you come up with a theory that you believe is better than the one we came up with today, contact me. I do not have any more evidence than do any of you. Your theory is as good as mine! Better, if you are right."

Detective Strange was more than pleased to be hooked up with this snappy Lieutenant.

House wondered if Wellsy was married.

Wellsy new he needed to make that damn phone call.

Chapter 6—Day Six
BI YAN

Nabulio held in his hand the latest copy of the *Mace and Crown*. He loved this Old Dominion college newspaper, as it had already offered him his first two participants that opened new rounds of battle in a much older war. It gave him everything he needed for this second clash as well. He was looking carefully at the Deans' List: the smartest of the smartest students on campus. There were scores of names to choose from. Except—of course—for the two names that had already been lined out: Nowicki, Carolyn Ann and Andersen, Jessica June, and, of course all other girls whose last names began with an "A" or a "N" were now safe; as were those whose last name did not fit within the framework of his needs of war. Presently, he was looking for the right girl, the female whose last name started with "B".

While there were many to select from—twelve in all—his choice was made easily. As soon as he saw her name, it felt right, she felt right, she even sounded right. She was most intriguing. Once chosen, he began his investigated of her—Bi Yan—to make sure she would be a realistic candidate. He found three pictures in the previous year's yearbook: her student picture among the rest of the students; another, she was sitting poolside with legs in the water, chatting with a friend, and a group photo of the debate team. She was, indeed, perfect.

Her Chinese surname or family name, or xing was Bi. Her given name, or ming was Yan. She was a third year junior, smart as a whip, and unquestioningly pretty, bordering on gorgeous. She was a member of the Chinese Student and Scholar Association at Old Dominion (CSSA-ODU), another plus. She was on the colleges swim team, and the schools debate team. And, as an added bonus, she was the Captain of the debate team; refreshing news!

The fact that she was a scholar really pleased Nabulio, but then again, everyone on the Deans List was qualified; of course! He also liked what the

CCSA stood for, especially the fact that its' associates were "to protect its members against various possible injustices, to facilitate the mutual helps within the community." He loved the humor in it. After all, none of her CCSA members would be able to do anything for her by way of protection against long overdue injustice. Nope, they couldn't help one lick! She was merely a casualty of war, almost picked at random. Yes, Nabulio like that very much.

Nabulio took but six days to cross-reference everything he had found out about his newest candidate volunteer. He had all he needed to know, where she lived, what classes she was enrolled in, her daily schedule, and her part-time job at Tupelos just three quarters of a mile from campus. He liked the fact that she biked wherever she went. However, Nabulio didn't like the fact that she had two roommates in her off campus apartment, Connie Shay and Beverly Simons, neither of which were ODU students. That was fine by Nabulio; as those two weren't going to be participants anyway, except—more than likely—one or both would find Bi Yan's charred body and scream and such, and then be asked and have to answer a zillion police questions which most of which, they would have no clue. None!

Nabulio caught a break when he found out that housemate Connie also worked at Tupelos, and that she seldom worked the same shift as Yan. The other housemate, Beverly had a steady male friend and they were most often gone, together, but there were still some snags that had to be ironed out with Beverly and boyfriend. Knowing when Beverly would and wouldn't be gone for an entire evening or night could be dangerously tough to work out. Worse, yet, if Beverly happened to come home on the evening of the battle with her male friend things could get really ugly. Well; there are always dangers in war; weren't there? Yes, Nabulio would regulate sufficient contingency plans.

With all this in mind, Nabulio decided on a mid-morning plan of attack, but—of course—that meant no darkness to steal away in, and no perfect way to wander about with a bloody rubber suit on, and the equipment he would have to lug around. *Even to W that might be a big clue*, Nabulio chuckled. So, his decided mid morning plan became the negated plan. There wasn't any hurry, after all, his entire mission needed to take exactly 101 days from beginning to end, and he had two of the seven bodies in hand, already—well—actually two of eight already in the bag. No worries!

He continued his investigation. He followed Yan to class, to work, to home, to the library campus and back, again. Incognito, he visited a swim meet, and watched her. Little by little, he knew her, became one with her. He liked her. He liked her, a lot, and he liked the fact that she was beautiful—no, not beautify, she was darn right gorgeous, beyond description. But Nabulio wouldn't ever cross that line, but he could certainly admire, just not touch. This was war, but he didn't believe in ravaging the conquest. Though throughout history, *to the winner often went the spoils*, and all too often women were the spoils of war. *Something to ponder*, he gave consideration too. He nearly hardened at the thought. He had to shout 'NO' to his mind. He was angered.

The thing that intrigued him was the fact that though Oriental, she seemed to have rather large breasts. He remembered his last comment to Carolyn about her breasts. Yan's breasts were certainly much smaller than Carolyn's were, but by Chinese standards, Yan's were gigantic, especially considering her petite figure. Nabulio put those teasers out of his mind for the present. *A future bonus*, he thought. At length, he told himself to get his head out of the gutter, that this was war and his personal desires had nothing to do with combat; nor of winning the battle. But, on the other hand, again, he pondered, to the winner go the spoils of war. *Stop it*, he thought. *Pull yourself together man*. He actually contemplated finding another girl to take her place so he could date her. He quickly realized that he was losing focus. His appetites would have to way until after the hundred and first day.

Nine days after his initial opening of war, he made his strategic plan to further his cause, the origin of total revenge, nothing more. The plan was for 9:30 p.m., two days hence. Like the previous engagement of war, he would wear a rubber suit, but this time, the suit would be under his jogging pants and sweatshirt. Nevertheless, when he left her house, the suit would be just as bloody as his first battle, but his jogging pants and sweatshirt would soak up much of the blood, when he re-donned them over the blood stained rubber suit for the casual get-a-way. *Perfection*, he thought; he mused.

He pre-tested everything. Inside the pizza box, all the necessary items easily fit, and it gave the box the right feel and weight of a real pizza housed, inside, and it included the iron "W"; which took considerable time to make. Nabulio placed the needed items in the box in the order they would be needed for that evening's use. Later, the folded and crumpled box would return to his home along with everything else, including a very small part of Yan.

He wrote up a list of things to be left behind: the discarded cigarette, ashes, partly burnt matchstick, saucer from her kitchen, and finally, a couple short strands of black hairs, pretty much the opposite of his own dishwater blonde hair, a jean that traced back through his mother's ancestral line. He taped the note to the rubber pant leg, outside were his right knee would be inside the suit.

Two days before the assault, Nabulio planned to get a hair cut, and—while at the barbers—he would be sure to collect a few strands of black hair from a previous customer. In fairness, he had to give W a break—some free DNA—albeit, someone else's; which made him chuckle at the notion. Nabulio loved the game of war. He loved toying with W's mind, and he knew Wellesley was brilliant, but not quite as brilliant as himself, of course. He wrote a note and taped it to his medicine cabinet in the downstairs bathroom. "Be sure to wash your hair several times before night of engagement." He wanted to be sure no loose hair follicles of his own would find it's way back to Miss Chinese.

Unlike his first escapade, this time, he would leave but one simple carved clue, and it was a dandy. Every thing was ready, well prepared two full days before the operation he called *China Night* was to commence!

The day before the event, he stopped by Tupelos. He asked for the pretty redhead that worked there. "I'm sorry she's not scheduled to work this week." He thumped himself on the head and said he'd forgotten that she was going out of town for a few days. Estelle, from behind the counter, acknowledged, "Yes, she's in Baltimore visiting with her family. I'm sure her *boyfriend* went with her! She placed a lot of emphasis on the word boyfriend; least this guy thought he had some chance with her! Estelle didn't like the vibes she got from this intruder, either.

Estelle would later tell Detective Strange that very thing—that she got bad vibes from the guy who asked about Connie—but no, she didn't remember what he looked like, but he had hair above his lip, dark or black, I think. Yes, Nabulio had a stash, but he had removed it when he was back in his car and headed down the road after leaving Tupelos. Estelle wouldn't remember how tall he was, and he had on a hooded sweatshirt with Old Dominion pressed on it. She couldn't remember anything else; after all, she sees *tons* of people, everyday.

Three blocks away, Nabulio put the PT window down and dropped the mouse-stash to the pavement. The stranger—Nabulio—was long gone, and out of Estelle's mind, until Strange would pay her that visit; later. By then, her memory would be too foggy to be of much help, except that the guy had a mouse-stash and wore an Old Dominion sweatshirt. A police sketch artist couldn't do justice with Estelle's remembrance of the man that came to her shop.

The warrior turned the corner and headed home, his sanctuary.

Tomorrow night was the night; he thought. Everything was ready. The swim photograph that he had seen in the yearbook, taken at the side of the pool was just what he needed, and he was a math wiz anyway so doing the computations wasn't all that hard to take the photo measurements and translate them in to actual living dimensions. By his translated measurements of her, the print from the apparatus should work just perfectly. Its brazen mark would confuse the living hell out of the Lieutenant, the mine duke of Wellington. Yes, Nabulio knew all about this man named Arthur Wellington Wellesley. Everything was ready for the second battle. A battle that he would win, and this time, it would greatly bamboozle the Lieutenant.

Nabulio was having more fun than a body ought to have; so much so, that he rewarded himself by calling an escort service and had a beauty of beauties toy with him for the night.

Chapter 7—Day Eight
THE DISCUSSION

Eight days after the massacre in Landrum Hall, the case was going nowhere, or as John Madden might say, "going nowhere fast." One really couldn't call it a massacre by definition; two slaughtered co-eds could hardly be considered a massacre. Make no mistake, for those two women and even April wouldn't argue, disagree with the terminology. April still didn't have her life back. She would wake up in the middle of the night and not be able to budge because of the bans of tape that were nailed to her hospital bed. Over and over again, she was told, that it was all in her mind. With her own clarity, she knew better. Anytime the door to her room opened, she saw their killer; man or women, it didn't matter; he lurked after her all the time with many different faces; the faces of death!

The same could be said of Alexandria and Arthur. There relationship was going nowhere, fast. It was stalled. As hard as they might try to draw closer together, the more the case—Case Number H1122242—would unwillingly close in. Part of the problem was that Arthur couldn't stop thinking about it. Therefore, he had to talk about it. So, from Alex's perspective, the case was still the unavoidable wedge. So, when they were together, it was the case. And, when they weren't together, Alex worried about her Wellsy. Together, or apart, there was always at the center of their life Case Number H1122242.

What was even stranger was the fact that while Alex actually wanted it to all go away, as did Wellsy; it was also a fact that Alex was very interested in the whole case, if she only had to look at it clinically that is! She had to observe the case as if her Wellsy wasn't actually a player, thee player at the center of the case. So, they offered—together—a sort of compromise. She would actually help him solve the mystery, if he wouldn't drudge up the nasty stuff and, or the always danger of his own life. He so avowed.

It was agreed. But, it was also agreed that until the case was completed, there wouldn't be any more talk of engagement, let alone, marriage. It was difficult for the both of them. They both wanted the marriage, badly, but not badly enough that they would just lay aside his work. They, would, however, talk about the case as a daily practice. Doing so would fill them both with great anxiety, to the point that the only release was passionate lovemaking, sometimes just plain raw savage sex. The case seemed to bring out the beast in them both. So, the case wasn't completely bad; and finally, the case had its fun side to it for the both of them, too. Afterward, the reality, however, would always come back. The case was ever there, yes, and all the brutality as well. That just wouldn't go, away either.

One full week and a day had passed since the girls' destruction by the madman. Alex's Wellsy awoke with a new idea. It was a strange one, but he kept it to himself for the time being. It had to do with the females' names. He wondered? He got out of bed and used the facilities, brushed his teeth and turned on the shower. He was still thinking about the females' names. Suddenly, he felt her bare breasts on his back. He reached around and grabbed her and puller her into the shower. For nearly forty-five minutes he forgot all about the name thing.

An hour later he found himself at his desk playing the name game.

CHAPTER 8—DAY EIGHT
THE SECOND BATTLE

Nabulio parked the PT. He put on the hat. He looked in the rear view mirror, and then both side mirrors, no cars coming from behind. He looked out the side window on his left, and then on his right. He checked the rear, again, and then looked out the front windshield. *Praise to the gods, no one coming or going.* He stepped out of his car, and walked around to the passenger's side door and opened it. He clicked the door lock closed by depressing the little plastic box that was part of his key chain and all the locks went to the locked position. He grabbed the plastic bottle that lay harmlessly on top of the pizza box. With his other hand he unscrewed and removed the lid. He doused the handkerchief. He put the object in his hand, and then placed the pizza on top of the turned up hand that held the smelly wet hankie. He looked in all directions. Still, no one was coming. It was just twilight time outside her apartment.

He walked as calmly as a summers breeze across the street, stepped up the four steps of her stoop and rang the bell. It was all rehearsed in his head. He was prepared. He rang the bell, again. Yan said from within, "Just a minute." He waited for thirteen seconds. It didn't faze him. Yan opened the door, cocked her head and peeked around it. Her long wet jet-black hair drooped off the side of her head and danged toward the hardwood floor. She was gorgeous beyond belief.

"Hi, I'm Tim from the Corner Pizzeria on Wilson. I have a pizza for Beverly Simons."

"I'm sorry, she is not here."

"Huh? She left?"

"No, well, yes, but that was over two hours ago. She won't be back until late tonight."

He cleared his throat, "Well, hum, I don't know what to say, are you sure she is not home?" He paused, just as he had rehearsed it. "I mean we got a call from her," he looked at the paper tab taped to the box, "she called 26 minutes, ago, and ordered this pizza." She gave her number." Yan verified that this was their number all right, but truly, she wasn't here. He thought for a second, pretending, anyway, and then offered. "Look, I'm really sorry to burden you with this, but may I use your phone to call Corner Pizzeria, it will only take a sec, okay?"

"Well, normally I would, but I'm not dressed. I just got out of the shower."

"Oh, I understand, what with what the world is today. I don't blame you. I have an idea, if you have a cell phone, could you let me borrow it and I'll call from out here."

She offered a heavy sigh; it's upstairs I'll have to go get it. She turned away, and then turned back to him, changing her mind. "Oh, okay, come on in but make it quick, please. I don't understand how this could happen. She stepped back from him, as he entered and pushed the door closed. He made two steps and then stood still. She openly stared at him. "What," she said?

"Where is your phone?"

"Oh," she giggled, "I'm sorry it's in the kitchen, follow me." She turned to her left. She hadn't taken two steps and he popped the pizza box on a small end table, made two quick steps toward her as she started to turn toward him, hearing the noise. She didn't even get to a three-quarter turn. He was on her in a flash. With his left arm he whipped it around her head and drew her tiny frame toward him hard. His right arm and hand flew around her other side and the chloroform handkerchief found her nose and mouth. Seconds later, she was sound asleep. The struggle could hardly be noticed, and hardly took anytime at all. She was strong, but he was so much bigger and stronger and—after all—he did have a death grip around her throat, if he wanted to use that grip as such its purpose.

He could not believe her pure beauty. She really was the most beautiful woman he had ever seen. He scooped her up and looped around and headed in the opposite direction, moving toward the stairway. He took the steps two at a time. In the bedroom, he gently laid her on the carpeted floor. He was so curious, and had been for days. Under the robe would be her true beauty, his fantasy.

It was those darn breasts that he could not stop thinking about for days on end. He unhurriedly, bit by bit undid the loop of her robe, and unwrapped it as slowly as he possibly could. This wasn't something to rush. He peaked with excitement. Oh, my, there they were, indeed, perfect, *simply perfect*, he thought. He so wanted to touch so badly, but he didn't. Instead, he raced back down the stairs and opened the pizza box. On top were the first items he needed. But, before donning the rubber gloves, he removed his shirt and pants, revealing the rubber suite. He then put on the gloves, and locked the door; Nabulio then raced to the kitchen and took the phone off the switch hook. Next, he put on the plastic shower cap, and then walked up the stairs with the pizza box in hand.

He gently removed her white robe and discarded it to the bed. She was completely nude now. Completely. He gazed at her whole beauty for over two minutes; just gendering, lovingly. Her loveliness took his breath away. *Perfect*, he thought, and then Nabulio gazed the better part of three more minutes at her curves and crevices.

Finally, he got to work. He stuffed eleven cotton balls into her mouth, making her look like a gofer with her cute cheeks bulging outward. He then heavily taped her mouth shut with two pieces of duct tape, over lapped. He then hammered the nails into the floor, and carefully taped her hands to the nails like he had the lovely Jessica and Carolyn. He then placed her legs together, not as his previous victims legs had been placed in their spread eagle position, though. Instead, he gently placed her right heel over the arch of her left ankle, and wrapped the tape around them firmly, five times.

The next part was difficult for him as he drove the nails into the floor on either side of her hips. He could not help but stare. That is when it happened. That is when he became angrier with himself then he had ever been. He was becoming aroused. He stopped his activity, and fought the notion. He wanted them. Only them, mind you, after all, he did not believe in rape, even if in the throws of a savage war. He walked away until he found his apparatus back to normal. He crossed back to her body and continued his work, avoiding any peaks of her breasts, whatsoever. He was a professional soldier and he would act accordingly.

He removed the metal object from the pizza box. He looked at her, then, the design, again. He laid it upon her body. The fit was perfect. The first end—the top end—went about one half an inch above the top part of her right breast. The metal structure then angled downward, and inward as if it wanted to go from it's starting place to her navel in a direct line, but it stopped well short of going that far. The metal structure stopped almost perfectly to where he had designed it to stop—his calculations were perfecto—stopping perfectly just one inch below and in the middle of where her right breast nipple was, but below the bottom of the entire breast. It formed a perfect V design with the entire right breast resting perfectly inside of the V, yet, not touching it at all. Her nipple was dead center in the V. Nope, not one particle of the breast touched the metal part of the V. It was perfectly designed.

Added to the structure, another V, equal in size to the first had been welded to the outer top of the first, so the two together offered a double V as in VICTORY! Or so Nabulio wanted W to think. The two V's looked like this-> VV with each having a full breast inside each letter, and neither breast had touched the apparatus—no scar tissue to the breasts whatsoever. There was just enough added room that the mark could be made without fear of actually touching either perfect breast. He removed the metal for the time being.

He rose and walked toward her head, and drew back all of her hair above the top of her head completely baring all of her forehead. He then pulled about eighteen inches of duct tape from the roll, tore it and placed the middle of the tape across her forehead and tapped the rest to the floor. He then took nails and nailed the tape to the floor at the point where the tape angled to the floor from her head. He didn't want her to force her head up to look at his work, though he wouldn't mind, but the double V's needed to be perfect and if she saw ahead of time what was coming, her head would thrust upward and it could cause her body to surely move some, and perhaps forcing him to miscalculate. That would never do, this job had to be executed with exact perfection, for the sake of the job, and for the sake of his strongest desire not to disfigure her breasts at all; after all, he was going to immortalize them. He smiled at the thought.

He waited another five minutes. She was still asleep, so he tried to revive her, gently slapping her facial cheeks. She moved, but did not wake up. He sauntered to the kitchen to get some ice. Having returned, he made little circles about her face and neck with the ice cubes. That did the trick. She finally opened her eyes. Before she could figure out why, she thrust at her pinned position. She saw him standing above him. She tried to talk. She couldn't. She tried to move. She couldn't. She tried to move her limbs. They would not move. She tried to lift her head. She could not. She was justifiably terrified. Her eyes were open wild with fear, anxiety, and pure terror!

He said, "We need to take care of our three tasks, but don't worry, I'll do all the work. Oh," he remembered, "that funny taste in your mouth is cotton-batten. Sorry about that, but there will be some pain involved; Jessica and Carolyn, kind of taught me by their example that I should have used more cotton then I did, you know, to get rid of the muffled screams; sorry! Of course," he added, "their pain wasn't nearly as bad as yours will be, but it's necessary; sorry!"

She was already scared, but when she heard to two women's names, her eyes went wild, darting to and fro, and her heart flew in beats; she knew, she had read the paper and watched the news. She tried desperately to shake her head side to side to nonverbally say no. Her head would not move, and she couldn't even hear her own vocal muffs. Her breaths were coming in rapid bursts. She needed desperately to breath though her mouth. She was suffocating. Her body was shaking violently. "Okay, okay," he said. Just a minute, I'll help you." Her eyes followed his every move. He undid his leg patch that was taped down and took out the small jack-knife. He opened it and said, "Try to move your lips apart. I'll stick the knife between you lips so you can get some air. He thrust the knife too high; it sliced her upper lip and the knife cut into her top gums. "Oops, sorry," he said. He saw the blood bubble so he knew she was getting some air. "Good!" he said.

"Now, Yan, this will hurt some, but it won't last too long, and it will help prepare you for the second part, because that is really going to hurt, but you'll probably pass out I would think. Oh, and one more thing. I really don't want to have to tape you down anywhere else, so please cooperate and let me do my work. I know this will be tougher for you, because you know what happened to the others, but I can't help that. He smiled. He wanted to kiss her, but that was out of the question, DNA, and all that business. "Well, shall we begin?"

With every bit of strength she had, she tried to wriggle away. It wasn't any use. She couldn't lift up her head to look, but he was still standing. She watched him tear off a piece of tape from his leg and underneath it was another knife, a much larger knife. Her cheeks bloused in and out, fast, and her blood was actually flying out of her mouth now with every gush of panted air. She remembered seeing one just like it in her uncles tackle box. It was called a Buck knife. She was paralyzed with fear, and nearly hyperventilating. Her mind was screaming *I don't want to die, I don't want to die; I don't want to die, please, please, please let me live.*

He knelt down, turned and looked at her. "I want you to know. You are the most beautiful woman I have ever seen, truly. You are perfect in every way." He paused, and then volunteered a question, "Would you like to know what I'm going to carve?" She lay motionless, yet her eyes were searching everywhere for some miracle of hope. He twisted about and looked dreamingly at her, just one more time. "Try not to pass out, because I will have to wait for you to recover, before I will be able to go on, so let's be a team, okay?" He then added, "Here we go."

The cotton helped, a lot. He could barely hear her muffles. It also helped that he put a lot of pressure above her abdomen with his left palm so she couldn't wriggle as much. Her taped feet however jerked about with every cut. He found that annoying, but understood. She wreathed in agony; helplessly! He was relentless, cut after cut after cut, but no deeper—for the most part—than three-eights to one half of an inch deep. He was pleased she bled much less then the two others because there was a lot to write and he need needed every part of her stomach. He needed so much room that the last word had to be carved right over her pubic hairs. So, he had to stop his designed work, and take the knife and shave her. Only then did he finish.

She was still conscious, but going into shock. Somehow, she was still with him, alive and awake. Actual puddles had accumulated on the floor from her tears. The teardrops would dissipate before the body would be found, however. He was so proud of her. *What a great partner*, he thought. He looked at her, "You did really good, Yan, very well, indeed. Thank you!" He paused, and then stood, and said, "I'll be right back. I need to get something to clean up this mess. I'll be right back and we'll finish." He walked away. He stopped, and came back. He offered; "By the way, the other girls were not raped. I know there were a lot of rumors about that, but it didn't happen, so be of good cheer, you are safe; you'll not be raped; though I'd like…" His voice tailed, off! Nabulio started walking away. He stopped, and came back and offered, "Oh, and one more thing, you truly are the most beautiful woman I have ever met, and your breasts are literally perfect, womanly perfect." He paused, slightly then added, "In a minute, I'll frame them for time and all eternity, but W will misunderstand the message. Poor, W."

He went to the bathroom and brought back two towels, one of them was wringing wet, the other was dry. He washed and cleaned her stomach several times. Involuntarily, she squirmed in agony, every time. Through foggy eyes she watched him get out this metal contraption of some kind. It looked like a big W with a prong sticking out at the top in the middle of the W.

She saw him take something cylinder looking out of the pizza box. He took a match and ignited it and the cylinder blew out a yellow-bluish flame. He held the prong part that was made of iron, but had a looking casing around the prong handle. He held the wood part and put the flame to the end of the metal part, moving it around for the longest time. It never got to red heat, but she could see the waves of heat spilling off of it, nevertheless. She knew she was going to get branded. Fear alone caused her near to shock. Her eyes were glossing over; yet, she still comprehended it all; well, what was going to happen, anyways.

He spoke to her, lovingly, but she couldn't understand his words, but she could smell the heat that poured off the metal. He placed his feet, spreading his legs over her body near her pelvic area; facing her. He was telling her not to move or it might get all messed up. He told her, "I only have one chance in getting this right." He held the prod as planned and slowly brought the scorching, smoking V to her upper torso. She could feel its heat from seven inches away.

Nabulio paused, and looked up at her. "Now you know this is going to hurt, so brace yourself, but I will be quick and efficient." He was steady, and his mark perfectly scorched into her surrounding breast without touching at part of the breast, itself. Actual noise came from her lips and her torso arched as far as her shackles of tape allowed. She could smell her own sizzling flesh just as she was quickly passing out. Fortunately, Kim barley felt the pain, but her senses smelled her pain. With that, she was totally out cold! Nabulio reheated the instrument and unceremoniously branded the second V, creating the double VV about her unblemished breasts.

He was glad she was out. He didn't want her to know about the last phase, only the W, and his hoard of onlookers—the other less minded idiots—needed to know. He hated to spoil that which was already perfect but, but Nabulio had to be thought of as a true serial killer and this would help. He removed the glove of his left hand. He most carefully leaned over and took the nipple of her left breast with his thumb and index finger and pulled it up, firmly. Then, cautiously he removed her right nipple with one quick swipe of the buck knife. He took a piece of tape and taped her nipple to his suite. A tear spilled from his eye, realizing that he had just destroyed a perfect breast. The severed nipple would later be incinerated with everything else. Nabulio didn't need the souvenir; he just needed W and his lot to think he did. He put his glove back on.

He wiped her stomach some more. The blood had slowed its leaking. It could be easily read, now:

Power is my mistress. I have worked too hard at her conquest to allow anyone to take her away from me.

#3.

He smiled at the number three. Now they would know for sure, he was numbering them, one by one, and in the correct order. That was most important. It was an intentionally blockbuster of a clue, now. Now W could add to the previously number one and two. Nabulio loved the individual battles of the greater war; the war that so far; he was the only one who knew; but the time would soon come. The days were clicking down; he knew, only!

He was done, except for the last of the last. He cleaned everything up, and took the metal piece to the bathroom, stuck it under the showerhead and turned on the water and watched it seam away to nothingness. He looked at his watch. He had been there 47 minutes; well within the hour he had allotted. He thought back to when he pulled up to her apartment, she must have been just getting out of the shower, so full of life. It was sad that she would be dead in less than a minute, but his work was done. It was perfect in every way; yes, he was so perfect in every way! He gave a last look in the kitchen, the bathroom, the doorway entrance, and the bedroom, again. He left the few strands of black hair about seven feet from the body. He did the cigarette thing, again, but he figured W had already figured that out.

Nabulio brought the knife blade gently to her throat. He was just about to cut when her eyes opened. She saw him. He saw her deep shock look, but a look of life, nevertheless. He put his lips to her ear. "You are the most beautiful woman God ever gave to this world." She didn't hear his words or the gush of air that slipped though her severed throat.

He put the telephone receiver back where it belonged. He donned his blue jeans and sweatshirt over the rubber suit.

Once in his car, he smiled a smile of success and relief. When got home he would do all the necessary clean up and burning, and then shower and relive today's battle. A block away from her apartment, he turned on the radio and pushed the CD button, and listened to the serene sound of the Beatles, song, *Let it Be.*

CHAPTER 9—DAY NINE
FIRST AND 2ND WITNESS

Beverly Simons decided not to go home last night, the night her roommate was butchered. She tried to call Yan five times. The first two calls were met with busy signals; the last three calls were answered by the answering machine, so Bevy—as her roommates called her—only heard her own-recorded voice at home. She was sure that Yan had said that she was staying home all evening, but, hey, even Yan went out from time to time.

This morning at seven minutes after nine, Bevy tried, again, and again, all she got was the same recording. That was way strange. Yan didn't ever stay out all night. But, Bevy dismissed it, anyway; *who knows*, after all, Yan often did the workout thing; she could have been out running, gone to the store, or as she some times did, just didn't want to answer the telephone. That irked Bevy, but she was used to it. The final time she called, she merely left a message for Yan. "Hey, girl, I'll be there about noon so check you out, then. Make us some lunch. Love, Bevy." She added as a afterthought, "Oh, by the way, were are you?"

At twelve sixteen, Beverly biked up to the house, put the bike lock on, and opened the door. "Hey Yan, you home girl," she half yelled! Other than the fact that there was an odd smell about the house, she paid it little notice. She went to the living room, and popped on the TV. She channel surfed for a few seconds, then tossed the changer on the sofa, and left the TV on an old Gunsmoke episode, that wasn't worth watching. She went to the kitchen and made a chicken salad sandwich, and grabbed a coke and returned to the TV Land network. Forty-five minutes later, nature called, so up the stairs Bevy went.

* * * * *

On the other side of town, Wellsy had spent the morning totally frustrated. He played the name game at work from noon yesterday until six-thirty p.m. This morning, he got up at six and looked at the girl's names, again, first, last, middle, and made as many combinations as he possibly could. He got nowhere. He wished he hadn't left the paper work at the office. Before leaving the office, however, he had given what he had accomplished to Alex by way of fax to see if she could muster though it as well, hoping to find something, significant. On the cover page, he had written, *I've tried everything, and Alex, it has come up a big fat zero. You play with their names and see what you can find—if anything—but for me, right now, the entire case nowhere.*

He went to bed at 11:22 p.m. and slept soundly until almost six thirty. He got up and put on his running shoes and took a three-mile run. Afterwards, in the shower, he cleared his head. Nothing was working. He wasn't any closer. At 8:22 he ran up to the office to bring his useless name game paperwork back to the house, so when Alex called, they could compare notes, as if his notes were significant enough to share. He had nothing else to do. His case appeared to be stone cold dead.

He hated Saturdays, and it was Saturday and he virtually had no clues that led anywhere. On the way back home from the office, he stopped at McDonalds and gobbled up a breakfast sandwich of some kind. He didn't bother to eat the greasy potatoes. As he pulled into his driveway he looked at the clock. "Ten, eleven," he mumbled to himself. At eleven thirteen, his cell phone droned the announcement of the caller, Alexandria. Good morning, love," he said.

"Napoleon Bonaparte," was all she said!

"Al Kaline," he replied, back.

"Who is Al Kaline," she asked.

"A baseball player with the Detroit Tigers, retired. He's in the Hall of Fame, love."

"Lucky him; whose hall of fame; not mine?"

"Major League Baseball," he said, and then added, "never mine." He paused, waiting for her to say something, so he took the bait, "What about Napoleon Bonaparte?"

"Thought you'd never ask. It's his quote."

"What's his quote?"

"'Le plus dangereux le moment vient avec la victoire,' He said that; Napoleon; that's who said it."

"Did he, and, did he also say, 'le secret de guerre mensonges dans le communications'?"

"I don't know. I only fine out one spectacular thing at a time, but I know he said that, first one."

"First, you say, what do you mean, he said it first; first before, whom?" He paused, "Who said it second?"

"I don't know who said it second, maybe he did. Actually I don't know that he said it first, but he said it over a hundred years ago. It's a quote attributed to him, so I guess he did say it first, or he's the first to be quoted for saying it, anyway. I'm getting confused here." She thought for a second and continued, "Look, I don't care if he said it first, seventh, or eighty-eighth, but he just said it is all I know. Anyway, it's recorded that he said it, so it's his quote as far as I'm concerned. He's quoted as having said it, so I suppose he said it first. It's his quote, anyway. Stop making me talk in circles"

"According to who?"

"According to whom, you mean."

"I don't care if it's who or whom, when did he say it?"

"Say, what? Wait, stop," she said. "We're playing a game and losing sight of what I called for. Look, I'm talking about what he—the killer—carved—you know—what he carved on the first girl. That's a quote from Napoleon Bonaparte. Bonaparte also said 'the most dangerous moment comes with victory!' That's what Bonaparte, said."

"Okay, I got you. When did he say it?"

"I don't know. I only know that it rang a bell with me, and today I remembered where I saw it, or rather heard it. It was in fifth grade, we were talking about him, you know, Napoleon, and I remember it from then."

"I can't remember what I learned a week, ago, and you remember fifth grade. What kind of mind does that, anyways?" He didn't wait for her, "What else do you know?"

"I know I'm on my way to the library to find out. I'll be there in less than two minutes."

"Ok," he said; and then he said, "Hold on, my cell is ringing." She waited three minutes. Arthur came back on the phone, offering, "He's struck again." I'm gone!" He clicked off and raced to the crime scene.

She fully understood his comment, *did he butcher two more*, Alexandria wondered as she continued on to the library.

* * * * *

Seven minutes before Wellsy was churning fast toward Yan's house—outside Yan's house—Alice Fay and George Seams were passing buy, holding hands and smiling. They both jumped and froze solid in their tracks when they heard the curdling screams from the house to their right. Alice grabbed George's arm. They looked at one another in amazement and with some fear. Alice wanted to run. George wanted to help, sort of. The shrill scream wasn't anything but that of one involved in some kind of terror. Their look at the house was interrupted by another blood curdling scream from Bevy, inside, upstairs. "I better go," George offered.

He pulled away as Alice suggested that perhaps he'd better not. He rang the bell. From inside the house, all he heard was, "Help, help, help, God, help! He tried the door. It was locked. He furiously pushed the bell button, wiping out any partial print that Nabulio may have left behind. Bevy flew down the stairs and fell as she miss-stepped the last stair step. She more than wrenched her ankle she actually broke it. The pain was streaking though her as she hobbled to the door, and flung it open, "God help, she's dead, butchered." Immediately, without thinking, George raced by her and ran up the stairs. Bevy sat on the floor, crying, shaking, and cradling her broken foot, and her shattered heart.

George saw the hapless nude body and vomited on the spot. He could not comprehend the awful scene before him, a massacred woman. His mind couldn't accept what he was looking at? He reached for his cell on his belt, and punched 911, frantically. It took him three tries to get it right.

Patrol officers Julie Hardwire and William Acworth were the first officials on the scene. They beat Wellsy by only eight minutes. They un-holstered their firearms, and walked toward the stoop, cautiously. The apartment door was open. Beverly was seated on the cement slap where Nabulio had stood the previous evening. Alice was seated beside her, arms around her shoulders. Beverly was cradling her foot, and sobbing. She looked at the police officers, "She's up there, she's dead."

"Who is in the house," Hardwire, asked?

"A guy, who came to help, ah…"

"George, George Seams, my boyfriend is up there with her."

"Who are you," Acworth, asked?"

"I'm Alice Fay. Me and George were just walking by, and…"

Hardwire, asked, "Who else is in the house."

Alice shook her head, Beverly said, "Just him and Yan."

"Yan," Hardwire asked? "

"Bi Yan, or as us Americans would say, Yan Bi. She's Chinese," Bevy started crying and sobbing, again. She looked up and finished, "One of my roommates."

"One, where is the other," Hardwire asked? "Is she, inside?"

"Connie, Connie Shay, no, she is away for a long weekend. She's in West Virginia."

"You're sure no one else is in the hours."

"I'm pretty sure."

"Pretty, sure."

"I was out all night, I came home about an hour ago. I ate and watched TV and then went up stairs to go to the bathroom," with that, she exploded into tears, shaking her head. "I don't think anyone is in the house."

Both officers' head snapped toward the street as they saw a green Jeep come screeching to a rocking stop. Wellington stepped out of his vehicle and help up his shield. He half trotted up to the officers. "What've we got?"

Two minutes later, Wellsy lead the way with Hardwire right behind. They interred the house, firearms drawn and held upward. At the foot of the stairs, Wellsy yelled up, "George Seams, you up there?" He replied in the affirmative. "Walk out of the room, slowly. Walk towards the stairs. Put your hands on top of your head, with fingers laced. When you get to the first step, stop, and turn around with your back to us, and keep your hands laced behind your head."

"But I didn't do anything."

"We know that, just do as you are told, and you'll be fine."

"She's dead. He massacred her. She's all bloody. He wrote on her with a knife."

"Just come to the stairs, now." He did as instructed. He was never more scared in his life.

As Hardwire escorted George out of the house, Wellsy searched the upstairs. Satisfied the perp wasn't upstairs, he called down and gave instructions to the two officers. Bevy was interviewed until the ambulance came to take her to the emergency room. Alice and George were interviewed and allowed to leave. They would be contacted again.

Wellsy looked at the body, and immediately saw Carolyn Ann Nowicki, and Jessica June Andersen, all over, again. His quick mind immediately noticed seven things that were different. First, there was but one body, or at least at this point, only one corpse.

Secondly, he noticed the perfect branding between and below her breasts.

Third, he noticed that her legs were crossed, and not in the V pattern, which seemed to contradict the double V's that was branded between her breasts, and the first murders of Nowicki and Andersen. He thought about that for a few seconds. This just wasn't consistent. For only a couple of seconds, he thought, copycat. He quickly dismissed that notion. The carving on the stomach was by far too consistent to be anything else, but the first perp; the only perp.

Forth, he noticed that her nipple had been sliced off, or at least he assumed that for the present. *Trophy*, he pondered. If it was a trophy, then why didn't they notice what trophies were taken from Nowicki and Andersen? What did they miss? *Damn*! He also noticed the amount of blood that appeared where the nipple had been. It was evident; the perp sliced it off, before he slit her throat.

Fifth, he noted that there wasn't any other note from the perp, upstairs, anyway. Nothing had been written on the wall.

The sixth difference wasn't noticed at first glance—anyway—necessarily inconsistent with the first homicides. The woman was of Asian decent, but—of course—she was female.

The seventh difference was that along side the head, there was a small amount of water, or a watery substance on the floor, along side of the cheek area. There was too much liquid for the two small puddles to be that of tears, but too little for them to anything else he could think of. He made a note on this notepad: Small water drops aside the cheek area of the face, hmm! He then stood and looked around the room. Everything else seemed to be in order. He took out his cell phone and punched two buttons. Two rings later, she answer. "Write this down," he said, "and write it word for word, okay!" She said, *okay*, and then said, *shoot*. He then quoted the preps carving, "'Power is my mistress. I have worked too hard at her conquest to allow anyone to take her away from me.' I need to know if his quote belongs to Bonaparte.

No jokes were made. She said, I've checked three books; one is called Napoleon Bonaparte; Raymond and Loretta Obstfeld edit it. The second is Napoleon and Wellington. And…"

He interrupted her, "I've read that one. Nothing in there you will want, I don't think."

"Have you. Then, we should talk," she offered.

"Okay, but not now, now I need to know if the killers scrawl is a Bonaparte quote."

"I'll get on the internet for that. That will probably be the fastest way. Anyway, the third book…"

"Look, Alex, I don't have time for this, okay. I'm sorry, but it's another massacre, but a massacre of only one this time, but it's even more gruesome."

"How is that possible?" She didn't really want to know. "Okay. I don't want to know. You be careful."

"Always, bye."

Detective Earnest L. Strange, and Ted Castle, Forensic stopped at the opening of the doorway. "The same," Strange asked?

"Yeah, kind of, sort of. It's the same perp that is for sure. You got your team here, Ted?"

"Just me, so far, we've got two more coming."

"Well, go ahead after the photos. I'll come back up and tell you what I need! This may sound strange, but I'm curious about the wet spots next to her cheeks."

"As in eyes, or buttocks?"

"Eyes" He looked to the Detective. "Come out in the hall, and we'll go over what we have. Then you can come in and note what I've said, and then look at her and figure some things out. Okay!"

The detective took one last look at the body before he left the room. "She's hot, that's for sure."

"No, Detective, unfortunately, she is stone cold dead! The bastard," he added!

"Yeah!" was all the Detective could muster.

CHAPTER 10—DAY NINE
THE NAME GAME

Alexandria couldn't get her mind off the fact that her fiancé was gazing at some unknown dead women who had probably been hogtied and carved on and then had their throats slit. And, just like the other two women, these unlucky ladies probably had had their legs spread wide apart for her Wellsy to gander at. It made her want to vomit. In an attempt to keep on the subject, but less on the details, she delved into the Internet, looking for Napoleon Bonaparte quotations. It didn't take long and she hit solid pay dirt. There before her green eyes, she had found a website called brainy quotes dot COM.

Alex however had to look deeper into the net because *brainy quotes* didn't have all three of the notes or quotes left behind by the killer. It didn't take her long and she hit gold, again, at http://www.military-quotes.com/Napoleon.htm. She was excited beyond measure as she was finally—actually—contributing to the investigation. She had found all three quotes.

She highlighted and copied all of the quotes she found and put them into a file for future needs, of both hers and Wellsy. She was excited with the opportunity to show Wellsy. She wanted to call him on the spot, but thought the better of it. After all, he was deep into the victim's crime scene of this serial madness. Nevertheless, she was full of positive energy, so she went back to study what Wellsy called the name game. She liked the name of the game; it had a certain ring to it!

Her subconscious mind was a tremendously wonderful tool to work with. Her mental powers could regurgitate almost anything, from months, even years, previous. Seven minutes later, the things, the items, and the truths she had been storing in that section of her mind—the subconscious—suddenly spewed forth its latent information, exciting her even more. A wonderful realization seized her, swept over and enveloped her. *Holly cow*, she half whispered to herself, *could it really be this obvious, this simple? No, it's not possible! No one is this lucky.* However, she remembered a saying that went something like, luck is where persistence meets opportunity, or somewhat like that.

She decided to throw caution to the wind. Alex decided to make the call to her, Wellsy, anyway. She knew he'd look at his cell phone window and notice it was she, and then he'd just click her off without even answering, as any male *prick would do.* She also knew what he would be thinking, and what he would do. *He'll breath a swear word at me for calling now, now of all times.* She could nearly hear his words behind his steadfast resolve to let him work and leave him the hell alone, especially now. She rid herself of caution—took the chance—and called, anyway. After all, this was immensely important, regardless his attitude.

Along about the same time Alex began her quote searching, Captain Rodgers had stopped by the crime scene. He didn't bother to talk to his lead investigator. He knew Wellsy would be busy and he also knew that the Lieutenant didn't need his Captain interfering, or even poking around. Rodgers had a short interview with Detective Strange, got fully updated, and then went up stairs to the study the situation. Rodgers had been around for a long time, but the body of Bi Yan wasn't a pleasing sight by any stretch of the imagination. She, obviously suffered a great deal, and more than likely—in the end—death came peacefully, and happily. *What kind of animal*, he contemplated.

Nineteen minutes later, he left the premises, pondering the number of inconsistencies from this murdered victim compared to the previous two. His mind seemed to work in tandem with that of the Lieutenants. He couldn't help wonder why Bi Yan hadn't been staked out—spread eagle—as the other two victims had been. He also wondered if her nailed position and posture was in some odd way, emulating the Savior on the cross, and if so, why? But mostly he wondered why she had been, indeed, staked out differently? The removal of her nipple troubled him a great deal. He decided to return to the office and take closer looks at the photographs of the first two butchered women. Had they two had some part of their person removed as a souvenir that somehow had not been noticed? Had Wellsy and his team dropped the ball on this, somehow? *Not likely*, he thought, but he had to look, anyway. He made a note to talk to Wellsy about this very thing, but he well knew, Wellsy, knowing that Wellsy had—most likely—already contemplated the same conclusion. *But, it never hurts*, he thought.

Rodgers walked outside and immediately the local and the national press was all over him. He suggested they wait and see what Lieutenant Wellington would decide on the matter. As he walked to his car, the reporter's questions didn't stop spewing forth. He ignored them all. He stopped, placed his hand on the door of his car, turned, and said. "Look, we will cooperate, just give Lieutenant Wellington a little time. He's deeply involved with the investigation right now. I will answer the one question you are all wondering, however. "Yes, it would appear that the there is a connection with this murder and two women who were slain last week. Other than that, you'll have to wait." More questions flew at him as he quietly got into his car. Danny Pepper from CNN said, "Captain, you said 'This murder,' does that mean there is only one body this time?"

Rodgers didn't even lower his window, he merely said just loud enough for some of the throng who were closest to his vehicle, "Very perceptive, young man, very perceptive." He drove off forgetting the press. He was thinking about the severed nipple, and a host of other inconsistencies. For a brief moment he thought, *copycat.* Less than a half-mile away from the crime scene, he dismissed any copycat theory, altogether!

Detective Strange made his way back up the upstairs. As he approached Wellsy, he watched the Lieutenant grab for his cell phone. Wellsy looked at his caller I.D. and was about to click it off. Instead, he pushed the green button. "I know this must be important," he said, "or you wouldn't dream of interrupting me right now, right?" Without waiting for a reply, he added with a bit of irritation, "what is it?"

"Two things," Alexandria volunteered. "First, Alex, give me just the first three words of what the killer carved on her abdomen."

"I'm not sure I want to give that out right now! Why?"

"Look, Lieutenant"—she kept it official—"I can make this quick, just the first three words. Please!"

"Okay, the first three words are 'Power is my...' that's it, that's the first three words, Alex."

"Okay," she offered. "I was wrong, I need just one more word, please. What is the next word?"

Wellsy offered a grimace into the phone. "Okay, but I don't want this to turn into some damn name game right now, I'm up to my ears in this investigation." He went over the entire carving message in his mind before he spoke. "Okay, the next word is mistress. Why do you ask?" Alex didn't answer right away. She was scrolling done the list. "Alex?"

"Okay, sorry!" She took an anxious breath and continued, "Starting from the beginning, and don't interrupt me. Here goes, 'Power is my mistress. I have worked too hard at her conquest to allow anyone to take her away from me.' That's it, isn't it?"

"Yes, but how could you k…"

"I've got them all, all of his quotes. I've got the three from the last time, and I'm sure I have the others from this one too, Wellsy. All of the things the killer has left—so far—are quotes from Napoleon Bonaparte. What else, what other messages did he leave this time? You start them, and I will finish them."

"Nothing, nothing more, that is all he left this time."

"Oh. I just assumed he would leave his carving on both girls, again, and then something on the wall."

"Alexander, you are very astute, but no, no he didn't leave anymore. Furthermore, he only killed one woman this time, but I'm not going to share any more information, after all, this investigation is only getting started."

"Actually, Arthur, I may be more astute then you know. I can also tell you what this woman's last name is, too."

"What? No, way! You can't possibly know that! That is totally impossible!" You would have to be the killer to know that. You can't possibly know her name, Alex." He then remembered how truly bright Alexandria was. "What is it, what is her last name, then?"

"I'm sorry, I misspoke myself, you are correct, I can't tell you her last name, but I can tell you what letter her last name started with."

"No, way! Even that could be remarkable. Okay, go ahead and give it to me."

"Okay, here it is. Her last name started with a P, correct."

"Yes, how did you know it started with a B?"

"Wait! What did you just say?"

"I said 'her last name started with a P."

"Are you saying B or P, which?"

"I said B, like what someone gets from a bee sting. I said the letter B."

"No. That can't be right. It has to be a P, P as in Paul, Arthur."

"Sorry! It isn't. Why were you so sure it was a P?"

"Never mind. I guess I'm really way off track. I am embarrassed, now. I will hang up. You have work to do; I'm going to ring off. I have to figure out where I went wrong. I was so sure, Arthur, I was so sure. I'm embarrassed, now, I'm sorry I called."

"Wait, Alex. You were right about the quotes. That is purely phenomenal." They talked another few minutes. She was definitely on to something with this Napoleon business, "His quotes and all," he reminded her. He told her to keep up with the name game, and to somehow extend that to all of Napoleon's quotations, suggesting that they somehow tied together. He, however, warned her not to tell another soul about the quotes. Wellsy told her that he was grateful for her call, and that she was very much a part of the team, now! He ended with the perfect words. "I love you, Alexandria."

"I won't see you, today or tonight. Will I?" He had already clicked off.

Three minutes later his cell chirped, again. "What, Alexander?"

"Does the dead woman have roommates?"

"Is this important?"

"Please."

"I don't like this Alex, but yes. Yes why?"

"Maybe he killed the wrong woman. Does either of the other women's name begin with a B?"

Wellsy had to think. His concentration had been gravely interrupted. He withdrew his notes from his pocked, opened them and scanned. "No, Alex, no such luck!"

She uttered a simple "Dang!" and clicked off, embarrassed, again.

Chapter 11—Day Nine and Beyond
LONELY HUNTER

Nabulio was still on a high the morning after his work. *Ninety two days to go*, he considered, happily. He had returned home after his completed task and did his routine clean-up thing, incinerating all evidence, etcetera. He then dressed and casually went out to dinner at the Purple Hippo. Afterwards he went to the latest Tom Cruise movie, returned home, and fell fast asleep. While driving home, he scanned six radio stations, hoping to learn that the police was on the scene of a new murder. No such luck. Home, he ran two miles on his treadmill, showered and went to bed. His last conscious memory was that of Yan's perfect breasts. It was only tarnished by the recollection of the severed nipple, which had long sense, been incinerated. The thought of her perfect breasts aroused him, a little. He pushed the thought aside, rolled over and went quickly to sleep, without so much as a twinge of guilt. War!

He woke up this morning—day ten—after seven hours of sleep, and flipped on his radio. He was invigorated. Life couldn't get any better, except for the fact that in just ninety-one days from now, utopia. Eight minutes later what he was hoping to hear was broadcast. Other bodies were found. He smiled. *The news was almost always wrong.* He hated the press. In his mind, the press printer or broadcast what they hoped was true, and later confirm their own wisdom, or correct earlier reports that they indicate what other networks got wrong. *Bodies*, he smiled. *Idiots are the press*, he thought.

Nabulio needed every thread of wisdom and caution to keep his self from driving by the murder scene. He knew better. Some flunky cop or cops were assigned to write down every make, model, and license plate number of every car that went by, assuming the idiot *serial killer* would happen by to see his carnage. A lesser man might do so. *Fortitude*, he mumbled to self.

Yan's killer turned off the radio and searched for television news on the matter. He found it on Fox news. "Republicans," he offered weakly into empty space, meaning nothing of significance. Everything FOX offered was sketchy, but he was gratified that he was making the national news, already! That added to the flavor of the war. He was in the winning column by all network standards. Poor W was losing, badly. He smiled, and then laughed out loud. They really didn't know much. Nabulio quickly gave up on their incompetence. He had work to do. His pattern was set. He got to work.

As before, Nabulio held in his hand the latest copy of the *Mace and Crown*. It was the last time he would use that source for his volunteers. He was—again—looking carefully at the Deans List. His choice of last names this time started with the letter U. His choices this time was limited to just four women scholars: Kirsten Marie Udvardy, Colleen Royal Ufer, Whisper Katharine Ulrich, and Kathleen Summer Urbana. Both Urbana and Ulrich were juniors. Ms. Ufer was a senior, and Udvardy was a sophomore. Urbana was quickly ruled out when he saw that her name was listed as misses. Kathleen was married; therefore, she was disqualified from the selection process. Being married may well have saved her life, though she would never even know she was a considered as a possible casualty of war. She was further saved by the fact that she was with child. Nabulio would never harm a baby, born or unborn for that matter.

He loved the name Whisper. It just jumped out at him. *How cool*, he thought. Therefore, he settled on studying her background, first, hoping she was a perfect fit. The first thing he learned about Ulrich wasn't especially good news. Her place of residence on campus was Landrum Hall of all places. For that reason, alone, he should have dismissed her. On the other hand, who would ever expect lightening to strike twice in the same place, and wouldn't that just smack W in the face. He liked the idea, after all; war often has battles on the same battlefield more than once. He was actually pleased with the notion. He would still consider her.

He found her sophomore class picture. He found yet one other picture of her, nearly full length. She was perfect. Her jet-black hair fell freely to nearly her buttock. She was tanned, slim, and pretty. Her breasts were ample, but not overly, but seemed so because of her slight built, just like Yan Bi, by comparison, anyway. Her smile was engaging. She was very long legged. She rode horses. She was born on a farm. Her major was Library Science. She didn't work. Her eyes were dark brown, or so he thought, as the pictures were in black and white. He wanted her to be the choice. Nevertheless, he knew he had to study the other women as well and find out a whole lot more about Whisper on his second investigation of her. But, for the moment, she was a prime candidate. He needed to see her, look at her. He ran his fingers over the page, over her face, her neck and her swelling breasts. He stirred.

Just as Nabulio began his search on Kirsten Marie Udvardy, Constance and John Ulrich were making a call to their daughter Whisper. It was the second call she received from them in five days. "We want you to come home, Whisper," Constance pleaded, back. Mother was insistent. "It is just way too dangerous." Whisper replied that they had already talked about that. "Yes, we have," mother said, "but that was before this second episode."

"What episode are you talking about, mom?"

"What you don't know, another woman has been slain in Norfolk," Constance said with amazement. "How can you possibly not know that, Whisper? It's all over the news. What have you been doing that you don't know?"

"Mom, you woke me up with your call. I haven't heard anything, yet."

Never one to be subtle, Constance bulldozed forward, "Well your dad and I want you to come home, stay here until this thing blows over. It's not safe for you so leave."

Whisper rolled her eyes. "Mom, I'm sure I'm safe. I am very car..."

"You are not safe, and you are no more careful then the two dead women were. No women are safe in Norfolk these days. Now be sensible young lady and just come back to Cincinnati at once, right now where you belong."

"Mom, will you listen to yourself. If a couple your age were killed, would you move out of town?" She didn't give her mom a chance to respond, "Of course you wouldn't, and I wouldn't expect you to, either. Besides, I'm in Landrum; and yes, that is where he first struck, and yes it was God awful horrible, and yes, it makes me shutter to think about it, but it happened. It happened and it is over. He isn't going to strike three times in the same place. Besides..."

"Don't besides, me, you don't know that, you don't know if he would or would not do that!"

"Mom, for heaven sakes. Security is so tight right here right now that it's ridiculous. They have campus patrol cars out every minute of every day, and so are the local police department cars flinging around. It is safe, mom. It's ugly, but it's safe."

"Well, if it is safe, how come another was killed last night? Huh? Answer that Whisper." She stopped, and then added, "Just a minute, your dad wants to talk to you." Whisper let out gush of air. She wanted to know more about the murders that had taken place, this time. She lifted the TV remote from its home along side the easy chair. She channel surfed, and finally saw a picture of a dozen police cars, lights flashing, and traffic stopped. The view was made from a helicopter circling above from Fox 43.

"Cookie," her dad called her. "Honey, we are so worried for you. Please just come home, okay?"

"Daddy, I can't, it's the middle of the semester. I just can't do that. You know momma is over reacting, she always does, daddy."

"It's not just your mother, we are sick over this. Just take the rest of the semester off." There was a long silence. Neither knew what to say. He wanted to demand that she come home, now, but he knew she would just dig in. She was that way, because he was that way. "Look, honey, if you are resolved to stay there, I can understand that, but at least let Gary come and stay with you."

"Oh, daddy, come on, be realistic. Landrum is an all female dormitory. He can't hang around here. He just plain can't stay here, daddy. This is all so silly…"

"It is not silly. There is a maniac out there, and you could just as easily as anyone else become his next target. I'm sure the others thought they were safe, too. Now, be wise and come home." She let out a deep sigh. She didn't know what to say, but she knew she wasn't going home, and she knew her younger brother wasn't coming to Virginia, either. The droning went on for another fifteen minutes. Most reluctantly her dad finally hung up in disgust.

She hung up the telephone, let out a huge sigh and walked into her bedroom and looked into the mirror. She wiped a tear from her eye and collected her thoughts. She knew she had been firm, but her resolve was important to her. She was on her own now, and nearly twenty, and too old for running off to mommy and daddy, even at situations such as this. She turned and looked into the mirror as she peeled off her sweater top, and slipped off her bra. She liked what she saw, which made her think of poor deprived Parker.

It was time to stop putting her steady off. After all, she didn't want to lose him. Tonight, she decided. After the rally she would lead Parker to Landrum. On this night of nights she would let him touch her, a little anyway, or maybe a lot. She smiled at the thought of teasing him some. She began to tingle and she knew that that would swell within her, and probably him, too, well—most definitely—him. She discarded the rest of her clothing and skipped into the shower; pleased that his goodies bounced firmly as she moved along. Tonight would be heavy jaws and extra play, a little extra, anyway, more than enough to excite him. She tingled some more!

As Whisper stepped out of the shower, six miles away, Nabulio ended his preliminary research of her. *She was definitely a possibility, but Landrum Hall would be a big risk, big, maybe too big*, he played against his mind. He turned his attention to Kristen Marie Udvardy, one of the two sophomores. She was all-athletic and while Nabulio was strong—very strong, indeed—he felt it unnecessary to engage in anything physical, DNA, wounds, and all those possibilities. He passed on Miss Udvardy, immediately.

Colleen Royal Ufer was the last to be initially evaluated. She was a fifth year senior and a co-captain of the woman's fast-pitch softball team. She had hustle, looks, and was engaged to one Thomas Edison. Nabulio wonder the obvious about Edison, but decided not to investigate Edison's history. He had plenty history of his own, and one day soon, W would all to well, know that history. Nabulio also wrestled with the fact that she was spoken for, and that could mean trouble if her engagement with Edison were played out. He needed a woman that was predictable. Colleen was a Political History major, and an all "A" student, destined to play women's softball for many years to come. In the end he finally dismissed her for the wrong reasons. She had small breasts! He would never admit that to, himself, no, never! There had to be another reason, after all, he was not a sex feign.

The following day, Nabulio dismissed Ufer. He went into a phase two with Whisper Katharine Ulrich. For a few days, he studied her from every possible angle. He tailed her on campus. Once, he even brushed by her on campus. She apologized for the bumping, but it was his fault—unintentionally—intentional of course. He turned to her and said, "You're welcome!" She shuttered, and then, kept moving away from him, walking a little faster. There was something about him. She walked faster. She shook it off; it was a brief interlude, she would never remember. Whatever part of her life that didn't fit into his scenario, he made it fit, firmly, perfectly. He forced her to be the one, though from all aspects, she indeed would have been chosen, anyway! Seeing her up front and personal, he was most pleased to see that her breasts where much larger than her pictures offered, and they offered, plenty!

He memorized her school habits. Mondays, Wednesdays and Fridays she left the dorm at 7:45, and was in school from 8:15 a.m. to 3:45 p.m. On Tuesdays and Thursdays she had a lab class from 10 to 11:40 a.m. At noon she ate a sack lunch, and by twelve thirty, she was at Perry Library on the ODU campus. She always studied until 5:30 p.m. That was her school cycle. Privately, she was difficult to trace. She didn't keep much of an organized routine. She biked here, and there. Took the bus. She ran. She rode with friends. She jogged. She cycled. She was always on the move. If he chose her, it just couldn't happen at Landrum. It would just plain be suicide for him. Security was way too high on campus. It had to be elsewhere, but where?

Nabulio was on the edge. He wanted the battle to begin. He needed it. He needed it now. It was now the fourteenth day, and he was behind schedule. Not that the schedule was all that important, after all he had all the time in the world, as one hundred and one days are a lot, and he still had plenty of them left. And, he only had to dispose of four more bodies in four more battles, and then—of course—the crème de la crème on the one hundred and first day of his rein of terror, capturing all that W stood for.

Nabulio ached for her, his little Whisper; little frame, but ample big boobs. After much decidedness, he had determined that he'd take some pleasure with her, though risky, as it would be. His heart was heavy; he hadn't seen her in two full days. She had just disappeared. He was losing sight of the big prize, W. He longed for her, but tried hard to stay focused. On the fourteenth day he got lucky. He was headed west on I-170 toward I-60, where he turned South heading toward I-166. He turned right on Wesleyan Drive. He turned into Virginia Wesleyan College. He planned to scout out the possibility of finding new candidates at this institution, next. As he slowed to get a feel of the landscape a car passed him exiting out of the College. He couldn't believe his eyes. In the car was none other than Whisper. There was some guy in the car, too. He was driving. It was a white Ford of some kind, maybe a 2006 something or other.

The Ford turned right onto Wesleyan Drive. He followed staying three cars behind Whisper and her *male* friend. Wesleyan dead-ended at I-166. He turned right following them, now only one car separated him from his prey. A short distance later they crossed Diamond Springs Road, and proceeded on I-166, which was now labeled Northampton Boulevard. The couple made the first available turn to the left. Nabulio pulled perpendicular to the road and watched the Ford go to the very end of the road, to the last house on the left. He watched them get out of the car and disappear into the house. We waited nearly five minutes. He backed up, and then preceded forward turning onto the dead-end road. The road wasn't named or, rather it didn't advertise its name.

A mailbox posted the name Erick L. Parker. Underneath and screwed to the nameplate was a makeshift board which announced, W. K. Ulrich. Immediately, Nabulio knew two things: First, he was hurt, offended, and secondly, she was living with him, and out in the middle of nowhere. It was all going to work. He made mental notes. The house was small with two bedrooms, maybe only one. The car in the dirt drive had a bumper sticker on the right side of the bumper. It proclaimed, Virginia Wesleyan College. Ah, he's a student, here.

Nabulio had more work to do. He left, pleased as well as pissed.

CHAPTER 12—DAY NINE AND BEYOND
THE PROFILER

Seventy-seven year old, retired FBI Agent Katrina Cowlings had been working off and on in an ad hoc capacity with the Norfolk police agency, and others for the past sixteen years. She came to them with a broad base background and foundation in sex crime investigations and strong interrogation methods. After a through investigation of the third woman's murder, Lieutenant Wellington requested—on the eleventh day of the investigation—Cowlings' service. Budget dollars were tight, but Captain Rodgers approved the request. If not for any other reason, this killer wasn't about to stop his carnage on Old Dominion coeds.

Katrina Cowlings was a big woman, with deep sunken dark eye sockets. Her grayish silver hair snarled and twisted itself into a bun at the back of her head. She wore silver rimmed spectacles and if one looked closely enough they would see the traces of a mustache about her upper lip. Though her demeanor was composed, she always moved in straight lines, as did her mind. She seemed to be a walking computer, as everything she thought was analyzed before it came through her lips with complete accuracy.

Cowlings seemed to take after the likes of England's legionary Paul Britton, their best-known profiler. She came to Wellington with many questions rather than advice, initially, anyway! There would be scores of queries from her, long before any possible answers could be generated. Initially, she didn't want to talk at all about the killer whom they wanted profiled. Instead, she wanted to know exactly what had happened to each girl, specifically, detailed, precisely. And when she had that; she had more in-depth questions. This profiler wanted to know exactly what happen to each girl, specifically and in great detail. She wanted to know all the similar facts and those, which were different with each woman, what the murdered did in common and differently with each coed. Only after she had asked voluminous questions answered did she want to know who the individual victims were, personally. She then asked more in-depth questions to each preliminary question as each was answered. Her first three questions lead to scores upon scores of other questions that swallowed up over a day and a half.

Satisfied with her answers, on the fourteenth day from the first set of killings, Cowlings moved toward the motivation for the assaults. Specifically, she wanted to know what drove or motivated the assailant to muscle these offences? The investigation—with regard to profiling—hit a huge snag at this juncture; for this was exactly why Wellington wanted to bring in a profiler in to begin with. The Lieutenant and his group hadn't a clue why this killing monster did what he did. That is what *they* wanted to know. So, each team member was taken aback when Cowlings asked him or her the very questions that they were looking for answers from her.

Just two weeks after the team had initially met, most were again assembled. Seated around the same table were: Wellington, Detective Strange, Captain Herrington from Strategic Management, Hank Blister from Operations, Captain Rodgers, Detective Castle from Forensic, and even Campus Security Guard, Jessica House was also invited, because Wellington liked how her mind worked. Rounding out the group was none other than Captain Ernst Herrington from the Strategic Management. Wellsy also wanted Alexandria there, but his Captain thought the better of it, but told him, "Lieutenant, that is up to you, but I'd advise against it. This is a wily group and she would definitely be considered an outsider without any law enforcement knowledge, experience, or credentials; therefore, it would be risky." Wellsy decided not to invite her.

Katrina Cowlings strongly suggested to the group that when their answers met her satisfaction, that only then could she begin to look for proper motivation of the culprit. Only then could she begin to piece together a background foundation, education, where he lived, what he might do for work, excreta.

Blister posed his own question, "Dr. Cowlings, Hank Blister, Operations, why are all these questions of us important to you?"

She offered a Paul Britton-esque type answer. "I need to have clarity with regard to the victims. For instance, were the victims randomly selected or specifically selected? I need to be clear whether or not each fatality was merely a person of opportunity, or a person whom the killer, if that's what we're calling him, came across intentionally, deliberately followed, groomed, and/or stalked. That is the only way I can place each victim on a risk hierarchy. When I can do that, I will understand how hard this individual works to get to each person, individually selected."

By the end of that fifteenth day, she had exhausted them all with her questions, her probing. After that, she left them. She needed to be alone. She demanded that she not be called or interrupted for any reason. Well—of course—there was one objection that would be tolerated; another killing, or killings!

* * * * *

Reassembled, her first report was sketchy but she determined that the killer was, indeed, male, somewhere between 30 and 40, but likely closer to thirty. She was sure that he had higher than standard intelligence, and because of that, "He does not do well with understanding other people, nor does he try. Therefore, for the most part," she suggested, "He is by and large a loaner. He cannot identify with others," she offered or, rather regurgitated to the team, "he most likely has an inability to have or, perhaps, show sorrow any way. Repentance is not a word he understands as might you or I, but," she added, "he wants forgiveness all the same." She then explained that everything to him is centered in him, and is centered with a sense of self-awareness, or self-belief, that he is at the very core of what all do when near him.

I doubt that he is married, I would think, probably not, nor has he ever been married. However, if he found the right woman, he would do anything for her. He would cleave to her first and foremost in all things, perhaps even before himself."

House introduced herself, and asked, "Would he stop this madness if this woman were to present him with an option of her or his killings."

"A skilled question, Ms. House. I think not, but I could be wrong there. It would depend on how driven he is in his purpose, but overall, I would say, no!" She continued, where she had left off before the questions. "Let's see, where was I, oh, yes, his victims are in part merely tools to accomplish his higher goal, perhaps spiritual, or something that to him is even more important, perhaps a coming together of many parts to fulfill some distant hegemony, some completion of some great work, unfinished."

She went on and reiterated herself by, again, reminding all of them "He has a relatively low capacity for any form of guilt, unless he steps outside of his own plan. "And trust me, his plans are worked out in every detail." She took a breath, and said, he will not stop killing until something is fulfilled, but," she stopped talking, looked about the room making sure all would receive the deep seeded gravity of what she was about to say, "God help us if he makes a mistake, or something doesn't go according to plan. He will become the butcher of all butchers."

"He isn't that far from that, already," Herrington offered. The Captain also wanted her to elaborate on that, but held the thought inwardly, for the time being, anyway.

"Listen," Katrina said, "and make no mistake about this, he wants to talk directly with Lieutenant Wellington. He won't do that, at least not now! However, know this, he wants to more than anything." She looked up. "I believe his final goal—but only on his own timetable—he wants, you, Lieutenant." She pointed her index finger directly at Wellington.

"Why," Wellington, asked?

"What are you asking? Are you asking why he wants to talk to you, or why he won't talk to you, yet, or why he wants you?"

"Well I mean the first, but as you so well put it, I guess I am asking both, or all three."

"Well, his carvings clearly suggest this is a game between the two of you, he isn't the least bit concerned with anyone else." Captain Rodgers piped in and asked if she were sure about that? Now, it was Katrina who was puzzled. "Why do you ask?" Rodgers immediately cleared the room—for a fifteen-minute break—except for Wellsy, himself and the profiler. And, he did it much to the aggravation to one Captain Herrington.

Rodgers crossed to the door and closed it after all the uninvited were excused. He spoke directly to Katrina but looked at Wellington as he said, "What about the possible danger to the Lieutenants' fiancé, Alexandria Mae Southerland? She is indirectly part of this investigation. As a matter of fact, the Lieutenant was going to invite her here, but I suggested, no." He then added as an afterthought, "No one else on the team is aware of her involvement."

"How is she involved?" Wellington filled her in on all that had happened, including the engagement, the name game, the Napoleon Bonaparte quotes, and excreta. Cowlings wanted to know more, much more about this. She was very concerned; very! But, she withheld her concerns for the present, anyway. She suggested that she have a one on one with Wellington after this meeting, and then, if necessary, with Ms. Southerland with and without Wellington. Before there mini-meeting ended she asked, if there were any possibility that the killer knew about Alexandria? The Captain and Lieutenant exchanged looks. The guess spoke up; "You bet your ass he does," she said, "My guess is he is following—in some manner—Wellingtons' every move, unless his ego is so out of whack that he assumes he knows all your moves and isn't bothering with you at all, but that is most unlikely. "Gentlemen, "she said, "He knows her. It is my opinion that your fiancé is at great risk."

With that, the rest of the day was put on hold. A new plan of safety was required.

Chapter 13—Fifteenth Day and Beyond
PRE-BATTLE PREPARATION

Two days before Whisper moved in with Parker, she called home to her parents. Her mother Constance answered the phone. Before Whisper could get two words out her mouth her mother asked if she was coming home. "No, mother I am not, but I listened carefully to both you and dad and I have made a decision you will like. I'm moving out of Landrum, but not permanently. When this whole thing blows over, I will go back. Does that make you happy?

Constance offered back a reserved, *yes*, but still she had many concerns. Whisper was ready for them, and she was ready to give her parents all the answers they were seeking, but first she asked if her dad was home. She was glad he was, she didn't want to go over this information more than once, least she get caught in some misstatement, later. "Mom, tell dad to get on the other extension; okay?"

There was an uneven silence while they waited. John Ulrich picked up. "Hi, pumpkin!"

"Hi, daddy."

"She's moving out of Landrum, but still won't come home."

"Well?" asked John.

"That is true, but I'm moving into a home that belongs to two students that live south east of here. They are students at Virginia Wesleyan College, daddy. They are brother and sister, Sharon and Erick Parker; they are both seniors." She was talking so fast that she was afraid her nervousness was going to shine through, so she cleared her throat and continued more slowly. "Sharon has one class a week that she is taking at Old Dominion, so she won't be one class short of graduating and then have to go another full semester at Wesleyan just to make up one class. I guess Wesleyan will accept that class." She took a breath. "I don't actually know how that works, but that is what she is doing, anyway. They have an extra room that I can stay in. They are not going to charge me, either, because Parker—oh that is what they call her brother Erick—likes the idea that there will be two of us in the house when he cannot be there; so he is happy about that. So, I imagine the two of you are happy now, too, right?"

Reluctantly, both parents accepted this as a far better situation, though they still preferred her to just come home. Everything she told them was the truth, except for the fact that Parker didn't have a sister, and for the fact that she—would, indeed—from time to time be alone in the house. So anything about her or in connection with the sister was a lie! Facts were facts. Fact one was that Whisper had moved into Parkers' home, and fact two, she was sharing his bed. As far as Whisper was concerned, her parents knew all they needed to know, and they certainly didn't need to know those other things.

By the thirteenth day, Nabulio knew Parker's weekly schedule. Erick worked early mornings Monday through Friday at a discount tire dealership. He put new tires on older cars. He worked from 6:30 a.m. to 9:30 a.m. He had classes on Monday, Wednesday, and Friday at 11:00 a.m. and 2:45 p.m. and he had two classes on Tuesdays and Thursdays as well, one at 10:45 and the other at 1:15 p.m.

Nabulio compared Parker's scheduled to that of Whispers. He found the openings he needed for his purposes. Daily, Erick Parker was always gone from his house by 6:15 a.m. for his tire job. Whisper was always gone by 7:45 a.m. on her way to her classes. Nabulio knew he could strike safely—anytime—between 6:20 to 7:25—the time Erick was gone and Whisper was readying herself to leave. Parker wouldn't return home from work before 9:45 a.m. to clean up for his class that started at 11:00, M-W-F. Parker was the only real consideration, after all, on that day; Whisper would never go to class, anyway. Never again!

A schedule for Tuesday or Thursday would also work, but Nabulio realized that he would have about fifteen minutes less time, and fifteen minutes less time is just that, fifteen minutes less time to complete the battle, so he flatly decided on the Monday, Wednesday, Friday schedule for the campaign. A Monday would be the perfect day for a battle. However, before making his final decision, he checked out their evening schedules as well. Yes, there were openings, but he decided daytime would work best, though the cover of darkness was always better, but—on the other hand—their evening schedules were more open to slight alterations. He was resolved; a Monday morning was in order.

He tingled at the thought of it. Unfortunately, he was focused clearly on two juxtaposed objectives; one, a job he needed to complete—execute—flawlessly and, secondly, his continued urges of not only gazing upon her bare breasts while she was still alive, but also, actually touching them. He knew she would both love and hate that. He struggled with the thought that flawlessness meant flawlessness, and in touching them, or even focusing on any part of her body, didn't that—he argued with himself—contradict any thought of flawlessness?

He thought of just removing them, altogether, and then taking them home. It took him less than a second to realize that that thought was disgusting. That was emblematic of a serial killer trophy taking. He would have no part of that! He was disgusted with the whole scenario. He pushed the whole of it out of his mind. *Stay focused to the battle* he demanded of himself.

The plan was decided on, the twenty-third day of the one hundred and one day campaign. Whisper would be Nabulio's "U" in his offensive attack on Lieutenant Wellington, i.e. W. He looked to his legend and worked to two hours to find the right quotation to inspire W and his band of idiots! Idiots, yes, but idiots that were lead by a great general that was to be hated, yes, but also to be revered. And, at this battle, for the first time Nabulio would most intentionally leave an even more powerful message. He would leave an addition single letter! He was excited with anticipation.

He closed his eyes and offered up a prayer to the Gods of War! Monday, the nineteenth day since the battle began, that was the scheduled day of days for battle number three.

Chapter 14—Day Eighteen
FULL DISCLOSURE—WRITTEN REPORT

It came by special currier right to his house. Alexandria was cooking breakfast. She had spent the night; actually, she had spent the last three nights playing endlessly with the name game, and now the letters' game. Was the killer spelling something out? If he was, what, if anything did it have to do with Napoleon? Furthermore, what—if anything—did any of this have to do with the concerns of the Profiler?

The ringing of the doorbell disturbed her thoughts. She saw the little man in a kind of brown uniform, with a mailer under his armpit. It didn't add up. It was Sunday. There aren't any deliveries on Sundays. She pressed herself against the north wall of the kitchen, out of view from the front door. She got down on hands and knees and scampered to the hallway. She didn't bother to get up once she was out of sight of the front door. She continued crawling towards the bathroom.

Just as she was about to stand, the door opened. Wellsy looked at her as he stood with a white bath towel wrapped about his waist. She cocked her head upward at him. He smiled, "Not now," he said, "maybe later." She ignored his attempt at humor. She stood and whispered, "There is a man at the door with a package. It's Sunday, Wellsy, no one delivers packages on Sunday." He removed his towel, reached behind the door and grabbed his trousers that hung freely from the hook. He zipped to his room and grabbed his Glock G37, and tossed on a sweatshirt that ironically stated with embossed letters, Old Dominion University. "Stay here." He went out the back door, circled around to the front, and leveled his Glock at the back of the man's head and said, "I'm a peace officer, turn around slowly."

The man nearly wet his pants. Three minutes later, Wellington accepted the package and returned to the house, via the front door. He yelled, "Honey, I'm home," he said. Alex peered from around the hallway corner, and smiled, but still scared. She ran to him. Wellsy stated, "It's a packed from a currier service is all; everything is okay, love." She held him tightly. He held her warmly. "It's okay," he said, "everything is okay!"

"What's in the package?"

"I have an idea, but we won't know until we open it, will we?" A brief note lay on top of the report. It was addressed to Lieutenant Wellesley. It stated: *I'm not finished but I thought you would need to have this immediately. Lieutenant it's not a PROFILE, I'm afraid, but read it, and you'll understand why I say that, Regards, Cowlings. Oh, one more thing. I'm sure that from time to time you may wish to discuss this with me, so each paragraph is numbered, beginning with number 1 through paragraph 392.* Oh, yes, and one other thing, Lieutenant; in the latter part of this report, I have typed some of my personal remarks to you. Those I felt extremely important are typed in bold. Please pay close attention to those bold items.

"It's the profile Alex," Arthur yelled to his significant other, "but she says it's not a profile, but in part it is. I don't know what that means, yet; I'll have to read it to fully understand and appreciate it.

Alexandria made it clear that—for the present—she didn't want to know what the profiler wrote. "I don't want to be grossed out, so you just read it and then tell me what you want me to know, if anything."

He began reading slowly, deliberately. His senses were astute, he took it all in as if it were gospel truth. Much of the beginning was pure stereotypical. According to, Cowlings the killer was a white heterosexual male, mid to late thirties. However, unlike most serial killers, Cowlings did not think he was sexually dysfunctional nor did he have low self-esteem, but he may be living some kind of non-sexual fantasy in the throws of sexuality, because she found inconsistencies with regard to his methodical rampages. While they seemed sexual in nature, she felt the killings were only being conveyed to represent sexual killings; when, in fact, they were just the opposite. *Just the opposite,* Wellington thought, *what does that mean?* He noted the paragraph, 69. He circled it. He'd talk to Cowlings about this at another time.

The Profiler sighted the killers 'left behind notes' as having an underlying purpose, but the notes—in and of themselves—had nothing to do with the killings per se. "He kills to complete part of an ongoing agenda that will ultimately bond himself with Lieutenant Wellington—specifically Wellington, the man—not the cop on the case, who just happens to also be Wellington. This is all specifically, personal. His true agenda is Wellington!" Cowlings then added, "I don't know if it is the name Wellington, or the man, Wellington." Wellesley noted paragraph 84, and circled it.

Katrina Cowlings also noted other deviations that were atypical of this specific serial killer. She was skeptical as to the unusual habits concerning this serial killer and his victims. Too many things just didn't add up! "In general," she wrote, "these types of killers normally murder unfamiliar persons at random. Our man—I believe—may well be killing strangers, but by the time he actually kills them, he has studied them. His prey may not know him, but he definitely knows them;" whereupon, she gave several indications for her findings, including her belief that he was faking his trophy taking, i.e., the slicing off of the nipple. Wellsy noted and circled paragraph 107.

Katrina believed that the cutting off the nipple was either an after thought, or he forgot to take a prize from the first two women killed. Either way, it was her opinion that the killer was pretending to take a trophy. She added, "It's also possible that he had an infatuation with her breasts and wanted them, but constrained himself to just one nipple. His cooling off periods were—by and larger—shorter then the normal, but it was too soon to really be sure of that, with respect that there have been only two attacks thus far. "I believe he will strike again within the next two to three days, maximum." Wellsy so noted paragraph 199 and circled it.

Wellsy stopped reading and looked at the date of her writing. It was dated, yesterday. As per their earlier discussion, the report made clear, that he—like many serial killers—was specifically taunting Wellington with fake DNA, (pieces of hair, the cigarette, etc.). At this point she made her boldest statement, "Yes, he is definitely a Serial Killer, *but only by definition.* This killer has researched the role of Serial Killers and he is now playing out the roll of being one of them for the Lieutenants' sake. She wrote, "He obviously knows when he started his killing, and he knows exactly when he is going to quit. "That," she said, "separates him from other so called Serial Killers. He's pretending, or he wouldn't quit."

She stated that all three of those he has killed were previous strangers to him. He studied them. He already knows his next victim, or possible victims. However, the victims between the next killing and his last are—by know— known to him, today, because he doesn't have a cooling down period like most serial killers do. His time is spent in investigation his next prey. But the next person or persons are definitely known to him. His date is also known, and I believe he already knows the place as well; house or apartment.

"The last victim he will kill (butcher might be a better word)—in his mind— is none other than Arthur Wellington Wellesley, Lieutenant, from the Norfolk Police Department. This killer has some personal hidden agenda that is driving him to take out Wellington in the end, and he is on some kind of timetable to administer this. Therefore, and I want to make this crystal clear, this man is NOT a SERIAL KILLER. He is a PRETENDER from the word go." Wellesley noted paragraph 222, and so circled.

"Note: this man, this feign does not care how many he kills, but he kills them specifically. He has numbered them one, two, and three so far. Therefore, he has a timetable of sorts, and some specific agenda. I don't know how many he will kill, but he knows. I am amazed that he is numbering them 1, 2, 3, etc., With what he is doing, I would have expected him to have numbered them 10, 9, 8, etc. (not that he will kill 10—I've chosen that merely as an example; an indicator) Nevertheless, he will continue to number them. The last woman he kills—I believe—will not be numbered. He may leave a word on her like, finished," or "you're next," or something like that. He will warn you Wellington, that you are next, but he will not come right out and say it that specifically." Arthur circled paragraphs 241-244.

"While on this thinking, with each killing new killing, he will become more aggressively sadistic, more ferocious vicious, and far more atrociously brutal. Each succession murder—or perhaps battle is a more specific word—will intensify in brutality. In his mind he is working up to his grand triumph, his greatest brutality and carnage he will inflict on his true prey, Wellington. I'm not sure why, but Wellington is his foe of foes.

As an aside, the department may want to see if Arthur's father or grandfather had some run in during their life with someone from this area who might now be looking at some type of revenge motif."

Arthur stopped reading and called for Alex. She came. He asked her to read just this one little section. She did. He stated, "This is what I want you to work on, Alex, this comment here." He read it, again: "'I'm not sure why, but Wellington is his foe of foes.' Alex, I want you to work on this, see if you can get a line on it?" she accepted the challenge. She walked away as he continued his reading.

Next, Katrina suggested that, "It's all about the final battle. He wants to embarrass the Lieutenant. Figure that out and you will find him before he finds you. Figure out his code. It is there. He is giving hint after hint. He is taunting you. He is trying to belittle you. Give it back to him, Wellington. He is leading up to the big battle. Get him out of his game plan. Come up with your plan, a better plan. He is controlling you, Wellington, so you must control him! That should save lives, but be wary, he is cunning, and will stop at nothing to devour you!"

Arthur stopped reading again and asked Alex to come back. He read to her this last part that he had just read since she had walked away. He emphasized Cowlings last sentence of paragraph 300, which he had circled. He told Alex to "Think about that, too, okay." She acknowledged that she would. He continued to read as she left.

"He has no sympathy for them—the women—and no feelings toward them. They are nothing more than victims but participants of war—any war—take your pick. He has some war in mind, but he is careful about that, but figure out the war and you have him figured out. Those killing are nothing more than an opportunity for him to communicate with Wellington, drawing the two of them (himself and Wellington) closer together to fulfill some outlandish destiny, real or imaginary that has transcended from his mind to his reality. So the war may or may not be real. I cannot say. Nevertheless, I tell you; be aware!"

Cowlings continued: "The inclination to remove Wellington from the investigation—in my opinion—would be catastrophic in every way. To remove Wellington for this case would cause this killer to greatly escalate his killing by hoards of numbers, making or turning himself into an actual Serial Killer of chaotic proportions. As long as Wellington remains on the case as a lead person, he—Wellington—is safe until that last moment, whenever that may be. Of course, that is the rub, only the killer knows that time, and that place, and why!

I would keep Ms. Alexandria Southerland out in the open, too. If he knows who she is, he will not hurt her if everything looks, and appears, normal. Unless her last name—which starts with an S—is the same letter that is needs in his alphabetized killing spree. If that is the case, I would be most concerned. That being the case it could be a big win for the killer. Therefore, it behooves us to learn fast what he is spelling out. I would not impart any of this to Ms. Southerland." Wellesley so noted and circled paragraph 218.

"Remember, this is war to him, and yes, there are innocent causalities of war, but he will not target her indiscriminately. In war the enemy doesn't interrupt the war to go after the family of the soldiers. So, for him to kill her he would have to step outside of the box. He won't do that. As a matter of fact, I'm sure he wants her alive to deeply mourn Wellington's death and destruction. That would be her part of the war. On the other hand, taking her out of the loop could be calamitous. He would sense something was up. Furthermore, at no time should any police official, including Wellington or others, warn or caution him to leave her, alone. First, by doing so, places her as part of the war effort. The killer will take that as a definite challenge! From that believed challenge, he will add an addition battle for him to win.

Ms. Southerland would be discovered nude, tortured beyond measure with her reproductive organs removed, probably hacked out. But first, she will have been repeatedly raped, savagely—he would enjoy this more than life, itself— why, because this would be personal, outside of the war effort, but definitely, she will be left alive, for it is Wellington who must feel the pain. To this slaughterer, she would be nothing more than a participant, as have been the three women thus far; they are to him only pawns, little players in the battle. He gave no thought to their death. They are nothing more than causalities of war to him. However, the gruel, brutal assault on Ms. Southerland would be nothing more than light practice for what he has in store for Wellington." *So noted,* Wellesley thought!

Cowlings began winding down by reminding the readers of this report of the killer's comments: 'the most dangerous moment comes with victory!' and, 'The secret of war lies in the communications.' "He is crying out, Wellington. He wants you to communicate with him. Do it or pay the consequences. Finally, he writes, 'Victory belongs to the most persevering.' Lieutenant, make him believe that you are more persevering than he is. If he believes you, he will not back off in his communication, he will increase it giving what he believes to be crucial communication. However, the opposite is also true! But, he will not be able to help himself; he will give you the clues you need to get ahead of him by the final battle. Remember that!

She then offered a personal note to Wellington, "Rethink the double V's between Yan's breasts. I think you have misunderstood. It is not a double V as you suggest, rather it is a *W*, as in *Wellington or Wellesley*, meaning that the message is for you, Lieutenant. Mark my word on this Lieutenant"

Holy shit, Wellesley thought, *how could I have missed that?* He yelled out to Alexandria. She called back. He yelled back, "Never mind." *Stupid, stupid. stupid, this is the last thing to tell Alex*, he realized, so he went back to his reading, "This man has an infatuation with the female breast. That may be a weakness. Though, admittedly, I'm not at all sure."

A W, Wellington pondered, *not double V's*.

Cowlings then copied the last note from the killer: "he writes, 'Power is my mistress. I have worked too hard at her conquest to allow anyone to take her away from me.' "Lieutenant, find a way to take his power away, and make him think it has transformed to you, somehow. That will keep him thinking and make him jittery. The more he thinks the more mistakes he will make, and—in the end—it will add to lengthening the times between killings, because you will give him more and more to contemplate. Remember, he is bright, but he is alone. Trust your instincts. He says, 'at her conquest.' Find out what he means by that and take it away, too." Arthur circled paragraph 392.

With that, her report ended. It really wasn't a profile, after all! Wellington was not dealing with a Serial Killer. He was scared; scared for Alex, scared for the thousand of women out there that would have no chance if they were selected. He was scared for his lack of experience and knowledge, scared that the Captain might reassign the case, though Cowlings had warned not to remove himself from the case. He was also sacred that the Captain wouldn't reassign the case; he was scared for all of Norfolk. But, he wasn't scared for himself. *How foolish is that*, he thought.

Alex walked up to him just as he finished. She looked at him. "Should I read it?" He didn't have a chance to respond. His cell hammered at the silent air. It was Captain Rodgers. Wellesley confirmed that he to had received the report and that he had just finished reading it, but only once through. His Captain had read it five times. He wanted to meet. He told the Lieutenant to meat him at the station. Wellsy suggested that the Captain come to his home. "Alexandria is here, he said. You come here, okay!" Rodgers left his home, forthwith.

Alexandria made meatloaf for the three of them. She was not invited to their little meeting. She was hurt, but more so, she was glad.

CHAPTER 15—DAY NINETEEN (MONDAY)
THE THIRD BATTLE

Nabulio sat two houses down from Parkers. He had arrived at precisely at 6:20. Erick's car was long gone; therefore he knew he had the green light. He went over in his mind what he was going to say, and what he was going to do. He had rehearsed it several times in his head on the way over from home headquarters, just as he had several times before leaving home. Nabulio was confident and totally ready.

The battle had been planned. It was time to execute with precision. He drove to the dead end road and pulled over. He rehearsed it all, again in his mind. He then drove the last few yards, going just past their driveway. He eased to a stop and backed into the Parkers driveway and stopped. It's one thing to expose ones car, it is quite another to display the license plate to neighbors. He snatched up the fake report that lay on his passenger side seat. He had on gloves. It was okay, it was a late cold fall morning; wearing gloves was most appropriate.

Over his rubber suite, he wore his new sweatshirt with Wesleyan college plastered on it, and blue sweat pants that draped over his work boots. He was, after all, incognito. A late fall stocking cap adorned his head and bled a little over the top of his ears. He bounded up the walkway with enthusiasm and onto the porch, just as planned. He took a deep breath and wrapped on the door. He waited. Twelve seconds later he knocked, again.

Whisper cracked the door open, exposing very little of her bathrobe that covered her otherwise wet naked body. She had just moments before stepped out of the shower. *How delicious*, he thought. "Hi, I'm Michael Collins," he said as he thrust out his hand with the report in it, and placed a broad smile on his face. I know that Parker already left for work, but I won't see him before class today so here's the report he wanted. He needs this," waving the report, "before tomorrow morning. I hope I didn't wake you, "he added. Nabulio quickly added, "I hope I'm not disturbing you, I know it's early?"

Normally, she would have just cautiously accepted such a report, thanked the stranger and closed the door, immediately, but today was a bit unusual. She said, a few words that shocked him. He heard some of what she said, but the rest was lost to him at his surprise as to what he had just heard. All he heard was what he wanted to hear, "Well, come in then…" What he didn't here her say was, "and I'll tell Parker you're here, Michael."

So, excitedly, gladly he entered through the door, and at the same time, asking, "Excuse me, what did you say?"

She was a good three feet in front of him by now. She stopped, made three-quarters turn which opened her robe just enough that he knew she was nude, or at least from the waste up. He thought he had actually seen a nipple. He stirred ever so slightly. His time was close. "I said, I'll tell Parker you are here."

"What, wait! What did you say? Parker's here?"

"Yes, he's sleeping; I'll go get him."

"No, he's at work, his car is gone."

"Huh ah, no he isn't, he's taking a day off to do his research paper. That's what this is for, isn't it," she said waving the paperwork back at Nabulio?" She hesitated, paused just for a second, and then figured it out, "Oh, the car, no, Todd Christensen borrowed it, yesterday; he's bringing it back her soon."

Nabulio spoke fast, too fast. "Hey, no, don't wake him," he said as he grabbed her arm "Let him sleep. I got to run, anyways."

She shook his hand off her, not with any fear, but to let him know it was okay for her to wake Parker up. She stopped, and turned toward Nabulio. It's okay; he wanted me to get him up, anyway. It's cool." She smiled that smile that Nabulio had learned to love so much. She poked her head into the bedroom, and flatly stated, "Hey Parker get up, Michael is here with the paper you're waiting for."

Nabulio quickly excusing himself, saying, "It's really okay, I have to run, anyway, really!"

The bedroom door opened, Parker stood in his boxer shorts. "Huh? Who are you?"

Nabulio was in mental torment; his knife was taped to his leg over his rubber suite, but under his sweat pants. He had no defense. It all happened so fast. Whisper looked at Parker and then at Michael. Nabulio looked at Whisper, and then at Parker. Parker just looked at the stranger, Michael; bewildered. Everyone looked at each other, and all seemed confused.

Nabulio wasted no time. He lowered his head, and sprinted forward and bulldozed into Parker hitting him, driving him with his head right in the sternum, jamming him past the open bedroom doorway and across the room, slamming Parker and himself against the far wall of the bedroom. The sill of the window caught Parker right in the middle his head. Erick Parker went down; out like a light. At the same instant, his attacker had tumbled, and sprawled to the floor rolling in to Parker and the north wall of the bedroom.

Nabulio quickly spun up and around so fast that Whisper still hadn't comprehended what was happening. He dove at her thrusting his right arm around her right thigh, twisting her body, slamming her to the floor. She bounced on her back, which slammed her head to the old hardwood flooring. The assailant quickly straddled her body and tore at her robe, exposing those swelling mounds of delight; he had dreamed about so many times. For the present, he ignored them. It wasn't those breasts he was interested in, now?

Her attacker was totally out of control. He pulled, tugged at her bathrobe cloth belt. Receiving it, he flipper her over, and as he did so, her chin jammed into the hard floor catching a small sliver of the flooring that cut deep into her chin, tearing, nearly an ugly inch and a half long gauge out of her lower face; seven stitches worth that she'd never receive. She screamed in agony, as she pulled her hand up towards her bleeding face. He grabber her right arm that was pinned under her thigh and forced it behind her. Her left arm was outstretched up and above her head. He snatched it up and down with such force it dislocated her elbow. She screeched in horrific pain. He could care less. He grabbed her by the back of her head, raised it up, and slammed it down, breaking her nose and placed her unconscious.

Nabulio then tied her hands so tightly that eventually they would lose all their feeling. He ran back into the bedroom. Packard was motionless on the floor, blood oozing from the back of his head and his right ear.

The maniac quickly looked for the bathroom. It wasn't far away, just off their bedroom. It was small and cozy, painted yellow. He looked into the mirror for signs of blood. He looked fine, perfectly fine. He then grabbed a roll of toilet paper and ran to Parker. He wrapped the TP around and around his left hand, eight times and then crushed it into a ball with both hands and then forced it in Parkers mouth. He ran back to the woman and did the same to Whisper. He looked diagonally out the window; the neighbor's house across street still didn't have any lights on; *good*, he pitched to his active mind.

The Perpetrator took a deep cleansing breath and calmed himself, and casually walked outside through the back door to his car. He got in and started it up and then backed it all the way up the dirt drive to the end of the house. He then cut the wheel sharply and backed in and behind Parker's house; out of sight from the road. Nabulio brought his box of supplies into the house through the back door.

Nabulio's mind was still reeling. He was way off his game plan. Yes it was to be a battle, but not like this. He had plans for his Whisper; fun plans, games, and assorted activities. But this Parker character screwed it all up! He would pay dearly for that miscalculation; misadventure. Innocent bystander or not, that shit-face would truly pay, and so would she for betraying him; Nabulio.

The attacker put that behind him for the moment. He had a battle to win. His heart was pounding. He demanded himself to control it. He was most unsuccessful. *Mind over matter* he screamed into his brain for comfort, release, and destruction. Nevertheless, rage continued to build within him at fervor's pitch.

Inside he laid the box down near the door. He withdrew the duct tape, crossed to Parker wrapped it around Parkers mouth and head three times. He then went to Whisper and did the same, but he wrapped it only twice about her head. She almost immediately began to gag. Air wasn't passing freely through her broken nose. He ripped the tape off her face, which tore off a small piece of skin near her left cheekbone. He assessed the problem. Even in sleep, she wreathed in pain.

What to do, he thought? For the time being, he left her, but not before picking up her head and popping it back to the floor with some force, just to see if she was faking. She didn't show any signs of being awake, or alive for that matter.

The destructive villain took a deep cleansing breath. He stood perfectly still for the next minuet or so, relaxing himself and regaining his composure. Satisfied, he walked into the bedroom, and sat on the edge of the bed. He had to think! After three minutes, he made his irrevocable decision. And, at the same moment, he heard Whisper mumble, half crying out, "Parker!" She couldn't figure out why her speaking sounded funny. She got scared. She hurt everywhere, and she couldn't move her tongue, couldn't talk, and couldn't move. She felt paralyzed. Panic seized her at every groggy thought.

The Perp crossed back to Whisper. "Don't speak again or I will kill you, now! Is that what you want you stupid witch! You want to die, now? Your nose is broken, your mouth is filled with TP, your face is a bloody mess, so if you try to talk, you will not be able to breath very well, as I will tape you up across your mouth that you will suffocate a slow miserable death. So just shut that pie hole in your face, woman!"

She was crying, shivering, quivering, sobbing and gasping for breath the whole time. She tried to tell him that her arm was broken or something! She mumbled something. Further pissed off, he kicked her in the ribs, breaking her third rib, and said "Shut up whore!" The pain shot through her like a hot bullet. He wanted to be sure she was totally submissive, so he kicked her again, cracking another rib. He bent over her and ripped the top half of her robe open. He openly ogled at her wonderfully swelling breasts. He wanted them so, but he forsook his wants and grabbed both of her breasts, hard, lifting her up off the ground by only pulling at her breasts; only.

She felt as though her glands were going to rip apart. His fingernails under the rubber gloves actually dug through the rubber and into the underside of her breasts where they met her chest cavity. The pain was excruciating. On the topside, his thumbs had so much pressure on her breasts that immense pain pulsated, and shot through her like a hot pokers.

"Look, missy," he said through clenched teeth, "if you don't cooperate with me every second of every minute I will cut these damn things off right here and now!" As he said that he shook them up and down, causing her feet to go to the balls of her toes, then to her flat feet, and to the balls again. She felt like she was being ripped apart. The pain was excruciating. Then, he just released her and let her tumble, crumble to the floor with a deadening thud. Her elbow was screaming with throbbing pain as she hit the floor. Her chest was on fire. Her ribs cried out in agony, and she was literally gasping for breath. She was terrified out of her mind. She couldn't think, only sobbed, desolated.

She so wanted to be quiet but she couldn't. She peaked up at him from the floor, "Your him, aren't you?"

"No. You are safe from that," he lied! "Just shut up, bitch or you will end up like the others. *I he or isn't he?* Just come with me and shut up. He grabber her by her beautiful but snarled wet hair and lugged her, dragging her into the bedroom. She kicked, but it was useless. Her elbow hit the edge of the bedroom door, and another sharp pain sliced up her arm into and through to her neck. She nearly fainted, but withheld from making any voluntary noise. Once in the bedroom, she snuck a peak at the crumpled body of her Parker! She wanted to ask Perp what was going to happen. She remained wisely silent, terrified and wreathing in pain from nearly every part of her body.

Between her inability to breathe well, and the crippling pain from her broken and cracked ribs, she was quickly giving in to his madness. He retraced his steps and went back into the small living room and collected his box of goodies, and set them on the bed in the bedroom. The killer gathered up his spikes and his hammer and laid them at her side. He removed his sweatshirt and blue sweatpants, exposing his rubber suite. He sat Whisper up and untied her hands.

She thought she was moving them, but she could not feel them. Nevertheless, the slightest movement sent chilling pangs up and down her arm, and deep into her neck. The lucid pain squeezed out of her as tears freely fell. Nabulio then removed her robe. She knew she was going to be rapped, now, just like the others.

Defensively she crossed her legs at the ankles, and she took her right arm and reached across her chest, which covered her right breast, and she cupped most of the left with her hand. Her dislocated arm fell helplessly towards the floor; yet screaming with sharp pain. The protection she offered herself for her breast worked for only six seconds, until he grabbed her hand and pulled it off her breast and put her arm and hand up above her head and wide apart like a small child might make an angels wing in the snow. She looked down at her naked body. The topside of her breasts was nearly bluish purple, already. She couldn't see any more as he pushed her head down. "Don't worry about them missy, I'll tend to them in a minute!"

He then dove the nails into the floor, and taped her hand as he had done to the three other helpless victims. He kindly said, "I will tape your other arm in place where it lays. Do not attempt move it. I will spare you the pain of stretching it out and up." At that point, Whisper knew for sure. *He's the one.* She then began her involuntary chant. She half whispered, half mouthed over and over again, "Mommy, daddy, I'm so sorry, mommy, daddy, I'm so sorry, mommy, daddy I'm so sorry, mommy, daddy I'm so sorry." She just kept repeating it over and over again, while she remembered her parent's pleas to just come home until the madness ended. This madness she was living would soon end. Each time her chant went faster and faster, unending! Her entire body trembled. Nabulio ignored her. She knew she would be raped and then her throat would be cut. "Mommy, daddy, I'm so sorry..."

Whisper became numb to the reality of what was happening. She tried to move her hand. A prickly feeling jettisoned though her fingers. It hurt. She didn't even feel him open her legs up and hammer them and duct tape them home to the hardwood floor. In her mind she was somehow floating above her body. She could see herself, spread eagle on the floor, but it was as if she was looking at someone else. Nabulio propped a pillow from the bed under her head. He wanted her to watch an innocent civilian of the battle be tortured, mutilated because her Parker had ruined his plan, the plan of himself and his Whisper, or her for him into immortality!

He drove four nails into the wall opposite of her—so she could clearly see—he would use this cluster of nails to assist in his work. He drove four more nails in one cluster and another four nails in a cluster about 20 inches past the first cluster, horizontally, and about 3 feet below the first four clustered nails. He tied Parker's hand together, tightly, and put him up and over his shoulder and flopped him to the wall. Nabulio had to sling Parker four times before the tied hands looped over two of the four nails, above. He let some of Parkers weight hold to the two nails assisting in supporting the weight of his captive.

Nabulio stretched out placing one of his hands hard against Parker's stomach and grabbed the black duct tape. He turned and pressed his back against the tall; his thin slouching body. The killer pulled nearly a three-foot tape strip off and spun around and leaned his head into the stomach of the sagging body. The goon quickly wrapped the tape around the four nails, stretched the tape across Parker's abdomen, and wrapped the tape around the other four nails.

Nabulio then dragged a corner of the bed over, stood on top of it and securely taped the outstretched arms and hands to the four nails. He then put tape over poor Parker's forehead and taped it solidly to the wall. He did the same around Parker's neck. Afterwards, he nailed two more nails on each side of Parker's forehead and also at the neck. More tape was applied sealing any movement, and helping to support the weight of the drooping body. He repeated the procedure at the waste, knees, and ankles.

Helplessly, Whisper watched all of it as she continued her parenting chant, but it was done in silence now, nevertheless, the chant went on, *Mommy, daddy, I'm sorry, mommy, daddy, I'm sorry, mommy, daddy, I'm sorry, mommy daddy…*

She watched in horror as her assailant remove a knife from a patch in his suite. She watched him cut off the boxer shorts Parker was wearing. The knife was so sharp it took almost no effort at all. Nabulio then stepped to the side, so she could see, and watch. More tears filled her eyes as looked upon the hanging body of her Parker, nailed so helplessly attached to the wall. She wondered if he was dead. Something told her that that would be best.

The assailant looked at her, and then he took the point of the knife and placed it under the head of Parker's rubbery penis. Nabulio gently lifted it up so it pointed directly at her. Her attacker then moved, putting himself—his body—between her and Erick, with his back toward Whisper. The madman made some jerking moves, looked over his shoulder at Whisper. He smiled at her, smugly. He turned back around. The procedure only took about a twenty to twenty-five seconds. Whisper heard a groan come from her Parker. *He's alive.* Her attacker stepped aside, reached up and took the toilet paper out of the dangling man's mouth and replaced it with something, else. The attackers rubber gloved hands were dripping with Erick's blood, as was Parker's chin now dripping from his own blood. The assailant stepped aside.

In horror, Whisper screamed. All of Parker's genitals were gone, severed, removed! Nabulio had stuffed them into her fiancés mouth. The attacker whirled about and puncher her face. She was not out, just staggered, and dazed. He reached down and grabber the nipple of her right breast and pulled it out hard, and way too far. He then methodically sliced off the entire nipple and almost a half-inch of her breast behind where the nipple had been. Blood gushed out. She fainted dead away from both pain and shock. He did the same with her left breast and stuffed both breast parts with nipples attached into Parkers mouth with his genitalia, and then taped his bulging cheeks and mouth shut! "Live you bastard. Tell them what happens to the innocents in war!" Nabulio walked away.

Nabulio sat on the edge of the bed. "Think," he demanded aloud! *Okay, they will ask him to describe me. No way will he remember. Not good enough! Think! A sketch artist will help, but if stupid Parker can't see what he has described they will not be sure if what they sketched is sketched correctly. No matter,* he thought, *Parker—if lucky—saw me for less than five seconds.* It didn't matter, Nabulio played it safe.

He got off the bed, took a nail, made a fist about the nail with an inch sticking out past his curled littlest finger. He reached up, and jabbed each of Erick Parker's eyes, twice. Parker's body twitched at that event. *That should do it you prickles wonder! You can describe all you want, but you can't see what the artist has drawn from your words, so you are worthless to them now!*

For the first time in the killings, Nabulio laughed. This—to him—was that funny!

The Perp then looked out the window; the sun was offering a reddish yellow tinge against the morning sky. He had to hurry; time was fleeting. He went to Whisper and decided to carve on her a different note than that which had been planned. He had planned to carve *"Courage is like love: it must have hope for nourishment!"* He thought that that was no longer appropriate. As he placed the knife to her lower chest and stuck his knife in to begin his writing; she let out a scream, as her body snapped back to life. He taped her mouth shut, again. He could here her pulling hard for air, choking and wheezing. She was getting some air at least. He started to carve. He was in a hurry and she wasn't complying. He began one more time, but the body twisted and turned in terrifying agony. She was making his work impossible with her stupid twisting and churning. *Dumb bitch. Enough is enough!*

Methodically, he picked up his knife and shoved the blade deep into her vagina and ripped upward with all his strength. He heard and felt the blade slice thought tissue, cartel edge, and bone. He twisted the knife, again, and withdrew it. Her body twisted, wreathed. She was still alive, and somehow through her taped lips passed, "Mommy, daddy, I'm so sorry…" That pissed him off, even more. He stood up and looked deadly into her open eyes. Her eyes were open; she could see her death coming. He slashed though her neck with one whisking swipe.

Her head listed to the left and fell, making a gurgling noise, and exposing more than a full inch of her inner throat. All noise ceased, except he heard the release of bodily air escape in death. He finished carving, uninterrupted. Finished, he read:

Never interrupt your
Enemy when he is
makking a
mistake!
#4.

He stepped back, and admired his masterpiece. "Figure that out, W!" Immediately, however, he was mad as hell. In his hurriedness he had added an additional letter 'K' to the word 'making.' Knowing that W would think he misspelled the word, and W's team would think that he was an idiot, he was overly pissed. On the other hand, perhaps he could confuse them by his intentional double message. Erick Parker had made the mistake of being where he wasn't supposed to be, and Nabulio's miss lettering was also a mistake, not a misspelling. *What will W make of that? Let him think on! Let him stew!*

He felt like hacking the whole phrase into oblivion and redoing it on Parker. After all, it was Parker who interrupted his plan. He deserved it! Nabulio decided against it. Deserved or not, he was merely an innocent bystander who was nailing Nabulio's girl, Whisper. The whole of it was her fault, *the slut*. Nabulio had intended to have some fun with her. *Well, I did, didn't I?* No doubt her damn breasts had excited the now ball-less Parker! He had nothing left to ball with; it was all sleeping in his mouth between her nipples. *Let him chew on that.* Exercised, by it all, he withdrew the blade from her private section and drove it deeply into her heart as was humanly possible. One of his knuckles actually broke though her skin from the plunging thrust of the knife.

The mad man collected all of his things, and laid them on their bed sheet. He wrapped the sheet up and took off the pillowcase of her pillow and wiped up as much of her and Parkers blood he could off his rubber suit. He tossed the sheet into the corner of the room. Leaving bloody footprints; he retrieved his outer clothing and donned them over the blood smeared rubber suit. He took the contents to the door, leaving his knife deeply imbedded in her dead heart. *A souvenir for W, a souvenir of war.* Nabulio, smiled.

Before leaving, he slapped Parkers face a few times. His body moved slightly. He would live. Good! *Tell your story how you brought her life to an end, bastard.* "Think of her often you dickless wonder!" Before leaving, he went to the front door and locked it, but left the back door unlocked, intentionally. He forgot to do the cigarette thing. Later he would remember that he forgot that. He wouldn't care. He took the phone off the hook. Went to the front window and as he looked out, a light from across the street came on at the same instant.

He got in his car, started it and began to pull forward. He suddenly jammed on the breaks; the car sallied back and forth. He jumped out and ran into the house to the bathroom. He searched the vanity drawers. He found what he wanted. He thought for a second and then wrote on the wall with Whispers lipstick:

He who fears being

conquered

is sure of defeat!

The serial killer raced back to the car and jumped in, quickly. *Damn*, he thought.

He raced back into the house and collected his phony research paper and its folder.

Back outside and into his car, he pulled around the house. At the end of the drive he turned right. As he turned, he looked at the neighbor's home. Not a sole watching him. He drove less than fifteen yards and turned his headlights on. Just as he came to the stop sign at the open end of the dead end road, another car turned to the left in front of Nabulio and onto Parkers road. The stranger slightly waived. Nabulio waved back at what he saw, Parkers car. He didn't notice who the driver was; it hardly mattered. What did matter was the fact that in less then a couple of minutes the police would receive a call from Todd Christensen. Christensen would make that call, but not until he vomited twice.

* * * * *

Todd Christensen had borrowed Parker's car the night before. He promised he would have it back Monday morning by eight at the latest. It was 8:11 a.m. when he waived at the unknown Nabulio. Had he arrived on time, he may well have been another innocent victim. At 8:49, Todd—in a bit of a shock—would tell Detective Strange that he saw a dark green or blue car pass him by as he had turned the corner. He didn't actually see the man, but he waived and the man waved back. He guessed he was forty-five or so! He didn't know! How could he know, he didn't see him, really?

Wellington arrived at 9:00 a.m. on the button. He could not believe how this poor dead woman resembled his Alexandria. They may not have been twins, but certainly sisters. He massacred this woman in humiliation and senselessness. Erick Parker was rushed to the hospital. It was there at the hospital that the contents of Erick's mouth revealed more disgusting truth! Almost unfortunately, he would live.

The war had taken a much harsher step; turn! Why? Former FBI Agent Katrina Cowlings in her report had warned Wellington and Rodgers what would happen if things didn't go as planned by their non-Serial, Serial Killer! She was right on target! That mattered not at all to Whisper anymore!

Chapter 16—The Nineteenth Day (Monday)
WELLINGTON FINDS WELLINGTON

Wellington took one very fast look around, and told Strange to get a hold of the Captain and tell him that he needed Katrina Cowlings here, pronto, "and tell him, I need him here too, and ASAP!" he added.

Wellsy knew one thing was for sure. This non-serial, Serial Killer had taken things to a new level. *If he's not a Serial Killer then this guy was the best pretender of one in the history of Serial Killers.*

Of all the things for Wellington to take in—and for whatever reason—he zeroed in on the lipstick note in the bathroom. He looked at it and tried to imagine the killer writing it. *I was written so deliberately, so carefully, and yet he knew it was the last thing he did before he left.* He looked at it for the tenth time:

He who fears being

conquered

is sure of defeat!

Wellsy knew the killer was referring to Wellsy, himself. This diabolical man was playing on the fact that he knew that Wellington was beginning to play it cautiously safe, waiting for the next victim. The press was all over Wellington and the police force. The press wanted to know when they—the police—were going to do something to stop this maniac. The burden was lying heavily, squarely on the young Lieutenants shoulders.

Katrina Cowlings was right; the devastation that this maniac left behind this time was way over anything he had previously committed. Something unexpectedly must have transpired. Wellsy knew that he had to respond, immediately. This foe had carried out his carnage just as Katrina said he would. Ten minutes later he was still looking at the quote, thinking! He picked at his cell phone and called Alexandria. He asked if she could find what date was it that

Napoleon had made the two quotes that he had just left behind. He wanted to know exactly what was happening, historically when Napoleon made these two statements. What were his contexts for the quotes? He also gave her the names of the two victims, but that she was to only focus on the girl for the name game. "What are you thinking," she asked?

"I think I want to know about Wellington!"

"Wellington? That's you!"

"Yes, and no. I want to know about the Duke of Wellington from Britain."

"Why?"

"Because his quotes might be helpful for me to better understand this whole Napoleon quoting thing. According to Katrina," he said, "our killer wants me to respond. So I'm ready to do that but I want to respond as did the Duke of Wellington counter to Napoleon; as best I can!"

"Why!"

"I don't have time for why, and I'm not sure myself, yet. Look, I'm too busy for you to ask why questions, okay, so please just do it, quickly and get back with me as fast as you possibly can. I want a list of at least ten quotes."

"Consider it done!" She had never seen him so up tight and edgy.

"I already did." He cut off the call. He thought about Cowlings and what she said in her report, 'He is crying out, Wellington. He wants you to communicate with him. Do it or pay the consequences.' *Could the consequences be any worse than what he did to this man and to this poor woman?*

Ted Castle's assistant Trudy Hawks walked up and gave him the list of what he wanted to know. Whisper Katharine Ulrich died from her throat being severed. She had two broken ribs, a dislocated elbow of her right arm, her nose had been broken, a cut to the face that would have required six or seven stitches, she had been stabbed through her vagina and the assailant had taken the weapon and drew it up and out causing extreme destruction to her organs. Castle's opinion was that this man had tortured her in about every way possible. After her death he stabbed her thorough the heart with enough force to inlay is knuckles of his first and second fingers of his right hand into her person. *He's probably right handed, then.* "Additionally, we found sixteen hairs from her head from the outer living room to the bedroom. They came out of her head while he dragger her to the bedroom." The last bit of information Hawks was pleased to tell the Lieutenant. She told him with a bit of excitement. "We have DNA samples, Lieutenant."

"Where, how?"

"Come, I'll show you." They walked back to her body. "Look," she said, look at the top of her breasts, both of them. Extreme pressure was placed on each. "Now look," she said as she took a tongue swab stick, and placed it under Whisper's right breast and lifted up. "Right there," she offered, "see those two small indentations and cuts in the swelling area at the base of her breast?" Looking carefully, Wellington nodded, yes. "We are about ninety percent sure that those are fingernail gauges from the attacker."

"Well, I'll be go to hell! Wait, he offered, all that means is that her DNA is under his fingernails; it doesn't mean his DNA is there, does it," he asked hopefully?

Trudy ignored his comment. She carefully removed the stick, and repeated the action to the left breast. This time there were three such marks. "We believe he picked her up off the floor, by her breasts with thumbs on top, and fingers underneath." She paused and looked directly into the Lieutenant's eyes. "We believe he pushed down hard with his thumbs and dug through his gloved rubber gloves…"

"Rubber," Wellington asked?

"In a second, okay." He nodded in agreement. "Anyway, he held on to her and lifted her. Her own weight caused him—forced him to push down hard with his thumbs and dig in and up with his fingers—to have a strong enough hold to lift her! The pain for her would have been excruciating, but for him as well. He was digging fingers and thumbs hard and deeply into her flesh. We believe the force was so great that his fingernails actually went though the glove and into the bases of her breasts. Certainly he has her DNA under his fingernails, but hopefully we have his too!"

"The rubber gloves?"

"Some very small pieces of something, we believe rubber, were found in the area of his fingernail cuts. We'll know more after the tests. We're hopeful, Lieutenant, that's all I can say."

"Thanks," was all he said."

"Just catch the bastard, Lieutenant. This girl suffered beyond anything realistic!"

"So did he," Ted Castle said, pointing to where Erick Parker's body had been. He was gone, taken to the hospital. At the same time, Castles cell when off. A minute and a half later, he confirmed what they suspected regarding the contents in his mouth. "However, Lieutenant," he added, "the assailant didn't keep her nipple, well nipples and a small portion of her breasts as souvenirs; they were also stuffed in Parker's his mouth."

"Bastard," both Wellington and Hawks offered at the same time.

"That's all we have for you now, Lieutenant. Anything else for us?"

"Yes, when Katrina Cowlings gets here, be sure to tell her about the lifting of the breasts for him to carry her, and also about the contents in Parker's mouth." Hawks, nodded. Wellington stepped to the body, again, and again her read: Never interrupt your enemy when he is makking a mistake! #4. He pondered it all. Who interrupted him? Had he planed that note or did it come out of something else, like Erick Parker, perhaps? He thought of other things to, like '*Victory belongs to the most persevering*,' and the Profiler's comment, '*Lieutenant, find a way to take his power away*.' Wellington's head was swimming. He knew he was way over is head in this whole damn mess. On the other hand, who else would have enough experience to solve this madman's plight? *This lunatic had opened a whole new door to craziness, why?* That was the question. The question was *why? What was his motivation? Why was he doing this to these unfortunate women?* Cowlings' was sure it was about himself—the killer—and Wellington.

The lead detective turned his thoughts to the misspelling of 'making,' the attacker had added that second "k." It perplexed him. *Wait*, he thought. *This whole thing when wrong for him this morning, yes, it went all wrong. Parker wasn't supposed to be home, that has to be it. But parker was home, but the killer didn't know that because this Mike Christensen had borrowed Parker's car. Parker surprised this guy. So, he went into a rage and took it out on Parker and Ulrich. That had to be it. He was hurrying at the end and simply misspelled or added an additional "k." inadvertently.*

That had to be it. He called for Strange. He told the Detective, "I need to know if Parker was a student here at Wesleyan, or Old Dominion, and if so, and I'm sure he was, I want his class schedule, and if he worked, where did he work, and did he work with Parker, and..." He stopped in mid-sentence. "No, Detective, I don't need all that. Is that kid still here who found all this?"

"No. His name is Todd Christensen, he was pretty shaken so I had him taken to the hospital."

"Get over there, find out what he knows about Erick Parker's school and work schedule."

"I have all that information, already. I got it from Christensen." Strange told Wellington exactly what Wellington had suspected, that Erick Parker was supposed to have been at work, but took the day off, and he must have surprised this Angel Killer. *Angel killer? Why did I call him that?* That got Wellington to thinking. Just as quickly, he knew! It was how he staked three of the four out, like Angles. Wellington was on to something, but what it was, he wasn't exactly sure.

Two things interrupted his thoughts at once. First, Katrina Cowlings had arrived, and secondly, his cellular phone when off. He told Cowlings to look around, that he had to take this call, and he'd be right with her. Alex rattled off her several quotes from the Duke of Wellington. She said it wasn't going to be easy to get each quote, dated, but she wanted him to have what she had found so far. He told her she was a gem.

She wanted to know more about what he was thinking. He promised to tell her later, that he actually couldn't wait to tell her. He needed her keen mind. He asked her to read all the quotes she had, again. She told him that she had dozens, but that he had only wanted ten. She read them back, again. He told her to download them into is cellular. She said okay.

Wellington went to the bedroom doorway. He didn't say a word, he just watched Katrina Cowlings observe, work. He watched her get very close to Ulrich's body. She wasn't looking she was studying. She was amazing to watch at work.

His cellular vibrated. He went to his download. There were two quotes he liked. He decided to combine them together as one. He read them back-to-back: "The whole art of war consists in getting at what is on the other side of the hill. All the business of war, and indeed all the business of life, is to endeavor to find out what you don't know by what you do; that's what I called 'guessing what was at the other side of the hill.'" He took out his note pad and wrote down what he had read. He then added to it. "Angel Killer, I know you. You left me too much. I see you on the other side of the hill. Remember, I am watching you! I now know what I didn't know by what I know now. Now, you must learn to know what you don't know that I know on my side of the hill!" *Let him chew on that!*

He allowed Katrina Cowlings nearly an hour before he approached her. She asked, "Tell me what he did to the man he had taped against the wall." He told her all that they knew and what he had surmised of the whole thing. "You don't need me any more detective. You know that don't you? Oh, yes," she continued, "you think you do but you don't.. It's your case. Follow your instincts, Lieutenant. There isn't anymore I can add. I assume you know why he went on a tirade, don't you?" He simply nodded yes. "I want you to answer me one question, and then I'll be done with this." She took a step back, and asked, "Have you decided what you are going to communicate to him?"

"Yes, let me read it to you."

"No! I don't want you to, just tell me who you are quoting, it's not Napoleon is it?"

He smiled, "No, no it is not!"

"Good then you are on the right track. Using the Duke of Wellington is a good choice, then. Congratulations, you are about to take away his power.

However," she added, "he will change the game, somehow, but that will tell you that he is running scared, but never forget, he will not quit. He has an agenda, but now he will communicate back, and to that, you must be ready." With that, she turned and left, not even asking what quote or quotes he had decided on. She didn't need to. He had asked for her to come. She did! She came, and did nothing, except to offer the Lieutenant the one thing he needed, confidence. She left knowing he had it!

"Ms. Cowlings," he said, "One more question?"

She stopped, "You don't need to ask, just do, Lieutenant." She turned to leave, and turned back toward him one more time. "But, if I can make one more suggestion," she offered before he had a chance to respond, "no one but you should tell this young women's parents. This was a vial, sick execution; you need to find the muster to tell them, yourself. And, Lieutenant, you need to do this not only for them, but also for you. I know police leaders such as you. You feel that you have to remove yourself from the death, the pain and the anguish, and that is true for the most part. However, Arthur," (when she used his given first name it sent a shock though him) "until you feel the pain through the parents, you'll never really understand. On the other hand, if you accept my challenge, I promise you that for the next forty years, you'll be a great investigator and a great cop. If you ever want to understand this mad-man, then you need to truly understand the true pain he is inflicting." She paused for a brief second; "You will find that in the eyes and heart of mister and misses Ulrich." She left him standing in a deep stupor of thought.

He mumbled back to her as she was leaving, "Angel Killer."

She stopped in dead tracks, turned and looked directly into his eyes from twelve feet away. "You're on the right track, ANGEL, now, go and find the KILLER!" She walked, away!

He needed his Alexandria for help, support, and courage. Maybe she would go with him, he wanted to run after the Profiler and ask if talking Alexandria with him would be best. He looked around the room and saw the devastation, truly saw it for the fist time. He was standing in a trance trying to make sense of it all. Suddenly he felt pressure on the back of his shoulder. He turned around. "Sorry Captain, I didn't know you were there."

"I know you didn't, but let me tell you something, Lieutenant, I've been where you are right now, just one time. I see it in your face. I see it in your countenance. It has just become really real, hasn't it?" He paused, "Look, son, I need to make a suggestion to you, privately, man to man, not cop to cop or subordinate to Captain." Wellsy looked up at him. "Twenty-seven years ago, a man by the name of Trevor O'Donnell said to me what I am about to say to you. He then left me alone to my thoughts. Here it is son, get away from this crime scene. Go off somewhere and take a cleansing breath, then muster up your courage and you go to wherever this woman's parents are and tell them yourself. You will only need to do that once, Lieutenant." He paused, "Lieutenant, it will make all the difference."

He paused again, as the Lieutenant looked up and into his eyes, amazed that he was hearing this message twice inside of just a couple of minutes. "Tell me you need a vacation day or a sick day, whatever. Tell me what you need to about this case, and then get yourself to those parents. Don't try to escape it. Go! Learn! By the way, the department will not pay for your trip, either. If you need a loan, I'll help. Do you know where they live?" Wellington shook his head, *no*!

"Okay, get Detective Strange here and fill us in where you are on this thing, and then get the hell out of here!"

His meeting with Rodgers and Strange took 44 minutes. He was on his way to where he needed to be. It was the only place he ever felt secure. He rushed to Alexandria and begged her to just hold him as he cried, hard, just as he cried hard when he was twelve years old and his Labrador retriever, Smoky, died. She cradled him just as she had hopes that one day she would cradle his children.

CHAPTER 17—THE NINETEENTH AND TWENTIETH DAY
THE VISIT

Their plane landed at one minute to midnight. They picked up their rental car, and made the two-hour drive from Columbia, South Carolina to Laurinburg, North Carolina, and stayed at the Holiday Inn. Other airports were closer, but connections would have been far worse. This was their best choice; their only good choice. They were up by eight a.m. and on their way to Wagram, North Carolina by 8:45. It was a lazy but nervous twelve-minute drive. They turned on to Bundy Street—of all names—looking for the Ulrich address. The Ulrich's mailbox announced that they had arrived at the their exact location.

Wellsy took a deep breath, and just blurted it out, "Let's do it!" Arthur hated the deception he used, explaining that he was involved in an investigation and felt they could help. He had called just last evening, about the time that their daughter had been placed in the morgue. Alexandria squeezed his hand one more time before they got out of their car. They walked to the front door of the house and rang the bell.

Constance offered a welcoming southern hospitality smile. By habit, the Lieutenant used his law-enforcement credentials to offer proof of their identification. When Constance glanced at the word Norfolk, she staggered back, and cried out, "Oh God, no!" Wellington stepped forward to brace the stricken women, but Alexandria was faster. She actually ushered the older woman to the couch that rested in the formal living room of the house. Constance cried "Oh, God," again and called for John. The tone of her voice scared him. He burst though the archway opening, and saw his wife with a shattered expression.

"What is it?"

"I'm afraid there isn't any other way to tell you Mr. Ulrich, but we've come to tell you that your daughter was murdered yesterday morning in her apartment."

Both parents were paralyzed by his news. Neither parent was thinking. The words just blurted out her mouth. "Did she suffer?"

He glanced at Alexandria, "I would be lying if I said otherwise, Mrs. Ulrich. I'm afraid she did!"

John just let the words slip by his lips, unaware, "Oh, Cookie, oh Cookie!" He looked at the policeman, and grabbed at his heart, and slipped backswords off the chair. "Why, why her, why?" he asked falling, slumping to the floor?

Arthur leaned down to grab him. Alexandria cried out, "Oh, Lord, no!" Constance ran to the kitchen.

She returned with a flash, "Open his mouth officer; open it." He did, she inserted the pill under his tongue. "He'll be fine now. Just let him lie there a minute. He'll be, okay!" Again, she dashed off to the kitchen, retrieving a glass of water. For the better part of ten minutes she cradled him, whispering to him all positive things. She had been though this six previous times. She was an old pro at it, now! Another ten minutes passed. He was up and on the sofa next to Constance.

Reality came crashing back in an instant. Alexandria reached into her handbag and withdrew a few pages of notes. "With the permission, my fiancé," she turned and acknowledged Wellsy, "Lieutenant Wellesley, who is in charge of the investigation, allowed me to make copies of the last few days of Whisper's life from her personal journal. You should know that Whisper was very happy with her life over the last few days. These notes, Mister and Misses Ulrich—while she wrote them for herself—there is a good deal in them that directly addresses the two of you. Did you know she was in deeply in love?"

The Ulrich's looked at one another; each shook their head, no.

"She was. She was excited about that. According to her journal, she was very happy. I took the liberty and borrowed this picture from their apartment. She handed John the picture of Parker standing behind Whisper with his arms around her waist. Whisper was smiling, looking upward at him over her shoulder. Her smile was engaging. They looked loving; yet tears in their eyes betrayed their happiness. Alex, offered, "You might want to know, he tried to save her life."

"He's okay then?" John asked. "Could we talk to him, Parker I think his name is? Alexandria looked at Wellsy. Wellington told the couple that he was alive but that he would be in the hospital for some time.

The Ulrich's had so many questions, most of which they didn't receive sufficient answers for. How could they? Arthur went over the events—as he knew them—doing his best to leave out the gore of it, or her pain, and her suffering. It was basically impossible. What he didn't say became obvious to them. John asked with a quivering voice, "How did she, my, my…" he couldn't breath, "my Cookie actually die, Lieutenant? Wellsy started to answer, and John waived him off, deciding he didn't really want to know the ugly truth, at least not now, anyway.

At length, John did ask, what the Lieutenant needed of them, now. Before he could answer, a young man entered the room, and immediately sensed something wasn't right. Without thinking, John just blurted out, "Gary, I'm afraid Cookie has been murdered in Norfolk just as we feared." His sentence caused Wellsy to look up, at mister Ulrich. *Had they been warned in some way?* He knew he had to wait to ask! He shot a glance at Alex; she wondered the very same thing.

"When, how, why?" Gary asked. He took a breath, "Who did it? Are you sure she is d…" He couldn't get out the word.

Constance put his arm around her only son, and now her only living child. Tears swelled in her eyes, as she stated, "This is Detective Wellesley from the Norfolk Police Department. He is the officer in charge. They came here to tell us Gary. Things in the Ulrich home stayed in turmoil over the next fifteen minutes. Gary said, "Why wouldn't she let me come there, like you said, dad? Again, Wellesley's ears picked up. John hadn't any reasonable reply. Finally, John said, "Lieutenant, what was it you were saying before Gary came in?"

"Well," he stammered, "hold on just a second. A few minutes ago you mentioned that your daughter was killed just as you feared. Had she been threaten by someone, or have any of you been threatened? Furthermore, Gary asked why she wouldn't come home as you had asked. Had something happened along these lines?"

John was the first to respond. Lieutenant, I know where you are going with this, and no. "Neither Whisper nor us were threatened, but yes, something certainly did happen. On the heels of those first two women killed, there was another. We called Cookie and pleaded with her to come home. She said she could take care of herself, and I told her, that I was sure those other three women thought they could t…" He could not finish his sentence, as; again, the reality of his Cookie's death betrayed him.

Constance held her husband, while she said to the visitors, with her head buried into her husband's chest, "We begged her to come home. She said, no!

She said that she would be all rig…" She got nothing more out. She spilled into a heap on her husband's chest bawling into it. Her body quivered and shook, as did her husbands as he gripper her tightly with his arms. Gray walked over and placed his hand on his mothers back and his other hand went atop of the back of his father's head. He knelt down to be closer to them and to support his weakening body.

Only then did Garry offer, "And they told her that I could come live with her until this killing stopped." After a minute, he added, "She said that that was stupid, because she lived in the all girl dormitory, and said I wouldn't be allowed to stay there." He took a cleansing breath and offered, "And then she called home a few days later and said, she had moved in with two friends…"

"Landrum," Wellington asked, and then repeated, she had lived in Landrum? Gary merely nodded, yes.

"When did she move out?" The Lieutenant asked.

Gary started to answer, then stopped in mid-sentence, "Oh, heavens, is Sharon dead, too?"

"Who is Sharon?" Wellington asked?

Constance was the one who was now confused. She broke her hold from her husband, "Sharon? Sharon is Parker's sister, she lived with her brother Erick, and our daughter, Whisper." She paused, and then asked, "I take it that Sharon wasn't home then?"

Wellington and Alexandria figured it out at once, but what to say? Alex took the high road, but made sure she didn't lie. No, Sharon wasn't there, Mrs. Ulrich."

"Then she is safe."

How could that question possibly be answered? Wellesley offered. "We were not aware that Erick had a sister, perhaps she was away. We will have to look into that."

"Wait just a minute, Gary said, "you had to have seen a second or third bedroom that Erick used, or… I imagine that…" He said no more. Everyone by now had it figured out, too. Whisper had lied to her family! The term—*shacked up*—went through John's mind, and a similar thought pierced though Constance.

They were heart sick all over, again. The day had just turned darker for the Ulrich family. There were more issues to be considered. Constance handed the picture of her daughter and Erick back to Alexander. "We won't be needing this after all."

"Are you sure, Misses Ulrich, she loved this boy very much." Constance broke down. Quiet minutes went by. Constance reached out for the picture. I'll take that. Alex handed it to her, smiling. She also handed out the copies of the journal. "Please take these. It will help you, your husband and Gary. She was a most happy woman. You need to learn that. It will help."

"Nothing will really help," John quipped. More silence stilled the air. All were feeling quite remorseful. It had all been said. "Lieutenant, you said something earlier about what we need to do now."

Arthur looked at the forlorn family. He cleared his throat. He had said this more than once before, that that was basically always to strangers. The Ulrich family wasn't strangers any longer. "John, Constance, someone needs to come to Norfolk and identify the body that indeed, it is your daughter!" He paused, "And you'll want to make arrangements to have your daughter's body brought back here, I would guess. That brought on more tears. They stayed another twenty-two minutes. They left, but not before Alexandria gave each family a hug. Gary wept on her shoulder longer than was comfortable. Alex let him get it out of his system.

Captain Rodgers and the Profiler were dead on. This case took on a whole new level for Wellesley, and for Alexandria as well. For the first time, Arthur understood the pain of death outside of the agony that the any victim ever felt. That agonizing pain swept though families, too.

As they were leaving the house, Constance gave Arthur and Alexandria another hug for coming personally. "I will read these papers right away," she lied. She didn't intend to lie, but she found she didn't have the capacity to pry into her daughter's life, that that was somehow wrong, for the present, anyway.

Eleven weeks would pass before she gained enough strength to read about her daughter's love for Erick Parker. As they turned to leave, Arthur heard something. He looked up, John latched on to him as if he were a long lost buddy, returning. It made Wellington most uncomfortable. He then saw deeply into this grieving man's face, and then focused into his eyes.

Katrina was right, he saw into the soul of this poor man. He looked at Constance, her eyes piercing into his. The three of them, their lives would never be the same. The Lieutenant saw the pain of death, and understood it for the first time. He felt so alone. *How they must feel?*

* * * * *

The Ulrich family ignored, as best they could all the press and hoopla surrounding their daughter's and sister's death. Newspapers were stacked up near the door. When Constance got around to reading her daughter's copied journal notes, she was happy for her daughter's love. When she finally took courage and read the discarded newspapers, her heart sank lower when she read what the monster did to Parker, as well. She grieved for him, too.

* * * * *

Three weeks after Wellesley left the Ulrich's home, Constance received a package from him. A brief note stated, "By now I assume you have read the notes from your daughter's journal. Here is the hard copy of her journal. Alexandria and I care for you and your family. Give our best in these trying times to John, and Gary." He simply signed it, Arthur Wellesley.

* * * * *

As the couple returned to the car, Wellesley realized that by now, his comments to the Angle Killer had hit the streets of Norfolk. They decided to forego taking the plane back. They decided to drive their rental car back to Norfolk, and on the way they'd look at this murder case from every possible angle it had already been looked at and many new angles as well. For three hours of that drive they played the name game.

After a late lunch, he asked if Alex would drive for a while. He wanted and needed a nap. An hour and seventeen minutes later, he woke up. They stopped and had coffee, after which Alex slept for forty-seven more minutes. When she awoke, they chatted for nearly an hour, and then stopped for a late dinner. Back in the car she decided to read a book she had brought with her, *Napoleon Bonaparte*, by Alan Schom. She read the Preface, and then the Acknowledgments. After the Acknowledgment page she studied the Bonaparte Family Tree. A puzzle was developing, but she couldn't put it together, yet. Time needed too incubate for that one, so that puzzle would come, later, much later. But, it would be the key to this whole mess!

The second sentence of the first chapter caused her to suddenly stop reading. She didn't know why. Something was shouting at her, but she couldn't figure it out. *Come on girl think*! She read the sentence three more times.

"Wait," she half screamed!

"What, Wellsy screamed, back?"

"I'm on to something, but I don't know what!"

"On to what?"

"Holly, cow. This is unbelievable. I was right all along, but wrong as well. Remember when I mistakenly told you that I could tell you the name of the next victim."

"Yes, I remember, but you were wrong, what you had meant to say was that you knew the first letter of the next victim."

"Yes, right but I was wrong, wasn't I?"

"I'm afraid so."

"Well, I'm not this time," she asked, "Give me the names of the first four victims?"

He spat them back in nothing flat, naming them one by one and in order of their death: "Nowicki, Carolyn Ann, Anderson, Jessica June, Bi Yan, or more specifically, Yan Bi, and of course Whisper Katharine Ulrich." He had added that he hoped she would be the last. Both knew better!

"I'm afraid not, Wellsy." She continued with her newest triumph! "Remember that later I told you I thought he was going to spell out his name, the Angel Killer's name, and I thought that his name was..."

Wellington beat her to the punch, "Napoleon."

"Right, but I was wrong, dead wrong."

"Yes, we already know that, but I was amazed when you were right about the third woman, Bi Yan, or Yan Bi. I still don't get that."

"Forget about that," she told him that that wasn't important now. She knew exactly how many he was going to kill, and the first initial of the victim's last name. She told him that the next girl's last name would start with a 'L', and the next would be an 'I', and finally, she snipped, an 'O.' "After that, I don't know." She added, "Maybe that will be all. Maybe he will be done then. But, forget all the maybes because I am sure about the 'L', and the 'I' and then the 'O'. I'm dead sure this time, Wellsy! Dead sure!" She paused ever so slightly and then asked, "How do I know this, Wellsy, how?"

He obviously wanted to know the obvious. *How did she know?* He was perturbed that she was actually making him ask. *Let her have her victory. Ask!* He was so excited to know. "Okay, okay, let's have it. And, stop being mean!"

She gave credit to the author of *Napoleon Bonaparte*, Schom. "Let me read you the first two sentences from his book. The second sentence is what gives it away, but I'll read the first as well. Here goes," she read "'On December 17, 1778, thirty-two year old-Maria (or Charles, as he now called himself) Buonaparte boarded a coastal vessel in the Corsican port of Ajaccio. At his side, Joseph, ten, his eldest son; Napoleon, or "Nabulio," nine, the second surviving son.'" She took a breath. "Our killer was not, as I thought, spelling out Napoleon, but the name by which Napoleon was called by his father, and or others as well, Nabulio." She spelled it, a letter at a time, "N, A, B, U, L, I, O." She took one last breath, and finished, "Arthur, he is spelling out Nabulio, N, for Nowicki, A, for Anderson, B, for Bi, and U, for Ulrich," which Arthur said at the same time with her.

"Next will be some poor woman that her last name starts with 'L', the next one will end with an 'I' and finally, an 'O'."

Arthur didn't have a chance to respond. He couldn't believe what he heard. He opened his mouth, but his cellular went off. He didn't recognize the number. He took the call. It was Justin Thompson from the Norfolk Gazette. Justin began by thanking Wellington for the scoop to be the first to tell the public and inform the Angle Killer with his statement. "My telephone has been ringing off the hook with tips, or leads. You won't believe what we are hearing." Wellington took it with a grain of salt. There could well be tons of leads, but he would now need a task force to document and follow-up on them all. It would take a lifetime. *Hell,* he thought, *I will need a task force to run down the possibilities of L, and I and O, as well.*

"Look, Justin, I'm excited about this, but right now, I'm involved with something much hotter. Do you have something specifically for me, or not," Wellington hoped.

"No, not exactly." Thompson sputtered back. But I have something, that I want to release so badly but I need your approval, according to Robert Jenkins our editor, because it is explosive. I've found the key." Wellington asked what he had. "I know the source from which source the Angel Killer selects his victims."

"Tell me!" He then interrupted, himself, with a thought, "Wait, what did you just call him?

"The Angel killer."

"Where did you get that from?"

"The police department."

"Who said you could use it?"

"Your words are of public domain, you did, and that is what I printed, you are calling him the Angel Killer, right?"

"Well," Arthur threw out some air, "I guess we are now. *Wow, is this a day of days, or what,* Wellsy thought. "Okay, tell me what you have found."

"No! You must come here, now!"

"I can't. I'm on the highway returning from an out of State trip. I will not be available until tomorrow at the earliest, and not before then."

Jenkins fired back, "Okay, I will tell you, but you must come in here tomorrow morning and discuss this with me or I'll not say a word, now! This is explosive, Wellesley. It's bigger than you can imagine." Wellington agreed to meet. Jenkins had always been straight with him. "Don't be late, or I'll run my story!" Wellesley agreed to meet in the morning at 7:30 at the Gazette. Jenkins said but three words, and then added, "Tomorrow, or I go to press!"

"I'll be there," he said, and clicked off his cellular. He looked at Alex, "Holy, shit," Wellsy whispered between his teeth. Alex asked what that was all about.

He didn't answer; instead, he pulled off the interstate onto the shoulder. He got out of his car and opened the trunk. Two minutes later, Alex had Arthur's laptop on her knees and was accessing the Internet through Goggle. First she went to Old Dominion and from there she easily found the reporters source, the three words he said to Wellington, *"Mace and Crown,"* she then went to the Deans list, and found the four names: Nowicki, Anderson, Bi, and Ulrich.

Wellsy began to speak. She was way ahead of him. She had already anticipated his next question and rattled off eleven more names all starting with the letter "L": Larkin, Karen O; Lashbrook, Jill Susan; Lewis, Terry Ann; Lillian, Karen, Kay; Lincoln, Angelica May; Lincoln, Sharon Margaret, Lindsey, Janet May; Lions, Marcella Peoples, Linville, Cynthia Ann; Locus, Deborah S. and. Lucy, Connie Marie."

The two sleuths realized and discussed the fact that 11 women were a lot of people to investigate and attempt protection all at the same time. Time, and money expenses were also an issue. Additionally, they didn't have a clue how long it would take the killer to make up his mind, if he hadn't already done so. They discussed several scenarios as to how to go about everything. One possibility was to expose the list of names, through the newspaper, forcing the attacker to switch tactics, but that would leave them, like before, clueless as to what he would do next. That would never help, or would it? They didn't know! Who, could?

Both, Wellesley and Southerland assumed—felt—that by exposing the names to the community through the press—and—to the killer at this same time, had its pluses as well. For instance: allowing the Angel Killer to know that he, Wellesley, knew who the next targets were could only elevate the Lieutenant in the mind of the Angel Killer? Alex offered, "Look, Wellsy, in the mind of the AK, this announcement will acknowledge as well as add insult to injury."

"What did you just say?"

"I don't know, what?"

"You said AK!'

"Right, AK, Angel Killer!"

"What is this, everybody takes a take off me? What is up with that?"

"You're the man, Arthur, you be the man! The main stain, you are it big fella, like it or not!"

"Not," he said.

"Tough noogies. Suck it up, big fella!"

He just stared at her. She went on, as if she hadn't been interrupted, "Combined with your comments to AK that you not only know what is on the other side of the hill, but, also, you also know what is going on, on the other side of the hill; that will expose his plan. Remember, Wellsy, you will make him think that you are about to close in on him. Don't miss that opportunity. Force him into a mistake."

He started to speak, but she interrupted him; rolling over him. "I think you are on to something here, Wellsy. Blow it up in his face. Show him how smart you are." She thought for a moment, "Wasn't that what Katrina said you should make him think? I remember what she said about the Angel Killer stating that "Victory belongs to the most persevering.' She said to you, 'Lieutenant, find a way to take his power away.' By exposing him now, the next time might be a long way off. He may even quit. This could scare him to death." *Or, go on some rampage*, Wellsy thought. "That is what can happen if you take away his power!"

He had to admit, what she said made a lot of sense! He looked at his watch. The day was shot. He needed to sleep. They got home at 11:15 p.m. They made love, and talked until one or the other fell asleep.

When the alarm went off 5:40 a.m. Wellsy fell out of bet trying to answer it. He was dead tired. He needed more sleep. That would not come for days.

Chapter 18—Over Two Hundred Fifty Years Ago
Family Tree—Nabuilo to Nabuilo

Carlo Maria Buonaparte married Letizia Ramolino in 1764, thus beginning the Buonaparte family tree. Years later the spelling would change to Bonaparte. Twelve children from that family tree were presented to the world, only eight of them survived infancy: Joseph, Napoléon, Lucien, Elisa, Louis, Pauline, Caroline, and Jerome. The second son, Napoléon was born in 1769, and lived 52 years, passing in 1821. He is the focus of the Buonaparte line that must be followed to reach today's consideration. In 1796 Napoléon married Josephine de Beauharnais. They divorced 14 years later. In the same year of their divorce—1810—Napoléon married Marie Louise of Austria; they had but one son, Napoléon-Francois-Joseph-Charles, born in 1811. Napoléon's son, Napoléon, ultimately became the Duke of Reichstadt and later the King of Rome. He lived until 1832.

Napoléon's second wife, Austrian born, Marie Louise brought to their marriage her son, Eugène de Beauharnais, from her first marriage with Alexandre de Beauharnais. Buonaparte immediately took favor with his stepson, adopting him. Buonaparte nurtured and directed the boy, treating him as his own son. Eventually, Napoléon advanced Eugène's career by appointing him as aide-de-camp of Bonaparte in Egypt.

Later, yet still under the hand of Napoléon, Eugène became a Colonel in the military and later, promoted to the rank of General. Ultimately, Eugène became the Arch-Chancellor of State, and Prince of the Empire. Eugène's list of achievements didn't end there, either. After Napoléon had formed the kingdom of Italy, he appointed Eugène his Viceroy. Eugène served in that position until the kingdom dissolved.

Because Eugène wasn't natural born to Napoléon, he was not considered—legally—part of the Dynastie Franchise, or French Dynasty; therefore, he did not hold rights of succession to the throne. He was—however—a *prince français*, which meant that he was, indeed, an official a member of the French Imperial family, but without rights of succession.

Eugène de Beauharnais—stepson of Napoléon—married Her Serene Highness Princess Augusta Amalia Ludovika Georgia von Wittelsbach of Bavaria, the daughter of the King of Bavaria. Together, they offered seven children to the world. The seventh child of that marriage, born in 1818 was named Maximilian Josèphe Eugène Auguste Napoléon de Beauharnais, 3rd Duke of Leuchtenberg. In 1838 Maximilian married Maria Nikolaevna, Grand Duchess of Russia, second child—first daughter—of Tsar, Nicholas I of Russia. Maria was just two years younger than her husband.

After Maximilian, passed, Maria watched over their eldest son, Prince Nicolas-Maximilian. Prince Nicolas would later become a strong candidate for the throne of Hungary. That advancement—however—would never come to pass as Maximilian and Maria's children were given the title of Prince or Princesses, but were never considered true members of the Imperial Russian family. Maria petitioned on behalf of herself and Maximilian's children to collect their due inheritance. Notwithstanding her attempts, the Ministry of France, invoked the decree of 1811, which deprived Maximilian's offspring their due title as members of the Russian Imperial family. Maria appealed the decision but to no avail. The outcome was complete. Their titles were revoked, forever.

Nevertheless, Prince Nicolas' linage exists, today through his mother Maria Nikolaevna, Grand Duchess of Russia, and his father, Maximilian Josèphe Eugène Auguste Napoléon de Beauharnais. However, many scholars in this generation question the validity of his posterity down to this day.

One questionable line seems to trace the following; today, one Maximilian Napoleon de Beauharnais is earnestly convicted to, and convinced of his direct linage that traces back to the great Napoléon Buonaparte born in 1769. According to this procession, Maximilian's father (Joseph de Beauharnais, born in 1946) just as Napoléon father (Carlo Maria Buonaparte, born in 1745) called his son Napoléon, the nickname of Nabulio. Joseph de Beauharnais also called his son Maximilian, the same nickname, Nabulio. (Maximilian's, stepfather—of today—also calls Maximilian, Nabulio). There isn't any question—in Nabulio's (Maximilian) mind—that he is a direct descendent of Maria and Maximilian Josèphe Eugène Auguste Napoléon de Beauharnais, 3rd Duke of Leuchtenberg. Which means to thee Nabulio of today that he is—in fact—a direct descendent to Napoleon Bonaparte through the authenticated adoption process of Eugène de Beauharnais.

Today, in this generation, to Nabulio, this is all that matters! He is a descendant of the Great Napoléon Buonaparte. Nabulio's entire life centers in and on that distinct fact. As a matter of fact, it is an obsession to today's Nabulio. He lives this obsession. In his mind, it is his legacy—his destiny—to carry on the great birthright of his Napoléon, by avenging that which rightly belongs to him. Nothing will stop this transformation of power!

Supposedly, in tracing this questionable hierarchical line, Prince Nicholas was married three times. The first marriage lasted 15 years years, ending in 1877. The second marriage came two years later, lasting only twenty-five months as this wife—Annette—died in childbirth, as did the child. According Nicholas' third marriage was to Josephine Ramolino, two years later. They had four children from that marriage.

In 1895 Nicholas' last child—Joseph Carlos Eugene de Beauharnais—was born. When Joseph was 14, his family was exiled to Austria under complicated circumstances, irrelevant to today's Nabulio. Three years later, 1912, Joseph's father, Nicholas died by way an unknown virus. Two years later, Joseph's mother married a final time, Joseph Agapito; an Italian born immigrant with about equal amounts of Italian and Spanish blood in him. Joseph—at the time—had just turned twenty. That was late in the year of 1915. He married just six months later, October 22, 1916. Joseph's wife, Katrina Piercefield, supposedly could trace her linage back to Colonel Valentine Morris. Morris—1779—the governor of St. Vincent, the British Caribbean Island, whistled up an embarrassing surrender to French forces. Just sixteen months after their marriage Katrina gave birth to Joseph Carlos Eugene de Beauharnais, February 21, 1917. Devastatingly, Katrina died giving birth to Joseph junior.

Four years later the family fled to America, by way of Ellis Island. Shortly thereafter they traveled to the Detroit, Michigan area. After struggling for another four years the family, in 1922 traveled east to Pennsylvania, near the greater Philadelphia area. Joseph was 26 at that time.

Struggling financially, Agapito found himself involved in some minor racketeering operations. When the police cracked down, everyone involved scattered to the four winds. At the time of fleeing, Agapito had been left holding the bag, the money that is. He fled with his family and a colossal amount of money, $6,822—a pile of money at that time—to the Virginia area where Agapito started his own Italian Restaurant, simply calling it, Agapito's Ristorante Italiano. Joseph worked with his stepfather in the restaurant. That same year, Joseph met Angelina Russo, daughter of Apollinaris Russo, an immigrant from Athens who had come to American just eleven months before Agapito and his family.

Angelina was—at that time—the only one earning any money for the family. Her father struggled deeply with his health after his wife lost her life crossing the Atlantic. In loving-kindness Agapito hired Apollinaris to do light labor and dishes in the restaurant, while both families lived in Agapito's home. Nine months later, Joseph and Angelina, married. Five years and ten months after that 32 year old Joseph and Angelina on January 3, 1928, brought Joseph de Beauharnais into the world.

Six years later, Agapito broke his hip falling from the stoop of the Restaurant. While he lived 11 more years, his ability to stay ambulatory continued to plague him until his death in 1945. In same year Joseph Sr. took over the running of the Restaurant, and ran it until Joseph Jr. took it over in 1947; the same year his mother died, and only seven months after his father died. The business became Joseph's everything, including his wife. He was too busy for any other life, including women. He rebuilt, redecorated, and enhanced the business to a place of posterity and elegance with formal dining. For another 14 years he stayed single until he went into the flower shop across the street from his Restaurant and bought some flower to put on the graves of his parents.

In 1961, love smattered the 33-year-old man. Agnes Weathers Thompson, also an immigrant from Europe—England—snatched away his heart. She had been married once before, but lost her husband from a chase of the chills shortly after the marriage. She was young and full of life at 31 when she met Joseph. Contrarily, he felt old at 33 and knew he was way too old for marriage and certainly too ancient to have children. Nevertheless, he popped the questions all the same.

She said she would marry him, but conditionally. She confided with Joseph that her purpose in life was to have children, lots of them. She was, however, logical. She understood that at 31 she could not have a lot of children. However, she said, "Joseph, I can not leave this world without offering at least two of our offspring to replace ourselves. That is our obligation to the world." He laughed, until he noticed the sincere look upon her face.

He offered that he was too old to have and then tend properly, a child. Nevertheless, he accepted the bargain. As often happens in life, things didn't work out as they had planned. They married right enough and built a wonderful life, but it did not look as if their bargain would or could be kept. Their restaurant was their only child, and it too was getting old. After ten years, they knew their lot had been cast. There would be no child of that marriage. She was heartbroken, as was he, but he was inconsolable for her, only. It looked as though child-baring time had passed them both.

Then—miracle of miracles—finally, fifteen years later, 1976, he was 48, and she was ancient for child-bearing at 47, but she had their only child. While the baby was born, healthy he was also born breach. The ordeal was beyond her capacity, and while she survived the day of his birth, she succumbed four days later. Her final words to her Joseph were, "Let him carry on your great legacy. No man have I adored as much. You were my life, Joseph and now the life of my…" She wasn't allowed enough of her final breath to release her final word, *child.* He wept for what seemingly seemed days. She was his entire life. In her eyes, he saw life, forever. Now, he wanted no part of life. He was empty, void inside.

After eleven days, he took hold of his senses and realized he must be the best father and mother he could be to their boy. He put the restaurant up for sale, replacing that child (the restaurant) for his newborn. It was his pleasure to name his child after his long legacy, as Agnes had wanted. Proudly, he named his son, Maximilian Napoléon de Beauharnais. Joseph said to his sweet wife's headstone, "We"—he wanted her to be every part of this child—"must, however, darling, call him Nabulio, for his great-great-great grandfather called his son, Napoléon, Nabulio as well.

Joseph would dedicate his life to their son, Maximilian (Nabulio). Just beyond three months, the restaurant sold. Joseph took the money and his savings, and moved to the downtown Norfolk, Virginia area. He then planned a trip to visit that world where his family began in America. He went to the Detroit, Michigan area, but didn't like it there, so he brought his son back to Virginia and settled permanently in Norfolk. There, he hired a nanny, and he spent his time, raising his son in the memory of Agnes.

When Maximilian was sixteen, his father taught him his history, his legacy. "You, Nabulio", he said, "are a direct dependent through my line of the great Napoléon Bonaparte, the greatest hero, the greatest leader, and the greatest general the world has even known. Therefore, Maximilian, you must live accordingly." Nabulio hung to those words. Seven years later, at the age 70 his father passed. Immediately, Nabulio's connection to Napoléon passed as well with his father gone. Maximilian had lost his closest friend. He laid his father to rest next to his mother at St Mary's Catholic Cemetery.

At twenty Nabulio began in earnest to know all there was to know about Napoléon Bonaparte, or Buonaparte. It became his obsession.

At the time of Joseph's passing, Nabulio was a student at Old Dominion, a sophomore. After his father's death he dropped out of school. He had had a part-time job at the Blue Hippo, washing dishes. His dad had $34,991 in his savings account and another $4,200 in checking. Nabulio was also left his father's house. He had twenty-four months left, and that house would be paid off. He had an appraiser come in to find out the houses' value; $154,000. *Not bad*, he thought. That was his total inheritance, except for the wealth of knowledge that he was heir to the Bonaparte line. Certainly $39 thousand dollars, available cash wasn't a cascade of money, but at twenty-one it seemed like a mini-fortune.

After spending his ninth day in a row at the Jordan-Newby public Library studying his Napoleonic history, Nabulio decided to go home and take a nap. On the way, he stopped to fill his car with gas, bought a beer and also made his regular—on going—purchase. Four days later he nearly died of heart failure when he discovered all his numbers matched, even the mega ball number. Maximilian was a mega millionaire.

Life changed, immediately. He took the far lesser amount of the lottery money, but got it all at once, up front. He could live as a king on the generated interest, alone. He bought everything in sight. He had every toy he wanted, and then some. He had all the women he wanted, and then some and he wanted them frequently. He also wanted and purchased a new home overlooking the ocean; it had beachfront property too boot.

He lived the Life of Riley, but that still wasn't enough. He hungered, but he wasn't sure what he hungered for. After three quarters of a year, he realized that his wonderful home on the oceanfront was nothing more than a snare for his appetite for more women, more women with large breasts. He left it abandoned and went back to the simple house he had lived in well before all his dreaded wealth fell upon him. He quickly became bored, disenchanted. He needed a challenge.

Out of sheer monotony he took active research on his legacy, and the life of Napoleon Bonaparte. He was so enthralled in his heritage he made a pilgrimage abroad to study Napoleon. Nabulio began his visits with Napoleon's birthplace, Corsica. From there he then went to Egypt, then India, and then France. He followed Napoléon's legacy. He visited Marengo, where his hero had defeated the Austrians. He went to Trafalgar where Napoléon was defeated, and then to Elba, and then back to France where Napoléon reinstated himself for his auspicious 100 days of power, Emperor. He studied those 100 days of supremacy. Lastly, before returning home to the United States he visited the battle sight of Waterloo where he became greatly depressed.

Nabulio learned that that battle was fought just south of Brussels. Napoléon, the commander of the French and Wellington, the commander of British ended twenty-three years of war that had started with the French Revolutionary War and had moved into and through the Napoleonic Wars. Napoléon's defeat at Waterloo ended Napoléon's 100 days of supremacy as Emperor. Nabulio was angered, more; much more, indeed!

In 1804 Napoléon had coined himself, Emperor. That was just one year after Britain had declared war on France, which brought on those aforementioned Napoleonic Wars. However, Napoleon had wanted more, much more; he wanted to conquer all of Britain, the world for that matter.

Nabulio felt it wickedly unfair that Britain, Austria, Prussia and Russia had assembled together—teamed up as one—to defeat his Napoléon, bringing disaster to his legacy. Together, they closed ranks and descended on Paris, from about every direction possible. *Bastards, Unfairly*, Nabulio thought. Napoléon had to fight against several foes at once; even Wellington had to have help. Alone, Nabulio knew that the likes of Wellington could never have defeated the greatest leader the world had even known. The Prussian commander Gebhard Leberecht Blücher was at Waterloo with Wellington. Napoleon well knew Blücher, as he had once before defeated Napoleon in battle. *The prick*; Nabulio so considered. Furthermore, Arthur Wellesley, or the Duke of Wellington (as he was ordained after his defeat of the French in 1814) as he was called had never tasted a loss by the French. Nabulio felt everything was against his hero, unfairly.

Nevertheless and notwithstanding the odds against him, Napoléon had his battle plan well laid out. He planned to divide Wellesley and Blücher's armies. The Emperor ordered Marshal Ney to attack at Quatre-Bras crossroads between where Brussels, Charleroi, Nivelles and Namur were. The plan would have been perfect had it been executed just a bit earlier. It came too late. The enemy was already positioned, and thwarted Ney's attack. However, that battle ended in a standoff, otherwise the French may well have been victorious because they greatly outnumbered the opposing forces, and those forces may well have retreated; instead, they mightily dug-in and regrouped.

There was, however, some victory, Nabulio learned. Napoléon had succeeded in keeping two different armies apart, but Napoleon was wrong in thinking that the Prussians had lost their battle, and that came by way of miscommunication. Miscommunication would become the rub.

The fateful day of June 18, 1815, Napoleon knew that his potency resided in his cavalry, his artillery. He surmised his power was sufficient to overmatch that of Wellesley's. With this in mind, the Frenchman decided upon an aggressive surprise. His design was to rupture through Wellesley's line. Napoléon attacked the walled farm—Hougoumont—hoping the British would advance part of their army away from the hardened center to offer support at the Hougoumont farm, thereby softening the center so Napoléon's forces could advance upon it. Unfortunately for Napoléon, he greatly miscalculated his misadventure. The French Commander had obligated too many too many men on Hougoumont, and even with that they could not greatly weaken the British as he thought.

Later—when it was all over—Wellesley would suggest that the defense at Hougoumont was the very key to victory. Napoléon had, however, weakened Wellesley's forces, so Wellesley's thrust forward from the ridge and smashed into the French. Wellington, also directed his reserves to stop the opening gap. Napoléon was driven back. Wellington, now—having the advantage— marshaled his cavalry brigades and continued to assault the weakened French, which left his own left flank weak. Unfortunately for Napoléon, his right flank was diluted as well. Wellesley and Napoléon both need added support. Little was available for either.

Napoléon knew that that stronghold at La Haye Sainte was the answer to victory. Therefore, he ordered Marshal Ney to seize upon it. Napoléon had to smash the center in order to claim victory. As ordered, Ney charged to his mark. Wellesley was more than ready. His infantry had formed squares at the ridge, waiting for the attackers. Standing as a fortress in front of the formed squares was Wellington's Allied artillery. Gunners pounded upon Ney, until his army needed to fall behind the squares.

Though going badly for the French, more men were deployed to assist at La Haye Sainte to break it down. Though the French had to withdraw, a partial victory was found. A small infantry force managed to capture La Haye Sainte, and Wellesley was forced to give it up for the moment. On the other side, Ney requested more support. Napoléon's response sized up the ongoing war with the following response, "Where do you expect me to get them from? Do you want me to make some?" Ney found no humor in the retort.

Napoléon could not give Ney the men he desperately need, as the commander had other worries. He had lost Plancenoit to the Prussians. He couldn't give away and divide his forces any more, so he threw his elite Guard forward to make a final attempt to stop Wellesley's line. Wellesley and the Allies overmatched Napoléon's Guard; they retreated, having been tumbled with Napoleon scarcely making his get-a-way.

By evening the French-held La Haye Sainte folded after having a final thrust up the ridge. Wellington and company was waiting for them, hiding in the cornfield. Wellesley then ordered the Allied to advance upon the Guard, successfully crushing them.

Blücher wanted to name the battle *La Belle Alliance*, but Wellesley demanded that his tradition be upheld. It had been his practice that a battle would be known based on where he spent the night before the battle. In this case, his last night's sleep before the battle had been in Waterloo.

* * * * *

Exhausted from his findings, Nabulio sat back and just thought it all though. He whole of it just didn't make any sense. He kept asking himself, how could Napoleon have lost? He found a quote from Wellington that greatly aggravated him. Wellington said his victory was a "damned near-run thing." *What on earth was the supposed to mean?* That comment didn't make any sense, either. Nabulio came to realize that it was just plain luck, nothing more. He chose to define "dammed near run thing," to mean "just plain luck!"

To Nabulio, the whole of it seemed to depend solely on communication, or in this case, miscommunication. They didn't have telegrams, or cell-phones, or anything except foot soldiers or soldiers on horseback. Soldier or horses, either way you look at it was just too slow; and, of course there was always the chance of being caught while transferring messages. Nabulio knew that Ney lost the chance to gain control of Quatre-Bras, why? Why, because he waited for orders instead of taking the bull by the horns and doing something.

The fact that Napoléon didn't have any procedures or controls in place to be sure orders had been delivered was hardly his fault. Secondary leaders of Napoléon should have taken care of those mishaps. It was all about communications. *Stupid Ney; leaders lead; they don't wait.* Maximilian seethed. Nabulio learned that the weather hindered Napoléon far more than Wellesley. Everything was against Napoléon.

"Well this time, it will be different! Much different," Nabulio whispered to himself. "Much different, indeed; Wellington will lose"

Nabulio exploded when one writer suggested that Napoléon was overly convinced, and arrogant. *Bastards!*

The end of Napoléon's hundred-day reign ended with the Battle of Waterloo. Napoléon was banished to St. Helena, an island where he died in 1821. *Bastards!* Nabulio was more than provoked. He was exercised beyond imagination. *Bastards!*

Nabulio returned home after his exhaustive visits abroad. It didn't take him long before he found himself wrestles, so he purchased a book, *Napoleon and Wellington*, by Andrew Roberts. Before he read one word of it he flipped though the pages. An insert in the book just next to page 160 caused every fiber in his body to gyrate. There it was; the amazing great statue of his namesake and hero, Napoleon. But, below the photograph he read the following inscription:

"The ultimate trophy: Canova's statue of Napoleon that stands at the stairwell of Wellington's London home, Apsley House, the gift of a grateful nation in 1816."

Everything about Arthur Wellesley drove Maximilian Napoléon de Beauharnais crazy; but to see that that statue was a prize—a trophy—a symbol of victory—for Wellesley or *Wellington's* family to gloat upon infuriated Nabulio beyond measure. It was at that instant that twenty-one year old Nabulio made a vow, a self determined stand against a modern day Wellesley, some how, somewhere or place and finish what his hero was rightly cheated from. He decided to investigate the Wellesley family as he had his own ancestry. Nabulio would find out what was needed and then avenge his hero, Napoléon and mock the world of their unrighteousness toward the great Napoléon. There would be one last Waterloo, and this time today's Wellington would meet his Waterloo.

It would happen in Virginia this time! Nabulio so avowed to God and this ancestral right; victory at last!

CHAPTER 19—THE TWENTY-FIRST DAY
GAMESMANSHIP!

Wellsy was up at 5:15 a.m. Nabulio awoke two minutes after Wellsy had awakened. Nabulio couldn't sleep because of what he had read in the paper. Wellsy couldn't sleep because his thoughts were on Justin Thompson from the Gazette and what he wanted to print. It could be catastrophic. Nabulio was beside himself with anger. Wellsy was excited and concerned with anticipation. Maximilian Napoléon de Beauharnais grabbed the previous days Norfolk Gazette and read it for the twenty-seventh time, the quote that so infuriated him.

"'The whole art of war consists in getting at what is on the other side of the hill. All the business of war, and indeed all the business of life, is to endeavor to find out what you don't know by what you do; that's what I called 'guessing what was at the other side of the hill.' "Angel Killer, I know you. You left me too much. I can see you on the other side of the hill. Remember, I am watching you! I now know what I didn't know by what I know now. Now, you must learn to know what you don't know that I know on my side of the hill! Lieutenant, Arthur Wellington Wellesley.'"

Maximilian seethed on several levels. Who did *this* W think he is? He would kill Wellington right on schedule, and with great pleasure then he had ever known. *I dare that prick to call me an Angel Killer!* He then, again, read the name of the reporter that reported Wellington's words, Justin Thompson. *I'm going kill that prick too!* He knew he wouldn't, as it was not part of the war's battle plan, but just maybe, anyways! It was only then that Nabulio noticed the punctuation marks in the quote. There was a quote within the quote. The first part was W quoting someone else. He rushed to his PC and typed furiously, he needed to know, who? What he feared blazed across the screen. Those were the words of the prick of all pricks, the *real* Wellington, not the pretend guy of today. *Your dead Lieutenant Wellington, dead as dead can be, but now you will suffer, first.*

While Nabulio was seething, Wellesley raced to the Norfolk Gazette to see Thompson at their predisposed 7:30 a.m. meeting time. On the way, however, he stopped by the office to leave Rogers a cryptic note to have the Captain contact him at his earliest. Just as he pulled up to the Gazette his cell erupted. Before he went into detail, he told his Captain that he knew the name of the next victim of the Angel Killer. "Well," he said, "I know the names of the eleven women the Angle Killer will choose one from; one of these poor girls will be his next victim." He then rattled off the list, alphabetically by last name, first. Rodgers quickly scribbled down the names.

"How on earth have you deduced that information, and how accurate it is?" Wellsy told him about Alan Schom's book, *Napoleon Bonaparte*. He then filled him in on the name-game that he and Alex had been working on for weeks, and how Alex thought the Angle Killer was spelling out Napoleon, but by Schom's book, no, instead, the evidence strongly suggested that Angle Killer was actually spelling out Nabulio. He then shared with his Captain the conversation he had with Thompson from the Norfolk Gazette, and finally, how that dialogue led to the *Mace and Crown* information. Finally, he told his boss the hard news that Justin Thompson wanted to release the names of the potential women, and that he was about to meet with Justin right now. He looked at his watch; he was now four minutes late of the start time for that meeting.

"We can't let him print that, Lieutenant."

"Well, Captain, I'm not totally sure that is correct, there could be a lot of benefit in printing those names, however, but, I think I have the solution, anyway, Captain."

"Tell me!" The Captain thought for a second, and offered, "Or don't I want to know?"

"Want to know, trust me, Captain you do want to know. That was the purpose of this call. This is what I planned."

"Go on!"

"It's quite simple. I make a deal with him, Justin. I offer him the whole inside scoop, every jot and tittle of it, but he can't print it until I say so. I tell him about Schom's book, about Napoleon or Nabulio spelling out his name. I give him the works, Captain, but he can't print it until I say. Otherwise, I…"

"I got get the picture. If he doesn't agree, you'll slap an injunction on him. Therefore, he can't print a word, or he'll be interfering with a police investigation. You tell him that you'll nail him with obstruction of justice on an official police investigation."

"That's my hope."

"No, hope, it will definitely work, Lieutenant; good thinking! Look, you go in there and stall and tell him you will not talk to him without his editor present. In the mean time, I'm on my way to you and Thompson. We'll broadside him. I bring someone from the DA's office to show we mean business. I'll being the District Attorney, himself, if he is in.

As the Lieutenant got out of his car and as the Captain left headquarters they haggled over what to do with this knowledge. Their conversation didn't differ much from the discussion he had had with Alex that they had had just one day ago on their return trip from the Ulrich's. The Captain's mind worked much like Alex's. Then, in mid-sentence, Rodgers said, "I think you are on to something here, Wellsy. Blow it up in his face. Show him how smart you are." The Captain—just as Alex, had—recommended, that that was what Katrina had suggested as well. Everyone was on the same page.

However, Wellsy then reminded the Captain what the Angel Killer had said as well, 'victory belongs to the most persevering.' The Captain agreed on point until Wellsy suggested that in letting the killer know that they knew who is next, "Well," he said, "he will definitely know that I am seeing into his backyard."

"That is good, but what will he do about it?" the Captain asked.

"That is the sixty-four thousand dollar question, Captain. That is the question of a double-edged sword. It can cut either way. If we expose ourselves he just might quit, but he can also make new plans and we would be totally in the dark, again. However, I do not think he will quit. Alex and I are sure he has a much more hidden agenda then we know!" He paused. "I think he is playing a game that has almost nothing to do with killing young beautiful women."

"Meaning you can't see on his side of the hill, right? Is that what you are suggesting?"

"Right, no, wrong! I just want him to think that, Sir!"

"May I suggest we wait on this, Lieutenant? You need to get in that meeting. I'm on my way. He paused, and then added, "I think there are more pluses than minuses with going forward and enlightening the community. Just think about it." He hung up. Wellesley had a sudden stroke of genius. *Get Strange's idea on all this, he's your right hand man, not the Captain.*

Thompson stood at his office doorway that he shared with two other key reporters. He was looking at his watch, and offering nonverbal language that suggested, *you're late!*

"Thompson, don't start with me." The reporter tossed a large grin. This was going to be fun, or was it?

About the time that Wellington, Rodgers, and District Attorney, Harold Robison were beginning their discussions with Thompson and the Gazette,

Nabulio was finally calming down. He had made some serious decisions while defusing. He would strike immediately instead of waiting, and he would change his source, and then he would stop for sixty days, just plain stop. That would drive W crazy, all right. He got in his jeep and made the drive. He was in a hurry. Time was of the essence. He had to show W who was really in charge. He traced the same pathway he had gone the day he saw his prey and her boyfriend leave the campus.

He was ticked. He couldn't find anything like the *Mace and Crown* on the Wesleyan Campus. *Dumb stupid little college,* he thought. Nevertheless—back home—he persevered and found what he needed on the Internet. He found what he needed under Clubs and Organizations. It took him two hours, however, as there were over 60 organizations for him to muse. Finally, he found what he was looking for in S.V.E.A., Student Virginia Education Association. He looked up the names of several of the key women of the organization. The organization had on its membership 62 students, 44 of them, female. Most impressively, the organization's President was a diamond in the ruff. She was an undergraduate student, third year, female, an Education major (Special Education, emphasis), single, 21, and an honor student to boot. On top of all that, her last name was Litchfield. Nabulio uttered, *"Holy cow!"* He couldn't believe his luck. He was beside himself with joy. *She is screaming for me to select her! W will see her ravaged in a way that would make #4 look like a walk in the park.* Ms. Litchfield was the mark.

She had to have been chosen before he even looked for her. He just knew it. It was providence. She was that special—*a chosen vessel*—to be sure. Her name was just what he needed—too—she was, indeed, too perfect. Her last name not only started with an "L," but all three of her names started with an "L." Her full name was Labella Lucille Litchfield. She was the perfect candidate in every way. Her photograph was proudly shown in the Organizations officers' page. She was beautiful beyond measure, nearly as wonderfully beautiful as his last candidate, Ms. Ulrich. He had to see her up close, maybe closer than he had been with any of them. He had to be sure. He went to work on his investigation as he had previously done four other times. He wanted it all to happen within five days. Was that possible? He would make it so.

Under SVEA her e-mail address was listed. *It may come in handy,* he thought. He wrote it down. He easily got her physical address. She was listed in the telephone directory as, L.L. Litchfield, 2212. He went to the pay phone on the corner, and called her number. She answered, yawning, "This is LL." It was 8:18 a.m. when he called.

At the same time Nabulio was calling, LL; Wellington was wrangling it out with Thompson and his editor.

Nabulio gave LL Litchfield his phony introduction. "Yes," she told him, she would answer his short political questionnaire, but that she was in a hurry, because she had three classes, she had to get to, today. He found out she was 21, lived alone, that she did not work and that she was a Democrat, and had her own form of transportation. That was enough for now. He rang off!

Nabulio got in his jeep and headed toward her apartment complex to scope it out. A drive-by would be enough for now, he decided, but it turned into a lot more. His plan was to make the call, drive by her apartment, and then drive to the campus to dig up her class schedule. Getting a class schedule was always tough; such things are just not given out, protection to the student and all that crazy stuff. It didn't matter. Whatever it took, she was the one. He'd make it work! She was his destiny.

Nabulio got lucky—however—while outside of her apartment; he sat a quarter of a block away watching her at the bike rack. When she bent over, his eyes wanted to explode. She was gorgeous, and well built. Her dangling breasts—obviously braless—caused him to stir. He couldn't see them fully but he could tell. She was definitely competition for the looks of Miss Ulrich, but she went way beyond Ulrich in the stacked department. She too was extremely healthy, perhaps even more so than Ulrich. One day soon he would know for sure. She was braless, he could easily tell. He smiled. W had set new parameters of opportunities by his newspaper message. Nabulio could do whatever he wanted to this one. He smiled. He had quit an imagination. It was definitely payback time!

He twisted this way and that, but followed her through the campus. He spent the day watching her from afar. He followed her to her first class, and then to her second, and finally, her third class. It was, after all, a Wednesday. Therefore, he knew she had a Monday, Wednesday and Friday classes at 8:40, 11:40, and 2:40. While she was in class, he worked on discovering more about her, and the rest of her schedule. She ate a bagged lunch in the cold under a tree at 1:00 p.m. Nabulio was half way home. He knew he could do this within five days. As he traveled home, he thought, *what is going on, on my side of the hill, now, W? I own you, prick*, he thought and smiled.

Chapter 20—The Twenty-Second Day
AGENDAS EMERGING

Labella Lucille (LL) Litchfield was just two days from her twenty-second birthday. She was going to have a blow out party on her birthday. Her small one bedroom apartment would be jammed with her friends, most from SVEA and other classmates. She had been planning and looking forward to it for weeks, and now it was just around the corner. Her schedule was tight, with classes every day of week, Monday though Saturday. She both hated and loved and hated her 8 a.m.—three-hour Saturday—P.E. class. It was a grueling three hours of physical fitness. Her body balked at it, but appreciated the ardent workout, yet screamed at its intensity.

She had a strong propensity for underprivileged children, and couldn't wait to get into the mainstream teaching and loving them. Her younger brother, Sean was among such a group, autistic, and she loved him dearly. It was her habit to call him every Saturday when she returned home from her P.E. class. It was their special time together. It was nearly a ritual.

Tuesday's and Thursdays were her light days, only two classes, eight-thirty to ten, and then ten-thirty to noon, and then—thank God—done for the day! She was ritualistic; she always came directly home and did all her homework—all of it—every time until it was all done. So, Tuesdays, Thursdays, and Saturdays were her hard workdays, which made Mondays, Wednesdays, Fridays and Sundays her half work days and her more personal days. She was regimented to the tee. Being an honor student was no accident; she worked at it, earned it, focused on it!

As Nabulio watched her, traced her, he quickly found her disciplined. That was good. He needed that, especially with so little time to prepare. He loved disciplined people, especially, women. They could be counted on. And, he was contenting on her. Her very personal traits worked well for his precise planning.

He also couldn't wait to see her completely nude. He vowed to himself that he would find a way to touch her, skin to skin, or better yet, skin inside of skin. She was truly that kind of treasure. He was as dedicated to his task as she was with hers. One or the other's agendas and tasks would end abruptly, and then to be moved upon, nevermore. On this Tuesday morning, Nabulio followed her to class, but first he made special note of what she did when she left the house, her habits. He watched her leave the house, and again followed her to class. After seeing her go into her classroom, he jetted back to her apartment.

At the apartment, he sat. He watched. He noted others who came and went. He sat quietly. Within a half hour, he had his plan in place for Saturday, but there was one more thing he had to know, and the only way was to get inside the building to find out. He would find a way. Tomorrow, Wednesday, Nabulio would find that way, and it would be quite by accident, well, hard work opens the doors to positive accidents. But, for today, he only knew that he had to find a way to get into her apartment. Tomorrow he would realize that Saturday was very possible, very possible, indeed.

When LL reached home after class on this Tuesday, she did her thing, and completed all her homework by 4:45 p.m. She opened the refrigerator and decided upon cottage cheese and peaches for supper. After eating, she decided upon reading. She grabbed a book from the bookcase, and went outside and sat on the stoop in the twilight and read, unaware that across the street she was being gazed upon.

At five-fifteen she felt a shudder. She looked up and saw a man in a dark colored jeep across the street. He was looking directly at her, maybe staring! She got that eerie feeling that one gets from time to time when something isn't right. Goose pimples surrounded her arms and legs, neck and shoulders. She quivered, again. Her stomach tightened, some. She quickly removed herself from the stoop, used her passkey and re-entered her apartment. The jeep lurched forward and disappeared into the night!

Inside, she realized that he probably wasn't staring after all. She decided it was just her imagination. She felt safe inside, inside her sanctuary. Still, she felt completely strange inside her own apartment. Something just didn't feel right. She wanted to peer out the window, but caution prevailed. She clicked the dead bolt on the inside of her apartment door, and for whatever reasons, put on a bra.

She slept uneasy that night. Perhaps it was a prelude of things to come. Fortunately, however, her last awakened thought was about her birthday just a day and a half, away and not the man in the dark green jeep who would on the morrow leave his jeep in his garage for three days while he rented a plane brown Chevy Impala.

Chapter 21—Twenty-Second Day, Barely, and into the Twenty-Third Day
UNKNOWINGLY, SHE FINDS THE VERY KEY

She tossed and turned, fretted and fussed. She looked at the clock on and off for well over an hour. She and Arthur had made quiet love, routine-wise at 10:02, which meant that only he got off. That was okay with her; she thought of it as his manly needs. By 10:37 Arthur was sound to sleep. After using the bathroom, Alex intended to sleep as well. Nope, that is when the tossing, turning and fretting began. At 12:02 a.m. enough was enough and Alexandria slipped out of bed, quietly put on her robe and went into Arthur's den.

It all had been eating away at her since she had read Schom's book, learning that Napoleon had been called Nabulio as a child. What if, she thought, what if today's Angle Killer was also called Nabulio, but his real name was Napoleon, Napoleon Bonaparte, or Buonaparte as it once was. What if the Angel Killer was a descendant of thee Napoleon? Alex had also read a host of other books on Napoleon, and or Napoleon and Wellington, like the work of Andrew Robert, his book, *Napoleon & Wellington*, and three other similar books. Sudden enlightenment grazed across her mind. *Could it be that simple*, she wondered.

She went into the kitchen and removed the Yellow Book telephone Directory and opened it to the residential section. Nope, not one name in the book was listed as Bonaparte or Buonaparte. Shucks, she thought, wouldn't that have been a wild coo. She considered asking Wellsy if the residential section of the telephone directory could be downloaded into the police computers organized alphabetically by first names first, and then last names. If so, then, someone could see all the names of persons whose first name started with either of these two key names. If so, they just might have their Angle Killer. They would only have to look at two first names. After all, how many first names of either Nabulio or Napoleon could there be in the Norfolk area? A second thought was that Wellsy could just go to the utility company of Norfolk and get such a list from them. She was tempted to awaken him. She decided it could wait until morning. If this was possible, this case could well be completed in one day, luck permitting! With such a list, how hard would it be to interview these profiled names?

Her thinking was keen and astute, pieces of the mega puzzle might well be falling into place. She was convinced that the Angel Killer was a descendant of thee Napoleon, so she went to the computer to see what she might find with regard to the Bonaparte or Buonaparte genealogy. She found enough information that would require hours upon hours of investigation and consideration. More than she wanted at the present.

Her earlier readings on Bonaparte had also triggered other thoughts, somewhat far-fetched—perhaps—but on the other hand, maybe not. She had put it aside at the time. Now, at 2:33 in the early morning hours it seemed most logical, and the right place to begin searching the historical family tree of Napoleon's nemesis, the Duke of Wellington, and how that may have evolved with her sweet Wellington.

She glanced at her watch. She had to be at school by 7:45. Should she or shouldn't she delve into the history tree of thee Wellington at this hour? Was there enough in the websites that would lead her down the path that she was assuming, assuming that their just well might be a Napoleon & Wellington connection all over again in this day? She pondered, *to bed*, or *the computer* and Ask Jeeves? It was tough, she knew she should go to bed, but that wonderful history was just a few clicks on the computer away. She decided that she would begin and quit at 4 on the nose.

She started with typing in what she needed to do to get to the ancestral linage of thee Arthur Wesley. She learned the identical information that Maximilian Napoléon de Beauharnais (Nabulio) had when he too had delved into Wellington's history. It was all so remarkable that she got so caught up in the reading that she forgot to keep herself centered. She glanced at her watch realizing that 5 a.m. must surely be approaching fast. It was 6:22 a.m. Damn! What to do, she pondered. Should I *call in sick, just work for another forty-five minutes, or sleep for forty-five minutes, or what?* She decided to take a shower, and then ready herself for work, go, teach her classes until noon, and then take the rest of the day as a sick day.

She showered, had a toasted bagel, and drank as much coffee as was humanly possible. Before leaving, she woke Arthur up, kissed him, and then told him she loved him and that they needed to talk in the evening. She said, "I have had sort of what I could call a revelation on the case. I think we can break it wide open tonight, and have the Angel Killer in just a few days."

Wellington bolted up from the covers. What? No! Wait, what did you just say?" "No, if it is that important, tell me now, right now!"

"Honey, I can't. I have to get to work. I'll be home by twelve thirty. I will take a nap and then, when you get home, I'll lay it all out for you."

"But…"

She shushed him, putting her index finger to his lips. "This evening, no arguments, okay? I'm way too tired to fight or anything else."

"Have you been to sleep?"

She shushed him again. "Get up, get ready for work. I will lay it all out for you tonight. Okay? I love you. Bye!" She bent over and kissed him again on the forehead, said she loved him, again, and walked away. She stopped, turned, "Oh, and one more thing."

"Yes."

"Tonight, tonight it will be for me, I will have earned it, big boy."

"Anything you want."

"Don't say what you can't deliver, Wesley."

"I'll deliver."

"Oh, I know you will." She blew him a kiss and was gone.

Forty-two minutes later his cell phone screeched. "Wellsy," he said. It was his captain. Meet me at the hospital, Rodgers had said. "What's up," Wellsy returned.

"There has been an accident."

"What kind."

Rodgers took a cleansing breath, "Just meet me at the hospital, Alexandria has been in an automobile accident!"

CHAPTER 22—TWENTY-THIRD DAY
A PAPER IN THE WIND

Labella Lucille Litchfield was one of Heather Willingham's admirers, but, from afar. They weren't specifically close, but they had much in common. Both girls went to Capital High School in Charleston, West Virginia and both were football cheerleaders for their Cougars basketball team. LL was a year older so she graduated a year before Heather, and got to Old Dominion on a scholarship. A year later, Heater arrived at the prestigious University by the seat of her pants. LL had been an all "A" student, but Willingham had to work very hard in her senior year to even qualify for college. It was more her looks than her brains that got her into Old Dominion, on a Cheerleading Scholarship, but LL admired her college work ethic once she arrived.

As their 2nd period class ended, Heather put LL's note in her Fundamentals of Human Growth and Development textbook. Both girls, along with others closed their text and left their Fundamentals EESE 413 class. As they walked out of the classroom and into the beautifully warm late fall day, neither noticed the man standing leaning against the brick building behind them. Heather missed the middle of the last of the steps, and caught the heel of her shoe causing her to tumble onto the walkway spilling her textbooks and papers on the way to the cement.

By way of natural reaction, Nabulio sprang to the fallen girls aid. She had badly scrapped her knee. As LL kneeled to the ground to help he friend, Nabulio collected her books, notebooks, and lose papers. Her textbook lay open with the pages fluttering in the wind. A thin single sheet was attempting to flutter away. Nabulio snatched it up, glanced at it and shoved it into his pocket. "Are you alright, Heather," LL asked. She mumbled a *yes*, with some embarrassment. Though her knee really hurt, but she rose quickly, feeling self-conscious.

"Are you really, okay," the male stranger asked. Both women looked at him.

"Can I help you?" he asked. She merely shook her head, no. He looked at her, then toward LL. LL was still bending over; her open neckline exposed a good deal of her large breasts. He quickly looked away. LL noticed his look, and then saw his eyes divert. It was a common occurrence. No big deal, after all, that is what guys do all the time; ritual. Nabulio looked directly into LL's eyes. Was he caught, did she recognize him the previous evening, gawking at her from his car across the street. He saw nothing in her eyes, he was safe, and she didn't make the connection. *Whew!*

"Come on, let's get you to the restroom, and take care of that. They walked up the steps together. Over her shoulder she told the man, "Thanks."

"Don't mention it." He left, feeling he wasn't any closer to his task. He felt defeated, and walked a football field distance to his awaiting rented Impala. Once inside the car, he just sat, thinking and seeing those huge mounds of flesh that jutted toward him from Labella's top. More than ever, he wanted her. He knew it. He decided it. He would break every rule he had made. He definitely would have physical contact with this woman, skin on skin, forget the rubber suit this time. *DNA. Find a way.*

He sat in the car another ten minutes thinking of her breasts, and the rest of her parts that—for now—he could only wonder, or dream about. He would definitely have her, though, definitely. He realized he was aroused. *How unprofessional,* he thought. He rid himself of those thoughts and reached in his pocket for his keys. His hand touched the paper. He with withdrew it and read.

To One, To All:

Hey everybody, come to my Birthday party tomorrow night, anytime after 7. I'll provide the first drink and you are all on your own for more. After that, so BYOB! I will have snacks and sloppy joes, too. You all know my address, if you don't; it's on the SEVA page! Party ends at midnight! Don't linger longer!

LL

Nabulio could not believe his good fortune. It was all taking shape, he would go to the party and stay but five minutes tops, or as long as it took to find out what was needed to know about the apartment. He was surer now more than ever; it was providence that was bringing them together. Never had he known such joy as this moment. He was just one day away from having her and teaching W about knowing what side of the hill he was on. W would not have a damn clue. Nabulio definitely had the right L, Labella Lucille Litchfield. That was for sure. He spelled it out in his mind, accenting the L. *Nabu-L-io!* He then said it out loud, "L for Labella, L for Lucille, L for Litchfield, and L as in Nabu-L-io."

Tomorrow seemed so far away, but he had much to do. The day after tomorrow would be her day. The night she would join the others. The night, or perhaps the next day, a day that the Lieutenant would never forget, until, of course, his day in not the too distant future, either.

He adjusted his crotch, moving things around for comfort's sake. He then started the car, looked into the review and side mirrors, buckled up his seat belt, and drove off, smiling and singing with the radio, "do wa diddy diddy dum diddy do!"

CHAPTER 23—TWENTY-THIRD DAY
THE LONGEST DAY

The Captain was waiting for him at the front entrance of the hospital. While Wellsy sped to the hospital with siren spewing he talked to his Captain. Rodgers had already been at the hospital, looking in on patrolman Ken Witherspoon, who had accidentally discharged his weapon in the locker room at the precinct just after his night's shift. Other than a superficial wound and enormous embarrassment, the young cop was fine.

Rodgers said that she Alexandria had apparently fallen asleep at a traffic light. A car was waiting for her to move when the light turned green. "According to the driver behind her, she just sat there, asleep. The guy, a Rusty Schultz got tired of waiting, so he beeped his horn. Naturally the beep jarred her awake. I'm guessing that instinctively, maybe in daze, Lieutenant, she lurched forward. The driver, Schultz says she just stepped on the gas just after the light turned red, again and an early morning Gazette newspaper truck slammed into the side of her car. Her car rolled to it's side and skidded a few feet. Apparently, she hit her head on the driver's side window."

The Captain stopped for a second. Gave it another thought and continued, "She was out when the guy behind her and the truck driver pulled her from the car.

"They pulled her from the car."

"I'm afraid so. Look Arthur, they were afraid of a fire or something. They were thinking on her behalf. You can't fault them for that."

"Yeah! I guess not! What more do you know?"

"She's being operated on right now."

"For what?"

"I think, I'm not positive, but for pressure on the brain, swelling, something like that."

"Was she unconscious when they brought her in?"

"I guess so, I'm not sure."

"What about the other guys?"

"They are okay."

"No. I mean, have you talked to them."

"Patrolman Roberts has their statement."

"The guy in the truck hung around for a while. He was pretty shook up, but he's gone."

"Did he get a citation?"

"No call for it, Lieutenant. He was not speeding. Granted, he was timing the light, but that's not a crime, and the light was clearly red when she lurched forward, according to Schultz."

"The guy behind her, right."

"Right, the guy behind her." Both were quite for a minute or so. "Was she up all night?"

"Huh, what?"

"I said was she up all night?"

"Right, I think so. She woke me up before she left. She said something about tonight, that tonight she would fill me in, and then said she wanted…"

"Wanted what?"

"It's personal. Never mind."

"What is it? Maybe it's important."

"Let it go, Captain."

"Well tell me, it could be important!"

He said all too loudly and in anger, "She said she wanted sex tonight, and that it was her turn, to, well you know, to get it her way!" He looked up, people in the waiting area were chuckling, or snickering." The Captain let it go.

Wellsy walked to the desk to see if he could get any more information. Naturally they asked if he was family. Rodgers followed him over, flashed his badge, and said, "It's okay, tell him all you know."

She looked at the chart and asked him to have a seat that she was still in surgery and he would be called when they were done. It was another hour and a half before the doctor—Neurologist Simon Fischer—came to talk to him. Most of the words were gibberish to the Lieutenant, but the gist of it was she was resting comfortably and they felt she would be find, but that there were some concerns with vision, water and swelling. He asked if he could go to her room. The doctor advised against it for the time being, that he should check back in about forty-five minutes to an hour. He went back a half hour later. No change, "Pease be seated," Gloria Heart, offered.

An hour later, there still wasn't a report. Another hour passed. Wellsy was getting perturbed. After the first hour's wait, Rodgers had left, but called back every half hour or so. At 2:25 p.m. nurse Florence Fogg asked Wellsy to follow her. When they got to her room, he was informed that she had slipped into a coma. Her prognosis was up in the air.

Wellington called her parents in Hollywood Florida, and then Alexandria's sister in Chicago. He got a recording at Shelly's, so all he could do was leave a message. Alex's parents were on their way. He called them back and asked if Shelly had a cell number. They told him that they would call her. He sat at her bedside until 7:45 p.m. when he went downstairs to eat. He was beside himself with grief and pain. While eating, Detective Strange called. Wellington turned over the investigation to him. Strange said that Thompson from the Gazette was trying to reach him all day. "I'll call him!"

"What do you want me to do?"

"Well, fill me in on what you've got."

"I've got nothing. You've not given me much to do lately, Lieutenant."

"Yeah, you're right. I haven't, guess I've been thinking so much that beyond that, nothing is getting done." He paused, look, Sergeant, I'm really having troubles concentrating right now. It's getting late. Call me tomorrow when I can think. Beyond that, use your judgment; I believe in you Detective." They symbolically shook hands over the phone and the Detective was gone. Strange felt badly for his Lieutenant. He liked Alexandria, a lot. Who wouldn't?

Wellington rested with his head on the topside of her hospital bed. At 11:11 a.m. Shelly called. Their conversation was short, no changes. She was flying out at 6:40 a.m. tomorrow. He had to tell her the story all over again. He understood that, but he didn't understand why what happened to is Alex had to happen. He no sooner hung up with Shelly, and his cell erupted one more time.

"Why in the hell haven't you returned my calls, Thompson shouted?" Wellington wanted to tell him to screw off. He started to. "Just shut up and listen," Thompson shouted, "and listen good."

"Okay, okay, okay, what is it, what do you want."

"I got a call from an unidentified source. Are you ready for this?"

"Dam it, I'm not up to your games. If you have something, tell me."

"I received a call today, hours ago, from maybe a prankster, but he said, 'Tell Wellsy than I'm in a whole new camp now. I'm on another hill, and tell Wellington that within five days he will wish he never wrote to me.'"

Did he identify himself in any way?"

"Yes, he said he was the Angel Killer but he hated that name and it did not depict him."

"What else did he say?"

"Nothing, he hung up."

"Was it recorded?"

"Yes and no."

"Don't tell me riddles, was it or wasn't it?"

"Yes, all calls are tapped here, but he called in on a janitorial line, and that has low, old tapes, it scratchy as hell."

The call didn't move further. It was a waste of time. The Lieutenant called Strange and told him to follow up in the morning. And, that tonight wouldn't yield much. Furthermore, he doubted it was *our* guy. Wellsy also told him to get the tape, word for word and have the Captain have our Profiler look at the wording. "Get her spin on it!"

At 1:41 a.m. Wellsy fell asleep, finally, exhausted, and scared for his passion. He prayed!

CHAPTER 24—THE TWENTY-FOURTH DAY
POTPOURRI

LL couldn't wait for her party. Nabulio couldn't wait for LL's party. LL rushed home from school and tackled her home work as always, and then dusted, vacuumed, did the dishes, remade her bed, cleaned the toilet, watered her sixteen plants, shook the rugs out on the stoop, took a shower, made the snacks, went to the store on the corner and got more treats—over spending her budget—came home and made sloppy joes, put out the dishes of this and that, and put the four bags of ice in the galvanized tub and put in the beers. She put on jeans and a fall sweater, and no underwear, she felt frisky. She ran down the hall and put the notes on the other tenants doors. It said, 'Remember tonight is my party; I know it is Thursday; I'll end it by eleven. I promise. She signed it in her typical manner, LL.

All was ready. The sign on the outer door said, LL's Party, ring the bell for the bash. The very popular girl had forty-eight show up. The first to show up was Thad Hutchinson; he arrived at 7:01. He had dated her for seven months in her freshman year. He was too demanding for her. She called him a sex crazed little boy. All her girl friends had been warned about him. Thad kissed her on her cheek, brushed his hand against her right nipple for old times sake, a habit he never wanted to give up. The most—at any one time—in the apartment was 32. Then, there was little room to move, but all were enjoying the fun.

At nine twenty, Nabulio arrived. Her apartment door was open. It took him two seconds to see what he needed to see. He cased the apartment, the layout, and the furniture's placement. There were two interior doors; one—he assumed—must enter into the bedroom, and the other the bath. He opened the one he assumed to be the bathroom. He was right, however, there was another door off the bath. He assumed it lead into her bedroom. He opened it. Again, he was right. He made mental note after mental note of everything. He thought it chancy, but he had his story if it didn't go well. He liked the idea he could do it from the bathroom, no one would see him do it. He opened the door and interred her bedroom. There it was, right on her nightstand. He scooped it up and went back into the bathroom, shutting the door behind him. He took out her billfold, scanned it and saw what he wanted. He put it in his pocket.

Nabulio offered a relieved breath; it had been so easy. *Brilliant,* he thought! He knew LL wouldn't miss having her inside door key until she got home tomorrow when she came back from school; only then would she notice that her passkey was missing from her purse. She'd think once or twice where it was, realize that she must have left it in her bedroom. She'd fret for a moment to two and then do what she had to do.

Nabulio knew that people lose their apartment pass keys all the time, so she either had another key stashed somewhere in the hallway, or outside by the stoop, or in her mailbox, or, that, someone in the building had a master key when such dimwitted person—such as herself—lost theirs. LL was resourceful, she would just get what she needed and be in her room without another thought. He was sure there was someone in the building that would let her into her room.

He took the card from her wallet and put it in his own wallet. He reopened the door to her room to put the purse back. He did so. In crossing back, he bumped into the corner of her dresser. His hand gripped the dresser to steady, himself. He felt something under the doily atop the dresser. He reached under. *Providence,* he thought, simple providence. She purely was selected before he ever looked for the right one. Under the thin cloth was another room key, her extra, no doubt. Quickly he went—again—back into the bathroom, put her card back into her purse, and kept the second one, the one from the dresser. How perfect. Now, she could come home to him in her and his apartment. She would unlock her door as always and never lock it again, but he would!

Back inside the party, he said "hi," many times, sometimes calling himself Terry, or offering no name at all. Somewhat startled, he bumped into Heather. He smiled, and asked how her knee was? She smiled warmly back at him. It's fine, thanks, and then said, by the way, who are you, before he could answer, another beautiful female bulldozed into Heather, nearly knocking her off balance. When she regained her balance, Nabulio was gone, out of sight. She didn't give it another thought.

As he was leaving, he caught a last look at LL. She saw him and offered a strange smile. She couldn't place him, but she raised her beer bottle to him as a token of a toast. He mouthed "Happy Birthday," back at her. She smiled. *She's braless! Tomorrow they are mine*! He offered back an even broader smile, and winked. She started to wink back but Bobbie York kissed her birthday cheek. It was nine forty-four p.m. when Nabulio drove back home and readied himself for tomorrow's battle. As he lay down to bed, he pictured those full breasts that wanted to leap out at him on campus just one short day ago. Tomorrow. Tomorrow he would not rush any of his work; tomorrow was a time to have a lot of fun at W's expense, and LL's, too, but, war was war, but this would be a memorable battle.

As Nabulio was pulling into his driveway, Alexandria's hand twitched ever so slightly. Shelly's hand was on top of that of her sisters. "She's stirring, she's stirring, everyone, her finger has moved. Quickly, Wellsy pushed the button for the nurse several times. He heard a yes.

"She's coming awake," he said awkwardly.

Dr. Robertson followed the nurse into the room. Everyone stepped back. The doctor turned to Harriet, "Are you her mother." The older woman merely nodded. "Come here then, and sit down on the edge here and talk to her, calmly, warmly."

"What do I say?"

"Anything, anything at all. Be sure to smile, she may be disoriented. Remember she has been asleep for over a day and a half. She may be confused, or merely think it is yesterday morning. Just go with it! Assure her that she is fine. Say nothing alarming. Whatever strange things are said, we can straighten them out, later. For now, just go with it.

An hour later, Alex had all the signs of recovering, though she had a headache and some of her hair had been shaved away. Her speech was even and steady. She was even embarrassed that her family had to spend so much money to come to here like this.

As her parents were leaving for the evening, Wellsy's cell phone vibrated. He stepped into the hall. It was his Detective. They had one Timothy Jowls in custody. He was the one who made the call to the Gazette. He was harmless, seeking attention. He got more than he wanted to.

An hour later, the nurse shooed everyone away, the doctor wanted Alexandria to get a good night's rest. All promised to be back in the later part of the morning. Alex cried at their leaving. They had all touched her so. Wellsy was exhausted, but went to the office first to see what he had missed. He made a note to get his Detective more into this thing. It was the third time in three days he had made that promise to himself.

It was after one a.m. before he was in bed. He didn't set his alarm. He would sleep in, and then visit Alex, making sure she was okay. He planned two give her a week or so, and then revisit the conversation they had had two mornings, ago, just before she left for her destined accident.

She was safe, now, and getting well. He was grateful.

Tomorrow, however would thrust upon him a disaster beyond belief or words. Tomorrow would be a day he would never forget, and the battles with the Angle Killer would move to new heights. He would wonder if he was truly worthy of such an opponent. But, for tonight, in the wee early morning hours of tomorrow he was happy his Alexandria was back, meaning his life was back and on track. He loved her so. When this diabolical killer is taken care of, he decided he would propose to this wonderful woman. His last thought was, would this killer of killers let me live to be hers for time?

CHAPTER 25—THE TWENTY-FOURTH DAY
IMMEASURABLE TORTURE

He watcher her leave the building from over a half block away. He stayed where he was, and when she was securely out of sight; he drove the car up to and just behind the stoop entrance of her apartment. He was dressed appropriately, enough. He had a wool-stocking cap on that covered a good deal of his face and his ears except the bottom of his ear lobe. Fortunately, it was a brisk late autumn day, most appropriate for this warm clothing, and cap. He had on a dark blood-red sweatshirt, and over it a wool jacket with the last two buttons securely in place. He wore blue jeans, white socks, and dirty running shoes. He was definitely good to go. He said his opening line three times inside his head to be sure he had it right.

At the same time that he stopped on the north side of the street, a clearly marked 14-foot U-hall truck pulled up across from him on the other side of the street. *How perfect*, he thought! It had to be divine destiny. There wasn't any doubt in Nabulio's mind that LL was purely chosen before he ever put the plan of battle, together. He smiled broadly. He looked at his watch. His adrenalin was flowing madly. He had never been more excited in his entire life. It was all so very perfect. Everything wonderful was going to happen today. This would be his day of days. Nothing would ever surpass it, except for the high he'd receive in killing the little W prick.

He got out of his car and crossed the road, and introduced himself to the two guys in the van. "Hey, Chuck Albright, here, you guys moving in too?"

"Well I'm Sid Trainer." He offered his hand as he introduced himself. "This is my brother Jack." Jack swished his fingers though his hair and asked, "So, you moving in too?"

"Yeah, across the street, over there, Jack."

"Cool, you a student too?"

"Yup, sure, doctoral student at Dominion."

"Cool, I'm going for my Masters. I'll be here another full year, so I'm moving closer than I was. I've been commuting back and forth from Petersburg."

"Yeah, good move, moving here. Well, hey, I've got get unloaded myself. Catch yaw around; we'll have a beer sometimes. Good to meet you too, Sid, he said looking at his brother."

"No, I'm Sid," Sid said, "He's Jack."

"Right, sorry." An uneven moment passed, "Yeah, well I got to get moved in. Take you up on that beer another time, okay?"

"Sure, right. Let's get at it Jack."

Nabulio took two steps toward the apartment, turned back and said, "Hey, you two need some help, I only have a few things."

"No, Chuck, it's cool, we got it, thanks." He then added as an afterthought, "Hey, man, do you need some help."

"No, just a few more boxes, thanks." Nabulio, smiled back. He checked his watch, *about two more minutes*, he thought! He crossed the road, opened his rental car's trunk and got out the large, heavy box. He lugged it to and up the stairs of the stoop. He looked over his shoulder; the brothers had their ramp down and were walking up it and into the truck. He looked at his watch, again. Anytime now, come on girl. Thirty seven seconds later, Tricia Bakker opened the door, nearly right on cue, but close enough that his plan was already working fine. He then offered his well-practiced line, "Oh, hold that for me, please," he said as he hefted the heavy box up all on cue.

Tricia looked at the hunk of a guy, "You moving in or out."

"In. Thanks for opening the door it was going to be hard what with this box and all."

"What apartment?"

"Upstairs, B-19," he added, "Gads this is heavy," doing his best to end the conversation.

"Oh, cool! I'm in B-27, just down the hall from you." She paused briefly thinking of something to say, "Ah, are you going to school here?"

"No, Old Dominion. But I want to be away from the campus." He paused, look, ahhh…"

"Tricia, Tricia Bakker."

"Right, Tricia, I hate to be rude, Tricia, but this box is heavy!"

"Oh, I'm sorry, sure." She pushed the door a little more. "I'll stop by and say hi, tonight."

"That would be nice, Tricia, but I'm just moving in my stuff today, I won't actually be moving in until Monday or Tuesday of next week."

"Okay, well, I'll see you around, then."

From across the street, Sid, yelled, "You doing okay Chuck?"

"Yup!" he yelled back.

"They with you?"

"Yes and no, Tricia, they are moving in across the street and volunteered to help me bring my stuff here."

"Who are they?"

"Sid and Jack, look, Tricia this really, really is heavy!"

"Oh, I'm such a dunce, I'm sorry." She paused, "Do you want some help?"

"No, I'm all set, thanks. I'll be gone in a half hour, anyway. Hey, I'll talk to you next week!"

"Looking forward to it, Chuck." She held the door until he was all the way in, and let it go. She left thinking she wanted to get to know him better.

Inside, he breathed a cleansing breath. He walked to her door, put the box down, walked to the base of the stairs, and looked up. No one was insight. *Good.* He walked back to LL's door, removed the passkey from inside his hat and opened the door. The smell was rich and sweet. Fresh bread sat on the kitchen counter. Ah, the aroma of a woman's home. He liked it. He quickly went back through the door and grunted as he picked up his box of goodies. Inside he put the box on the kitchen table, turned back, closed and locked the door.

He had all the time in the world. She had three classes today. He opened the box and withdrew the gloves that were inside. They were brown, everyday work gloves. He took out a towel, more like a diaper, and went into the hall and wiped down her door entrance. He then traversed back into the home. Nabulio then went into her bedroom, took her fold up bed, folded it up and wheeled it into the kitchen/living area.

He put her bed where he wanted it, near the middle of the room. He knew where her head would be—at the extreme end of the bed—and how she would be bound. He took two of the triangular lag bolts and screwed them securely into the floor about a foot past where the top of her head would be on the bed. He no longer opted for nails. First they were noisy to use, banging and all that, and secondly too many things could snag on them, like his skin, DNA!

With her lying on her back he would pull her arms up, over and past her head so that her elbows would be on either side of her ears, pointed towards the ceiling. Her wrists would be wrapped with the heavy elastic cords with her hands and arms then being drawn down at about a 45-degree angle away from the top of the bed toward the lag bolts that were secured into the floor. Those bolts would receive the other end of the elastic cord, cinching her into place with little wriggle room. He was making sure he had full-unhindered access to any part of her body he wanted; any and all parts, well front side, anyway. Furthermore, by pulling her arms up and back this way would necessarily thrust her breast up higher. He hated the thought of any sagging breasts, though he doubted there was any sag in her at this young age even though her breast were more than ample.

He then estimated where her hips and pelvis would rest on the bed with her head all the way up to the front edge of the bed. Her head—by way of her forehead—would be strapped or taped back, just past any comfort zone to the metal part of the bed frame. With head, neck, arms and hands secured, Nabulio would then take each of her legs and open her up as far as her body—maybe a little further then her body—would allow. Her legs, at the bend of the knees would be pulled off the sides of the bed and pulled down and back toward the front part of her bed with the bottom of her feet nearly arched up toward the ceiling rather than the floor.

It would be as if she was in a squatting position, but—of course—her knees would be forced against the side of her bed. Her ankles on either side of the bed would then be screwed to the floor by the same process that held her arms in place, i.e. the triangle lag bolts, or screws. So, actually, her ankles would be pulled toward the front of the bed. Finally, a bans of elastic cord would be secured also to the floor on either side of the bed across her abdomen, just above her navel.

Her bottom would be placed on top of a pillow so she made for easy access. He knew she would be in great pain where her knees forced off the bed with her legs and ankles pulled toward the bed, but it was necessary.

Having secured the six triangular lag screws to the floor, he went about getting other things ready. Things he would need, like shaving equipment. While she was still asleep, he would carefully and completely shave her private area. That was the way he liked it, clean, uncluttered, and ready. Until the point of shaving, he would leave her panties and even her sweatshirt on. When he was ready he would cut both articles of clothing off.

He laid the other articles he would need on the kitchen counter, all lined up as would be needed. He decided where he would leave his messages as well. He finished much earlier than he thought, so he had a wonderful slice of her oven baked bread. It was delicious. He was in heaven. He turned on the TV and watched an old Gunsmoke episode. Afterward, he still had an hour and a half. That is when the phone rang. On the fifth ring it answered mechanically. He loved her voice. At the beep he heard her voice, again. LL recorded, "Hey, don't forget you promised to feed Arthur's cat at five." *How cute*, he thought, *she left herself messages.* That would never happen on this day! *Poor kitty*, he thought.

Nabulio made sure the door was locked; he then lay on her bed and napped.

CHAPTER 26—THE TWENTY-FOURTH DAY
THE ALARMING INTERVIEWS

While Nabulio was napping at LL's apartment, Detective Strange looked at the list one final time. He was trying to match the face with the name. Actually, he was just starring at the paper trying to look busy with something important. He was covering for time. *Where are you Wellsy?* Though his Lieutenant made it clear that he was to start without the Lieutenant there, Wellsy assured Strange that he would be there close to the scheduled starting time.

All the young women assembled were quite nervous. They weren't exactly sure why they were at the police station. Each had received the same letter; yet, each had no idea that the collected group had each received the same letter. Each woman was told to discuss the matter with no one outside their immediate family, that was to include boyfriends, friends in general, and all others. Strange knew that several of them didn't follow the letter as instructed.

"Okay, the Detective began, let's be sure everyone is here, but first, please be seated at one of these three tables. It doesn't matter which one you sit at. I know you all have questions, and I know that all your questions will ultimately be the same questions. We will get to them all, I promise you, but first I will begin by stating your name, and as I do so, please acknowledge that you are here, and who you have invited here to be with you, if anyone."

"He was getting nervous. Suddenly this was a shockingly real. "You will notice that also in the room with me is your Dean of Students at Old Dominion, Mr. Jasper McKay, and your College President, Dr. James E. Townsend. Mr. Thompson from the Gazette is also here. I will say more about him in a few minutes. Nevertheless, we welcome you all, here. I will now read your last name first, and then your first name and finally the initial of your middle name if you have one." He paused and looked at his list. "Larkin, Karen O."

"That's me, I'm here alone."

"Thank you, Ms. Larkin." He paused and looked at the next name, "Ms. Lashbrook, Jill Susan."

"I'm here," the Detective looked up. "I'm here with my husband, Thomas. And, Thomas has a question."

"Thank you Mrs. Larkin, but I will answer questions in a few minutes. He read off the next three women's names: Lewis, Terry Ann; Lillian, Karen, Kay; and Lincoln, Angelica May. Each acknowledged the fact that they were present and, alone. He continued, "Ms. Lincoln, Sharon Margaret?

Tom L. Gross, answered, "Ms. Lincoln is present with her attorney. T.L. Gross."

"There isn't any need for an attorney, Ms. Lincoln, nevertheless, Mister Gross is welcome at your individual expense." He continued, "Lindsey, Janet May. She acknowledged her presents as well. "Ms. Lions, Marcella Peoples."

"Officer, I'm Cynthia Ann Linville, Marcella isn't here. She told her boss that she needed the day off, but because she would not, or could not tell her why she needed it off, he threatened her with being fired if she didn't go to work, today. I'm also on your list officer."

"Yes, I see that Ms. Linville; thank you for your help, and she isn't in any trouble with us, but I do need to know where she works. Cynthia gave him the information. At that, Wellsy entered the room. The Detective nodded, Wellsy replied in kind. Locus, Deborah S."

"That would be me, officer. I too am with my husband, Darrin Fletcher. But, I go by my given last name which is Littlefield."

"Thank you, Mrs. Littlefield. Last on my list is Lucy, Connie Marie. Marie merely put up her hand and quietly waved. He nodded. "Again, thank you all for being here." Again he paused, and cleared his throat, "Allow me to introduce Lieutenant Arthur Henry Wellington." Wellsy walked toward the Detective. Strange continued, "You may have recently seen his picture in the newspaper, or on TV regarding the Angel Killer. The Lieutenant is the lead investigator in this matter, and unfortunately, it directly affects each of you." A mumble when though his small audience. "As you know, ladies and gentlemen, this Angel Killer has murdered four women. Though this maybe painful to hear, rest assured it is paramount to our investigation." He offered up the five women's names. I cannot and will not go into detail but we now have some very important information that we did not know until recently, and each of you needs to know! He stopped, looked at Wellsy, nodded, and said, "Lieutenant."

Wellsy thanked them for coming. He told them that they—the police—new how he was selecting his victims, but didn't go into great detail. "Let it suffice that we know, and here is what we do know that each of you in this room should know as well. Each of you are targeted to be his next victim." A gasp when up the room as each woman expressed herself. "Ladies, please, be calm, you are very safe. I repeat you are safe. Your Dean of Students and your College President have already been made aware of this situation that is why they are here with you. Each of you have major decisions to make, but I need to give you additional information, first."

The meeting lasted another three and a half hours. The last hour and 47 minutes of that time, Ms. Marcella P. Lions was at that meeting. Strange had left and returned with her. "For the next 72 hours the Norfolk Police Department will offer each of you a round the clock surveillance and escort." He encouraged each of the women to leave the University within the next 72 to 96 hours, and to stay away until the Angel Killer has been apprehended. Each were told they could make all the necessary out of State phone calls to family for whatever traveling arrangements needed to be made. Each woman was assured that Old Dominion would give them a free additional semester when they came back to school, but, for the present, their welfare and security was the number one priority.

Next on the agenda, Captain Ernst Herrington, from the Strategic Management Division offered the sound thinking and security that had been arranged by his department. His department would oversee their individual safety. Each woman was given a file folder as to what to do, who to talk to, what to say, what not to say, and how best protect themselves in the event of threat. He explained that the best thing to do was to keep quiet about the whole thing.

After Herrington finished, Campus Security Guard, Jessica House offered encouraging remarks as to how Campus Security was fully aware of the situation and would aid in their transition of safety.

Time was turned back to Detective Strange. When he asked if any of the women had a question, every hand flew up with multiple questions. Lunch was ordered for all. Much to the department's surprise, the attorney for Ms. Sharon M. Lincoln, Tom L. Gross was totally supportive with the Police and the College's handling of this episode. He was told that he was not allowed to even whisper a single note of what was happening, here, and that included the Law Firm he was part of. He offered back, "No problem."

Toward the end of the meeting, eleven police officers were ushered into the room. Each officer had already been briefed and given a full dossier of the woman they were so assigned. Each sat in conference with the woman they had been charged to watch over and protect. Each of these officers was trained for this type of surveillance and safety. They would always be in uniform as a visual sign of protection.

The final and toughest question came from Mr. Gross. He tossed the question to the Lieutenant, "Lieutenant, what do you think the Angel Killer will do when he sees that he is being outflanked? One of these girls may already be targeted. What do you think he will do?"

"That is a great question. If you have followed the newspapers, he knows I am looking over the hill from where I stand and I am watching him, though he knows that I don't actually see him. Right, Mr. Gross; we believe he will be silent for sometime to come."

"You hope, Lieutenant!" The room fell silent!

CHAPTER 27—THE TWENTY-FOURTH DAY
NON-SERIAL SERIAL KILLER

She arrived right on time. He heard the front door open. He heard her singing. He wasn't excited. He was calm. Ready. He heard the click, unlocking the door. She stepped through the door. He grabber her left forearm just below the elbow pulling her hard, quick in past the door. His right arm came up fast, swooping around the back of her head to the front of her head cupping both her nose and mouth with the chloroformed rag. At the same instant his buttocks slid into the inside of the door and pushed it closed. He thought he heard her exclaim, "What the..." That was it. She struggled for a total of 11 seconds. And she was out cold, limp in his arms.

He turned, walked 4 and one half feet and eased her onto her living room bed. He picked up her door card that she had dropped, and then returned to her inside door and secured the lock, again. He was amazed; his heartbeat was easy. He was calm. He closed her curtains that faced the street. He turned on the lights in the living room. For the first time he was actually close enough to her to actually study her beauty. He leaned over and smelled her. His body moved with delight. She was a prize; the prize of all time.

He nearly forgot. He walked to his box and removed the cryptic note. He opened the door to her apartment, again, and put the note—do not disturb, sleeping—on the outside of the door, taping it down.

He returned to her. Very slowly Nabulio undressed her, working from the feet upward. First, he removed her shoes, then her stockings, and then the little gold bracelet that was fastened around her ankle. He put it in his pocket for safekeeping. He spent a moment rubbing, massaging her delicate feet. They were warm, inviting. He kissed them, the arch of her left foot, and then the same to her right foot. She had a robe belt. He untied it, rolled it up and placed it beside her right cheek. Her assailant then took the metal button through the buttonhole, unzipped her jeans, and pulled them down past her hips and buttock. He then walked to her feet and pulled the trousers off her. Her shape was inconceivable, near perfect. He stayed true to his promise and left her panties on. They were cotton, white with little red hearts on them. *So cute!* He stroked her thighs, and her calves. An erection was growing. He didn't care. She would be pleased she had such power over him. He gazed at her beauty; it nearly took his breath away.

He moved up and around her to her head. Her hair, brown with a tinge of red, smelled like April showers. He pushed his face into her hair, relishing every second of it. He had too, for he knew the moment would soon come upon him and he would be gone from her, forever. He pulled the hair off her face, brushed it back with his fingers and let it fall freely towards the floor. *Beautifully soft!*

From her right side, he picked her up and moved her about five inches forward so that the very top of her head was slightly over the front edge of her resting place. He then removed a gold necklace from her neck. He leaned in and kissed that long, wistful neck. *Delicious!* He unbuttoned her jacked. It was most difficult to take it off her as her arms just dangled. Obviously she could not help. He laid her down, again, most gently and tenderly. She deserved his loving care. Standing about even with her hips, he leaned over and cupped both of her breasts over her sweatshirt. His heart skipped a beat, they were even larger than he had imagined, and her nipples were—well—way beyond what he had dreamed of. He so wanted to remove her top, but he held fast to his plan. Besides, it was a plan of total delight. He could wait. He touched again; to be sure they were *that perfect! They were!*

He stepped back and just admired her. She was beyond beautiful. She lay radiant before him, as a goddess should. He looked at her for long moments. He wanted to remember, her! He would be her last. It had to mean something to them both. He could hardly contain himself.

Fastening her to the triangle screws went extremely well, though spreading her legs as far as he needed them to go to get her knees over each side of the bed was more difficult than anticipated. Her body wouldn't open enough. It really meant that she would just have a little more discomfort in her groin and thighs then originally considered. After she was fully secured, he rubbed her stomach, occasionally allowing his hand to go under her shirt and touch the underside of her breasts. He decided it would be all right for him to lift her sweatshirt to see— to be sure—if how he attached her arms did—in fact—make her breasts rise. "Good heavens," he whispered to the sleeping body, "*it purely did!*" He received another growth spurt as it were from this exciting, and beneficial, activity.

Satisfied all was in ready, he crossed to her refrigerator and took two pieces of ice to help awaken her. Before using the ice, he put cotton balls into her mouth and taped her mouth closed. He ran the ice along side her cheeks, eyes and neck. It took about two minutes and she was coming back to life. At first signs of life she began to struggle with her position, but she quickly realize the more she tried to move, the more horrific the pain was in her groin, her thighs and her arms.

Nabulio pulled a kitchen table chair up along side of her. "Calm down. You are okay. You are tied in such a way that the more you struggle, the more pain you will inflict upon yourself, but you choose for yourself, but I'll show you. He pulled on her arms just a little; she screamed though the cotton and the tape, muffled as it was. Then he pushed instead of pulled. It offered her the same screaming pain. He did similar things with her legs, stomach, and head. It all resulted in more pain. "Don't move LL, and you will not have such ugly pain, okay? Neither of us wants you to have pain, do we? Her eyes said, *no.* "That's my girl, LL." Do you mind if I call you, LL. Again, her eyes said, *no.* Relax; I'll massage your thighs so the muscles loosen up, okay. Her eyes said, *no.* He did it, anyways. *Heaven!*

He put more tape on her mouth, just to be sure. After which he said, I have to inflict just a little bit of pain so you understand the philosophy here. In a minute or two I am going to un-tape your mouth so you can read a story out loud. I will record the story and tell you later it's importance; okay? Okay! The story will not make any sense to you at all, but it will to Wellsy when you recite it to him. Ah, you are wondering who Wellsy is? Well, he is the bad guy in this story. That is all you need to know for now.

He took a deep breath, and said, "Okay, prepare yourself for just a little pain, okay?" Her eyes went wide. He got up; she tried to raise her head, but it brought with it, instant pain. She could not see. He went to the counter took up his knife, crossed back to her and sliced her little toe off. Naturally, she wreathed in pain, but little sound passed the taped mouth.

He showed her, her severed toe. Her eyes went wild. Muffled sounds from her mouth would not allow him to know the words she used to describe him.

"Now, when you settle down, I will un-tape your mouth so that you can read. Remember if you scream or anything like that, I will cut off your ring finger on your wedding hand, and your big toe. I'll let you decide which big toe is to be severed. Do you understand that?" Her eyes said, *yes,* though tears flowed from them. "Good! Good, girl!" If you ask me a question or say anything at all, I'll cut your nipples off, and believe me, I don't want that to happen, okay." Again, her eyes said, *yes,* in defiance.

"So, did you hear me, because there will not be a second warning. You did follow that, didn't you?" Her head barley moved but he knew she got the point. "By the way, would you like a drink of water before we begin?" She indicated *yes*. He got the water, and the tape was removed and the cotton balls were withdrawn, and she got her drink, and he set up his recorder and the microphone. He held the story for her to read. It took 3 minutes, and it was completed. He complimented her on a job well done. Then, he re-taped her mouth, but not before he kissed her soft, luscious lips. It stirred him. *Hallelujah!*

"I have to admit to you, that while this isn't any fun for you, it isn't for me either. I hope you understand that. However, I have been watching you for days, and, quite frankly, you are a fantastic looking women, and in every war women are ravaged." Her eyes went big. "No, no, you are not going to be ravaged, but I do need my reward. It won't take long. Just try to enjoy it. He picked up the scissors and cut off her panties. He shaved her as he had promised, himself. It took much longer than he anticipated, but he accomplished it without cutting her. He explained why he did that—after all—this was his little treat. He then took warm water and bathed her private area, gently, softly.

He removed all his clothing. His manhood was flaccid, until he cut her sweatshirt off. Everything changed then. *Larger than life breasts with nipples that were perfect!* His demeanor changed. He became unintentionally savage. She closed her eyes, totally giving in. He pounced upon her, mangling her breasts with his hands and mouth. She was totally dry but he thrust into her with such savageness that he tore her in four different places. In less than a minute he was totally spent. Tears ran down her cheeks. He was done with her, but his hands keep grabbing her fleshy white ample breasts. In the excitement, he bit off just the tip of her right nipple. It was part of her, so he swallowed it. In his mind she loved it, too, so he licked the blood until he became hard, again. And then, again he thrust into her, and again he instantly released in her.

When finished he put the chloroform to her nose again, and she was out. He untied her, and carried her to the bathroom. The tub had been previously filled with just hot water. It was tepid now, perfect. He bathed her, cleaning out all of his fluids—washing away his DNA! He used special feminine soap he had brought for the occasion. She was bleeding from there and from there. He felt badly about that, but it was a battle of war, totally justified.

He left her in the tub as he returned to the living room. He took out a large sheet of plastic from his box and laid it on the floor. He removed the bedding and the plastic sheet he had previously placed on the bed. He then took clean bed sheets and remade her bed. He went back to the bathroom and carried her to the bed and gently laid her down and refastened all her restraints. He took cotton balls and placed them in her private area to absorb the oozing blood. He put a cotton ball on her right breast and then placed a band-aid over it. He re-taped her securely.

His work was nearing it's end, the rest was all for W! But, first he returned to the bathroom and drained the tub and cleaned it all up, so it looked nice. He wanted her alive for a little bit longer. He felt the need to tell her how special she was, and how she was picked before he even looked. He said to her, "Labella, you mean so much to me. You really are part of my team. When I destroy W…" He stopped talking for a few seconds and then said, "LL, you deserve to know, don't you? Yes, you do. He leaned into her and whispered ever so softly, "W is Wellesley, and it is also, Wellington. Keep that between us. No one else knows. It must remain our secret, okay?" He received nothing back from her. He sat in front of her for nearly ten minutes. *Fantastic!* "Now, I will have you in my mind, permanently, I will love you for the rest of my life."

With that he said, good-bye to her. A tear trickled down his cheek. He truly loved her. Her eyes begged *no!* Through great pain she found a way to move her head, saying *no* with it as well! He placed his hand upon her bare left breast, squeezed it gently and slit her throat. He, like times before, heard the small gush release from her windpipe. She was no more. He wept into his shirt. He mourned her loss! *I loved you!*

Nabulio carefully removed both of her breasts and affixed them to her living room wall with 16d nails, driving them though the center of her nipple and what was left of the other center of the breast he bit. He allowed three-fourth of the head of the nail to protrude from the breast. *Ah*, he thought, *the nipples on her breasts seem excited.* The breasts were separated by about four feet. He wrote between them in large letters, making nine trips in all—back and forth—to dip his finger, or fingers into her neck for sufficient blood:

WHICH SIDE OF THE HILL ARE YOU LOOKING UPON? NOT MINE! YOU HAVE NO IDEA WHO YOU HIDE FROM ON YOUR SIDE OF THE HILL! HERE ARE TWO HILLS! AND WHO COST THIS WOMAN HER lovely HILLS? WELLESLEY? Or WELLINGTON?

Written in her blood, BY WELLESLEY AND WELLINGTON'S soiled HANDS!

He took his handsaw and cut her up into ten different pieces: two arms, two legs, two feet and her headless torso, her head, and—of course—her two breasts that were nailed to the wall, already, framing his delightful quote.

He placed the body pieces in different parts of the apartment. He then did the disgusting thing and gouged her eyes out of her head. He nailed them on the wall where the note had been left.

To the left of the first word, on the first line—"WHICH,"—he nailed one of her eyes, and to the right of the last word on the first line—"IDEA?"—He also nailed an eye. *The eyes have it*, he laughed.

He placed her head on top of the refrigerator and wrote below it on the freezer door, again using ample blood that seemed to be everywhere, now: I'M WATCHING YOU FROM MY SIDE OF THE HILL. SHE CANNOT SEE ANY BETTER THAN YOU CAN! I owned her, I own you! WELLSEY—WELLINGTON—GET YOUR HEAD OUT OF YOUR...

He gathered up everything that belonged in his box, and put it into the box. He quickly took another shower, scrubbing hard all over his body, a matter of wiping away his sins, and so he would be presentable in public should anyone see him. Stepping out of the shower, he put the stop plug into the tub and filled the tub with water, again. He toweled off, and then got dressed. Finally, he put on his clothing, his coat and stocking hat. He zipped to her apartment door, opened it and removed the note he had placed earlier. He then went back into the apartment, and erased the message on the telephone that LL had left for herself. He lifted the telephone off the hook and dialed the number for the current time, recording. He laid the phone on the counter with the recorded voice churning and churning.

He took a last look around. He took out his checklist and read and checked everything off. He was done, except for draining the bathtub of any residue evidence, thereof. He gathered up her wet towels and put them in the box. It was 7:30 p.m., plenty dark outside. He opened her shades, turned on her bedroom light and turned out the other lights that had been on. He made sure that he had her room key was returned to her purse, and the other card had been replaced under the doily in her bedroom. He turned on the living room light one more time, crossed to her eyeless head on the refrigerator and whispered, "I love you!"

It was then he remember, fingerprints from the pervious night. He had touched her dresser, and her purse, and her credit cards. He removed all such possible prints, and smiled.

On his way out he stopped and gazed at her removed breasts that adorned the wall. In memory of her, he said thanks. He so wanted to remember those wonderful breasts. Nabulio turned off the light in the living room, and went out her apartment door, and then outside the outside door. He then made sure both doors were locked.

He then carried his box off the stoop and down the stairs to the sidewalk and ultimately to the trunk of his rented Impala. He opened the trunk and replaced the contents, the box and all else into his trunk, naturally all on large plastic sheets. He was as happy as a clam, there wasn't one living soul in sight. Inside the car, he sat on the plastic he had left for later use—now was the time of later use—and then he started his rental car. He turned on the CD and listened to the classical music of Rachmaninov Rhapsody all the way home.

Home, exhausted he did the plastic thing, the fire thing, and the normal clean up thing. The box would be taken care of early tomorrow morning, around 4:30 a.m., as nothing was more important than that. Afterwards, at the mansion—on the water—he'd take care of the message business. Then he would drive to Rocky Mount, North Carolina, and make a single call from a downtown pay phone with his gloves on.

From there he would drive back home and return the Impala, and go back to the mansion by way of a taxicab. He would offer up to the ocean things that needed to be cleansed and ultimately, disappear by way a salty ocean can destroy and dissolve. He would then spend the rest of the day there at the mansion, and then disappear for sixty days, letting the salty ocean water wash away any incriminating evidence that was left behind. That was his plan, anyways, that everything would be destroyed. Now, right this minute, he was more than exhausted. Yet, he had an extremely important meeting with himself at 4:30 tomorrow morning.

He crawled into bed and thought of her breasts. It aroused him, again. He fell asleep fondling his manhood.

CHAPTER 28—THE TWENTY-FIFTH DAY
REPORTING HER OWN DEATH

Labella Litchfield phoned in her own death to the Norfolk Police Department. The call came at 1:22 p.m., the afternoon after her previous evening's death. Officer Lucile Henderson answered the incoming call. She immediately knew that she was listening to a recording. The voice said, "Hi, this is Labella Litchfield. Humpty Dumpy sat on the wall, but Labella Litchfield is nailed to the wall. W's Angle Killer murdered me yesterday. Tell W to come to my apartment and put me back together, again. But warn W that this isn't some Humpty Dumpy Story, that he can't put me back together again, even if he has all the kings horses and all the king's men. I've been sliced and diced because of Lieutenant Arthur Wellington Wellesley's little hill story. Tell him that the story is on the wall, hills and all, and her eyes will watch his disbelief. Ta-Ta!"

The telephone on the other end clicked off; Henderson heard it. Nevertheless, she still said, "Hello, hello?"

Henderson immediately notified the Day Watch Commander, Hazel Paterson. Peterson then requested an immediate copy of the recorded message. That took seventeen minutes—how is that possible—for Paterson to receive her copy. She listened to the message three times. She looked up Labella Litchfield's name in the Norfolk telephone directory. She found the number, called it and listened to the busy signal. She hung the phone up and called for an operator. She gave her police ID number and the operator came back and told her that it was an open line calling out to Time.

Paterson pushed the button on her telephone system, and then mashed the four-digit number! He was in, he answered, "Wellesley." He listened. "I'll be right there."

* * * * *

At 4:30 a.m. Nabulio woke up without his alarm. He drove to the mansion. He got in his 57-foot 5-inch Azimut Fiberglass Motor Yacht—which he bought as a girl getter for $1.5 million—and took the box out 2.5 miles and threw each piece of its contents into the salty water to eat away at the evidence. He tossed the empty box in the dark water, too. He then flipped the yacht around and headed back to the mansion. He went into the house and played with his electronic equipment until he got it right.

It was 7:47 a.m. when the project was done. He got in his car and made the aggravating drive to Rocky Mount, North Carolina. He stopped at phone booth on Washington Way in downtown Rocky Mount and placed the telephone call. He dialed the number and listened to the rings. As soon as he heard the officer pick-up, he mashed the play button and all his hard work from that morning paid off as Labella's hot voice echoed over the distance. He listed to LL's beautiful voice for the last time as the deceased Litchfield told the officer and ultimately Lieutenant Wellington of her death.

Nabulio had sliced and diced it all together from the story Labella read to him, yesterday when the battle was just beginning! While the story was senseless to her at the time; Nabulio was making sure that she said every word that was needed to be part of her recorded death voice, twice, so that he, again was sure that he had each word recorded clearly and precise. Litchfield had accomplished an excellent task for her Angel Killer, and today, her AK completed the task for this single phone call to Wellington.

Before the officer had a chance to respond, Angel Killer pressed the stop button. He put the machine into his knapsack, and pushed the phone booth door open with his elbow. The then took off his gloves and walked a half of a block to his rented Impala. He drove to Roanoke Rapids and stopped the car. He tossed the cassette player into a large lake of some kind. He then took the recording tape and burnt it in the ashtray of the Impala. He then tossed the empty cassette tape dispenser into the water as well. Across the road, he scuffed and kicked at the dirt making a whole and put the ash contents into the ground and covered it up. "There," he said, "I've buried her proper." He looked heavenward, and said, "Amen!" He then crossed back over the road, back to the lake and washed the ashtray in the water. Satisfied, he got into his car and journeyed north for an hour or so until hunger struck and he stopped to eat.

Wellesley listened to the tape seven times. He had it memorized. "Make me a copy, he said. Mark and file this one." He walked away pissed. He called Strange, gave him the address and told him to meet him at Labella Litchfield's apartment. It didn't take a genius. He knew what they would find, but he never expected to see what he was about to see!

After eating, Nabulio drove straight to Norfolk, and deposited the Impala, and called for a cab to take him home. Four hours later he would again call for a cab that would take him to the Airport and then off to San Francisco for a scheduled three days, and then off for an extended trip, and a well-earned vacation in Hawaii. *The Islands*, he thought, *brown skinned, women.*

On his flight he envisioned the Virginia Beach's salty water washing away anything related to Ms. Litchfield. He closed his eyes and thought of her breasts, he smiled at the thoughts! *I did it all! I'm the man! Good luck W! Soon it will be your turn, but not quite yet, but soon!* With that, he drifted off to sleep as the plane took him towards paradise!

CHAPTER 29—THE TWENTY-FIFTH DAY
THE UNBELIEVABLE

Before they went inside, Wellington had the outside of the door dusted for prints. There were—naturally—none to be found. They got the apartment supervisor to open her room with his passkey. The super was immediately dismissed without seeing inside. Tray Croswell, walked away disappointed. If he only knew!

Wellington's eyes immediately went to the wall across from him. It was ugly. The eyes. The breasts. The Blood! The bloody writing was written too small to be read from the entrance of the apartment. The cop didn't move, in. He wanted to survey the place from the door. He knew no one had been in here since Angle Killer left. He didn't want anything touched. This was truly pristine! Would that even matter? He saw her bed in the middle of the room, clean, neat, no blood. He saw the triangle lag screws turned into the floor. Well, he saw four of the six, anyway. He envisioned two more on the other side of the bed. He could only imagine her torture. He leaned in and saw her head resting on top of the refrigerator. It was looking directly at him with holes instead of eyes. He nearly vomited! He stepped into the hall. Less than a half minute later, Strange had to do the same!

Within a half hour the entire team was in place, inside. Wellesley was disturbed beyond measure. It was obvious that this wasn't just another brutal slaying. This was payback to him personally for his note in the paper! Wellesley was determined that the press would not get any information on this crime scene. Strange found her purse where the killer had left it after it had been flung to the floor when LL had entered her apartment. The wallet confirmed her name. The Detective also saw her college I.D. in the wallet; she wasn't from Old Dominion. *Damn it*!

A new twist, a new corner to figure out! Strange crossed to his boss.

"Lieutenant, I got something here that may be somewhat upsetting to you and to this case."

"Let me have it!" Strange didn't say a word, he merely showed the card. It announced, Virginia Wesleyan University.

"Good Lord," we're starting all over again. A new kettle of fish had been opened. Wellesley uttered a vulgar four-letter word, and then he shouted, "EVERYBODY STOP WHAT YOU ARE DOING. JUST STOP!" A pin could be heard if dropped. All eyes twisted to the chief investigator. Wellesley lowered his voice. Folks this woman isn't from Old Dominion, she's a second year student at Wesleyan." A murmur carried throughout the apartment. "Back to work!" He yelled for Strange.

"I'm right beside you boss. I'm right here!"

"Look, Detective, I've got to get out of here. You take over. I've got to get what is inside of Alex's head. She's coming home from the hospital today. I tell you she knows something, Detective. I have got to find out what it is. Now! This crime scene is way over the top. Unless we find some real trace evidence that can narrow it directly to this guy we'll find nothing else here. I have got to get inside of him, somehow! I have got to get into his head, somehow!

He started to walk away and abruptly stopped, "Do not, under any circumstances let the press in here, and you personally see to it that not one word of what is seen here is leaked to anyone, anybody. People come in here on my say so only. Am I clear?"

"Yes!"

"Good! "That means you call me about anything, everything! Keep it that way!" He turned to leave.

"Lieutenant." A young officer stood right behind him. "I have something, Sir."

"Give it to the detective."

"It's a sort of a witness, Sir." The cop explained that across the street was an elderly woman named Julie Hartley. "She lives in the apartment over there. Sir." He pointed. "She said that she was two men today with a U-Hall truck moving into her building, and that through her window she saw them talking to a man that had a box, he was holding on to it on the stoop just outside." He took a breath. She said he was driving a white car of some kind. It looked new to her."

"Are the two men there?" Wellington asked.

"No, but she has their phone number!"

"Why?" He interrupted his own question, "Never mind. You got their names and numbers?"

"Yes, Sir." He handed his notes to Wellington.

Wellington handed his notes back to the officer and scratched down the names of Sid and Jack, and their phone number. "You did great work officer." He looked at his nametag, "Officer, Scar! Excellent. Is there anything else?" The cop smiled, and merely shook his head, no! Inside, the young officer was on top of the world. "Okay, Officer Scar, go inside and tell Detective Strange what you told me, and give him the number, and tell him I said for him, and him alone to go visit this Hartley woman, and then he is to call me. You got all that?"

"Consider it done, Sir."

"Good man!" Wellesley got in his car. He stopped. He got out of his car, and yelled, "Hey, Scar." The young officer turned around. "Tell Strange to take you with him." He added, "Now, son, you just listen and learn when you're over there. If you have anything to say you write it down, and you ask the detective after you're out of the house; you got that?"

"Yes, sir, and thank you, Sir; I appreciate it."

"You deserve it, son. Good job. Good jobs are rewarded." That said he slipped back into his car and put his light on top of the car and sped off to the hospital. Five minutes into his ride, he called Strange. "I want to put that elderly woman in front of a sketch artist. I then want you to get, what's their names, you know, those two guys…"

"I got yea boss, you mean Sid and Jack Trainer, right?"

"Yea, I guess so, I didn't get their names. Anyway, I…"

"Lieutenant, I'm already ahead of you. These guys are still in town. Two calls and I tracked them down. And, you want them with sketch artists, too, right?"

"Right!"

"The guy they were talking to, Sid, he remembers this guys name as being Chuck Albright."

"Right, his name is Chuck Albright. If there is a Chuck Albright in all of Norfolk, I'll wager he's not our Angel Killer, nor will he be the guy the Trainers' talked to, either. If there isn't a Chuck Albright, then the guy they are I-D-ing as Chuck Albright definitely our Angle Killer, but his name isn't Albright." He paused, "When we get those 3-ID's give me a call. I want to see what this prick looks like, because he is going to be plastered all over every newspaper across this land, and every TV network and station on the planet!

"You're right as rain, boss; right as rain, like, always!"

"Hey, what do you think of that young cop, Scar?"

"He's a righteous dude, I like him."

"Remind me about his; I want to look after him."

"Why?"

"He reminds me of me. I'm gone!" Wellesley clicked off! Immediately his cell went off. He looked at the face of his cell. Alexandria was calling. "Hey, love." It wasn't his 'love,' it was his love's mom.

"Arthur, Alexandria has been released from the hospital. Dad is driving her home, to your house."

Wellsy made the next turn to the right. "Tell her I'll be there in ten minutes or so. How is she?"

"She's fine, tired, but fine."

"Ten minutes! Bye…." He almost said, mom. He didn't, but he liked the idea, a lot. "I'm on my way, mom!" He smiled, he said it. It felt good! Two minutes later after driving two blocks, he stopped the car and got out and vomited until he was empty. He wanted to die. He couldn't breath. It was overwhelming! He wiped his mouth with a hanky. He stopped at a gas station and bought a ginger ale soda to settle his stomach, like anything could?

What do you know, Alex, what do you know? The eleven-minute drive home went buy in a buzz. His mind was on so many things, but he still felt the key was in Alexandria's beautiful sweet mind. Just don't push her, guide her. He pulled over to the curb. For the first time in eight years, he bent his head in prayer, seeking guidance to stop this reckless uncontrollable, diabolical Angel Killer. "If I have to lose my life, so be it, God, but this animal must be stopped, enough lives have been lost." He ended his prayer, asking for God to "watch over his Alexandria, and to open her mind to help catch the monster!"

He stopped the car, again, and again, vomited. As he pulled into his driveway, he took the last gulp of the soda. He sat in the car and whisked away more tears. Did that woman die today because of me? He cried; he knew she did!

Chapter 30—The Twenty-Fifth Day
FRISCO

Nabulio's plane landed without notice to most. He taxied to his hotel. Yesterday's ordeal had physically wiped him out. He slept off and on while in flight, but when he arrived at his destination he was totally drained. He deplaned and grabbed a cab that took him to his hotel, The Four Points by Sheraton San Francisco International. He checked in, went to his room, took care of his clothing, luggage, and went to the Yellow Pages and looked up Escort Services. He told the sexy voice on the other end *exactly* what he wanted in every detail, and that he wouldn't accept any deviations.

He described LL to a tee, and then made his point very direct: "If you don't have one of your very best with at least a 99 percent chance of her being exactly what I want, in terms of a perfect match, then forget it because I'll just send her packing with nothing. I'd rather give you a thousand dollars now for a good referral then to get something I don't want in an hour or two!"

They assured him that they'd deliver.

He also made it clear that he was looking for the best of the best. And yes, he wanted her for the entire evening and perhaps all of tomorrow and tomorrow night as well. "Have her show up ready for a night on the town, elegance, and additional clothing for tomorrow, carefree, jeans, comfortable, and no bra." he added. "She must be 21 to 25 years of age and no taller and five foot five inches." He gave his American Express credit card number and hung up. He took a nap, falling asleep thinking of LL. An hour later he was in the shower, reading himself for the evening.

Kristina—her working name—showed up at 7:30 and eased into the elegant posh elevator that went nonstop to the presidential suite. The elevator opened into his elegant expanse. She was dressed to the nines as expected, wearing an elegant, black silky dress, with touching silver trim that accented her figure. Her hair was exquisite as anticipated, and much like LL's. "There is a test you must pass, first," he said. "I need to have a quick look at your breasts, if they aren't right, you're gone!" She complied without hesitation. He looked. She was definitely the right one! "One more question, and the interview process will be over," he suggested.

Before he asked, she answer, "Yes, completely, do you want to check it out yourself?" He replied with a simple no. This service company was good, thorough.

"What is your name?"

"Kristina."

"No, I mean your real name?"

"I hate my real name."

"What is it?"

"Constance."

"Do you like Connie?"

"No!"

"What do you want me to call you?"

"Kristina, or just Kris will do, whatever you prefer."

"Kristina."

"Then Kristina will do. What do you want me to be? Your flirt, your whore, your lover, your date, what?"

"Can you be Constance?"

"No!"

"Why?"

"Because that is a different life, altogether."

"Meaning?"

"Meaning, when I'm on the job I'm on the job, I will be whatever you want me to be; as long as you don't hurt me. When the job is over, I'm Constance, and she wouldn't give you the time of day."

"Are you always so brutally honest?"

"No! Yes! Well, maybe, but definitely not always, who is?"

"No one, I guess."

"What do you want me to call you?"

"Max."

"Okay, Max it is." They were quiet for an uncomfortable few seconds. "So, Max, what do you want me to be?"

"Is there anyway you can be someone without acting out a part?"

"Not really, how could I do that?"

"Search me! Well, try to be Constance, what I mean is, try to be real."

"I can't, this is work, not my real world."

"That's not true, your work is part of you, and your real world, isn't it?"

"Point taken, I'll try to be me, but there will come a time."

"Later, you mean?"

"Yes! Yes, I mean later, unless you want me now. I'm on your time, your dime, your clock, I belong to you as long as you don't hurt me."

"You keep saying that. Don't worry; I will not hurt you. And the other, well we'll deal with that when it's time to deal with that."

"Does Constance find me attractive."

"Yes!"

"Does Kristina?"

"She doesn't care, but she will show you, offer you, give you whatever you want, as long as you do not get overly physical."

"Understood, sort of, anyway. What is overly physical?"

"We're beating a dead horse here. I don't want to be hurt! Okay!"

"Okay." Another uncomfortable moment passes. He asked, "Is Constance hungry."

"She is starved!"

"Good then I'll take her out for dinner."

"Kristina will be along, you know."

"Good, I'll think of it as a double date?"

"By the way," she asked, "What is your name?"

"Max."

"Max, you say."

"Yes, Max I say!"

"Do you have another name?"

"Yes!"

"What is it?"

"Nabulio."

"Nabulio, you say."

"Yes!"

"Is he along on this date too?"

"Do I want him to be?"

"No. You do not what him to be?"

"Ok, I don't, but Constance wants him to come. You know, to fill out the double date, so, yes, bring him along."

"Okay, I'll take Constance and Kristina can come along and be Nabulio's date. The two of us will ignore them."

"All night!"

"Yes, all night!"

"Are you sure?"

"Yes!"

"Max, are you sure Kristina will like Nabulio?"

"That is for Kristina to find out on her own!"

"How will we know if she likes him?"

"I don't know for sure, you can ask her!"

"I will, where will I find her?"

"He'll point the way."

"You are a dirty young man, aren't you?"

"He said nothing for nearly a minute. He then asked, "Do you like escargot?"

"I like anything that slides down."

"That was Kristina speaking, wasn't it?"

"Yes, but it just so happens that Constance likes that too."

"Interesting!"

"Why?"

"Because so does Nabulio."

"Who just said that, Max or Nabulio?"

"Think of them as one in the same, and I'll do the same with Kristina and Constance!"

"Which will have the better evening?"

"Let's go feed them both, and then we'll see."

As they got into the elevator, she asked, "Where are you from?"

"Norfolk, Virginia."

"Oh, my," she exclaimed, "That is where they just had another killing!"

"You mean today," he asked?"

"Yes, earlier this morning. You must know about it."

"Well I know about the situation, but I've been in the air all day. I had no idea there was another one today!" He paused, "Did he kill another woman?"

"Yes, but the police are being tight lipped about it this time."

"So we don't know anything, then."

"No! Nothing!" she said, and then added, "It scares me to death,"

"I imagine it would. I can just imagine," he said as the elevator door closed them off from the world!

"I'll protect you tonight then."

"That's good, but he is in Virginia, not California."

"You never know," he said, and then repeated, "You never know!"

Chapter 31—The Twenty-Fifth Day
ALEXANDRIA'S WISDOM

The Southerland family reached Arthur's home before he did. When he arrived, he was surprised to see Alex seated in his Lazy boy chair. He didn't mind; it's just that he assumed she would have gone to bed. He felt uncomfortable. Her parents had never been to his home before, and well, after all, he and Alex were living together, basically, shacking-up. He wondered if Sean and Katharine were feeling as awkward as he was? He rushed to Alex and kissed her on the cheek, and whispered, "I love you." He broke away and asked, "How are you feeling."

"She's doing great Katharine responded. He looked at his future mother-in-law and offered a genuine smile.

"She's tops, you know, my girl is, "Sean offered."

"Yes, Sir, she is." He turned to her, "Are you comfortable?"

"Of course. Look you three. I'm find, stop pampering, I'm just fine," she reiterated.

"Nope, pampering is my job," Katharine, offered with a beaming smile, "Besides, we've decided to turn this into a bit of a vacation. There is a lot to see in Norfolk and the Virginia Beach area!"

"Good." Wellsy volunteered.

"Let's change the topic, Sean offered. How is this case you are working on, going, young man, I mean Lieutenant."

"Please just call me Arthur, Mister Southerland."

"Nonsense, Mom, Dad, call him Wellsy, it fits him and he likes it!"

"Wellsy?" Sean offered.

"Yes, Dad, but we'll go into that later." Her parents exchanged a look, but accepted it and each, smiled.

"Well, look, you two, we're going to shove off. I think we'll just go to back to the hotel and take a rest. We're not as young as we used to be." Sean offered.

"Yes, we'll call you in the morning, and go from there, okay?" Katharine added. There was the traditional this and that, about how everyone was glad that Alexandria was okay, and that her parents had taken the time to come, etcetera, etcetera, etcetera, blah, blah, blah. They left, and Wellsy and Alex offered up a sigh of relief. In the car, Sean mentioned to Katharine that Arthur was such a nice man, but" she shuttered, "that awful case." She asked Sean if he thought Arthur was in danger."

Sean merely replied, "It's a murder case, of course he is." She was hoping for a more positive response. None came!

"Do you want to lie down?" Wellsy, asked. She told him no, that she was comfortable. He asked if he could get her anything. She made it clear that she was fine. She asked about the latest killing, and why he wasn't on the premises. He took the opportunity to ask if she were up to a discussion. She assured him she was fine. "Well," he said, "you were going to tell me something about what you had discovered after you had stayed up all night, and then the accident happened."

She was taken aback. She had forgotten about all of that. A sparkle became noticeable to Wellsy. He could see her enthusiasm flaring. Color was coming into her cheeks. She told him how Schom's book had excited her, about Napoleon having the nickname of Nabulio as a child. She leaned forward in her chair, and said, "Look, this may sound strange, but what if your Angel Killer is or was also called Nabulio, and what if his real name is Napoleon, after Bonaparte?" She took a breath, "What if the Angel killer is a direct descendant of thee Napoleon?" Wellsy didn't respond. She didn't expect him to as this was crazy thinking. "Could it be that simple," she offered.

He didn't respond, so she told him about her telephone directory idea, but had discovered that there weren't any Bonaparte or Buonaparte last names in Norfolk. He liked her thinking. She had peaked his curiosity, and encouraged her to continue. "Arthur, could the police department request of the utility company for a down loaded list of people by their first name, first and then their last name?"

"You want to find out how many Napoleon's there are by first name, right, and Nabulio, too, right?" He didn't wait for an answer. "You are a genius." She ignored his accolade and suggested that there couldn't possibly be that many, especially the name Nabulio.

"Honey, I am sure that this guy is a direct descendant to Napoleon."

"Why?"

That wasn't what she wanted him to say; because she thought that he would think that her idea was too bizarre. So, she deflected it by suggesting that she was glad that she was home, that she needed some computer time to do some research on her theory. She asked him to just give her that without going into detail. He wanted to know, but was conciliatory to her wants. "Okay," she said, "steady me as I walk to the bedroom. I want to get started now." He helped her, though neither thought she needed the help."

"Look," she offered, I'm fine. I want to be left alone at my work, okay?"

"Okay!"

"And," she continued, "I don't want you sneaking up on me, either. Just let me be, okay!" He kissed her on top of the head and, with little willingness, agreed. "And, don't come in here every half hour or so and ask how I am doing, after all, this is all pie in the sky, okay?" He agreed. He told her he needed to make several phone calls, and so some thinking of his own!

"Is it worse this time, or like before."

"Don't ask, because I will not tell. It is unimaginable, Alexandria, unimaginable." She only nodded in agreement. "I love you, you know!"

"Oh, speaking of which," she offered. He stopped, turned to her, and offered a pondering look. "Tonight," she continued, "you owe me remember?" Oh, he remembered, all right. He then reminded her that there was certain parts of him never forget such things. So, she reminded him that his parts had an obligation to totally and completely satisfy her parts—several times—before his part could have it's concluding or climaxing enjoyment. He said that he was up to the task. She responded with "Well, then, you keep your part *up!*"

He asked is she was truly up to that, what with the clunk on the head, the hospital stay, and all. "Hey, she said, "you have to do all the work, it's a free-bee for me!"

"Gads, the things a man has to do to keep some women happy." He smiled and kissed the top of her head. "Happy searching," he said, and left the room. She watched him leave. *I love you* she whispered in her heart, and then added, *be safe my love, be safe.*

He went into his den and called the department, and made his request for them to get the alphabetized list from the utility company. He made it clear that he was only interested in the names of Napoleon and Nabulio. Next, he called Strange. As they spoke, he said that the elderly woman was at the station with the artist, and that the other two men were on their way, that they would be at the station within the hour.

He made one last call to the Profiler. She was unavailable. She was working on a profiling case in the state of Washington. She would get back to him. He needed to use the facilities so off to the bathroom he went. When finished, he washed his hands and when he looked up, in the mirror, he saw her vacant eyes looking at him though the mirror. He shuttered. *How could that animal do this?* He did his best to shake it off. It left. It was gone, sort of, but her eyeless face would haunt him for months, years. He felt as if he had killed her, by his newspaper release. He took a cleansing breath, and moved forward. He called the Strategic Management Division and asked for Captain Ernst Herrington, "I'm sure you've head it all, Captain, but may I ask you to take care of getting with all those women from Old Dominion we had in and offer their clean bill of health?"

"I was just about to call you, and offer the same."

"Thanks, Captain!"

"My pleasure! And, Lieutenant?"

"Yes!"

"It's not your fault, son, you know that, it's not your fault at all. He already had her targeted. He must have. He made the switch from one college to the other, because he sensed or was afraid that you were on to him. Don't read more into that than what is there. It is not your fault." Wellsy, knew better, but at least he could make the Captain feel better. He replied with simple *thanks*, and signed off, after, again thanking Herrington for his support and willingness to handle the Old Dominion women whose last name started with L.

"I" is next he said to himself, "and the then what?"

His cell phone went off. Captain Rodgers wanted an update. The conversation ended with the captain reminding him that what this animal did to Labella L. Litchfield wasn't his fault. Shortly thereafter, the call ended. In the privacy of his bathroom, he slumped to the toilet seat, and cried like a baby. *I killed her!*

CHAPTER 32—THE TWENTY-SIXTH DAY
CONFUSED PERSONS

Kristina, or Constance did something she had never done before. And then she had something that she had never had before, too. The date could not have been more perfect. The meal, the discussion, their games, the two of them—Max and Constance—played with the other two of them—Kristina and Nabulio, the whole of it was simply mind boggling. Personalities blended, meshed and were played off one another over and over again. The two of them, the four of them had a most delightful time. They laughed together, sometimes so hard they cried, together. They had more fun than either could remember in a long, long time. She forgot that she was paid for, and he forgot he was paying for her. It was magical, a never ending story.

When they got back to his suite, Kristina or Constance, one or both of them did what she had never done before. As a matter of fact, it was the one thing in her profession they had never done, unless—of course—the guy requested it beforehand, and then the professional had to get a second confirmation before she so engaged. So, what was this rule that she broke? She made the first move—that's what—and in her profession that was a big no, no. But, she (Constance) had to have this guy. She just took over the whole evening once they returned from date. He was standing near the bed, loosening his tie and she flung herself at him, tackling him and thrusting the two of them to the bed.

He was taken aback, but didn't complain; naturally. She was clawing at his garments, removing them with her hands, her teeth. He was so excited. She was so excited, too. This had never happed to him before, or her! She was kissing him everywhere. He asked within himself, was this Kristina the high-class hooker or Constance the conservative one who always removed herself from this activity. He was confused but went with it, totally. She did more to him in three hours then he had personally witnessed in his entire life. She was as surprised as was he. She had never done this before, either, and in the course of it all, she also had something she had never had before with a client. She had climaxed, and not only once, not even twice, but six times, or maybe it was seven. Who cared? It was magical, even mystical.

When it was over, she was still sitting on him, with her knees digging into the mattress over his groin. A drip of sweat fell from her chin to his chest. He looked up and for the first time noticed her breasts. Never before had he been so involved in the love making quest in and of itself that he didn't even noticed them; of all things not to notice, his favorite of favorites. As he looked at them now, he felt a stir, and she felt it, too. She moved her pelvis, wiggled it. "I can't" he said, you'll kill me." She got off. He pulled her down and they just held each other, until they fell asleep. That was 5:46 on the morning of the twenty-sixth day.

He woke up at 8:52 a.m. She wasn't beside him. He called out, "Constance!" She stepped out of the steamy bathroom, and looked at him. She was fully dressed in blue jeans, a white button up blouse, and she wore a frumpy tan corduroy cap off the side of her head that made her playfully engaging. It gave her a good-humored teasing spunky look. It made her cute. Last night, she was beautiful; today she was as cute as a button. He loved it. Her hair was pulled back into a ponytail that came off the back and side of her head away from the cap. She had a silky orange ribbon that dangled and twisted down with her hair. She looked pleasingly wonderful, youthful, young, charming, and had an air of tease about her. She flat out looked great, beyond great, terrific! He smiled at her and said, "Come here you."

She let out a sigh, stepped back, and said, "No," and then replied. "I'm leaving. I have to go!"

"You can't leave. I have you for today, all day as well, and now I think, tonight, too."

She took yet another step back, "Don't worry about it, it's all on me. I will cover all your charges from last night and today as well." She went backwards another step. "Sorry, I have to go!"

"Go! Wait! No! I'll not have it! Something happened to me last night. Something I can't explain."

"Me, too! And, because of that I have to go!"

"Wait, please" he said, as he climbed out of bed, stark naked. She couldn't help but look. He had given her such pleasure just a few short hours, ago. "You can't go! I had the best night of my life last night! It can't end this way. It just can't!"

"It has to. I'm leaving." She started to turn, away.

"You owe me a why, at the very least! Why are you leaving? Have I offended you? Have I crossed the line, what?"

"No you have not crossed the line, it is I who crossed the line, and in many ways. I was most unprofessional last night, and while you may have enjoyed it, I crossed the line! I must leave, don't make this any harder than it is, please!"

"I don't know if you did or did not cross the line, but what I do know is you are my everything! You cannot walk out, now."

"I have to!"

"Why?"

"You would not understand!"

"Try me!"

"No!"

"Yes! For heaven sakes, woman you owe me that!" She took a step toward the elevator. He too, took a step. Her hand hit the button for the elevator. He walked within two steps of her. The elevator opened, she stepped in. "Please, don't do this, at least help me to understand!" She let the door slid closed. He reached out as if to stop it, but she was gone! He stood there, nude, helpless, feeling stupid! His heart was low. He turned, crossed back past the bathroom and into the bedroom, and sat on its edge of the bed. He felt awful. Dejected. Alone! Unwanted. He sat there for what seemed to be a lifetime, but it was only four minutes. He heard the dinging noise, the elevator opened. She rushed to him, tackling him onto the bed's surface.

"We have a big problem, she said, but first things first." She raped him, again! What men have to put up with, he smiled; afterwards.

CHAPTER 33—THE TWENTY-SIXTH AND TWENTY-SEVENTH DAY
THE RESULTS

Wellsy got the results from the Utility Company; there were surprisingly 11 men whose first name were Napoleon in Norfolk proper, and an equal number in the surrounding area. On the first day of interviews, 15 of the 22 would be visited by the Norfolk Police Department. One of the 15 died six months ago, another was seventy-four years old, the rest just didn't match the profile, or they had a solid alibi for at least one of the killings, if not more. There was only one person with the name of Nabulio; he too was visited that first day. When the police arrived, Nabulio Fascine was in a wheel chair, but still, he fit the description so well that his doctor was a follow-up call. Indeed, this Nabulio was wheelchair bound for the rest of his natural life from an automobile accident that happened nine years ago, and "No," the doctor said chuckling at the policewoman's question, "he could not be faking it!"

On the twenty-seventh day, the remaining Napoleons were interviewed. One was in the county jail lock up and had been so for five days. Of the remaining group, four were prime candidates and two of them were taken to headquarters and examined. Both suspects had a secure alibi for at least one of the five killings. Over the next six days, each of the possible Napoleons' one at a time was scratched off the possible list. The good news, several had been eliminated from consideration. Bid deal! The progress crawled.

The press learning of the Napoleon and Nabulio police search had a field day with the Lieutenant's waste of funds. One paper called it worse than looking for a needle in a proverbial haystack. Only the Gazette praised Wellington's initiative. Nevertheless, all the papers splashed all three of the artist sketches in their rag papers. Calls started to come in fast and furious. Each of those calls had to be researched; causing time, money and inefficiency as all the leads went nowhere.

The two sketch artists that did the three sketches of the man who had identified himself as Chuck Albright had accomplished a great feat. They obviously caught the identity of the Angle Killer, if, indeed, he truly was the Angel Killer (AK). Unfortunately, this Chuck Albright was all coat, gloves, and that damned stocking hat covered way too much up to even get a hint of his face. Additionally, they couldn't remember if his hair was brown or black, curly, wavy or straight, perhaps, blonde. All three witnesses agreed that the mouth on the sketchpad matched the man, but they couldn't agree at all on the bottom part of the nose.

When each witness was asked if they could identify him, again, each agreed, probably not unless he had on that hat! Both men agreed that they could identify his voice, however. But when they were asked if they could identify his region by his accent, they offered two different answers, the south and perhaps the mid-west. That made no sense at all to Wellesley. When asked if they could identify him if they saw him walking down the street, each said "probably not unless he had on that hat," and then they were not sure.

Wellsy spent the first part of the day in the police DOG (Defensive Organization Group) Room. He studied the photographs, looking for similarities that might offer a clue. He also looked for dissimilarities, or patterns that might offer the slightest clue. He poured over the diagrams, or the position that each woman had been placed in. He read and reread chalkboard notes, and then adding to them, more notes. He pondered, reading over and over, again the Napoleon-like quotes of the AK. He looked for any obvious patterns that might be hidden in the pins that were stuck in photographs of the tortured women. Those pins had a threaded line that went from the photos to the map area where they were murdered. The DOG room seemed to have all the answers, but nothing was barking out to the lead cop. There was a mountain of information that he knew. In that mountain was the answer to the whole riddle, but he couldn't see it, and neither could his hard working team; including his hopeful bride to be! The solution was tougher than finding a needle in a haystack. *If I could only come up with a motive, he pondered. If only!*

He thought about what he did know. He knew that AK killed girls that were bright, smart, and go-getters, achievers. He knew AK used an outside source to select his victims, the *Mace and Crown*. He also knew that he stopped using the *Mace and Crown*, too. *Why!* Wellesley assumed that the AK assumed that we—the cops—were getting close. "Never assume," he told himself.

The Lieutenant knew that the killings were not exactly equal days apart, but, that they were averaging 5 days apart, or 6 if you considered that the first two women were killed at the same time, and/or the same day. With that in mind, he realized he would kill, again, in just 3 to 4 days. "Forget that! Stay focused! Get back to what you know." Wellesley knew that each of the killings were becoming more and more aggressively horrendous, but he wasn't sure if that was planned, or if it was because, the 4th girl's boyfriend surprised him by his presence, meaning that his perfect plan went haywire. And, poor LL was brutalized beyond any amount of sensibility because of Wellesley, himself, because of his speaking out to the AK though the newspaper.

After six hours of study, he threw his notepad on the floor, and bolted out of the building. Pressure and fatigue was eating at him. *Who is next? Who next can't I save the next time? Who, damn it! Who?* He tried to be positive and conjure what he did know, and that is when he realized something he should have thought of immediately. *Maybe the Perp just switched schools so he wouldn't be figured out.* Wellesley went to the far NE corner of the room and triggered on the computer to assist him. He couldn't find a compatible school student newspaper like the *Mace and Crown*, at Wesleyan College. He spent another hour searching, looking, and digging. He found LL. She fit the description of the girls from Old Dominion. She was bright, on the Deans List. She was a leader, the President of SVEA. Her picture was prominently displayed on the Internet. "Okay," he said. Now think, he demanded. Will the next victim be from SVEA, or another female leader to some other campus organization? He decided the ladder. He began his search. Over the next two hours he whittled the list down to 4 women. As an addendum, he added their leaders, either Presidents, or Vice-Presidents.

He knew the killer was going to strike a woman with her last name starting with an "I," taken from the "I" in Nabul-I-o! Here were Nabulio's choices, according to Wellesley's theory: Cheryl R. Insley, Christina L. Ireland, Trudy Izzo, and Michelle W. Isaac; were carried by police cars to the department.

Wellington called Detective Strange, and then had Strange call in the team. They had two days to find a way to thwart Nabulio's carnage. He laid it out to the team, seeking a plan to get AK. Everyone bought into it! They needed to bring these 4 women in, quietly, protectively, and without fanfare! "I want them brought in by policewomen, no uniforms, and no marked cars. Have them visit the girls, and vaguely explain what is going on, and have them leave their dorm, or house or whatever, casually, talking, giggling, etcetera. If this guy is watching them, he must not be alarmed, no, not one little bit. Furthermore, have the officers take the long way to the office. I want another car tailing behind to see—

to make sure—they are not being followed. If someone is following, well get a team on him, and we damned well might end it there. Let's not make a scene, okay! Let's keep the press totally out of this. Think of it as a covert operation on a need to know only, basis."

Wellesley looked up at the group, "I need someone to get the girls class schedule, and their dorm or off campus address. Folks, we need to do this immediately, somehow, and without excuses." Hank Blister from operations said he would take care of that. Strange said he'd talk to the day watch Commander to have the female officers assigned. The plan was quickly taking shape. "I want Campus Security Guard Jessica House invited here for this, too." Herrington wondered why, so he asked. "I'm not sure," Wellesley, said, "but someone from Campus Security should be involved, and beyond just knowing what we are doing. The woman has great instincts. Bring her in!" Strange said he would take care of it. "Okay, everyone, let's see if we can get everyone in here by three-thirty." He paused, "Any questions?"

"To get them here by three might mean that one or more of them would need to miss a class. Might that not send up a flare," Blister suggested.

"I don't think so, after all, coeds miss classes all the time. The officers will deal with that sufficiently," Wellesley suggested.

Captain Rodgers was sure they were on the right trail. He praised, Wellesley, and in turn suggested, "Horse feathers, it's only a theory, Captain," and then he repeated, "Only a theory!" He made more assignments; the College President and the Dean of Students needed to come in as well. "They can make up their own reasons for changing their schedules, today. Hell, they are used to that." He asked Captain Herrington to handle that process.

"I will, and someone needs to be sure every little detail is working out. Would you like me to be that source, Lieutenant? After all, it is what I do!"

"Excellent! Thanks! Do it!" He paused, and then asked, "So, does everyone have the plan, what you are to do, and whom you are to report to?" All heads bobbed, yes! "Okay, Captain Herrington, you lead out on this but I want to know about any and every snafu."

"Consider it done!" Wellesley asked if there were any questions. Everyone in the room seemed to look around. "Okay, let's get it done." Wellsy called home, Alex answered. He told her that he didn't think he'd get home much before seven. She understood, hated it, but understood. Next, he went to his office and studied everything that had just been accomplished. He looked for holes in his theory. He couldn't find any, and that troubled him, too.

The meeting happened. One woman—Trudy Izzo—said she was going home, no matter what! She wanted an escort to her dorm. She was packing up and leaving, immediately. No one complained, so she left with the female officer that escorted her to the meeting. An hour later she was in her own car and driving home to Beckley, West Virginia. For over an hour she was sure she was being followed, she wasn't! The rest of the meeting went well. The other girls were staying.

Each girl was interviewed. Each was asked if any of them had an extended conversation with a male, recently? Each was shown the three sketches. Each was asked if she ever saw the man in the stocking cap. Dozens and dozens of questions were asked. It appeared that they were barking up the wrong tree. Nevertheless, the cops pursued every avenue of possible disclosure. Decisive plans were laid out for each woman.

Wellesley told them all, "I don't mean anything personal about this, but for the next week, I don't care where you are, or where you go, but wear a bra, dress modestly! Cheryl Insley asked why. "Well Ms. Insley," Wellington offered, "Wearing a bra just might save your life." He paused. "No offense, Cheryl, but I can tell you are not wearing one now," she crossed her arms, "and rest assured, the Angel Killer can tell, too. Cheryl, that act of wearing a bar, could well save your life. It may well diminish your chance of his selection process! It's my advice. Do what you will." Secretly, she decided to wear a bra for the rest of her life, and she did.

Wellesley arrived home excited and somewhat depressed; he had hoped for more, much more. In the house he was met by the best smell, a smell that he wanted to remember forever. Mrs. Southerland had made apple-dumplings. It was a smell of home and of heaven. He liked it a lot. It was a smell he had longed for sense he had moved away from his parent's home. The food, the meal was a delicious feast. "I think your mom should stay here," he barked to Alex.

"Nope," Alex's mother said, "today we saw too many cockroaches."

"In our home," he quickly asked, and then he just as quickly wanted to take his comment back, but too late. He couldn't believe he said *our* home. All three Sutherlands sat quietly for some time. In the stillness, Mr. Southerland said, "No, not in your house, but them cockroaches seem to be all over, Norfolk." His wife added, "Yes, this is the cockroach city, for sure."

"Well, I'm feeling better," Alex suggested, just to change the topic. "I think I've got all my strength back from the accident. I'm glad it passed so quickly. Her mother warned her to not to do too much, yet. She suggested she keep still for another day or two.

Alex's parents stayed until 8:30, and then were off to their cockroach-infested motel. After closing the door, Wellsy said, "They don't like me much, do they!" Alexandria walked behind him, but her arms around his shoulders, and offered a conciliatory hug and suggested that they just didn't know him, yet. She asked him to be patient. He twisted around and looked up into her hazel eyes. "I hope you are right. I will try." He then added, "I have never had a more wonderful meal than I did tonight. Do you know how to make your mom's dumplings?"

"I taught her how to make that meal, actually." She turned away from him and walked away. He asked where she was going. She tossed a comment over her back, "I'll be right back. I want to show you something that needs immediate attention." He cocked his head, just like George Clooney does about twenty-five times in every movie, or every TV, ER rerun show he ever made. She noted the look—the craned neck—and went around the corner of the hallway and turned down the hall. Waiting, he snatched up the newspaper that rested upon the coffee table. The headlines pissed him off. Angle Killer Foils Police, Again! The subheading offered, Police/Wellington Have No Clue! At first he was pissed, and then he realized, the paper had it all correct. He tossed the paper down in disgust. He was feeling depressed again. It wouldn't last.

"Hey," was all she said. She stood eight feet in front of him, in a golden negligee that that left nothing to the imagination. "You owe me. It's time to pay up, big boy." She took one side of the dressing gown and parted it just past her right nipple. "Interested?"

He was up and out of his seat in a flash. He made three quick strides and scooped her up and carried her to the threshold of happiness. "Hey, slow down Big Guy, remember you owe me big time, this is gonna take you a long time, so save that energy."

An hour and forty-seven minutes later she said he had accomplished her mission with style. Somewhere, angels were singing, *hallelujah*. She laughed, "Did you hear them, too." He didn't answer. They took a shower together, and cuddled for a half hour. She was thinking how wonderful it was. He was wondering what to do about AK! There just didn't seem anywhere to go with the whole matter! *I need a break, I truly do*; he whispered to his mind.

CHAPTER 34—THE TWENTY-SEVENTH DAY
THE QUESTION

He woke up. He was lying on his stomach. His right arm reached across the bed. He was pleased that his hand was still cupping her right breast as she lie on her back. Her nipple poked through the separation between his index finger and middle finger. He raised his hand up and brought his fingers and thumb together and lightly squeezed his prize. She didn't mind. She moved just enough to let him know that she was awake. He felt it harden a bit.

"Hay," he said. She made an audible noise just so he would know she heard him. "I need to ask you something. He heard another noise. He asked if she was awake enough to talk to him. She mumbled something that he accepted as a yes. "Good," he said, put on a robe or something." She wanted to know why. He told her that he wanted to talk to her but if he saw her, well, if her saw her nude, it would change everything, and then he would be dog tired, again. She laughed and rolled away. His hand, his fingers felt lonesome, immediately.

He rolled off the other side of the bed and put on his silk pajama bottoms. Shall I order up some food or do you want to go out to eat. She asked the time. He had no clue. I think it is afternoon isn't it? She told him no, that he was on the west coast, it was only ten in the morning or something. "Well, then, I'll order up breakfast for you and lunch for me." Again she mumbled something that he took for an okay.

He called and placed an order. He then suggested they sit at the small round table next to the expansive window opening. She did. He opened the curtains. Light shattered the subdued room. It was a beautiful day. He looked out over the city from their presidential suite. He scratched himself, by habit. It made her smile. "Want me to help?" He didn't get it. He asked, her, what? She just smiled and said, "Sit down, big guy."

It started as small talk. Each expressed their fun, their enjoyment, the engaging dialogue, sex, all of it! But, he had to know, so he asked her up front. She smiled, and replied, "I have to admit, last night, and again earlier this morning, you were with Constance, me! It was not Kristina!"

"I didn't think so, or perhaps I should say I hoped not."

"No! It was all me!" He paused. He wanted to respond, but he couldn't, as he was so unsure of himself. "Max, I suspect there is something on your mind, please, just come out with it and say it. Get it over with; I'm a big girl. *I hope*, she thought, *don't dump me, now*!

He reached out for her hand, and she accepted it. He placed his other hand on top. He sputtered, and stammered, he he'd and haw'd, but finally got it out. "Look, you know I said I was going to the Islands, you know, Hawaii and such. Well, I could still go there, or anywhere, St. Lucia, New Zealand, Australia, Tahiti, anywhere, but the thing is, I don't want to go now. Well," he continued, "that isn't exactly right." He paused again, broke his hands from hers and stood up. He paced back and forth, cleared his throat, and tried to prepare himself for rejection. "The thing is, it doesn't matter where I go. I want you to go, too."

She wasn't shocked at all. She smiled at him. He couldn't figure out her smile, what was that smile saying? She wasn't talking. He was nervous. So, he tried another feeble attempt, "Look, I know you are a working woman, I know what you have to do, but I have money, lots of it. I don't know how much money you make, but I will pay you for your time and all your expenses, just come with me. Please?"

"No" she offered without even thinking about it!

His heart fell, sunk to the bottom. He started to speak, but she shushed him and put her index finger to his lips. "Don't talk; just listen, okay?" He nodded. She told him that she could not do that, that it just wasn't possible. "Too many complications," she offered. He wanted to ask why, but he knew why. He opened his mouth, but nothing came out. "So," she continued, "lets say we were gone a week, two weeks, a month, and then what. You would tire of this hooker."

"But…"

"No, no butts shush." Constance would never put up with being shelved for a week or a month, and that would be wrong for me, me Constance." She studied his eyes, and then continued. "And, if you were with Katrina our magic would not be there. Remember, Katrina is a hooked, high class, yes, but a hooker all the same, and you would tire of her, and want another, because she could never give you anything except organisms, and while that might be delightful, you would soon tire of it. So, no, I will not go that way. Sorry!"

"Is there a way you would go?" She nodded yes, but said not a word. "Would Constance come with me?"

"She would want to, but she cannot afford to go, and she would soon tired of being the kept woman if you picked up the tab."

He hated the fact that she was so sensible. She made too much sense and it was driving him crazy. He felt doomed. His hand slid off her hand, and as it did he touched something and sudden enlightenment struck him. He said, "Do me a favor. Stay right here, I will be right back, okay? Promise not to move."

"May I take a shower?"

"Yes, you can do that; I'll be right back. Whatever you do, don't leave! Promise me that!" She nodded, smiling at him, actually, loving him.

"Okay, but if you are leaving you should wear more than your pajama bottoms." They laughed together. He quickly dressed and left. Just over a half hour he returned. She had just stepped out of the shower. He opened the bathroom door; she was naked except for the towel that was wrapped up in her hair. He grabber her hand and led the nude woman to the little round table, again. He seated her.

"What are you doing, let me get dressed, I feel a bit conspicuous."

He stood up, and removed all his clothing, and then ran to the bathroom. He turned on the water and stuck his head under the sink and got his hair all wet. He took a second towel and rubbed away most of the water and then wrapped the towel about his own head, and raced back to the little table and sat down. "No need to feel conspicuous now, we're even." She smiled as she saw water trickle down his face.

"Okay, he said. "I have some questions I'd like to ask, and I only want to talk to Constance, okay? I mean, tell Kristina to go away; I just Constance here, okay?" She bobbed her head in agreement. *What are you doing Max?* "Okay, this is going to sound silly, but forget what it sounds like, okay; just stay with the conversation, okay?" Again, she bobbed, puzzled, but bobbed, anyway. "Okay," he said, and then let out a deep breath. "Okay, question number one." He cleared his throat. "Do people get engaged and then not marry?"

"Why do you ask that, yes, of course people get engaged and don't get married?"

"Please, Constance, just answer the questions and don't editorialize, okay?" He got the bobbing head, again. "Okay, why do the get engaged then?"

"Well, it gives them time to think about their life together, to make sure it will work out, to plan for the future, etcetera, etcetera, I guess. Is that what you are looking for?"

"Only if that is your true answer."

"I assure you it is!"

"Good." He let out a deep engaging breath. "Now another strange question. If a guy asked you to marry him and you thought there was a good possibility that things could work out, would you say yes?"

"That's a loaded question, Max. I'm not sure!"

"Okay, that's a fair answer, totally acceptable." He thought for a moment. He couldn't come up with anything more, so he bent over and grabbed the trousers he had taken off. He stood and turned his back to her as he fumbled with his pants. She smiled; she liked his little touché, each cheek of his buttock had such a cute little dimple in it! He turned back and sat at the table with his hands under the table. "Okay, I'm almost done," he said. He leaned into her and asked, "Is love blind." She shrugged her shoulders; she was never quite sure what that saying meant. She shrugged again. "Well, I think it is. I think it just happens, you know, love."

"Yes, I would agree with that. One never knows where or where or how it happens, it just does; right?"

"That's how I feel, too, Constance. I mean, you could know someone your whole life and never have had any really strong feelings about that person, and then all of a sudden, wham, bingo, you are just heads over heels in love with that person and your whole world changes, right?" She nodded and verbally agreed. "Or," he continued, "you could meet someone and bam, love hits you right in the kisser from the very first 'hello,' and bingo, you're head over heels in love, and it can happen immediately that way, can't it." Again, she nodded, though he wasn't expecting any answer. So, he smiled at her and went on, "That's right Constance, one never knows about love, I mean no one really does know, not really, anyways. Do you agree with all that?"

She didn't answer, just bobbed her head, and then added, "But sometimes it happens to just one of the two and then both are hurt, because it is a lopsided relationship." He hated that answer, but he pressed forward, anyway. He had nothing to lose. So, he nodded as she had already done several times.

He threw all caution to the wind. "Okay, just one more question, okay?" He got the bobbing head, again. He didn't have a clue as to how to get there, so he just freelanced it, "Constance, I really do want you to come with me to the Islands or to Jamaica, or Cancun, or Alaska, or Switzerland, or anywhere for that matter, and I want that more than life itself. I would give up anything on earth for that. I truly mean that, anything at all, and I know you said you would not go with me because of the money situation, but I do know one way that would make it possible." His mouth went dry. He could scarcely breath. She saw the perspiration sliding down his brow, his nose, and even his cheeks.

"Look, Max…"

"Not now, please!" He took courage, and brought his shaking hands up above the table. He held a small box in his hand. She knew. She started to say something. She shook her head. He fumbled with the box in opening it, but it opened and the ring fell helplessly to the table. He scooped it up. "I will marry you Constance if you will marry me back." Those were hardly the words he wanted to say, but that is what spilled out! He was trembling with anticipation. He sat there looking at her. She sat looking at this wonderful man, but, what to say or what to do. "Darling, we can take a vacation as a couple, and as a man I would be honored to give you this vacation to get to know me, us. I am not buying or bribing you, I'm asking you to be my wife, and we can go on a trip to learn of each other, to feed our love. I love you so, I…"

She put her finger to his lips. He was silent. She just peered into his eyes. She was looking for truth in the deepest part of his soul. Was it lust or was it love she felt, she did not know! She loved everything about him, but knew so little of him. She just gazed at this humble man across the table. She bowed her head into her open palms and let her fingers slide and rise up to and past her hairline as her face sunk into the palms of her hands. Her eyes penetrated the tabletop, as if it could tell her what to say, or what to do. She slid her fingers and palms up and past the top of her head and her palms ultimately rested over her ears with the support being held by her elbows grinding into the tabletop.

"Constance…"

She said, "No! Just be quiet for a moment, Max." She raised her head up, allowing the face of her hands to rest along each side of his face. She gazed into his eyes. He gazed back. "Will you ever hit me?" His head shook no! "Will you love me when I am fat and sassy and pregnant and ornery as a hoot owl, and when I'm in my eight month of pregnancy carrying your child?"

He smiled, a tear fell, while he shook his head, yes, while he said, "I will love you for all of your life and beyond the grave most eternal one, and love of my life."

"Will you love me more than you love yourself?"

"I already do."

"Will you promise me that from this day forward, your penis will never be inside any woman other than me?"

"I swear and oath before God!"

"Max, or dear Max, we do not even know each others last name!"

"Does that matter?" She shook her head, no! "Good woman, will you be my wife? I pledge my life to you, and I pledge I will do whatever it is that that you ask of me. As God is my witness, I so pledge."

She smiled. Can I trust that most mornings—even when I'm sixty years old—that I will wake up in the morning and your hand will still be resting, or caressing my breast?"

He smiled, and said, "Yes, if it hasn't shrunk to nothingness."

She smiled back, and said, "Yes, Max, I will marry you, and I will let you take me around the world if you want to, or you can just stay here with me now and make love to me until our bodies give in to exhaustion and we expire, together."

"What a way to go. I pick that way." They laughed together. The ring didn't fit her finger it was a size and a half too large. "I can get that…" She hushed him again, and suggested that he not worry about it. She told him to scoop her up and take her to bed one more time. "Gads, what a man has to go though, just to get engaged." "How about St. Lucia," he suggested.

"Why there? Heck, I don't even know where there, is!"

"Oh, I don't know, it's an exotic place, and a few years back there was a Serial Killer. His name was Trumpet, I think, yes, Darryl Trumpet. Anyway, he took his new wife there. I don't know. It just seems fitting to me, somehow. It's supposed to be a wonderful place.

"Okay, then St. Lucia it is, but I don't have a passport."

"Details," he said. "We've more important things on our mind, now! Are you ready to be scooped up."

"Ready for that and more!"

CHAPTER 35—THE TWENTY-EIGHTH DAY
SHE FINISHES: NAPOLEON AND WELLINGTON

By the time she woke up, 8:20 a.m., Wellsy had been long gone. She got out of bed and realized she fell fully well, finally! No headache, no stiffness of the neck, she felt she was back to normal. She called the school and told them she would be back to work on Monday. She chatted with the principle for ten minutes. Katharine Macintosh was a great principle in the eyes of Alexandria. She was fair, supportive, and consistent. Though 62, Ruth May was one of those people that one just liked to be around, always upbeat and productive. Quite frankly, Alex found her charming, wholesome, someone to emulate; she tried.

Alex hung up the phone and went to the refrigerator to get some juice. She knew Wellsy would have made some for her, he always did. There were two choices, and one of the two had a sticky note attached to it. The note said, *try the Cranberry juice, it's good for what ails you."* She giggled at his humor, but she felt that she was no longer ailing, so she had the orange juice, instead. Two quick sips right out of the bottle and she went off to the shower.

At 9:00 on the nose she sat down at the computer to hopefully finish the first half of her dual task. She had been stymied by her initial results. She could not find direct lines that would trace this AK Napoleon or Nabulio directly to thee Napoléon. She went back to Schom's book again and found what she needed and decided to trace Napoleon's stepson, Eugene de Beauharnais. It went fine for a long while, but then ran murky deep in scholarly skepticism. *Crap!* The historical line seemed to bleed into total speculation. Cops hate speculation, though they engage in it all the time. Wellsy would put down the work if was totally based on speculation. Unfortunately, several Internet sources did the same.

There was or seemed to be—at least—one account of Eugene de Beauharnais' family members through a Russian line that came to America, that made sense, but, it was still hard luck speculation. She took painstaking time and checked records of immigrants that came though Ellis Island. She found what she was looking for, a name, a family, but she didn't learn anything more about that family once they completed passage into America. She only knew that a small group had—in fact—traveled to American soil. What happed to them thereafter was—at best—a guess! She was stymied.

Alex made the decision to leave it where it was for the time being, and moved into the direction that excited her. Was it possible? Did her Wellsy have an ancestral lineage back to the Duke of Wellington? When they first began dating, she asked a few questions about it, but her Wellsy didn't care to reply. She thought it might be some kind of sore spot with him, so she let it go. He was—however—impressed that she even knew the real name of The Duke of Wellington. Few do! Well, in the United States, anyway. Heck there are throngs that don't even know who the United States President is, currently.

She began her study and almost immediately she ran into significant roadblocks. One source indicated that The Duke of Wellington's real name was Arthur Wellesley, whose father was Garret Wellesley, the 1ˢᵗ Earl of Mornington; so far, so good. A second source, however, indicated that the Duke of Wellington's father's name was spelled, Wesley. And accordingly, Garrett Wesley, the 1ˢᵗ Earl of Mornington had a son born to him whom he named Arthur Wesley, who would later become The Duke of Wellington. A third source, *good grief*, she thought, muddied the waters even more by indicating that Arthur's last name was originally Wesley, but supposedly, later, the last name changed from that to Wellesley. Furthermore, Wesley, or Wellesley (whichever is correct) was either born in Dublin, or County Meath. No one seems to know or have the real facts in the matter. She cursed!

How on earth can I follow his family line with such questionable beginnings? The only thing she knew for sure was that Wellington's father's name was Garret Wesley, or not! *How confusing is that,* she asked Jeeves on the web. Two and a half hours later, she was forced to give up, but there was a much shorter distance to her theory, anyway. She would have to get past the veneer of her Wellsy, and ask him. She devised a plan to do just that! And because she had a workable plan, Alex was no longer frustrated. If she got the truth out of him one way or the other, well then she could disclose her theory, and, if she was wrong, well, then, she could disclose her failure theory! She was nervous and excited with the prospect of him coming home.

Wellsy came home exhausted. It had been a busy day. He laid it all out to her, sharing with her all the business with the key women, that, that part was working out, satisfactory. He was assured they were fully protected, save from AK. He told her that he was exhausted, though. She asked when he'd know more. He shrugged his shoulders and then asked what smelled so go. "Lasagna yaw big lug; your favorite," she offered. He smiled. She realized she had been had. "Are you ready to eat? He was.

They ate pretty much in silence. As they were clearing the dishes, together, she told him that she had a serious question for him, and that he needed to bring along his patience. He willingly agreed. Tonight wasn't any night to have conflict. There was too much going on with the case and he didn't need any unwanted or unneeded tension.

"Well," Alexandria began. "I think I have something that is crucial, and I think I can basically prove it. If I'm right it will certainly add new intrigue to this whole AK case." He assured her that he was always interested in her theories. She reminded him that she needed a lot of patience from him, and to trust her. He promised! "Now," she said, "We need to begin with your patience, so control your emotions." His lips tightened, but he promised. "On more than one occasion during our relationship I've asked you if you were a descendent of the Duke of Wellington…"

He offered a huge sigh, "You're not really going to go into this, again, are you, Alexandria? How many times have you started up with this and…"

"Please, Arthur, bare with me, please. I'm serious; this could really help you tie up this case if I'm right. Honey, I promise I'm asking for pure investigation purposes on this case, and if I am right, your genealogy is paramount to the case. If I am wrong, well, then we are no further off the mark then we are at this very second. Please, give me that, at least." She then added, "Please have patience with me, please!" He asked exactly what she wanted from him. And, again, she made it clear that she needed to know if he was or was not directly related to the Duke of Wellington."

"I don't know for sure. Are you sure this is important?"

"Deadly, sure, Arthur, five young women are no longer alive, and one man who will never ever be even a shadow of who he was, Lieutenant."

"Don't remind me," He offered, "Okay, but you'll probably still have more work ahead of you, but I will—do the best of my ability—give to you what you want, or more importantly, what you need. Arthur, I need you to totally trust me and the work I've done!" She paused, briefly and stated, "I don't want you to give me anything, just tell me if you are or are not directly related by birth to the Duke…"

He interrupted, "I know, Duke of Wellington. It's not that easy! I have issues."

"Why? Never mind just put those issues aside for a few minutes." He said, "Hold on," to give him ten minutes, he needed to go into the attic. "The attic," she posed back to him? He told her to just wait; that he might be able to help her! He left. She was confused. She heard him in the hallway making odd noises. Arthur pulled the rope cord down which—in turn—brought down the fold up ladder that went into the attic. He unfolded the bottom piece and gently placed it on the floor. He dashed into the bathroom, and removed a towel and folded it in half and placed it under each leg of the ladder, so his weight on the ladder would not scratch the hardwood floor. He climbed up, and pulled the string that hung down almost to the floor of the attic. The light was out, so down the ladder he came to retrieve a flashlight and get a replacement bulb.

"Do you need help?" he heard her ask from the dining room.

"No!" he shouted, "I'm doing fine; it just that nothing ever seems to go easy in life."

"Poor Arthur," she said, and then wished she hadn't.

He didn't hear her. He offered, "Give me another two minutes." After accomplishing his task he saw the dust covered suitcase lying on its side. It was very old, dirty and extremely dusty. He picked it up, eased down the folding stairs, and toted it to the living room. On his way to the dining room he grabbed the newspaper and handed it to Alex and asked her to spread the pages over the table to collect the dust and yucky stuff, whatever. After she accomplished the task, he put the suitcase in front of her with the latches in front of her.

"What is inside of here?"

"Alex, I've never looked inside this suitcase. I have been told that in this suitcase are many family historical records, and many family secrets." *Secrets*, she thought. "The reason I've never looked inside is that I've been scared what I might find with regard to whatever family secrets there are. I'm not one much for skeletons in the closet, or attic in this case. Alex, this is something that I've never wanted to know anything about. I've always assumed that family secrets are secrets because they are bad, and not good. I hope you can understand that, because I'm not sure I do. Anyway, I know that this suitcase was last in the hands of my great-grandfather Angus Arthur Wellesley, whom—I guess—I'm named after, to a degree, I guess, or at least in part. I don't really know for sure. I have never looked inside the case, nor have I ever even opened it up. If you want to snoop, okay, but I'm not sure I want to know, okay?"

She simply said, "Okay," back to him. Nevertheless it baffled her that he, anyone wouldn't want to know about their family.

"I'm going to my den, Alex and ponder where I am in this case. I'm sure I will turn in early, so, if you find or don't find what you are looking for, it can wait until the morning. He turned and walked away to put the ladder back, and spend time in his den. In a strange way, she understood his point of view, but could not imagine him not having a more overriding desire to know truth. He *was* a *cop*, after all! Therefore, she was hesitant what might be inside, what secret or secrets that she mind find that she could never tell him, or be able to tell him, but would have to keep hidden in her heart. She nearly decided against the whole idea, *curiosity killing the cat and all that!* Her apprehension—at least—helped her to understand his apprehension.

On the other hand, she was excited, after all, how many opportunities are there in life like this one? To Alex, it seemed more like a treasure hunt and she and Wellsy had discovered the treasure chest at the bottom of the ocean—or— in this case, at the top of the mountain, up in the attack. Just two clicks away was the revealing of his family treasures, regardless what was in it! *What is inside?* "Truth," she mumbled back to her thought. She unsnapped the metal holders that secured the valuable contents inside.

With the case unfastened, she took a deep breath, and lifted up the lid slowly. She stopped. She thought? *Should I intrude?* She felt she was part of his family, so it was okay to intrude! "Here goes," she mumbled and opened it up, slowly. There appeared to be but one document inside, a large and very thick book, a *Bible*. She ran to the kitchen and put on the rubber gloves that she used to wash the dishes and to clean the oven with, and other such sundry jobs. She then returned to her task just as fast. Carefully, she took out the very old book and laid it flat on its side. She then removed the suitcase to the floor and put the book in front of her. In Olde English letters it announced, *Holy Bible*. Alex carefully opened the cover. It made a slight crunchy noise. To the left of the title page someone had written: Wellesley Family in what looked like a quilted pen on the inside cover page at the very top. *Wellesley, well there's a positive start*, Alexandra, thought.

Lying on top of the first page of text, the next page, she noted that there were several other papers that had been stuffed between the inside front cover and the first page of the bible text. Alex carefully picked up the papers and for the moment she put them aside. Under the stack of papers she had removed there was much to read, and at quick glance, she noted that two different hands had written that which was left for her—or someone—to read. Alexandria was very excited and nervous at the same time. She was in awe of the date that preceded the first hand written message:

Alex read; 'I am Lady Elizabeth Wellesley, born in the year 1918, December 26th. I am the daughter of Gerald Wellesley, the 7th Duke of Wellington (1769-1852) and Dorothy Violet Ashton his wife. I am pleased to say that I am the great, great granddaughter of Arthur Wellesley, the 1st Duke of Wellington.'

"Holy cow," slipped by Alexandria's lips," *I don't believe this; this is from the hand of the Duke of Wellington's great-great granddaughter, and it is in the home of Arthur Wellesley. I'm touching it! I'm reading it. She wanted to fly to the den and tell Wellsy. Instead, she continued her reading of the words of Lady Elizabeth Wellesley.* Alex continued to read Wellesley's words.

'That is my (our) royal heritage. His—the 1st Duke of Wellington—actual and full title was Field Marshal His Grace The Most Noble Arthur Wellesley, Duke of Wellington, Marques of Wellington, Marques Douro, Earl of Wellington, Viscount Wellington of Talavera and of Wellington, Baron Douro of Wellesley, Prince of Waterloo, Duke of Brunoy, Duke of Vittoria, Marquis of Torres Vedras, Count of Vimiero, Duke of Ciudad Rodrigo, Grandee of the First Class, Knight of the Garter, Knight of St Patrick, Knight Grand Cross of the Bath, Knight of the Golden Fleece, Knight Grand Cross of Hanover, Knight of the Sword of Sweden, Knight of the Annunciado of Sardinia, Knight of St Andrew of Russia, Knight of St George of Russia, Knight of Maria Teresa, Knight of the Crown of Rue Saxony, Knight of St Hermenegilda of Spain, Knight of the Red Eagle of Brandenburg, Knight of the Golden Lion of Hesse-Kassel, Lord of the Privy Council.'

"Holy cow," she muttered at letter's end.

Alex's concentration was interrupted when she noticed that Wellsy had entered the room. He kissed her, and told her that he loved her. He suggested she not stay up to late, and reminded her of her recent accident, that rest was required for full recovery. He, then, again said that he loved her, and then quietly removed himself from the room, without looking at the papers or the Bible that had been removed from the suitcase. She watched him walk out of the room. She wanted to get back to reading, and studying, but she couldn't help but focus upon the forlorn look on his face. His stress level was at its maximum. She worried for him.

She sat quietly worrying and then praying for her significant other, Arthur! After the prayer, she arose and went to the kitchen for a cup of instant hot chocolate. Returning from the kitchen, she looked in on Arthur; he was fast asleep, already. She was pleased, so she with hot chocolate in hand returned to the den to complete her study. She found her spot and continued.

'I record this to remind our family of his greatness—the Duke of

Wellington's Greatness—of which we are all a part. I wish to make a small list of just some of the things he accomplished. In 1805 he was knighted. In 1806 he married Katherine Pakenham. In 1807 he was the Irish Secretary. In 1809 he took charge of the British, Portuguese and Spanish forces in the Peninsular War. In 1814 Napoleon abdicated, and Great-Great Grandfather was made the Duke of Wellington. In 1823 he was made the Prime Minister. He did other great things as well. He was mentor to Queen Victoria and late in life; he was the Commander in Chief of the Army. We are all proud of him and his example! And, such are we Wellington's made of. My Great-great Grandfather, Wellington's son Arthur Richard Wellesley (1907-1884) was the 2ⁿᵈ Duke of Wellington in 1852. His son, Henry, (1846-1900) the grandson of the first Duke of Wellington became the 3ʳᵈ Duke of Wellington. His brother, Arthur Charles, (1849-1834) an English Soldier became the 4ᵗʰ Duke of Wellington, and his son, by the same name, Arthur Charles (1876-1941) became the 5ᵗʰ Duke of Wellington. Henry Valerian George Wellesley, (1912-1943) becane the 6th Duke of Wellington, was the son of Arthur Charles Wellesley, the 5th Duke of Wellington He married Kathleen Emily Burkeley Williams. Arthur Charles, the brother of Henry, (the grandson of the first Duke of Wellington and also the 3ʳᵈ Duke of Wellington), (1885-1972) is my father and he is the 7ᵗʰ Duke of Wellington.'

Alex got bit confused regarding the fifth and sixth Dukes. No matter it was all there. Whew! Alex sat back in awe. She was mesmerized. She could not believe what she was looking at, or what she had just read. This was real historical stuff that probably belonged in some museum archive or someplace. She gathered her wits and read the words of the next and last writer.

2/18/60. My mother gave this Bible to me and asked me to finish her writing. I don't have much to say. Arthur Valerian Wellesley is part of my family and is the 8ᵗʰ Duke of Wellington, today, as I write this completion. He was born in 1915. I don't know much about him, though, but I'm sure his history is recorded, somewhere in some encyclopedia, or in some assessorial book kept by the Wellesley line. I have no more to say! I gave this book to my Aunt for her keeping. If she gives it to someone else, I haven't any more obligations to this task. I'm sure it will be important to someone, somewhere, somehow. I now take my leave. R.C.

P.S. I am pleased to be a Wellington! God bless all those of the Wellesley family line! I added this line the day I gave this to my Aunt. 3/19/62.

Alex had no idea who R.C. was, so—for the time being—she ignored this writer's initials. Notwithstanding the identity of this unknown person, she didn't really need much more. She had all that she needed. It didn't matter why Arthur didn't want to talk about it. The fact that this Bible and a written family history were in Arthur's home was proof enough for her. The pile of additional papers was, however, worth looking though.

One paper, actually a photograph caught here eye, and it offered fuel to her thesis. It was a photo that she had seen before in one of the books she read. It flashed back to her, now, "Napoleon & Wellington, subtitled, The Battle of Waterloo and the Great Commanders Who Fought It," by Andrew Roberts. The photograph was a photo of a statue of Napoleon Bonaparte. The significance of the photograph was not so much in the artwork, but where the statue was situated, or rested. For the Wellington family, the statue was a trophy as indicated by author, Roberts. According to the description under the photo of Napoleon's statue, in Robert's book, page 160 the statue rests in the stairwell of Wellington's London home, Apsley House. The statue was a gift from "A Grateful Nation," in 1916 to the Duke of Wellington. It was, is still, a true prize to the victor over Napoleon at Waterloo, i.e. the Duke of Wellington.

Alexandria fueled her own thoughts as well. This statue of the great Napoleon resting in the home of Wellington is the greatest slap in the face to any admirer of Napoleon, or worse yet to any descendent of Napoleon? Indeed, she thought, perhaps to the AK, if my theory is correct. Would that photo fuel greater hatred, to the point of retaliation against Wellington, himself, or in this time, his decedent; "of course it would, or could," she said aloud. She was trying to decide if all this truly made sense or was she merely grasping at straws for the sake of her own Wellington.

Ultimately, she decided it made perfect sense. So, she practiced her sentence she would offer to her Wellington! "Arthur seeing how you are Arthur Wellington, or Wellesley, and are a direct and literal descendent of the 1st Duke of Wellington, or, more specifically, to Arthur Wellesley, doesn't it make sense that in the mind of an unbalanced ancestor of Napoleon, that you could be at risk as per retaliation?" She knew he would have to admit he was, and once that was confirmed she could offer the fullness of her theory!

She looked at her watch; it was well over an hour and a half since he'd come to wish her good night and then kissed her, offered a warm hug, and then went to bed. On his short visit, he had ignored all that she was doing. He had just come and gone. She looked at her watch. It was five of midnight. This would have to wait. She used the facilities, and crawled into bed beside him. She was restless, wrestling within herself. After five minutes the man resting beside her, said, "Well!" Not three seconds passed and she had the lights on.

She forgot her plan and just blurted it out, "Honey will you admit that you are related to the Duke of Wellington."

"You know that I am."

"I thank you for that." She took a deep cleansing breath and let it fly, "I haven't all the proof, but I'm reasonably sure that the AK is a direct descendent or perhaps he might be an adopted descendent through Napoléon Bonaparte's second marriage."

"And, if this is true, how does this relate to our Serial Killer?" he asked back.

"Oh, Arthur, that is an interesting statement, or question, and I'm not so sure you'll accept this very well, but I do not believe he is a Serial Killer, but rather, he is faking it to get to you."

"Me?"

"Yes, you," she touted.

"And why would that be? After all, he follows the line of Serial Killers, doesn't he?"

She ignored the second part of his question and answered the first, "Because of his quotes, and because of his anger against you, and more specifically, the Duke of Wellington which is how he sees you! He is getting back at the original Wellington through you. That's why! It is all because of what Wellington did to Napoleon."

"Could you go more into detail?"

"Yes, but wait, I have something to show you." She retrieved the Bible and laid it on the bed. She withdrew the photograph of Napoleon, his statue. Do you know what that is?"

"I've seen it before, yes!"

"Do you know what it stands for?"

"The statue itself or what the statue stands for," Wellsy asked?

"Well I guess that could be answered from two different perspectives." She offered.

"Well, love, what do you think it stands for if our AK killer is playing my game?"

"Your game?" she asked.

"Well, no, not exactly my game, but my position, you know, what you are leading up to in all this, I suppose!"

"You are correct." She affirmed.

"Then I would guess that the family sees this statue as a constant reminder that Wellington defeated Napoleon, and that this statue rubs it in the face of all relatives that are still alive and connected some how with this man, Napoleon Bonaparte!"

"Yes, but do you know where this statue of Napoleon rests, now!"

"Actually, I do know. It is in the possession of the Wellington family in England!"

"And, what might that mean to a zealot who believes that Napoleon is his forefather?"

"I suspect he would be rather mean spirited about it?"

"Mean spirited, you say? That is awfully polite, how about the fact that he might be exercised, how about un-rational, or how about beside himself so much so that he pretends to be a Serial Killer, and that murder after murder he's tossing it all in Wellington's face—your face—does that make sense?'

"You mean my face, right?

"Right, that's what I just said, Wellington! Right! Now you're seeing it!"

Arthur was quite and reflective for some moments. "So, according to you, our AK is killing only to thwart the works of me?"

She sighed; "Yes, something like that, but more so to embarrass you, and ultimately to destroy you!"

"Like he did to the last woman, Labella L. Litchfield, is that what you're suggesting?"

"Exactly, yes, you've got it Wellington, exactly!" She started to tear up as she indicated that she had not actually seen what he had done to Litchfield woman. "He kills them so he can talk to you. He kills them, and does his best to make you feel that you are at fault"

"He not far wrong in accomplishing that task; is he?"

He didn't exactly answer her, but he offered, "I know that, and that it will get worse, not better, until…"

"Until," she mustered up all her courage to say it, "he kills the Wellington in his life, and reigns superior over him, the total victor!" With that she fell apart and fell to his arms, exhausted, and scared to death.

CHAPTER 36—THE TWENTY-NINTH DAY
THE NEW BEGINNING

She told him a lie. Of course that was no way to start a honeymoon, but she did it anyway, but with good intentions on her own behalf. Her lie was simple. She merely said, "It's done, and I'm done!" Just like that. The inference—of course—was that she had quit her high class hooking job, when—in fact—she had merely told Escudo Savants, her Manager at the escort service that she was going to take a long, overdo extended vacation, immediately, because she needed it, but more importantly, she had a yeast infection. How could that be argued?

Constance still had every intension of marrying Max, to be sure, but—but what if—kept creeping in and ringing in her ears. What if it just didn't work out between them? After all, she only knew him for two and a half days; hardly long enough to walk away from the best paying job for any women on the planet for a working girl. Did she really want to start all over, again if she and Max didn't work out? *No!* It was that simple. However, right now—this very minute—all her energy was on making this engagement and ensuing marriage work! And—quite honestly—the sex was really something, and while sex isn't enough to build a romance around, it was way ahead of anything else she could think of at the present. Perhaps it was because sex had been a thoughtless job, and now, well now, wow, it was just plain wow, and wow was enough!

Max suggested they hang around San Francisco for a couple of days, to allow her time to adjust to the whole idea and to get her affairs in order before the long trip. She countered by suggesting they fly to his home on the East coast. She wanted to see his luxury home, and his life style, and furthermore, they needed to decide which coast they wanted to live on. He said that was a great idea, but deep inside, he knew he wouldn't live anywhere but on the Atlantic side of things. However, on this the twenty-ninth evening after his first killings of

Carolyn Ann Nowicki, and Jessica June Andersen he was prepared to bring home a woman that he found love in. She was perfect in every way.

At 7:22 p.m. they boarded a Northwest Airline jet that would take them non-stop to Detroit. After a one-hour and twenty-two minute stay in the Motor City, they took the hop to Norfolk, Virginia, and then taxied to his mansion on the Atlantic. They arrived at 6:02 a.m. She was exhausted by the trip, even though she did sleep on and off for about four hours. Nevertheless, she was overjoyed with his digs when they arrived. However, she quickly let him hastily know that his home desperately needed a woman's touch. "And," she said laughing, "we need furniture. "You have a mansion, and a few scattered pieces of furniture. This house is missing, everything." He said fine, that they would take care of that tomorrow, or later today even. They decided on tomorrow.

So, he said, "Tomorrow, we'll go to the bank, get you an immediate checking account and a credit card and send you off to buy furniture and whatever."

"Are you going to put a limit on my spending," she asked, somewhat timidly.

"You can bet your butt I will."

"Hmm, Okay, how much" she paused! "I mean, what's the catch?"

"Only one," he said, "We need a bigger bed." He then added, "A queen size is fine for me, but we need a king-size for us!" He then added, and I like those vibrating ones, too, like at our hotel in Frisco."

"Why," she laughed, "Why such a big bed, are you going to run from me?"

"Never run, but I've watched you in bed. You get around, lady. You do get around. With all your flinging, flailing and such, you could hurt the two of us in a small bed."

She chuckled at his silliness, and kissed him. She then asked, "What can I buy, just furniture, or furnishings too, I mean what is the spending limit, and what is the limit on how much decorating and designing I can do?

"It is my home, but it soon will be our home." He thought for a moment. "Well, lets see, I don't really want you to go hog wild. But I do want a nice home that is properly furnished, and certainly I want it to have a women's touch, and the entire trimming, except—of course—my den, which is across this room, down the hall and then its the third door on the right, oops, the left. Well, Constance, other than that, I think I should leave all the rest up to you, but lets say that I want you to call me if the furniture, trimmings and all that stuff go over a half million, okay?" He added, "Is that okay with you?" She could barely catch her breath. She uttered some sound that he took for an okay!

In her head, she restated, *half a million dollars;* Good *heavens, how much money does he have.* "We can afford that much?" He only bobbed his head in the affirmative.

Every second that passed made her realize just how much she liked this guy. She liked him a lot. He was so real, so honest, so handsome, and hey, he had mega bucks too. She wondered how much. It was too early to find out.

"Hey, he asked, can you cook?"

She, laughed, "Yes!"

"I'm hungry, but I'm also dead tired. Can we take like a four hour nap and then get up and face the day."

She laughed, "The day is here, already, max, "but, yes let's get some sleep, but not before…"

"Right, not before!"

"Where is that room?"

"Just follow me." He was starting to point the way, already!

CHAPTER 37—THE FORTIETH DAY AFTER THE FIRST KILLINGS
CONSIDERATION

Silence is golden, sometimes, and sometimes it can drive one completely nuts. Wellsy, certainly didn't want the AK to strike—to kill—again. That went without question. On the other hand, so much time had expired since his last rampage; 24 days in all. And, what was happening? Nothing! That was what was happening! The case was stymied, except for the team. Two days after Wellsy had had the conversation with Alex, regarding him being a true Wellesley, and a direct line to the Wellesley legend—The Duke of Wellington—it took him three full days to buy into it, totally. Nevertheless; he did, indeed, accept her theory, but only because every other theory went afoul. Perhaps this theory, too, would too die away.

He made an appointment with Captain Herrington, and discussed it, completely. At first, Herrington thought it was a bit silly, but—on the other hand—maybe there was something to it. So, the Captain suggested that Wellsy give him a couple of days to kick it around. Herrington then put his own team on Wellsy theory. They played with it for three consecutive days, after which Captain Herrington called his Commanding Officer Henry D. Rodgers, First Patrol Division, Blue Sector, and then he called the Sector Lieutenant, Wellesley as well as Detective Strange to his office for an exploratory meeting based on the Wellington's fiancée's newest theory.

"My team," Herrington began, "has spent countless hours reading, studying, theorizing, and gathering data of this Napoleon and Wellington thing that the Lieutenant has proposed. We have found and categorized all the quotes that the original Napoleon and/or Wellington have ever made. "Furthermore," he continued, "We have studied the specific quotes he has used in communicating with the police." He stopped, and corrected, himself. "No! He has not actually communicated with the police per say. Rather, he has specifically communicated with our Lieutenant Wellesley. I, we—my team, we've come to the conclusion that the Lieutenant is and his fiancée are 100% accurate." He continued, "In a conversation yesterday with the Lieutenant, he and I hashed this whole thing out. The results of that hashing are why we are all meeting here, today. However, there are two others who will be joining us shortly." He looked at Wellesley, and offered, "Lieutenant?"

"Thank you, I thought it was time that we get a new look at the Angel Killer, "the Lieutenant, began, "Based it on our new found theory, which—by the way—we have decided to take only that angle on the matter, today. And, we will stay the course on this theory until it is disproved otherwise. Our Profiler has restudied our AK based on this new light of theory and information. She is waiting outside with a new report based on what we are now accepting as reality."

"Gentleman, ma'am," he nodded to House from Campus Security, "Rodgers took the floor, again, "We have also invited to this meeting, Ms. Alexandria Mae Southerland, Wellsy's significant other. It was her hard work and her theory that brought this all together as it is now. I personally have met with her and Wellsy, independently, and hashed this out, thoroughly. Her—their—theory is rock solid based on her research, and the combined efforts of my staff, Wellsy and Detective Strange. Before we invite these two women in, and a few others, I want to make this abundantly clear; what we will be discussing is in fact theory, only. However, we feel it is the best we've got to nail this Perp. We do not have any proof beyond that. However, this theory makes more sense than anything else we have studied, or contemplated, or what we've already tried. This is no easy case, people." He looked at Wellsy, "Lieutenant, do you want to add anything else?"

Wellsy offered his concern with regard to the void of the last sixteen days. "We need to explore why this void has happened. Ms. Cowlings will also touch upon this. We ask that you take ample notes, but withhold your questions or comments until Ms. Southerland and Ms. Cowlings have concluding their remarks to us." He paused, slightly, "People, remember that Ms. Southerland may be nervous. She said she feels like she has to report to her principal for some great injustice she has done to one of her students. So, make her feel welcome, please; as you know, she is a civilian, and we appreciate her keen thinking on this case.

"Remember, Ms. Southerland isn't really there to offer a report; though she has a report to give. Actually, she's mostly here for the Q and A. that will follow her report, and then Ms. Cowling's report; nevertheless, Ms. Southerland will—as I say—give a report, nevertheless."

It was the Q and A part that each in the group was excited about getting to, anyways." Beyond Southerland and Cowlings report theory, the group wanted to test it so they could either comfortably ratify it and move forward, or, excuse it and then look for new avenues. Yes, the Q and A was what the meeting was to be all, about. It wasn't that they wanted to stump, Alexandria Mae Southerland, no, she was very much supported by this group, but their (hers and Wellsy's) theory had to be scrutinized, fully.

"Folks, if I might just offer one quick word."

"Yes, go ahead, Lieutenant."

"At the end of Ms. Southerland and Cowling's remarks, I'd like to be the first to ask Ms. Southerland a question. She is going to be very nervous, so I want to ask her a question which she can and will easily answer, just to help her get over her nervousness more easily, if you all don't mind?" There was an agreement made; Wellsy thanked them all in advance; "Okay, then, I'll ask the first question just to break the ice. Thanks."

The women and others, entered, and each of the two women were to give their report. Southerland gave her five minute report. The profiler was to go next, but she chose to defer until Ms. Southerland's questions there taken and answered. Immediately, as planned, Arthur asked Alex, "Thank you for that report, now, I'd like to ask, how you begin all this that started the nucleus for your theory, Ms. Southerland?"

His ploy, worked. It was an easy question for her, so she was comfortable, already. Alex talked about the name game; the reading of several books about the past and the call from *The Gazette*, reporter Robert Thompson, regarding the *Crown and Mace* information. Alex listed all the parts of the puzzle and explained how she built a frame around the perimeter of her thoughts.

There were three easy questions that came in quick in succession, and then Captain Herrington stood and asked, "So, Ms. Southerland, why do you feel that this serial killing is a reflection of your theory. She admitted that she had been waiting for this question because her answer was at the very heart of her theory. That too calmed her as well.

She cleared her throat, and began, "Each of his messages, or at least one of his messages from each crime scene uses the word *battle*. I believe, or rather my theory is that killer has what I would call a dual personality." She stopped for a second to look at the Profiler, wondering if she was going to make a fool out of herself. Ms. Cowlings; instead, offered Alex an approving simile.

Alex cleared her throat, again, and continued. "I don't mean that he sees himself as two different persons, nor do I believe that he takes on a second personality, but rather, he gets so into the *BATTLE*, to the degree that he loses control of his designed plan and goes wild; almost uncontrolled." She paused to let that settle in. "As some point, I believe the war rages within him—the *WELLINGTON WAR*—and he then finds himself with these soldiers—his chosen women—and he butchers them in *RETALIATION* of the *REAL* and *FINAL BATTLE* at Waterloo. He has so prepared himself to every detail that the slightest little thing that takes him out of his controlled element causes him to *JUST GO CRAZY!* He doesn't—in my mind—*CARVE-UP-WOMEN*, Nabulio *CARVES-UP-THE-ENEMY,* whose bodies just happen to be women. I'll come back to this in a few minutes."

"However, I also believe he kills the women that he sees in these soldiers, because they could bare more children, Wellington's, offspring, therefore, they must be destroyed. And he uses these victims to spell out his name; his *OWNDERSHIP!* I believe the spelling out of his name, is nothing more than a game for Wellington," she paused, and looked at the Lieutenant, "You Lieutenant," she continued, "he gives it to you to figure out. I also believe that these killings binds him to Wellesley; his nemesis! Therefore, each killing is more or less an opportunity to talk to Wellington, showing him, demonstrating that he has already started the *WAR*, by the *KILLINGS*, and that Wellington can't do a damn thing about them. I'm certain that the name Nabulio is the killer's nickname as was legendary Napoleon's nickname, Nabulio, given to him by his father." She paused, and took a drink of water.

"I can't help but wonder if our Nabulio of today was told why he has that same name today from his great, great, great grandfather. However, I'm pretty sure that Napoleon is part of his name, too. Either way, he knows that he must be very clever, wise, and most careful. I'm sure he prepares himself for battle, thoroughly. And, while I have not been witness to one of these murder scenes, I've heard enough to feel his brutality, and not just as a woman.

Gentlemen, ma'am, he's spelling out his name because he wants Wellesley to get the message too late. If you are wondering why he does it this way, I believe I can tell you. I've spent several days reviewing the actual WAR that Napoleon had with Wellington, and part of the reason Napoleon lost the war was because either his incoming messages either, did not reach him at all, or they arrived too late to respond to, or, the messages simply got intercepted, or whatever. I believe that all the communication he is leaving for Wellington—today—is to put the shoe on the other foot. His messages arrive all too late for Wellington to do anything about them. This killer wants to make Wellington have communication problems. This could be the very heart of him. He is just plain pissed that his namesake—Napoleon—lost because of bad communication; that he, Napoleon is sending messages to Wellesley after the battle is over, when it is too late for Wellington to respond." That, I believe this at the core; late messages!"

Alex then looked at Wellsy. "I'm sorry to say this, but when Wellington answered back in the newspaper, AK was so furious that he took the war to a whole new level to show Wellington who is winning this battle, this WAR; this war about communications."

Alex wanted to remove that that dagger out Arthur's heart, so she continued with the following: "He would have killed the poor girl anyway, and I'm sure as badly as she suffered, it was no worse than any of the other women he butchered." Butchered is butchered. Either way, the poor woman was going to die, a horrible ugly death!"

She took a deep breath, and continued, "Now, I will add one more thing, and then end." She cleared her throat. "I have not discussed this with the Lieutenant, either. I know that the AK bathed her, too, but I really don't know much more, but I know why he bathed her. I am sure that he had sex with her; first. Of that, I am positive. If I am wrong, then dismiss me without so much as a twinkle of an eye." She looked at each person in the room. Again, the Profiler smiled and nodded approvingly. "May I ask a question?" Wellsy and Herrington both said, yes at the same time. "Was she raped?"

The two men looked at Captain Rodgers. Rodgers acknowledged that she had been raped. He told her the evidence was solid based on numerous vaginal traumas. "Well"—he indicated—that they were about "ninety-five percent sure", so he reaffirmed, "Yes!"

"And none of the others were raped, that is correct, too, isn't it, Captain?" The Captain answered in the affirmative, again. Before she spoke, she turned to Cowlings looking for more support, "Mam, I'm right, aren't I?" Cowlings, for the third time, smiled. She nodded, indicating that Alex was correct.

Alex took a deep breath, and then looked directly into each of the men's eyes, "Gentleman, AK was offering Napoleon's seed within the Wellington camp." She paused to let that sink in. "I believe that he was taking ownership of the Wellesley namesake, symbolically, of course. He only needed to soil one soldier—one woman—because she stood for all the sons and daughters of the battle. He figuratively raped them all, raped them away from Wellington." She continued, "I also know that that is why he previously severed the man's penis and his testicles and stuffed them into the victim's mouth; the man's mouth! I asked myself why would he do that, why was he so upset? I believe it was because one of Wellesley's—in this case, the girl's boyfriend—*man* dared such a thing as to have command over this woman that belonged to him, Napoleon, and to him, alone! By command, I mean, physically, sexually speaking. It's all about ownership, ownership of the battle, and then the war, and then the glory of history that belongs to him, not Wellington, nor Wellesley. That, I believe is what is in his head." She was sweating, nervously, now, but her demeanor was—nevertheless—powerfully bold.

"Sirs, Mam, I am sure that he will kill two more soldier in two more battles, and then he will have you believe that he is done, that he has won, and that he has quit, and that he has walked away, free! But, alas, no, and after you firmly believe that, only then will he again kill, just one more time. And that last time, he will kill in the final battle, that killing ends the war, the rightful rogue, Wellesley! By doing so, in his life, he will reassume—in his mind—the role of Emperor, and his nemesis, The Duke of Wellington will be no more. He will have triumphed, and he will have had Napoleon's Revenge." And, lastly, and you may think I am nuts, but I think that after that…" She paused for affect. "He will never kill, again. He will just simply walk away, and who knows, perhaps he will build a statue of himself, or more likely one of Wellington, and keep that statue—that shrine—that symbol in his home, his shrine; marking this action as Wellington's last defeat!"

Alex immediately sat down, exhausted, and feeling quite faint.

Wellesley nearly stood up, but decided not to. His brain was busy. His mind was chewing Alex's words. He repeated those words over and over in his mind: *the roll of Emperor—he will reassume the roll of Emperor—what is it.* Think! *What is it?* Captain Rodgers, voice, broke his thought process.

"Ms. Southerland," Captain Rodgers, repeated, that was indeed, colorful, and more importantly, scary and I—for one—believe your every word; your thesis. You are a mind boggling woman. I believe you have hit the very motive of this AK on the very nose! Your theory makes total, logical sense. I applaud you!" He paused, "Do you have anything else?"

"No. Oh, wait, yes, yes I do, as a matter of fact I do have something else. I nearly forgot." She stayed seated, and offered, "Captain, I have just two more things. I'll be brief, I promise. First, I'm quite sure that—if not by now, or if not now, then very soon—AK will totally transplant in his mind, Lieutenant Wellesley for the 1st Duke of Wellington, and from that point forward, he will not separate those two individuals as divided individuals, any more than he will separate Napoleon Bonaparte from that of himself. He will, in his final battle of the WAR" she emphasized—*attempt*—attempt to kill his Duke of Wellington, our"—her voice cracked—"our," her voice sputtered, again, "our, Wellington, Lieutenant Wellesley." She collected herself, and wiped away the tears. She then reached into her bag and pulled out a single sheet of paper and unfolded it. Secondly," she said, I would like to read to you what I have written on this paper. First I'll read the banner, and then the quotes. She read:

PROBABLE QUOTES THE ANGLE KILLER WILL USE IN HIS NEXT BATTLE

There are only two forces in the world, the sword and the spirit. *In the long run the sword will always be conquered by the spirit.

*You must not fight too often with one enemy, or you will teach him all your art of war.

*A soldier will fight long and hard for a bit of colored ribbon.

The bayonet has always been the weapon of the brave and the chief tool of victory.

*There are but two powers in the world, the sword and the mind. In the long run the sword is always beaten by the mind.

These, gentlemen are the quotes I believe he will leave behind. Not all of them, of course, but definitely some of them. I have place an asterisk next to the ones I strongly believe he will use, next, and or the next two times. If he is successful in the last two final attempts he will use the last one—the last quote—on the list! The significance is simply this; he will be able to shout to the four corners of the world, 'Napoleon has outsmarted Wellington and his entire army.'" She sat down again, and said, "You need to copy this for those who need it, Captain." She handed the single sheet to Rodgers. Rodgers then asked if there were any questions of Ms. Southerland. The room remained silent, so he turned the remainder of the time over to Profiler, Cowlings.

She began. "I have in my hand a full and complete report, all 286 pages of it. I have a copy for each of you. Wellsy crossed to the table and began to pass a copy to each member, including, Southerland. "I had planned to go over it in detail. That, gentlemen, and lady, are no longer required." She turned to Alex, "Ms. Southerland, you are an amazing woman. As you read my report, you will—no doubt—feel as though you have written it. My professional hat is off to you."

She turned to Wellesley, "I know you are worried about the extended period of time that has elapsed between the last murder and now. I believe he will kill within the next three days. My reasons are in the report, but they will not help you solve this case, Lieutenant"

She paused to let that sink in. "However, based on what your fiancé has shared with us, I fully concur. However, and unfortunately, the dead body of the poor girl whose last name will start with an 'T', will be found like the rest, tortured, and her throat will have been sliced open. I do not believe he will sexually molest her, but don't take that to the bank. Whatever else he might do that is out of the ordinary—for him—will be because something happened that was not planned, or he wants to leave some other message to you, Wellington."

She took a considerable pause, "However, I want to address the last woman he will kill, the one after next. I believe he may kill a woman and a man at that time. The woman's last name will, of course start with the last letter of his name, Nabulio, an 'O' and man's last name will start with a 'N' as in the first letter of Napoleon." She continued, "Ms. Southerland believes that the female will be found headless. I differ, there, I believe the man's body will be found headless! Don't ask me what he will do with the head. I don't know, exactly, but I do believe he will make a public spectacle of it. It will be symbolic of the Napoleonic statue that adorns the Wellington homestead in England. Perhaps when it happens, you will figure it out, Lieutenant."

She looked about the room. "Questions?" There were none, all were busy reading her report, and scribbling in the margins. An exhausted team sat quietly reading.

Alexandria, sat terrified for the life of her Wellsy! She looked straight ahead, but her body was in prayer!

Chapter 38—The Forty-First and Forty-Second Day After the First Killings
PREPARATION

Connie thought it was a good plan. They had stayed at his home longer than had been anticipated, but it was okay with them both. They saw nearly every attraction that the Virginia Beach area offered. She taught him to play golf. They played almost every day. They drove to Kill Devils Hill, Kitty Hawk, North Carolina and discovered flight, or, rather they discovered how Wilbur and Orville discovered flight. They golfed in four South Carolina courses and three North Carolina courses; Pinehurst number three was her favorite.

They played nearly every day. Some days they walked, others, they carted. They just plain loved being together, and golfing was their truest togetherness time, accept—of course—the bedroom, lovebirds that they were. He was a natural according to her. "In golf or in…" He didn't finish, they just laughed, together. In their last round of golf he shot 85, and she 84.

On the day before they left North Carolina, while sitting in a restaurant, waiting for their table, Constance picked up the local newspaper. After reading some it, she asked, "What do you think of AK?"

He told her, "Not much, why?" She shrugged her shoulders, and indicated she didn't know, but she was just reading something about it. He asked to have the paper. She gave the paper to him. The Headline Banner announced, *Trudy Izzo Leaves Virginia Wesleyan Campus!* He read the article. While it was vague, it was obvious that the Norfolk, Virginia Police Department was watching three women from Wesleyan Campus. He wasn't happy with this new news at all. There wasn't much more in the story, so Nabulio decided that had to be far cleverer. Nevertheless he still needed a "I" girl. *Damn*, he thought! Was it a coincidence that it was Izzo, an "I" girl, and that was leaving town?

When they returned to his home after their six-day North Carolina trip. They sat down at the dining table and discussed their upcoming St. Lucia vacation plans. He told her he had some personal things that he had to tend to first, so he suggested that she go back to San Francisco and ready herself for that trip. She actually said, "Good idea, I need to visit my mom and dad, anyway. He said he needed to clean up some financial matters as well, so, if it was okay with her, he'd come to San Francisco in about ten days to two weeks. She thought it was a good plan, indeed. She wanted to ask what his business was, but decided against it. She didn't want to nestle him in too closely thereby creating a desire for him to want to run away.

The next day he took her to the airport, and told her to set a wedding date if she was so inclined. She was more inclined, but thought it best not to sound too rushed. "I'll let you know in St. Lucia, okay?"

He kissed her passionately, and simply said, "Okay!" He watcher her walk into the terminal, and then he scurried home. He had to work fast. What was the best tactic? He went to the computer to look up more successful women, but she had to have nothing to do with the Wesleyan campus, nothing at all, W would be planning on such a move. He spent the day, troubled. He couldn't find anything. He decided to take a shower, and let his mind whirl until the subconscious mind happened upon something.

After toweling off, and putting on his terrycloth robe, he snatched up the newspaper, drew some iced tea from the pitcher, walked to the east patio, sat in one of his new wicker chairs and watched the waves roll in. He loved the sound and the smell. Both enriched him. After a couple sips of the orange tea he picked up the paper, tilted his chair back and enjoyed the paper. There wasn't so much as a nod about the AK.

When he got to the entertainment section, he noted something of interest. He loved folk music and one of his favorite performing duets were performing at the TCC Jeanne and George Roper Performing Arts Center, downtown, Norfolk. How he wished Constance were still here, she would love to see them. They were the best, truly, the very best. Their music, their, stories, and, wow, *Overhang, and Isaacs* were performing for the next ten days. He really needed to buy tickets. He hadn't been in that old theatre space in a long time. He remembered that it had been totally rejuvenated; the old place was built in the early 20's and as he recalled, Tidewater Community College restored this old movie and Vaudeville house. Yes, he would go. Again, he thought of Constance, wishing she could attend.

It was in 2002 that he first saw Overhang and Isaacs perform. They were just barely 20 then. Sissy Isaacs was a year older then her cousin Samantha Overhang as he remembered. He picked up the telephone, got the number and order two tickets for three nights hence. After he hung up, he was angry with himself. Why did I order 2 tickets, and why am I going. I have more important things to plan. And then it dawned on him. *For heaven sakes,* he thought. He went back to the newspaper and read the whole story again. The article noted where they were staying. *Dare, I?* He pondered.

He went to bed to sleep on the idea. At 3:39 a.m. he awoke, suddenly. He would do it. *Go back to sleep, and work out the details, tomorrow.* He tossed, and he turned, and finally, he got out of bed at 4:44 a.m. He went to his den to see if he could get a good layout of the Prussian Towers where they were staying. He knew its location. It was less than 2 miles from his home, this home. It was eight or nine miles from his father's house; that, too, was important.

The Internet, once again, came through for him. You need to know which room. Easy, he thought. Wait for them to return tomorrow night. Follow them and find their room, and then make more plans. Time was of the essence. He looked to find out how many more days they would be there. That was simple too, five more days. *It could work. Okay, assume it will work. How will that change the overall plan?* He thought it through. He smiled. At 9:25 a.m. he went back to sleep. He slept until 11:47 p.m.

It was their last names. Because of their last names, Nabulio had his volunteers to bring the battles to a near end. He was excited. He worked the rest of the afternoon, thinking, preparing, and working out the smallest of details. When done, he couldn't help himself; he went to the Internet to find pictures, pictures of them and what he could see of their breasts. He wasn't too happy. They dressed pretty modestly. No matter, he thought, it will be a delightful plus when the time comes.

He ate. He hopped into his car and headed for down town. He stopped, ran into the store and made his purchase. He then drove the speed limit to the Prussian Towers. As he drove, he popped the new CD into its cradle and listened to the folksy songs of Overhand and Isaacs. Their voices were enriching, and there words were homey!

Nabulio needed to have his look see at the Towers. If it weren't right, he would cancel the targets without fan fair, and begin, immediately another target or targets. The more he thought of duet targets, the more he loved it! Either the plan is near perfect, or it's a no go! As he drove he thought about getting into the room, and getting out of it safely, after all, it was a high-end hotel. Security would be much stronger. Where he would park, excreta. In and out had to be perfect.

And, what of video cams? Don't miss anything! He reminded himself, winners win and losers have already lost.

He smiled as he turned up the long drive to the Towers! As he did so, he again smelled the ocean, an ocean that was still destroying DNA. Soon, he would add their blood to the salty grave of destruction!

CHAPTER 39—THE FORTY-THIRD DAY AFTER THE FIRST KILLINGS
SENSE, BUT NO SENSE—BUT SENSE AFTER ALL

Lieutenant Wellington was pleased that Alexandria Mae Southerland's thesis, or theory nearly paralleled the work of retired FBI agent and Norfolk Profiler, Katrina Cowling's report. However, the whole of it didn't jive with anything. *Big deal*, we know so much but we don't know what matters. He made a list of those items:

1. We do not know how to catch him before he strikes, again.
2. We do not know why he kills, well specifically, anyway!
3. We do not know when he will strike, again.
4. We do not know why he strikes, specifically.
5. We know that he has some vendetta with me, but we have no specifics, whatsoever! Well, Alexandria might argue that one.
6. We do know that he will most likely kill two more time, three if we count me!
7. We know a lot, but we don't know what it is we don't know; how obvious is that?

That thought made him think back to his thoughts at the end of Alex's remarks. He pulled out his note pad and flipped to the section where he had offered scribbled, somewhat unintelligible notes.

He read aloud to himself what he had scribbled down; partial thoughts "He will kill… that ends the war… the rightful rogue… Wellesley… By doing so, in his life, he will re-assume in his mind the role of the Emperor…his nemesis, Wellington, will be gone. He (Wellington) will be no more… He will triumph and will have Napoleon's Revenge…"

Arthur sat and pondered it all. It all made sense when she wrote it but it just seemed like fragments, now. *Hmmm,* he thought, *maybe that is the key.* He picked up his cell and pushed the button that would take the call to Alex. She answered on the 4th ring. He didn't even say, hello, he just blurted it out, "Alex, what did you mean when you said that He—meaning Nabulio—said, "He will triumph and will have Napoleon's Revenge?" What did you specifically mean by that comment??"

"Well," she said, "Napoleon lost at Waterloo, Wellsy." She thought for a second, and then added, "Nabulio wants to triumph over his Wellington, that's you, so that he can say—perhaps if only to himself—that he beat Wellington, and has therefore achieved revenge over The Duke of Wellington—you—therefore, he has captured Napoleon's Revenge!"

Wellsy got it, he truly did. "Okay," he said, "I've got it. I will have the upper hand if I can figure out how to use that information, right?" He paused, and then said, "Well, that will only take me a hundred years, but, thanks," he said to Alexandria, and rang off.

It must be more complex than that. It has to be. *Why all the killings? Why all the quotes? Why just women? Why did he kill Whisper Katharine Ulrich, and not her boyfriend, Erick Parker, too? Could it truly be that he is only really interested in killing his modern day Wellesley, me? If so, then, why hasn't he done it? What is he waiting for?* "Okay," he said aloud, "Why is he spelling out his name, or part of his name, first, before he tries to kill me?" *What is on his mind? What is the hidden piece of the puzzle?* And then it smacked him upside the face. "Holy, shit," he offered. "No," he said out loud. "Can it really be that simple?"

Arthur went to his calendar and noted the killing dates. Is there a pattern here? The only pattern was, was the fact that there wasn't a pattern, except they were all college students, so far, anyways. He was positive that Nabulio would kill again, and he was positive it would again be a female co-ed. His cell vibrating and ringing interrupted his thought. The face of the phone noted that the call was from, Alex. "Hi, love, what's up?"

"You Lieutenant are a genius. You gave us the answer, I think."

"I must have because I just thought 'could it really be that simple,' but then I just now realized that I don't even know what I'm thinking." He then paused, "So, Alex, now that I am a genius, tell me, what am I a genius about, because I am totally confused right now! Tell me about the genius I am!

"You are! What was the last thing you just said to me?"

"I said, 'okay, tell me about the genius I am.'"

"Stop that."

"Well that is the last thing I said."

"No, goofy. What was the last thing you said to me when we talked a ten minutes or so, ago?"

"I can't remember. I'm no genius, you know!"

She was in a serious mood, but that made her laugh; anyways. "You told me it would take you a hundred years to catch him, you know, the AK."

"Okay, if I said that, yes, I really did say that then. So, I said that, what about it?" He could hear her take a deep cleansing breath, and let it out heavily.

"Arthur, do you know how long Napoleon served or was Emperor?"

"No, I think it was like three months, not very long as I remember."

"You are very close, very close, indeed!"

"Okay, so how long?" He didn't wait for an answer; he figured it out from what she had said that he had said. "One hundred days; is that right?"

"Yes, one hundred days," Arthur, "One hundred days, exactly."

"Okay, so it jives with my comment about 100, days, so?"

"So think!"

"Nothing is coming, love, nothing."

She let out a frustrating deep sigh. "Lieutenant, how many more is he going to kill?"

"Counting me?"

There weren't any response. That answer caused her to want to slap his face. "I dare you to joke about this, Arthur."

He offered that he was truly sorry, that it was insensitive of him, that it was truly wrong. Dead silence filled the air space for several second. Neither spoke. He could tell she was crying. He felt like a jerk, hell, he was a jerk. "I really am sorry, Alexandria Mae. Not that it is an excuse, but honey, I am so wrapped up in the case. It is so heavy laden. Sometimes I need to find the humor in it or it will eat me up. I truly am sorry. Please forgive me. I'm a jerk sometimes."

"Yes you are, but—so too—am I. I am sorry, too, honey."

"Please don't be, I'll make it up to you."

She smiled. "Is that a promise?"

"Want me to put it in writing?"

"Is that necessary?"

"No!" After a few seconds, he continued, "Well, in answer to your question. We know he will kill two more times, and then…"

"No! No, don't say it. Yes he will kill two more women, right?"

"Yes."

"And we have been wondering why so much time has elapsed, right?"

"Right!"

"I may be wrong, and our Profiler may be wrong, too."

"What? How, so?"

"I think he will take one hundred days to kill the seven *NABULIO women,* spelling out his name, nickname, Nabulio!" She took a breath. "Along the way he is offering not only clues but predictions. He is—in fact—leading up to the final battle, the direct battle with Wellington, you, yes you, Arthur Wellesley. I have it all now, Wellington. I have it all." Wellsy was about to ask, but she bulldozed through the beginning of his question. "He is way ahead of schedule, Arthur, that is why he hasn't killed." It dawned on her, "Arthur, he isn't a Serial Killer at all, but he is an Angel Killer."

She lost him there! "He is killing your troops—albeit he is using woman—defining your army as nothing more than weak women. Furthermore, he has at least once left his sperm behind, just as a dog will pee on a tree, marking his territory. Each of his battles is his conquest over you." She stopped. Both were thinking wildly. "He will attempt to kill you on the one hundredth day from when he killed the first woman." She was silent. "Do you know why?"

"Yes, yes I do! I know completely, but you are wrong, I think!"

"What am I wrong about," Alex, asked?

"Napoleon served as Emperor for one hundred days, right?"

"Yes, so?"

"And, when he lost to general Wellesley, he lost his empire, and he lost being the emperor, right?"

"Right! So?"

"So, his attempt at killing his Wellesley must take place one day after the 100th day anniversary, so this modern day, Napoleon, will have surpassed thee Napoleon's record, making him the winner, forever and ever in his mind! "He will then, send some kind of message to the world, that Napoleon reins again, forever and ever! And then he will be at peace, and retire." Just like that," he snapped his fingers, and repeated, "Just like that, and then he will retire, forever!"

"Yes!" She thought for a moment, and then repeated, herself, as well, "Yes, Wellsy, that makes all the since in the world!" Neither of them spoke for a few minutes, and then she said, "But he will kill, again after that. A time will come that he will have to."

"Why?"

"Don't laugh at me!"

"How could I do that, you have figured out everything, so far, detective?"

She laughed, "I'm hardly a detective. But, thanks!"

"So, Alex, why will he kill, again?"

"Because," she said

"Because, because, why?"

"Because he loves killing women. He loves the power. He loves the thrill. He loves mangling them. He loves the sex appetite it fulfills. With each murder, he does a little more. I'm sure you and your cohorts have discovered that by now." That comment took Wellesley by surprise; they hadn't exactly noticed that! Well, not fully, anyway! She continued, "I don't think that it is planned, that that part happens because he loves it! He loves it so much, he will not be able to stop, because by then, he will have turned into a real Serial Killer, if he hasn't so, already!"

"You are way too smart for me."

"I know," she giggled.

"But, love, you are wrong."

"Why?"

"Because," the Lieutenant, said, "Because in your scenario you just gave, he completes his cycle. That will never happen. He will never kill his Wellington. His Wellesley will defeat him before his final victory; therefore there will never be another murder from him. The question is, can I, can we, stop the next two killings." He did his calculations. He was silent as he did the numbers. "Today is the 43rd day after he killed our two Old Dominion coed's. So, his plan over the next 57 days is to kill two more, and then 58 days from now, me! It will never happen. But, I have two more lives to save, first!" He paused, "Thanks for calling me back. You have solved this case."

"Yes, *we* did," she said, smiling! "Yes, *we* did!"

Chapter 40—The Forty-Third Day After the First Killings
FINAL TOUCHES

Nabulio knew what he was about to do was enormously risky, but it was the only way, of that, he was sure. He had searched his mind endlessly over the past 36 hours, but there were so many avenues of unexpected circumstances that could arise. He wondered if he was truly ready for such unexpected events? He didn't even have a contingency plan in place. On the other hand, the emergency plans he had for the previous battles were lame, at best. So, yes, he was scared that he didn't have such an alternative plan in view, but on the other hand, hadn't everything worked so far, even when that damned boyfriend didn't leave the house, as he should have. *Didn't I turn that lemon into lemonade, and didn't I teach him a lesson, and didn't I teach the prick cop W a lesson in messing with me! I put her hills and her looking eyes to point and stare at him when he walked unto my side of the hill.* Yes, Nabulio was scared, but that was nothing more than adrenalin. He knew what he was about. *Press forward!*

On the other hand, he thought of dumping the whole idea, but then he considered that there just wasn't any other way. He was lucky as it was. He hadn't expected to do both 'I' and 'O' at the same time. It was that darn entertainment section of the paper that brought forth this notion to begin with. It had to be providence. His thought of quitting was overridden by the providence of the newspaper article on these women. It had to be fate that offered an opening in the window of WAR; the battle was surely supposed to take place this way. Why else would external circumstances knock on his door and at the perfect time? No, he must go forward and on to the victory. Yes, *ON TO VICTORY* was his new born charge! He liked it; he liked it a lot.

So, Nabulio made the decision to proceed, but he needed to advise himself on all possible problems. So, at about the same time that Wellington was making his list of things he didn't know about the killings, Nabulio was listing the potential problems as he saw by attacking at girl's hotel:

1. Getting into the hotel, and then getting to their room, unnoticed.

2. Leaving their room, unnoticed.

3. Getting into and out of his work clothes, quickly, efficiently.

4. Unexpected guests.

5. Quick and efficient use of his stun baton, the SWMB750k Volt Mini Stun Baton, purchased in Texas three years, ago.

6. Use of the gun, itself, which could take up to 4 full seconds to totally control, probably less, *but* still it was a potential problem, and it was the *but* that worried him.

7. That he could stun only one at a time.

7a. The second woman could scream, or run out of the room, or call the front desk.

7b. What if the other assisted coming to the rescue of the first?

8. What if they came back with guests?

9. What if others were coming over to party—doubtful but certainly possible?

He sat for another half hour, and still couldn't come up with a 10th item to be concerned enough with to be added to the concern list. He read the list seven additional times, pondering. At length, he decided the mission of *WAR BATTLE* was, indeed, a go!

The mission to carry out the battle was scheduled for tomorrow evening, the forty-forth day after his first killings. Their show at the Jeanne and George Roper Performing Arts Center was to end on or about 10:15 p.m. Considering their habit from the previous evening, anyway, they would take a limousine back to their hotel by 11:00 p.m. Nabulio had decided that he would already be on their floor. Five doors down from where their room was vending machines were lined up. Next to and somewhat around a corner, there was a small alcove to the right of the machines, just large enough that he could, would easily stand in, and peer around the edge viewing whomever got on or off the elevator without him being seen.

To the right of where he would be standing was a shelf—why it was there, was anyone's guess, but it was a place that he could put his box on. The box had to be large enough for all his gear, his tools, his binding materials, triangle lag screws, and other sundry items. The box had to be large enough to also contain the object he would remove from their room. It would be impossibly for him to leave the hotel without being seen carrying the box. He decided that he would have to risk walking down a long corridor with the box at the extreme southwest side of the hotel, where less traffic would be engaged. He feared someone seeing him putting the box into his trunk. The slim likelihood of someone seeing that and then recalling it later to police was narrow in scope, but nevertheless a real possibility. Nevertheless, all battles have a certain element of risk. This was a risk of war that had to be taken. He decided it was still the best plan. It was settled!

Nabulio took a deep sanitizing breath. All he had to do now were the many details, yes, many of them, but he had done them all before, 4 other times to be exact. He smiled as he realized that he had started with two victims at one time, and he was ending the initial phase of the operation with two victims, again, and these two warriors, well, he admired them very much. The world would miss their music, and men their bodies, but this was war, and importantly, the next to the last battle. He was pleased. And, of course, there was the bonus in all of this, he pondered, the unveiling of their breasts, and from what he noticed, 'O's were ample. He was looking forward to the spoils of war; again! He had never touched a stars breast, before! *What a thrill for them both*, he thought!

Mentally everything was ready. He would spend the next four hours getting all the equipment in place, the notes to leave, the carving knife, all of it! He loved this part of the mission; it excited him. He loved the anticipation, the adrenalin flow! He loved the quest. He loved the operation. He loved the execution. He loved the thrill. He loved the fear, his and theirs. He loved the end results. He loved the plan. He loved the thought of W being stymied, again. He loved the fact that W was next. However, Nabulio would not let himself be sidetracked into dwelling on W, after all, he had 'I' and 'O' to think about, first!

Finally, carefully he finished the cardboard box that had hard plastic lining on the inside of the box, and then a small garbage bag that rested inside the plastic lining. The bag, and that box would later hold the contents from the girl's suite at the Prussian Towers to be shipped! He reminded himself to wrap it in plastic, to change his gloves. Actually he wrote every step of it down, step by step. He always, did. He was successful because he always did. Victory lies in the little things.

There absolutely couldn't be any mistakes here, no, not the slightest mistake, or he was doomed. One tiny mistake and the whole WAR would be for not. At the end of the very last step he remembered to have someone else hold the box for him. He added that to the list, naturally.

Afterwards, he would have to drive to his dad's house, and do the clean up thing, incinerate, shower, and excreta. Only then could he make the all night drive to Baltimore, Maryland, a good five-hour drive. He wanted to be there between 8:30 and ten. After Baltimore, he would drive to Washington DC, leave the rental car at the airport and fly off to San Francisco. Only on the non-stop flight would he finally be able to sleep.

He took a short rest, and then called Constance. He missed her so, and she missed him, equally. The lovebirds talked for twenty-two minutes. Afterwards, he went to his car and removed the diskette. Returning, he put the disk into his machine and the entire speaker system of the mansion vibrated with the songs of Overhang, and Isaacs, a lasting tribute! Listening, he mentally readied for battle!

Chapter 41—The Forty-Fourth Day After the First Killings
SAN FRANCISCO, HE'S THE ONE

Constance went to the Escort Service in downtown San Francisco. She took no more that three steps inside the office and Armando welcomed her back with open arms, literally. "Couldn't stay away, eh, kiddo, need some of that fresh meet, right?" he offered with his boyish snicker. Terrain Armando was crushed when she told him she was getting married, and that she had just stopped by to quit, officially and say goodbye to the girls. He accepted it with little grace. She was—after all—one of his better meal tickets. She went to the lounge and said goodbye to 3 of her co-hookers. The others were out doing someone or something. There were hugs and tears around, enough for all. It was always bittersweet when one flew the nest. There was always happiness when it was because of marriage, and sadness because it was happening to someone else. Constance left the Service, never to return. That life and that lifestyle were gone for good. Goodbye immorality.

She hopped onto 280 South to 380 East, and hooked up to 101-Bayshore Freeway, taking it all the way down to Menlo Park, the place of her parents, Lewis and Janette Middaugh. They lived on Virginia Lane off Fair Oaks Lane. She walked into their home, unannounced. Janette was cleaning up the lunch dishes. She heard the back door open, and was pleased to see the smiling face of her favorite daughter, her only daughter. " Hi, Mom!" After the hugs she asked if her Dad was home. Janette asked if she hadn't seen him in the garage. She said no; the overhead door was closed. The both turned looking toward the back door. They heard his footsteps coming up basement steps. Constance backed up and out of sight.

"What you up to, Mother?" Lewis asked.

"Glad you are here, I was thinking of driving up to see Constance." He said that that was a great idea, but why not just ask her to come down here, instead, where there isn't so much hustle and bustle. She smiled and said, "Turn around and ask her for yourself." He turned and immediately a smile embraced the additional twinkle in his eye. She advance and flung her arms around her hero, "Poppa!"

He broke the hold and stepped back. "Good heavens woman, can you possibly get anymore beautiful," he stated in his most prideful voice. She was the woman he cherished more than life, itself. "Give me another big bear hug, girl." She stepped forward and threw her arms around him. "OUCH," he bellowed. "You caught your watch or something on my ear." He reached up and grabbed his ear as he made the statement. He brought his hand back down and looked at it. It was stained with a little tad of blood. He laughed at himself for such a loud display.

"Let me see, Poppa!"

"No, I'm find, Turnip, I'm embarrassed I made a fuss in the first place."

Turnip was the name he gave were when she walked into the house after school on the day she turned fifteen. She said she hated the name Constance, and wrinkled up her nose and said, "I don't ever want to be called that again." He looked at her crunched up face, and how her nose just kind of shot up towards the ceiling. So, on that day, at that time, and since then, she was his Turnip, and hence, her name ever sense.

He checked his ear, again. Still bleeding, a little. He reached into his bib-overhauls and snatched up a hanky and dabbed it at his ear. "Come, sit down, child, and talk to us."

At the table, she said, "Sorry about your ear, but it wasn't my watch that scratched you Poppa." She looked at her mom, and then her dad, and then put her left arm straight out, and let her wrist allow her hand to dangle down toward the top of the table.

"Oh my word," her mother, exclaimed, look at the size of that rock, Daddy. And then she softly repeated, "Oh my word," and added, "Who's the lucky fella?"

"That's some rock, there, Turnip!" Lewis added.

Her parents exchanged a look, and then Janette let fly several questions as if they were all just one long question: "How long ago did this happen? What's his name? How long have you been engaged? Why haven't we met him, yet? Is there a wedding date set?"

Constance laughed, "Mom, calm down. I'll get to all that."

Janette was just beside, herself, "Oh, my baby, oh my happy baby," she said, bursting into wonderful tears! "What his name? Tell us all about him, and what lead to this?"

She gave them all the details, well all except for the first part, as they never knew, and would never know she was a hooker, albeit, a high class one. They thought she was a model of some kind. Anyway, she told them about him, his gorgeous looks, his kindness, and his undying love and devotion of and for her. "Mom, Dad, he is a dream come true. He is everything I've always wanted, and a lot more. He is the kindness man on earth. And Dad, you will love him too. You always said there would never be a man good enough for me, yet he is, he really, really is."

She spent most to the day telling them this and that about him, his home, his money, but mostly how he treated her as a queen. When her dad asked about meeting him, she told the truth that he'd be here in about a week, but then they were off to St. Lucia. Her mom had never heard of it, so that took some time and she told her mom all about it. "As a matter of fact, Mom, I've some literature in the car about that dreamland, I'll get it for you later, okay?" They asked if she could stay a few days, she said that she had hoped they would ask her at very thing. There were smiles, around.

The small family talked the day away. Her dad was always about working on something, but he was retired. He tended his garden, and made woodcrafts for three different consignment shops in the area. Her mother was devoted to cooking, cleaning and she was part of a quilting group that got together twice a month and quilted and talked the day away. She was part of the local Red Hat Society, with about 26 other women. They were a quite people. The Middaugh family was a good people, an open-minded people, and also minded his or her own business, and was a friend to most everyone.

Their daughter was home for a while, and her fiancé was coming soon. Could life be any better that that? Janette thought *no, not any better than that*. As far as Janette was concerned they should be married almost immediately, so within the year she could be a grandmother, and Lewis agreed, wholeheartedly. This was a happy time for the Middaugh family; plenty of smiles that day, and not a single frown from any of them. Paradise, and love was the topic for the day.

"Tell me about his family, Turnip."

She told her dad that his mother died giving him birth, and his father, too, had passed too, just a few years, ago. "So," She, "he really doesn't have any family, except me, and very soon, his new in-laws, of course."

"Well, by golly, girl, he's about to, yes sir, he sure is about to have a grand family. Hey," he said, "Do you have his picture?"

"Of course, it's in my purse." She removed the picture and both parents went on and on about how good-looking he was, and his infectious smile. She told that he even looked better in real life, but it is his wonderful personality that she loves most about him. He's nearly a Saint."

"Well, dear, I hope for you sake he is," Janette, offered.

"He is, Mom, you'll see, he truly is!"

"Well, daughter, I have to start supper, care to help this old woman?"

"That's enough old woman, talk, Mom, you've got years and years left in you." She turned and looked at her dad, "You, too, Dad, you too!" They all smiled for her good fortune, and now she had brought it to them. Sometimes life seems so perfect. Today was one of those days in the Middaugh family.

Later that knight, her mom would tell her husband, that Constance had a twinkle about her. He responded, "I saw that same twinkle in your eyes not but two days ago, old woman." After a slight, paused, he offered, "She comes from good stock, Mother, good stock, indeed!"

CHAPTER 42—THE FORTY-FOURTH DAY AFTER THE FIRST KILLINGS
NABUILO'S TIME OF TIMES

About the time Constance was helping her mother prepare supper on the East Coast, Nabulio was pacing in his den on the West Coast. Constance was going to eat. Max was going to devour. He was ready for the action of his assignment, and it was still two hours away. To better ready himself, he played their folksy music. He loved their sound, yet tonight he knew it would be silenced, evermore! He had even made it a point to purchase their last collector's edition. He was the only one in the word that knew it was their last CD. He was more than ready, he was agitated beyond measure; he wanted to get it on. He needed to do something to pass the time; a walk on the beach seemed appropriate enough, so he did.

He loved the smell of the ocean, and reveled in the noise of the waves washing up upon the shore. He loved its rhythm, so soothing, and mesmerizing. It was a peace offering from the Eternal God, and a reminder of an unending universe. He walked about a mile and a half, and then jogged back home, to shower, and don the clothing he would go to battle with. He sat in one of the cushy chairs Constance had selected, and thought of her. *You are an amazing woman, Constance, when this business is all over, I will give my entire life to you, and try not to over smother you with love and kindness. I will be your Napoleon, your conqueror, and your devoted husband; and, in many ways, your servant for all time. And, most importantly, I will be the father to your son, Napoléon.*

He looked at his watch, and noted the time; it was, indeed time to go. He knelt down and prayed that he would, again, be victorious. Upon ending, he asked for blessings over his beloved Constance. He went to the kitchen table and picked up the note he had left for himself. He read each and then checked off each items. Afterwards, he took the paper and burned it over the kitchen sink, and then let the ashes disincarnate down the drain. He took a deep cleansing breath and walked outside to his rented car, a dark blue Jeep Cherokee XJ that was housed in the garage. His large box, with another smaller box inside the larger box rested comfortably in the passenger's seat. He took a decontamination breath, depressed the button, and as the garage door slid up and above the Jeep, he backed out and was ready to the march to victory. He smiled. His adrenalin was flowing. He liked that. It gave him an edge.

The drive, the arrival, and the transporting of his boxes went smoothly. Once in the parking lot of the hotel, he scooped up his equipment, crossed to the back entrance and waited for someone to leave, exit. He saw a couple walking down the corridor toward him. He scooped up the boxes and waited for them to come to the door. They did, he said, "Thanks, I can't reach for my pass key, what with these boxes and all."

They couldn't see his face for the boxes. He had played it perfectly. "No problem young man, no problem," the older gentleman responded. Through the door, he offered a *thanks*, and he got back another, "No problem." The first of two large hurdles were over. The walk down the corridor was a piece of cake. It was a good thirty yards, and not one living soul saw him. It went exactly the same way it had the previous night, his practice night. It went well.

He slipped to the elevator and mashed the button. It opened, immediately. He was pleased. More luck happened when the car went all the way to the sixteenth floor without anyone else getting on board. He made it to the alcove just in time. Just six seconds later, two older women exited their room. The old ladies room was right next to his girls. *Good, be gone for a few hours, ladies!* He knew the gods were smiling upon him; providence smiled once, again!

He waited patiently, though very excitedly. However, when the girls hadn't shown by 11:10 p.m. he became uneasy. At 11:12 the elevator door opened, and three women stepped out, laughing and giggling. Sissy Isaacs was speaking, "…and wasn't it something when that old guy tried to rush up and onto the stage, and then fell backwards into that fat ladies lap in the first row. He couldn't get up, and she couldn't get out. She was just a wriggling and a twisting and a squealing about, I could hardly keep singing going!" She giggled all the way to their room.

Tammy Leblanc, added, "I grabbed the head-set and yelled for Tommy to get security down here in a flash."

Samantha Overhang offered. "And we are glad you did girl, you saved the moment, but it was funny as all get out. We sure followed that number up with some off the cuff remarks, didn't we," Samantha, offered? She stopped for a second to catch her breath, "Yes, and Sissy, I didn't know you were a comedian, when did that develop; the audience loved it. Maybe you ought to make it part of the routine, it was great."

Sissy laughed, "Neither did I." All three women laughed at that, too.

"Okay, Tammy, it's getting late, so if we are going to do parasailing tomorrow, here is my room key to let you in, in the morning. As you well know, we sleep too soundly for even phone calls to wake us up, so come by about 7:30 and just come in, okay? Sissy, asked.

"Just to be sure we're awake, okay?" Sam added. Sam then reached out and gave Tammy a big hug, "We really appreciate all you do, and you're the rock of this entire production, thanks!"

"I'm hardly the rock, but thanks just the same." She turned and walked past the girl's room." She then turned her head back and said, "Well, as you know, I'm at the end of the hall, 1622 if you need me, just call!"

"Good night Tam," Sam said, and then said to Sissy, "Get the lock I just gave my room key to Tammy."

Nabulio then had to do the tough part, wait a few minutes, hoping that one or the other would be in the shower. He waited eleven minutes. He took the stun baton from the box, and walked to room 1622. He offered a rapid triple rap with the back of his knuckles. "Who is there," came from within.

"We have received a telegram for Overhang and Isaacs."

"It's awfully late came from the other side of the door."

"It just this minute, well a couple of minutes ago, it, the telegram just came in; it's marked urgent."

"Well give me a second to put my robe on." Less than a minute later, Sissy unlocked the door, and opened it, but stayed a bit behind the door, so as not to expose any par of her nude body under the white terry cloth robe that had the PT hotel insignia over her right breast area.

Nabulio quickly looked both ways down the hall. It was all clear. He placed his right hand and on the doorknob, and thrust his weight against the door, pressing off with his right knee, foot and shoulder plunging into the door. The swinging inward door caught Sissy's left shoulder and then the left side of her face plummeting her to the carpeted floor. She let out half of a scream, yet, at the same time her assailant pushed past the door. Her right foot came up off the carpet, and went upward at an obtuse angel between Nabulio's legs tripping him. While falling toward her, his left arm reached out toward her body and connected with her right upper thigh with the baton. Its effect was useless; the door had knocked her out, already. Nabulio assumed the baton had done its work.

Without a second's delay, he shut the door, and locked it. Franticly he looked for the room key. It was right on the nightstand. He placed the card into his left hip pocket. He quietly slipped into the bathroom, and waited for the shower water to turn off. He didn't know if the water could shock him too. He was very peeved with himself for not thinking of that possibility before hand. He only had to wait a minute, but that minute seemed forever. She reached out from the shower and reached for the towel. Just as she reached for it, he juiced her right above the elbow. The baton slipped off her as she screamed. He ripped the curtain back and drove the baton into the right side of her torso just under the armpit and at the side of her breast. She quickly crumpled and sunk down; he smelled a tinge of burnt flesh, perhaps because of the water. He stopped her fall by grabbing her. He then eased her to the tub floor.

Nabulio then ran to the door, removed the passkey and held it in his hand. He peered down the hall. Clear. He half ran to his boxes, and collected them. Again, he looked left and then right and with that, he raced back to their door. He put the large box down, and keyed the room, pushing the door open and dragging the box into the room at the same time. He closed the door and was about to twist the dead lock, but he saw the dangling sign. He took it off the door handle, opened the door and placed it outside of the room, announcing to all who passed by, DO NOT DISTURB! He then locked the dead bolt. He gasped for air. He was overcome with tension and exhaustion, already. He gulped for breath. He was relieved. The toughest part next to the actual departure was over!

Nabulio raced to the center of the room and removed a coffee table from the floor, and placed it on the seat cushions of the sofa. He then pulled and dragged Sissy to the middle of the room, leaving rug burns on her backside. He removed her robe. He paid absolutely no attention at all to her nude body; instead, he placed her on the floor just like girl number one, Jessica June Andersen, exactly 44 days, ago. He put her arms out wide above her head. He then circled her body and spread her legs. He made quick work of using the 4 lag screws that would secure the four corners of her body—arms and legs—solidly. He did her wrists first. Done, with those, he went to her feet, first, putting them back together, briefly. He pulled on her legs, which caused her arms to stretch out to their limits. He wanted to be sure she would have little or no moving range. He then spread her legs apart as far they would go, and then screwed the lags screws down about four inches past the out side and beyond the end of her feet, also 4 inches. He wrapped her wrist with the elastic cord pulling the cords as firmly as possible, stretched the leg even further apart. Had she been awake, she would have shouted and squirmed in agony. Even totally out, an audible sound washed past her lips.

Nabulio raced to Samantha and gave her another burst from the baton, just to be sure. He dragged her and put her in the double V position with Sissy, just has he had done with Carolyn Ann Nowicki, and Jessica, and bolted Samantha into position, again stretching her body past the tolerant position. He was pleased with his work. He then, banded their mid-torso down tight to the carpet. Next he did the cotton ball thing, and the taping thing to their mouths. He sat down on the hard chair off the kitchenette. He was tired, hot and sweating. He got out a plastic bag, and then removed his clothing. He crossed to the bathroom and secured an unused towel and toweled off, placing the towel in the plastic bag when he was done! He offered a few words to himself. "Calm down, the worse is over! You're nearly home free."

After three minutes, he was still sweating, so he took a quick shower. Afterward, he walked back into the main room; naked. He looked around and saw the small mini-refrigerator. He put new plastic gloves on and removed a cold beer and took several sips. He sat on the sofa and rested. He then put the bottle down and sat on the carpet and examined each girl's breasts, first Samantha, *unbelievably perfect*. He looked up and over at Sissy's pair, *unbelievably ultra perfect*. He felt his manhood stir. He contemplated. *Better not.*

Just then Sissy stirred. She tried to move her toes first, and then her knees. Not being able to move seemed to awaken her faster. She offered an involuntary scream. It was totally muffled. She was confused. Her shoulder ached, badly, something was very wrong. Her thighs were killing her. She felt as though she was being pulled apart. She tried to sit up. She felt mummified. Fear took over as she struggled to move and nothing was working. She was scared, terrified, and confused. He stepped toward her, and straddled her bound body. As she looked up, she saw was his genitalia. She didn't want to know what would happen next. He stepped over her and sat beside her on the carpet.

"Calm down;" he said, "struggling will not help, it may even hurt you." He placed his right hand on her right breast. She writhed in disgust and concern. He was definitely getting aroused, now. He rubber her other breasts until he accomplished his goal. That was enough; after all, he wasn't a pervert. Sorry, he said, "I just happen to be a breast man. Please take no umbrage. I will not do that, again." He looked at Samantha; she was the pretty one, and the one with the larger breasts. *Perhaps in a few minutes*, he thought. "Well, he said, I have work to do."

As he walked away she noticed that he had a large birthmark on his left thigh. She told herself to remember it, to remember it for the police. It never dawned on her that she was the AK's next victim. Within twenty seconds, that all changed, when she saw the knife, and he simply said to her, I need to leave a couple of notes for W. Her eyes bulged. Her body writhed. Sweat poured from ever part of her body. Her back rose up off the floor. That ripped at her upper thigh muscles. "NO!" he screamed. I can't work if you are wailing around. *STOP IT, OR I WILL CUT OFF YOUR BREASTS. DO YOU WANT THAT?*" She stopped, but her body quivered.

He could deal with that. He pressed the knife into the upper portions of her lower ribs, just below her left breast. He pushed in the knife in about three-fourths of an inch. Pain reached her every fiber. He looked at her, removed the knife and pointed it at her breast, "Quiet! No more warnings, none!" He started to carve, again. She squirmed, naturally, but he knew it was involuntary. He carved as she writhed:

The bayonet has always been the weapon of the brave and the chief tool of victory!

He looked at her, and spoke, "I'm done. You have done very well. I'm sorry it took so long, but it had to be perfect for W, and no misspelling this time, either. Be pleased with yourself. You were a valiant warrior. You have done much better than the others. W will be pleased. However. There is one more thing, but it is symbolic, so do not take this personally, and I will wear protection, not for me, but for you! I will be right back. He crossed to Samantha and used her breasts to get himself prepared. He then lay on Sissy and thrust and thrust until he filled the sheath. I was difficult with Samantha's heel in the way.

He immediately got off her, and walked to the plastic bag and took off the protection. He looked at her. Don't be angry, it is part of war. I will be Emperor, so I must plant my seed in his business. Sorry, if not me, then perhaps him! She had a distant look, openly vague. She neither heard him, nor cared. He leaned over her and said, "I kept my promise, and I did not touch them, again. You were most brave. He would be most pleased with you. She looked deadpanned at him as she felt a little tug, and then it was hard to breath. Nabulio listened to the air escaping, bubbling in blood from her neck. She was gone!

He stood up, and nearly died. He saw a drop on the floor. His semen. He panicked! He cupped his privates and rushed to the shower and showered, again. He brought water and soap next to Sissy. He cupped her blood with his latex hands and finger and smeared her blood everywhere, covering up his cleaned area. He was still scared to death. He forgot to follow his directions. Her rushed to Samantha, and carved her lifeless body, her abdomen. She moved very little.

You must not fight too often with one enemy, or you will teach him all your art of war!

After writing the message, he examined it, and the carved beneath it, # 7.

He raced back to Sissy's body and carved beneath the wording, # 6.

He then clamed, himself, and took over the situation. He was relaxed, now and back in total control. As he stood over Samantha, for the first time she opened her eyes. She saw the nude man. Her stomach hurt, badly. She wanted to reach up and feel her stomach, but her arms wouldn't work. Her groin hurt. The inside of her thighs were screaming in pain. She was doing her best to figure it all out.

He asked, "If I take the tape off your mouth, will you scream?" She couldn't move but she moved her eyes back and forth, indicating she wouldn't talk. He held the carving knife to her eyes. He saw them; her blue eyes were dilated in total fear. She saw blood on the knife. "This is her blood, Sissy's blood. I told her not to talk, but she did not listen, so she paid the price. So, I warn you. Don't talk, not a word, one syllable and you are dead, too. You may talk if I say so. You talk otherwise and it will be the last thing you do. If you try to scream, all that will be heard in the next room is perhaps a little gurgling sound. You got that? Her eyes went up and down, wildly!

It was such a rush to see her mouth untapped, and the cotton balls, removed. "Don't talk but answer me, I'll read your lips, okay." She mouthed okay! "Are you scared?" She offered, *yes*! He smiled; "I guess I would be too. Do you know who I am?" She mouthed *Angel Killer*!

He smiled, and said, softly, "No!" *Are you going to kill me*, she mouthed? "No!" he said, and then added, "You are needed to communicate to W for me!" He was quiet for a moment, and then asked, "Are you hurting?" *Yes.* "Your stomach?" *Yes.* "Your groin area?" *Yes.* I had to carve a message with this knife to W. The worst is over; you are merely oozing blood now, it's coagulating! Do you want to know what it says?" *Yes.* He told her the truth, and read to her the message on her body.

"I have to write another note to him on the wall. Would you like to know what the message is? *Yes.* "This is it: 'there are only two forces in the world, the sword and the spirit. In the long run the sword will always be conquered by the spirit.' Do you understand what that means?" *Yes, I think so!* "The quote is taken from Napoléon Bonaparte, the greatest leader that ever lived." Her eyes were closing. "Are you still listening?" A weak, *yes*, crossed her lips. Do you want to sleep?" *Yes.* If you sleep, you will never wake up, is that what you want." *Yes.* He slit her throat and heard the noise.

He used her blood and wrote upon the wall, Napoleon's quote!

Satisfied, he withdrew his notes from the box, and one at a time, he complied with his own instructions down to the smallest detail. When the clean up was finished, he put on a new pair of latex gloves. Though both women were dead, he was curious, so he fondled each of the dead women's breasts. It meant nothing. It was a wasted activity. There wasn't any pleasure in it. He actually embarrassed himself. He was ashamed. He lingered a few minutes more before he took care of the final business. That was far more difficult than he had anticipated. And, it took twice the time, allocated. When finished, he took out his last list of instructions, and, again, followed them to a tee. After that, he stripped one more time, and took another hot shower, making sure there wasn't any residue left.

Out of the shower he put on plastic slippers, and then took the contents out of the bag and put his clean clothing on. Lastly, he removed the plastic slippers and put on his socks and running shoes. He put on yet another pair of plastic gloves and pulled a couple of pubic hairs out of Samantha, and placed them inside the drain of the bathtub. The gloves then went inside the large plastic bag, too. Finally he put on the last pair of gloves and tied up the plastic bag, first squeezing the air out of it. Everything went into the box, including the smaller box. Its contents had completed the mission, the battle.

He looked at his watch. It was approaching two o'clock, but that wasn't bad, he had an hour swing, anyway. He opened the door, and looked left and right. He took the large box and its contents and walked it to the elevator. He set it down, and ran back to the room, and took a quick look around. All was in order. He turned off the light and kept the passkey, just in case an hour or so later if he discovered he made a mistake and had to get back into the room, he could. He took the elevator to the 2nd floor and got off, then down the corridor and then down the stairs, and then the last leg to the side door exit. He peered outside, not a soul in sight. He pushed the door open. Held it open, took off the gloves, and stuffed them in his pocket, and walked to his car. He saw nobody and as far as he knew, nobody saw him! He was right.

Away from the PT hotel, he drove to his father's old home and did the furnace thing and all the rest. After that, he got in the rental and was on his way, just as planned.

At seven thirty-two that morning, the forty-fifth day after the first double killing, Tammy opened her bosses' door with Samantha's room key, and screamed bloody murder, because that is what she saw! Another gruesome double killing! She vomited, and collapsed to the floor at the sight before her, but it was a sight of who she knew had to be Samantha that caused her to faint dead, away!

Eighteen minutes later, Larry Cook was walking to the ice machine to get ice to make a cold pack for his wife's beaming headache. He saw a room door partially open with a foot wedged between the doorsill and the door. Carefully, and slowly he pushed the door into the room. A wrenching smell first swooped upon him; the combination of Tammy's vomit and other strange, ugly smells of death. When he saw what he saw, he turned to the hallway, and offered his own vomit, spilling the ice chips to the floor.

Cook then ran to his room, and scooped up the phone and called the front desk of the Persian Towers.

Chapter 43—The Forty-Fourth and Moving into the Forty-Fifth Day After the First Killings
POTPOURRI

Wellesley took the call from the dispatcher at his office. He had been in the building all of six minutes. It was 8:18 a.m. Wellsy called Detective Strange. Strange too had only been in his office three minutes. The two of them drove to the Prussian Towers in the Detective's car. "It's him, I'm guessing, right," Lieutenant?

"You are more than right, Detective. He's killed two this time."

"Two, you say?"

"Two is correct. The jackal has completed the spelling of his name; Nabulio"

"The team is on the way?"

"Some of them, I just got the word less than five minutes, ago! Dispatch is calling the rest"

"You said the Towers?"

"Yeah!"

"That takes some balls."

"He's got balls, and big ones. He doesn't seem to be afraid of anything, I'm beginning to wonder if he is invisible."

"Who found them?"

"I don't know, that seems rather unclear at this time. It's either some employee of theirs—the dead girls I mean—or another guest in the hotel. Like I say it is unclear."

"Who reported it?"

"The hotel dick." Wellsy paused, and then added, "He said one of the women's head is missing!"

"It's got to be a mess," the Detective offered.

Wellsy, asked, "You know all those cops turn House Detective, who is this guy at the Towers?"

"Paul Rood, he's from D.C. I think. I don't really know him. Can't give you what you are looking for, but I think he won't contaminate the evidence. That's just a guess, boss; sorry." He took a breath, "Her head is missing! That's not good. What do you think, Lieutenant?" The Lieutenant remained silent. Strange understood, completely.

* * * * *

His cell when off at 8:44 a.m. It scared him to death. "Where you at? I called you at home, no answer."

"Hi, sweetheart. Actually I'm on my way to you, indirectly. Right now I'm in Baltimore, Maryland."

"Baltimore?"

"Yes," he laughed. It's business, I'll explain later. Anyway, I was going to call you in an hour or so, anyway. I have to run some additional errands, and then I'm on the plane, coming to you, to take you to never, never land. Where are you at?"

She was excited. "You are coming already. Wow! I thought it would be almost another week."

"Well, that was the plan, but I just can't be away from you any longer, love!"

"I'm so excited with this news, honey. I'm home. I mean I'm at my parent's house. I want to pick you up at the airport and bring you to their house. You will come there, won't you?" She took a deep breath, and added, "And I have a wonderful surprise for you, too."

"Of course I want to come there, why wouldn't I. I'm looking forward to it already. Oh, what is it, what's the secret?"

"I can't tell you. I want to tell you, but I won't, that's why it's a secret. After I pick you up at the airport, then I'll tell you, so, you'll have to wait."

"I can wait, but I don't want too." He gave it another try, "Well, at least give me a hint to see if I can figure it out."

"You have no choice, my lips are shut tight!" She thought for a second, "Okay, I'll give you a one word hint, and that is all. Are you ready?"

"Yes!"

"Good, what you just said is the hint."

"What did I say?"

"You said, 'yes.'"

"I said 'yes,' and yes is the hint? That isn't any hint."

"Well, just because you don't think it's a hint doesn't mean it isn't a hint. After all, it is my secret and if I say that yes is a hint, then yes is a hint. That's it, you don't get any more." He merely grunted back at her, so she grunted back at him, and then they both laughed, and both were silent for a few seconds, and then she asked, "What time does your plane come in, and what airline?"

"Oh, yeah, no, I mean, no don't pick me up tonight. The plane gets in really late, the wee hours of the morning, so, pick me up tomorrow morning at about 8 or 9. I gave them your name, so they will give you the key to the private elevator. So go up to our love nest, where we first met. I'll get the same room we had, so quietly slide into our room, and get naked and have your way with me," he paused, "I promise I won't complain.

"Oh, heavens, get an earlier flight," she said, "I'm on my way and you can met me there tonight, you've got me hot just thinking about it!"

"Good!" He cleared the throat, "Actually it will be early tomorrow morning, around four I think. But come if you want, and then when I arrive at our hotel, I hope it will be you that is sleeping. Surprise me, but don't worry, I won't be mad if you are not there, either."

He flipped down the car visor and selected the ticked. "Hold on, I'm looking to find my arrival time. Got it! Yup, I land at 4:04 a.m." He paused, you decide, either is fine with me!"

That pretty much ended their conversation. She thought about it and knew the traffic would be lighter if she left her parents somewhere between and eleven and midnight rather than coming later the following morning.

Nabulio had a whirlwind of things to do. The most important was the mailing. That wouldn't come for another two hours.

Everything he had done with the box was set. It was a pristine box, inside and out. Not a print anywhere to be found. How did he know? He dusted it for latent prints, himself. He had a heavy string that that went from the bottom 4 corners of the box and rose up to his hand where the four strings came together. He tied them into a single loop. He could carry the box that way, three fingers though the loop; that way, he wouldn't have to touch the wrapped up box at all. The last thing on earth he would do would be to leave even a partial print. If the box was set down, all he had to do was to pull up the four strings at the four corners and then carry it with the loop at the top. It was perfection, and he loved perfection!

He drove to Georgetown University, and found the perfect student for the perfect job. It was that simple; he knew all college students needed money all the time. At a snack bar, he asked a young man if he could share his table. The student, said "Yes, no problem." Nabulio sat down, placing the box on the counter between him and the Georgetown student. He pulled the stocking cap well over his ears and it also covered some of his eyebrows. No, it wasn't the same stocking cap he had on, before. He wore a bow hunting jacket that gave him a more stocky looking body. His hunting boots finalized his image. He set the package down, and let the loops of the package drape over one side of the box. The two men had some small talk for a few minutes, and then Nabulio asked if the kid wanted to make some easy money? The kid asked, "Is it legal."

"Bet your ass, kid."

"What do I have to do?"

"Take this box to the post office and mail it for me."

"Why don't you do it yourself?"

"My wife works there and this package is going overseas to my lover."

"Really! Oh, I get the picture."

"I'm sure you do? Will you help me?"

"Depends!"

"How much, right?"

"Exactly!"

"Make me an offer, but remember I'll have to take a taxi from here and back here. This is DC, cabs not cheap."

"I know it's DC I live here, and have so for the past nineteen years." He cut through the clutter, "Never mind that, I'll drive you back and forth, you know, to and from the post office."

"When?"

"Now!"

"I can't do it, I have a class."

"Skip it!"

"No, it's important."

"You'd skip it for the right amount, wouldn't you?"

"Sure!"

"Name your price."

"Two hundred dollars."

"Okay, I'll give you two hundred dollars, and another five hundred to leave this second and get it done."

"I want the money now, up front."

"No, when we get into the car and we're at the post office."

"Done!"

On the drive over, he explained that the box was going overseas. Therefore, he explained the processor—the mailman, guy—would ask him how he wanted to send it. "Just say you want to get it there the fastest way possible. He'll tell you what you have to do, and then you'll have to sign, and stuff like that. Don't sign your real name. They won't check, so don't worry about it." The kid raised an eyebrow over that, but then, for seven hundred dollars, he didn't care. Nabulio went on, "Just make sure you don't sign your own name. Other than that, don't do anything illegal, okay?" Jason Ireland bobbed his head in agreement. He asked what and why he had to sign? Nabulio explained it all telling him why he had to sign, and so forth. "If you have to wave their responsibility of the package getting broken, just say okay, and sign away their responsibility." If asked, any other question, tell them the truth, that inside the box is an antique small crystal and brass chandelier valued at 4 to 5 hundred dollars. If they asked if you wrapped the package yourself, just say yes."

They arrived adjacent to the post office. He gave him the two hundred dollars and said "I'll wait right here by this post." He thought for a second. "Look, don't say much, my wife is very jealous, she's always suspicious of me, she picks up on everything, okay!"

"Gees, mister, I wonder why?"

Max laughed, and then said, "Okay, just say what you have to, okay!" Ireland started to walk away, and remembered, "Hey, you said I'd get all the money when we got here."

"You do your job and the rest is yours. I'll be right here, right here by this telephone pole. Don't dilly dally."

"You better be here, don't sneak off with the rest of my money. If you do, I will go back in the post office and tell them I forgot something and I need the package back."

"I'll be here, kid. Now move it."

He got out of the car and leaned into the window, "look, I'm 24, not that much younger than you, so stop calling me kid."

"Sorry you are right." The kid, Ireland, snatched up the box, and was off. Eight minutes later, he walked out of the post office, toward the stranger's rented car. Nabulio pointed at the telephone pole. Attached to the pole with two-thumb tacks was a brown legal sized envelope. Nabulio pointed to the kid, and then to the envelope, and then he took off. He kid yelled at him, and the ran to the envelop, opened it up and took out the ten bills, all crisp new hundreds, wrapped in a band of paper that was written in red crayon: *good job, bonus money, keep the money and toss the folder away.* He did exactly that! "What a world Ireland, said."

* * * * *

Ted Castle—Forensic—told Lieutenant Wellesley that they were finished with the bodies, that all the photographs were taken, and that they didn't need the bodies any longer. "Sir, can we have the bodies taken to the morgue?" Wellesley said yes, and then fifteen seconds later he said, "No. Leave them here for the time being. He walked away and yelled for Strange. He told his Detective what he wanted of him. Strange asked him if he was sure. "No, no I'm not Detective but we're going to do it anyway." Strange wasn't sure about this one, but he followed the assignment to the letter. He left.

Forty-eight minutes later he returned. He told the guest to stay outside while he got the Lieutenant. Two minutes later Strange returned with Wellesley. "He talked to you?" Wellsy asked.

"He did!"

"You okay with this?"

"No!"

"I will not make you, but if anyone can see anything you can. You've been right all along, Alexandria."

"I can't deal with the missing head."

"I know. None of us do well with that sort of thing."

"Once I look, life will never be the same, I know that, and Wellsy, you know that too. You know how I feel about your job, the dangers, and etcetera. I don't need this as a constant reminder of what happens, or what could happen!" She started to cry. "This could kill our relationship."

"You are right, Alex," he held her, "I won't argue that, but without you, this will not end."

"What do you hope for me to find in this mess? I've gone the distance with you, I don't think I can help anymore!" Her voice was quivering, as was her entire being.

Wellsy let out a deep sigh, "Perhaps you are right, Detective, take her home."

"Do you hate me, Arthur?"

He crossed to her, and held her tightly. Tears were streaming down his cheeks—as well—and he wasn't embarrassed that the Detective was witnessing this act, either. "No, it was a bad, idea. Just go home. I'll see you there." He then added, "I'm so sorry!"

She walked away with Detective Strange, stopped, and turned back, offering one more time, "I'm sorry!" He waived to her that it was okay. He then mouthed to her, *Sorry, my fault.* She commented back. "Bring me the photos; maybe I can look at them, later."

He said, "Sure," but he knew he'd never bring them to her. She stepped into the elevator and was gone.

Wellsy collected himself, and stepped back into the room "Hey, Ted, morgue them."

* * * * *

Nabulio drove to the airport. He dumped his sportsman coat and frumpy hat into the trash. He, thought, *Hmmm, didn't O.J. Simpson do the same thing with his coat at the airport when he was fleeing? No,* he thought, *it was only a theory that he did that. Well, let them theorize about this too.* He then checked in his rental, and waited for his flight, which was delayed 22 minutes. *No big. deal,* he thought, *they'll make up for the lost time once in the air.* He was in the air less than a half hour when he went into an exhausted deep sleep. When he awoke, he was 22 minutes from landing in San Francisco. *Will she be there,* he wondered.

At the hotel he asked if Constance Middaugh had arrived and had signed in. He was told that she had arrived several hours, earlier. He took the elevator. He slipped into the bathroom for a few minutes. He came out in his shorts. She was lying on top of the disheveled covers, dressed only in her slip. He quietly slid into the bed beside her. He cuddled her back with his front, wrapping his right arm over her torso, and cupping her right breast that gently rested on top of the covers, with his right hand. She moved ever so slightly. They fell asleep that way.

She woke up first at 12:44 p.m. She quietly slipped out of bed, shower and then called room service. Their brunch came at 2:22 p.m., just as he was waking up. "There is some food if you want some."

"No, I'm going to shower, care to join me? She did. At 4:30 p.m. they were on their way to her parents. On the road, he asked, "So, what's the secret?" She was happy that he remembered, being a man and all. He had to ask her a second time.

"We can still go on our extended vacation if you want, but we don't need to!"

"We don't need to, you say, why is that?"

"Well, I want to go, but one of the reasons for going is the fact that we were going to see how much we liked, or loved, or whatever, each other. The secret is, Max, that part is not any longer necessary. As far as I'm concerned, we truly are engaged right now, and if you asked me to marry you tomorrow, I'd do it. That is my point. I'm not trying to rush you into anything, I'm just letting you know that, I am totally your fiancé, and we can set a date for anytime you want."

Nabulio was all smiles; "And, what is your hope what I might be thinking right now?"

"If you loved me, that would be enough." They rode for a few more minutes, quietly. "Max, you are truly my everything. I want nothing more. I awake in the morning thinking of you and go to sleep the same way. We were only apart for a few days. Yet, each day seemed like a lifetime, Max. I want you to hold me, and never let me go." She leaned over and kissed his cheek. "I went to the Escort Service the other day, Max. I'm out of there for good—forever—no matter what. I love life with you. I love life away from that ugly past. Max! I love you so!"

She thought his next question was odd, but she answered it. He asked, "Tell me all about your mom and your dad, and tell me about their home."

For the next twenty minutes, she told him her life story, her love for her parents, her childhood in that old home, about the old tire that hung from a rope—still, today—that her dad had set up for her when she was eight or nine. She told him about her 15th birthday, and that she never wanted to be called Constance, again, so she is 'Turnip' to her dad, and her mom never calls her Turnip, but often calls her Missy, "or," she said, "if she is mad at me, it's 'Little Missy.' That's true even, today," she added.

"What do we do if they don't like me?" Max asked.

"You have to turn off at this next exit." She gazed at the side of his face. He turned three-quarters to look at her. "Oh, Max, they already love you, because I told them that you are perfect."

"Great I can't go nowhere but down, now," he laughed. She laughed, too, and then they laughed together.

The rest of the trip was filled with "turn here, turn there," and "there is where my old girlfriend Ashley used to live," and "that is the Bible church I went to, and that is my old elementary school." It carried on like that until they pulled into her parent's driveway. "Come on in, hurry, I want you to meet them, immediately."

"No, wait. I have a question?"

Impatiently, she said, "Shoot!"

"What if we were to get married in that little white church back there, or in your families living room, come two Saturdays from now?"

"Really? You are not kidding, Max, really? Are you asking me to marry you, now, I mean soon. Is this really true? Don't tease me, Max, please don't do that! Are you really asking me?

"Really!"

"Oh, Max, yes, yes, yes, I will marry you whenever." Her heart was pounding. She was the luckiest girl in the world. *Married, married to him!* Tears fell like a warm spring shower. Could life be any better? Constance snatched a hold of him and didn't let go for ten minutes and she wouldn't have let go then, had it not been for the fact that mom and dad Middaugh were standing outside of the car, watching the tears fall from their daughter, and the man holding her had a tear or two in his eyes as well. Her daddy wrapped his knuckles on the side window.

"Must be good news, daddy, Jeanette, suggested."

Startled, Constance offered back the best news a girl could have. Today was the dream fulfilled that every girl wishes for, hopes for. "Momma, daddy, we're getting married in a fort-night!

Chapter 44—Nine Days After the Last Pair of Killings
STONE COLD—HOT AS A FIREBALL

The case was stone cold dead, once more. Over two weeks had passed; nothing new on the case was disclosed. All DNA found in the hotel room belonged to the two dead girls, Tammy, or one of the cleaning ladies.

The press was all over the police for their inefficiency. The tabloids nationwide were offering the same, nonsense. AK was an official blockbuster story once Samantha's head was reported as missing. The Trumpet Star suggested that the Angle Killer was planning a mass murder of up to 50 women. Their source—of course—was confidential. Letters To The Editor, one of the Norfolk rags riddled the cops, Wellesley, in particular. Only the Gazette was soft on Wellesley. After all, Thompson knew he still had an exclusive promise from Wellsy, once the case broke, "If it every breaks," his Editor scolded him.

Tomorrow was scheduled for another Herrington Group Meeting. It was time for a new strategy conference, for strategy sake, only. No one wanted it, and no one expected any good would come out of it. The meeting would necessarily lead nowhere, but all had to play the game. Protocol demanded such meetings. Alex declined her invitation.

Though he was depressed, and feeling the failure, Wellsy and Alex were reconnecting in a most positive way. "Alex," he said, "when this is over, can we go away for a while? Do you have any vacation time, besides the end of the school year?

"Yes, yes," she said, "some time in mid to late November."

"Can we go someplace warm, and fun?" He suggested a cruise. "Perfect," she said, where?"

He told her that that would be up to her. He then asked, "and come spring, would you marry me?"

* * * * *

On the west coast, everyone was readying for an upcoming wedding. It was to be held in the living room of the Middaugh home. It would be a small wedding, with about 40 in attendance, all friends and family. Nabulio would have neither friends nor family in attendance; save it was Constants' friends and family. Max knew one of them well, Constance. None of that would matter. She was his universe, and her mom and dad were the stars in his life. They loved him, unconditionally, and he loved them without reservation. He was family. They were family. Family sounded good to Max. He needed to have that discussion with her.

Two days after the wedding, they were scheduled to board a flight to St. Lucia for 15 days of total bliss. They had booked the works. They planned to stay at the world-class honeymoon resort in St. Lucia, the Sandals Antiqua Caribbean Village and Spa, one of the most famous luxury honeymoon romantic getaway places on all the earth, situated on Dickerson Bay, which offered a picturesque Caribbean village. At the Antiqua they had ordered the special English Butler Service treatment during their stay. Yes, they planned to be pampered.

After discussing the activities, they decided on engaging in some water sports, mostly scuba diving. Mostly, however, golf would be their main activity. Most of the time they thought they would just relax and enjoy each other's bodies, and the elegant gourmet dining, unending. They wanted to taste the very best available. Trips were planned as well, St. Lucia's National Rain Forest Reserve, St Lucia's exotic twin peaks of Les Pitons, and Diamond Falls. Both thought sight seeing and shopping in the Capital of Castries would be fun, too. She wanted to spend a lot of money. He wanted her to spend it, too.

Contingency plans were worked out as well, should they decide to just up and leave. They had plans to free wheel anything that sounded good. The one constant in it all was that they would be together. They might stay for two weeks, or just one week, or a month, or a year, whatever. Why not? His 22 million dollar windfall had climbed to 25.8 million as of this day. If they spent the whole 25 million, they decided they would go home. She giggled about that, he frowned, a silly frown.

Constance reminded Max for the tenth time that he had a secret to tell her, too. He said he had forgotten, but would hold back on it until their wedding day. "Phooey," she said.

* * * * *

Just as Alex was about to respond to his wedding offer, Wellsy's cell phone erupted, naturally! "I have to take this, it's the station."

"Wellesley, here. No, don't patch him though. Give me the number and I'll call him right back." He waited nearly a minute, and then wrote the number down. He offered "Thanks," and hung up. "Wait he said to Alex, come to the phone, and listen."

"I don't what to hear that there is another killing!" she flatly stated.

"I don't know what it is, but it's not another killing."

They walked to the living room where the speakerphone was. He punched two buttons; the first button was to order up a dial tone, the second was to record the conversation. Wellsy then punched in all thirteen numbers. They waited for the ring and then for the pick up. Alexandria asked whom he was calling. "Just listen."

A female voice with a heavy accent answered, "Scotland Yard, Criminal Investigation."

"This is Sector Lieutenant Wellesley, Norfolk, Virginia Police Department, U.S.A. calling for Inspector Hemmingway.

"Please hold, Sir." Hemmingway came on and introduced himself and got straight away to the point. He told the Lieutenant that Apsley House, the former resident of the Duke of Wellington, received a package, a box addressed to the Waterloo Gallery. "Inside, the box" the Inspector said, "was a note written with what we believed to be red crayon. I will read the note: "Display this decaying masterpiece prominently among the other masterpieces from the Duke's extensive painting collection. Sorry this is not a painting, but it surely is a masterpiece. It comes as a token from a grateful nation." Alex immediately picked up on "a token from a grateful nation."

Wellesley let out a long silent sigh, he, too picked up on it! "My guess, inspector it that the contents inside the box is a head of a woman?" he offered in resignation.

"You knew it was coming?"

"No, but it couldn't be anything else."

"I take it that it comes from your Angle Killer!"

"Yes, I'm afraid so. Yes!"

"It disgraces all England, do you know this Lieutenant Wellesley?"

"Inspector, I do not need your sarcasm at this time. Did you not just say my last name? What do you think this means to me, of all people, and my family! Indeed, Sir, you are an Englishman, and I understand your embarrassment for such a thing to have happened. I do not live in England, Sir, but I am proudly of English blood. I, Inspector am a direct descended"—his voice cracked, choked, at this point—of the 1st Duke of Wellington, Sir." This animal has belittled my name, and disgraced all Wellingtons and me! And, and now, you insult me with your innuendo and your pompous attitude! You, Sir, owe me Sir, an apology, directly."

The Englishmen was quite quiet for several seconds. He decided on this retort: "As an English Inspector, Lieutenant, I am sorry for your *personal embarrassment*, good Sir, nevertheless, and notwithstanding your *personal embarrassment*, this trophy-head of *yours* is a total *embarrassment* to not only to London, Sir, but to all of England *especially*. Frankly, the personal *embarrassment* you mention should be your individual *humiliation*, to God and to Country; *England* I mean, Sir! Your *personal* ill treatment by *your* Angle Killer is of little concern of this proper nation. Fix it, dimwit, fix it! Please come here forthwith and tote your disgrace, away!" With that, the connection went dead.

"Now what," Alex asked?

Wellesley was beside himself with anger, embarrassment, and he hadn't the foggiest as to what to do. "I have to call the Captain at home. This will not go over well. Within the hour, my Captain will be talking to Inspector Hemmingway, and then, I fear, Hemmingway's superior. Mark my word, Alex; our governments will be in the middle of this before days end! He called Rodgers, and was vague. "Meet me at your office, Captain. We best speak there. Bring a lot of humor with you because it will evaporate fast."

Wellsy left in a hurry, forgetting to kiss her goodbye. He wasn't breathing very well; either. This was going to turn into a national incident, and he would be at its apex. He hoped for the best, and expected the worst, and beyond!

The stone cold case just got hotter than a fireball, and Wellesley knew it was going to get much worse before it would ever get a little better! On the way to the office he called Strange, and then Herrington. The last person he wanted in on this fiasco was Herrington, and he was the first one that should be notified. The four men talked for four hours. At the end, Rodgers called the Mayor. All hell was about to break loose in Norfolk, Virginia. A national story was brewing! *"Can it get any worse,"* Wellsy mumbled to himself?

"You had no business asking for an apology, Lieutenant, none!"

"Captain Herrington…"

Rodgers interceded, "Lieutenant, let it pass, now!"

"But…"

"No buts, let it pass, now; and Herrington, keep your fat mouth shut unless you have something positive to say!" This is not time to be a smart ass! He turned to Strange, "Order us up some food, Detective, we're not going anywhere." He looked around, "People, call your families, we're here for the duration." Herrington left the room mumbling obscenities."

"Is the Mayor coming here?" Wellesley asked.

"Yes."

"Whom, else?"

"That is up to the Mayor."

"You think the press are on to this yet?" As the Lieutenant asked the question, his cell phone rang out, as did Rodgers, and at the same time, three incoming calls came from the switchboard to the Captain's office."

Rodgers looked at his cell phone and Wellsy at his. "What do you think, Lieutenant? Is this answer enough?" He then added, "If you don't know who the call is coming in from, don't answer it!"

Rodgers called the switchboard and asked of whom the calls that just stampeded into his office came from?

CHAPTER 45—TWELVE DAYS AFTER THE LAST PAIR OF KILLINGS
MENDING AND SEALING

The marriage went off without a hitch, other than the fact that Reverend Leonard Smith fell off the small box Lewis had made for him to stand on while marrying his daughter to a bright, well mannered, and engaging young man, such as Max. Neither of Constants parent actually new Max's full name until the minister said "Do you Constance—blah, blah, blah take—Maximilian Napoléon de Beauharnais to be your—blah, blah, blah."

Lewis leaned over and asked his wife if she could spell Max's last name. She whispered back, "I can't even pronounce it, back." Lewis laughed so hard that heads turned to look at him. His wife quickly shushed him. "Hush, yourself, old man."

"Was your fault, old woman," he said. For that he got *the look*!

An hour later the young married couple were off by themselves in the back yard. Now, Max, now, what is your secret?"

He smiled that infectious smile he owned. "I was thinking, or wondering what you think of my middle name?"

"You mean Napoléon?"

"Yes, it's the only middle name I have." They laughed together.

"Why do you ask that?"

"Well, what do you think of that as the first name of our first child."

"Well, I would have to be pregnant wouldn't I? Or, are you trying to tell me that your secret is that you are pregnant, Maximilian?"

He ignored that part of her humor, "Yes, assuming you wanted to have a child and assuming that I was after your body steadily enough until you held one within you, yes."

"Well, practice does make perfect." She smiled at him, "Yes, I would like that! It's a name that has power and great strength, I think, don't you?"

"More than you can imagine, honey, so, good, then; in a little while we'll start on that project."

"How soon?"

"Is it too early to shush everyone away, now, this minute?"

"Oh, Max. Is that all you men think about?"

"Pretty much, yes." She laughed, as did he. "I hear it's about every fifteen minutes throughout the day, but I'm lagging behind by a minute or two."

She smiled. "But Max, what if our first child was a girl."

"He won't be! I could never tolerate that. He will be a boy. The gods have so offered!" He smiled, "After all what would we call her, Napollie?" She laughed hysterically, as did he.

"Yes, I like Napollie, so that's it then, our first child will either be called Napoleon or Napollie, depending on gender, of course." With that, she added, "Yes, sir, Max, yes sir!"

"Good, lets go back to the reception." He said, forcing a smile. She didn't pick up on his distain.

"Wait, what is the secret?"

"I'll show you that, later," he said deadpanned, but it was quickly washing away. He finally gave way to the humor in it.

"No, show me now!"

"Okay, he said and started to remove his trousers."

"WAIT, what are you doing"

"I'm going to show you the magic boy baby maker. It's a *BIG* secret." Again, they laughed together and rejoined the reception.

"Come on *little* man, back to the party," she teased.

"Ouch, that hurt." They laughed, again, together.

* * * * *

Wellsy was most fortunate. The calls that had come in all at once were not the National Inquirer or any other such publication. Secondly, the Mayor in a matter of minutes dissolved the entire problem with a single call to Hemmingway's English supervisor. He profusely apologized for what went down between the top constables, here and there. He happily took the heat and it was decided that the entire matter would best be a handled discretely within the confines of law enforcement establishments. So, discretely, that the Mayor took Lieutenant Wellesley aside and chewed on his fanny for several minutes, and then he did the same to Wellesley's Captain, ending by telling the captain to send someone to England and bring back the woman's head; pronto!

Before the Mayor left the station, he found Captain Herrington. He told Herrington to settle down and act likes an experienced professional. "It's time for you to grow the hell up, Herrington, or find some other city with all your power plays." He walked away, and then abruptly stopped, and turned, "I'm on to you Herrington!"

It was three a.m. before Wellsy pulled into his driveway. He walked into the kitchen having used the back door. There she was, still up, waiting. "You okay?"

"Yes! It all worked out, thanks to the Mayor."

"Why did he get involved?"

"Don't ask, just be glad he did!"

"Okay, I'm glad."

"Come here, and give me a hug." He did. They just held each other. Both were exhausted. "Yes!"

"Yes? Yes, what," he asked!

"Yes, I will marry you in the spring, conditionally." She paused, and then sat down. "Sit down Arthur!"

He had a most quizzical look about him, he offered, "I take it that this is rather important discussion we are about to have, yes?"

She acted as if he had not said a word. "Look at me." He did, *your gorgeous*. Get that look out of your eye; this is not going to lead up to that. You have to promise me something."

"For, that, anything!"

"Get your mind out of the gutter, and don't speak so fast, and just be quiet. You must..." He could see tears swelling up in her eyes. He reached over to whisk them away. She snapped her head back, and away, "Leave it, leave them alone. Sit there, and be quiet." He did as she ordered. He felt like he was about to receive another tongue-lashing. "You must promise me something, Arthur. You must promise me something that you cannot even control, but you must promise me, anyway, or I will not marry you!"

"How can I promise something that I cannot cont..."

"I am not going to tell you again. Hush! Do you understand, hush!" He nodded. "That's better!" She took a gulp of air. "I don't know when this case will end, or even if it ever will, but you must promise me that in the end—whenever that is—that you will not be dead!" He gave her a look, and opened his mouth to speak. She took three fingers of her left hand and pressed them to his lips, pausing. He sat quietly. "You must do whatever it takes to stay alive. I don't want some willy-nilly promise, either. You must promise me with every fiber of your heart might mind and strength that you will not leave me and your child without a husband and a father."

"Are you saying that you are…"

She put her hand to his mouth, again with more pressure. "*Hush,*" she offered with far more determination. She tried, again. "*You are a stubborn baboon. Will you shut up, now!* I am marrying you because I love you, and I need you, and I want you, but you are no good to me dead. I will only marry you—like I've said—if you will hundred percent guarantee me that you will be left standing when this mess is over. No promise, no marriage, no nothing! It is now, or it is never! Which is it Arthur?"

Two minutes of dead silence passed by, he said not a word. She continued to wait until she blurted out, "And don't tell me that you can't promise me that, or forget the whole thing. I want you alive, no other way. I do not want to mourn your death over this Angel Killer thing!"

"You are saying that I am to will my life over death, no matter what. Is that what you are asking of me?" She did not answer. She sat quietly, passive. Two more dead minutes passed. He took her hands in his left hand and then placed his right hand over both of hers. "Alexandria Mae Southerland, I Arthur Wellesley do hereby promise, no I don't promise, I guarantee that I will be alive, standing once the Angel Killer is in custody, dead or alive. I so testify in the name of all that is holy. I will remain alive if you say yes to my proposal." Her head fell, yet her heart was lifted. Tears filled the linoleum floor covering. She stayed that way for some time, with tears dripping to the floor, and body quivering, and trembling. Arthur didn't know what to do or what to say.

She did not look up, she continued to let the tear drops fall, but her head bobbed up and down, "Yes, Arthur, yes, I will marry you, and in June, I will give you your child, if you will have me!"

"You are pregnant, then." She wanted to say *DUH*, but the moment was far too tender for that.

Chapter 46—Seventeen Days After the Last Pair of Killings
MOVING TOWARD THE CENTER

They had just finished one full week of marital bliss in St. Lucia. It was everything the de Beauharnais' had hoped for, and even dreamed for; it was all surpassed in wedded bliss. The Sandals, St. Lucia was truly a heavenly gift from the Almighty. They had taken pictures galore, and discovered each others likes, dislikes, hopes and dreams. Or, at least, Maximilian had begun that process that would take some time, but started nevertheless; it had to be done. He had exactly 40 days left, meaning that 41 days from this day would be the one hundred and first day of his reign over W, and the day of W's last day on earth. It was his plan from the beginning; it was the plan until the end. Supremacy was his byword. He now began the process of indoctrination of his only love in life, save that of his hero, Napoléon.

It was just past eight when Max woke up in paradise. Constance was seated on the bed, her back against two pillows that her body pinned to the headboard. She was reading *The Broker*, by John Grisham, one of her favorite writers. "Is it any good?" he asked

I'm just starting chapter seven, so it's still building. But, yes. All his books are good. Have you read any?" He shook his head, no! "You should, he is very good." Max asked her how many he had written. "I don't know, let me look. She turned to the front of the book where all the previous titles were listed. "This book makes it 18."

"Have you read them all?" She bobbed her head up and down. "Which one is your favorite? She told him the first one, because it got her hooked. "What was the first one called?"

"*A Time To Kill.*"

"Really," he said! She looked at him. He had made his comment with a certain, well she didn't know, exactly, but a flare of some kind. He asked, "Do you think killing is ever justified, you know is there ever a time to kill?" She looked at him with a look of puzzlement about her. She shrugged her shoulders. He wanted to keep the conversation light, so he scooted closer to her, reached up under her black thin see through sleeping garment and fondled her right breast.

She smiled. "Don't start something you can't finish."

He told her he was not interested in finishing at the present, but suggested they let things go as they might. "About my question?" he asked. She thought and then answered in the affirmative, suggesting that in time of war killing was justified, and certainly for self-preservation, protecting families, law enforcement, and stuff like that. He liked her answer, a lot. Staying on the topic, but seemingly moving away from it, he offered, "Did I ever tell you that I'm a direct descendant to Napoléon Bonaparte?"

She put her book down, removed his hand from her breast, and leaned in toward him, "Really? I mean really, you are?" He answered positively. "Wow, I mean holy cow, you are famous." She paused ever so slightly. No, you are just playing with me, aren't you Max."

"Dead serious. Well," he began to add.

"Ah, I thought so, here comes the punch line."

"No, no punch line but let me ask you a question. Let's say you were married before I met you, and your husband died, and then you met me. However, before your husband died, you had a child with him, say a boy. Okay, with that as a background, let's say we had still met, fell in love and got married, and at some point in time, I asked you if I could adopt your son, and, for the sake of argument, you said, yes. So legally, he became my adopted son, but kept the last name of his natural father. Would you consider him as my son, legally?"

She didn't even have to think, she offered back, "Yes, of course." Then right on top of that she asked, "Wait, wait, one minute, has this something to do with the conversation we had on our wedding day. Do you already have a son by the name of Napoleon from some previous marriage? Is that it, Max?"

He laughed heartedly. "No, no precious not at all, ease your mind on that. I have no children, unless, of course…" He reached over and patted her tummy.

She smiled, "No, Max, no! Wait," she said, are you telling me that that is how you are related to Napoleon?" He bobbed his head and told her that Napoléon had been married twice and the second wife came to that second marriage with a son. Napoléon adopted her son and that that made him a direct descendant to the great Napoleon Bonaparte, though the de Beauharnais family line. "Holy cow, I'm married to nobility." Max loved hearing her say that.

"I have a passion for thee Napoléon, honey. I made a quest a few years ago and visited all the places he had been. I got so excited at it all; it still excites me today more than I can explain." He paused, and added, "Heck, I'd love to go, again."

"Oh Max. This is so wonderful. I know so little about Napoleon, sorry, but that is true. I only know that he was a leader, and Emperor, I think, maybe and that he was killed in a filed of battle at a place called Waterloo."

Max smiled. "Well, you have the gist of it."

"Sorry! I'm not much of a history buff, but, wow, you are a descendent of Napoleon. How cool is that!" He smiled. "Max, we don't have anything planned, today, do we?" He shrugged his shoulders indicating that he didn't think so. "Look, this has me so excited, I'm actually hot. Here is our plan for today if it is okay with you. First, I want you to make love to me, while I'm thinking of who is doing me, you know, like I'm getting it from Napoleon. I know I'm weird, but do that, let me fantasize, okay. Wow, this is really making me hot. Okay, then I want to spend the entire day learning all there is to know about your Great great great, father, uncle, what? I don't know how many greats, but you get the picture, your ancient grandfather or whatever he is to you. Will you do that?"

"I'll go you one better. We both have our passports, what say that you and I get it on, and then we pack up and we leave for Europe, starting with France, and then we'll visit his life all over the continent, okay? We'll take a month and discover the real Napoléon. Learn everything about him and…" He was out of breath, and out of dialogue. His heart was pounding. *Say yes, women say yes.*

"Oh, Max, can we really do that, really?" He hardly had time to bob his head. She was all over him. She ravished his body. She did all the work; she fought off any attempt he made to be part of the team. This was her time to bring him ultimate joy. She loved this reckless man with all her heart, and more!

Max thought he was going to die. Marrying an ex-professional call girl wasn't so bad after all. She was all over him to the degree that at one point he actually shouted out her hooker name, Katrina. When he did, she stopped everything she was doing. Looked down at him, and only smiled, saying, "You haven't seen anything yet, buddy!" And then she did something to him that he did not think humanly possible. Oh, my, life was good in the islands. But, happily, they were about to leave. *Hmmm,* he thought, *a time to kill!*

Six hours later they boarded a plane and were on their way to Paris France. They would spend two and one half days in Paris merely because it was Paris, after all, and, then on to Corsica—the armpit of Italy—but, nevertheless, still, where it all began for Napoléon Bonaparte. Max knew Constance would ultimately agree with this kind of killing as well; accepting the fact there is—indeed—*A Time To Kill!* It was merely a matter of time, and she would accept all the killings so that her husband would rule in righteous dominion over Wellington!

CHAPTER 47—EIGHTEEN DAYS AFTER THE LAST PAIR OF KILLINGS
DEAD CASE, BUT ONE HOPE IN BALTIMORE

Detective Strange caught the assignment to fly to England. He was invited to spend a day reviewing Scotland Yard, complements of Inspector Hemmingway. While there Strange visited the location of where Samantha's head was sent. Also, he took in the museum and all the touches of where his boss's legacy came from. Upon arrival back in the States he gave Wellsy the information regarding where the box with Samantha's head had been initially mailed. Two days later the Lieutenant arrived in Baltimore, and made a beeline to the post office, but not before stopping at the City of Baltimore Police Department.

Detective Sergeant Emerson Walsh then accompanied Wellesley to the US Post Office where the box with its contents—the head—had began its postal travel. Thomas Farnsworth was the individual who processed the paperwork. He was on duty, today, as well. The Postmaster gave permission for Farnsworth to talk to the police in the back part of the Federal building. "Normally, I probably wouldn't even remember, but the guy, I'd say age 25, or so, maybe older, I don't know, but I just remember something he said that was odd." Walsh asked him what that was. "Well, officer—Emerson let the title go—he kind of mentioned that he was a student at George Washington, and that he was finishing up his PhD in Postal Administration. I told him that I didn't know that that there was even a major or an option, or something like that in Postal anything. Anyway, the guy smirked at me and said, "Forget about it!""

"You have his signature don't you," Wellsy asked.

"Sure, but I can't believe he would have signed his real name." Wellsy told him that that was his worry, not the postal clerk's worry. "I'm sure we do, but,

I can't give that to you, it's Federal property. Wellsy looked at Walsh. Walsh shrugged his shoulders.

"Make us a copy of the signature, then."

"Sure, I can do that, I guess."

"What else can you remember?"

"Nothing."

"Tell me what this… Wait, I do remember something. When he left here, I started to wait on the next man, and that's when I heard a noise. I looked up and a lady upon trying to leave, following behind this guy we are talking about, well she stumbled, or tripped, or something, and nearly fell. She caught herself, but I tried to hurry around the corner of this counter to assist here. She was fine. I made sure and then pushed open the door for her, and I saw this guy, you know, the one were just talking about, I see him jogging toward a car, and then the car just took off without him. I then saw this guy snatch a folder, or something that was pinned, or nailed, I don't know, to the telephone pole, adjacent to, and across the street, over that way," he pointed.

"Is that it?"

"No, well, almost. He opened the top of the envelop and took out what looked like money or something, I'm not sure, but there must have been a note cause he read it, or it looked like he did."

"How long did you watch him?" Welsh asked.

"Not long at all. But I saw him toss the folder or whatever it was, maybe it was a legal sized envelope, I can't remember, but I saw him toss it into a trashcan by the telephone pole. The guy then jumped up into the air and hightailed it out of there. He was on the run. I don't know where he went from there. I went back to work." He laughed, and then added, "The next guy in line was pissed because I didn't finish waiting on him before I went to the woman's aid." He shook his head, and offered, "People," in disgust.

"We still need a copy of the signature." Welsh, demanded. Farnsworth said sure, then and went back to get it. It took him nearly ten minutes. While Wellsy waited for the signature, he asked Welsh to go across the street and see what papers were in the trash. "We'd be lucky there, Lieutenant."

Wellesley yelled after him, "If there is anything that looks close to it, don't touch it!

"Right, prints," Walsh yelled back! Wellsy nodded, though he realized that a lot of time had passed since the man had discarded the folder, or whatever it was.

The clerk came back and gave Wellsy the copied signature. "I'm sure he wouldn't have put his own name on it."

"Don't worry about it. Can you remember anything else about the guy?" He offered a simple no back to the officer. "Did you see the car that the guy drove away in?"

"Yeah, I think so, it was dark, maybe green, maybe blue, or maybe even black. It was a Jeep Cherokee, I think." He then added, "I really can't remember! I may not have been a Cherokee. I'm really sorry. I mean, it was, well, you know, it wasn't anything important in my life, at the time."

"You think, or you know?"

"I'm not sure, but it was dark, the car I mean, not dark outside."

"How well do remember what this guy looked like? Would you know him if you saw him, again."

"No, I didn't get a look at him at all. I hardly saw the car leave."

"No," Wellsy, said, "I mean the guy who signed this." He waived the copy in the guys face."

"Oh, sure, sure I could. Sure I could."

While Lieutenant Wellesley talked to Farnsworth's supervisor. Sergeant Welsh came up empty in fishing though the garbage. So, he went back inside the post office. Ten minutes later, Farnsworth and the two cops exited the Federal Post Office. Upon climbing into the car, Wellsy said, "I'll be right back." He jogged across the street, where a hotdog vender was setting up. He came back to the police car and climbed into the passengers' side of the car, and said. "The vendor doesn't remember anything." With that, Farnsworth was on his way to the police station to offer his description of the guy in question to the police sketch artist, Sandra Hill.

Next, with Walsh's help and the Director of Communication, Baltimore Police, Lieutenant Harold Thomas contacted: WJZ-13 Baltimore News Station. Within two hours the unnamed person's sketch was put on Baltimore TV, WJZ-13. Lieutenant Harold Thomas was standing next to the police sketch artist's rendition of Farnsworth's depiction of the unknown man. Thomas stated into the camera: "If you are this man, or if you know this man, who is believed to be a graduate student at Georgetown University, please call, or have him call the Baltimore Police and ask for Homicide Division, Lieutenant Harold Thomas." Under the sketch an 800 number was listed. This man may have vital information regarding the Angel Killer who has been stalking and killing women in Norfolk, Virginia. This man, the man in the sketch is only wanted as a possible witness that may be able to assist police in the Angel Killer's identity. He should not be concerned with being arrested; he is merely a witness with vital information that may help solve this Virginia killer known as the AK murderer."

After a two-hour wait, Wellesley made two calls, the first to his Captain and the second to his fiancé. His message to both was to tell each what he had learned from the Baltimore investigation, and why he was staying over night. He had high hopes he would be soon interviewing the unknown mailer of folk singer, Samantha's head.

Jason Ireland saw the news development the first time it was shown. He was scared to death. He vividly remembered what he thought when he heard the breaking news that a female head—absent its body—had been sent to England from the United States. He was quivering and shaking, now. He knew it had to be the package he mailed for the Angel Killer. He couldn't believe he spent nearly an hour and a half talking and then working for that monster. He had seemed to be so normal. *How could I have done this*, he brood over?

When Ireland got back to Georgetown University from the post office—to his friends, anyway—he had bragged about his mailing project that supposedly brought him $1,200. Hardly anyone had believed him because of the large money amount that he bragged about seemed so ridiculous; but then, when the news of the head broke, they all knew, and now Ireland wished that nobody knew. Now, all of his friends knew the truth, and they were all a buzz about telling others that Ireland had conspired with the Angel Killer. Jason was big-time scared, now! He knew he should call the police before one of his friends called them, because than it might look like he was guilty, of something; hiding something. He finally he got up his courage—his nerve—and Justin called the Baltimore Police just as Wellesley was hanging up with Alexandria.

At one point he said into the telephone, "I'm in big trouble, aren't I?"

CHAPTER 48—NINETEEN DAYS AFTER THE LAST PAIR OF KILLINGS
FIRST STEPS OF CONVERSION

Nabulio wanted Constance to understand that while Corsica was Napoléon's place of birth, he was not all that well thought of in Corsica, today, but there was a time that he was definitely beloved most everywhere he roamed. Therefore, the couple spent very little time in Corsica; but that's where it all started so that's where they started, too!

From Corsica, the couple followed the same path that Max had made several years previously when his life changed irrevocably. It was that trip—of years ago—when Nabulio fell in love with his great, great, great grandfather, Napoléon Bonaparte. So, on this trip of trips, Nabulio wanted to convert his dear sweet wife—line upon line—to that same love, that same heritage that he had and now wanted for their unborn son, Napoléon; for he—Napoléon Bonaparte—was truly the greatness of the world's greatest General, Commander, and Emperor of the world; albeit for only one-hundred days.

The couple traveled to Egypt, then India, and then back to France. They followed Napoléon's legacy. They traced Nabulio's greatness, their own legacy. They visited Marengo, too, where their hero had defeated the Austrians. And, to be totally fair, they traveled to Trafalgar where Napoléon was defeated, and then to Elba, where he served out his life. Finally, they returned to France where Napoléon reinstated himself for his auspicious 100 days of power as Emperor. Max talked for hours of those glorious 100 days and the importance they brought to the world. He then made a comment that Constance didn't understand, so she let it pass unexplained. Her husband had offered, "One day, I will surpass Napoléon's 100 days, by one day, giving thee Napoléon back all his glory, he so richly deserves." He went on, "I will beat—dear wife—the

Wellington in our lives; today, and make justice for the greatest of greats; Napoléon!"

Mrs. de Beauharnais became a Napoléon fanatical fan, after the path of her husband. Napoléon, as Maximilian cleverly laid out those 100 wonderful days rule of supremacy in such a way that his wife—his woman—fell headlong in love with the legacy of Napoléon, and that her husband that was part of the inheritance, which meant that she was, too, and their son—she hoped—would one day live as well. Neither she, nor Max knew that that child was developing within her womb, already; this day of days!

They spent an extra two days in Trafalgar, where Max offered the knowledge of the engagements and the battles, of Wellington, or Wellesley. His wife learned about the battles fought just south of Brussels. Max taught his converted wife his version of Napoléon, the commander of the French and Wellesley, the commander of British, and of how those battles had ended twenty-three years of war that had began with the French Revolutionary War, and drove through including the Napoleonic Wars.

Max had to wipe away his tears as he taught her of Napoléon's defeat at Waterloo; that crush that ended exactly his—Napoléon—one hundred days of supremacy as Emperor. Max shared his anger over this, with tears flowing, and nasal sniffing as she witnessed how angry he was over Napoléon's defeat. She felt his love, his passion, and his compassion to the degree that—she, too—cried out and even pounded her fist upon the table of the tavern they were in when she learned of the debacle in Napoléon's life at Waterloo.

Nabulio shared Napoléon's history, though he jumped around in telling it. He stared with 1804, when Napoléon had begun is reign as Emperor, and then Nabulio went back and forth, trying to give her the overall picture, historically. Britain had declared war on France, which brought on the Napoleonic Wars. He explained to her his great love for Napoléon and how he wanted so much more for Napoléon, now, even, yes, even today, so many years later. Nabulio admitted that he wanted to conquer all of Britain, all the world for that matter. "Honey," Max, said, "there was so much he could have done for the world."

He shared with his wife how utterly unfairly Britain, Austria, Prussia and Russia had assembled together—teamed up as one—to defeat all the goodness Napoléon would have brought to the world. "It was those ruffians that brought disaster to his legacy, my legacy, and yours and our son's Constance. Sweetheart—he implored—together, they closed ranks and descended on Paris, from about every direction possible. Napoléon had to fight against several foes at once. Wellesley, the Brit, was obviously the evilest of all. Yes, it was Wellesley that led the others to dethrone the greatest," he complained, crying, anew.

Max made it clear, that Wellesley, alone, could never have defeated the great Napoléon; himself." He added, "The Prussian Commander Gebhard Leberecht Blücher was at Waterloo with Wellington. Constance, Napoléon knew Blücher. That prick had defeated him in a battle, before. Additionally, Wellesley had never tasted a loss by the French. Everything was against our hero, and unfairly, too. Even so, love, Napoléon had a battle plan that should have worked. He was going to divide Wellesley and Blücher's armies." Constance was listening, intently. Max's excitement, and love for Napoléon was so strong, that it flowed into her with ease and deep appreciation for such a gallant man, hero.

Nabulio, continued, with a long narrative which didn't weary or worry her at all, she was mesmerized by it all; she wanted the whole of it. "The Emperor" Max said, "Ordered Marshal Ney to attack at Quatre-Bras crossroads between where Brussels, Charleroi, Nivelles and Namur were. The plan would have been perfect had it been executed just a bit earlier. Unfortunately, it came too late. The enemy was already positioned, and thwarted Ney's attack. Nevertheless, that battle ended in a standoff; otherwise Napoléon would have been victorious because he greatly outnumbered his opposing forces. Even, so; there was some victory in this, however, honey, while Napoléon had succeeded in keeping two different armies apart, he had thought that the Prussians had lost their battle." Max's face filled with tears at this point. He sobbed, uncontrollably.

Constance asked, "Why, what's wrong, Max?"

"It wasn't his fault, not at all. Napoléon received a bad communiqué. Had he had that information correctly, he could have quashed the Prussians and won the battle, and probably the war. It wasn't his fault Constance, not his fault at all. Really; it was, as I said; all because of bad communication, and because of that, the world has been turned upside down. The wrong people stayed in power."

Sadly, he continued, "On that fateful day of June 18, 1815, Napoléon knew that his power was in his cavalry, and artillery. He surmised his power was sufficient to overmatch that of Wellesley's army. So, he decided upon an aggressive surprise. He would rupture through Wellesley's line hoping the British would divert part of their army, thereby softening the center, the belly, and—if accomplish—then Napoléon's could advance upon it. "I will admit this much, though, Nabulio said, "My hero did miscalculated here, and therefore, it ended in a misadventure by having too many men on this one battlefield."

"Later, love, after the war's end, Wellesley suggested that that battle brought him the victory. Nevertheless, Napoléon had, weakened the British, but Napoléon was still driven back but Wellesley also needed added support. He couldn't have defeat Napoléon on his own merit."

He continued, after a sob of his own; "Napoléon knew that the stronghold at La Haye Sainte was the answer to victory. Therefore, he ordered Marshal Ney to seize upon it. He had to smash the center in order to claim controlled victory. As ordered, Ney charged to his mark; but Wellesley was more than ready. His infantry had formed squares at the ridge, waiting for the attackers. Standing as a fortress in front of the formed squares was Wellesley's Allied artillery. Gunners pounded upon Ney, until his army needed to fall behind the squares. Even then the army of Napoléon managed to capture La Haye Sainte, and Wellesley was *forced* to give it up." He paused, not wanting to say the rest, "but it was only for the moment. Ney requested more support from Napoléon. Napoléon could only respond with, 'Where do you expect me to get them from? Do you want me to make some?'" Nabulio paused, and offered, sadly; "In those remarks, it can be seen the stress and hopelessness of the situation.

"Honey, Napoléon could not give Ney the men he needed because he had lost Plancenoit to the Prussians. He couldn't divide his forces any more, so he threw his elite Guard forward to make a final attempt to stop Wellesley's line. Wellesley and *all his allies* overmatched our Napoléon badly. It was totally, unfair!"

Nabulio took a breath, and continued, but his heart was low, so he could hardly go on. She felt, no, she shared all Nabulio's pain. This wasn't just some story; this was Max's story, his life. After a deep sigh, he continued, "By evening the French-held, and La Haye Sainte folded. Wellesley, hiding in a cornfield—the coward—was waiting for Napoléon's troops to walk into the ambush." Nabulio added, "Just like the coward that he was, Wellesley was hiding in the cornfield. From hiding in a cornfield, the coward advanced and ended the battle."

He, continued, with little heart, "One of Wellesley's leaders, Blücher, wanted to name the battle *La Belle Alliance*, but Wellesley demanded that his tradition must be upheld. It had been his practice that a battle would be known based on where he spent the night before the battle. In this case, his last night's sleep before the battle had been Waterloo."

All Constance could think to say was, "Oh, Max!" She hurt terribly for him. As a matter of fact, she hurt for her family. She felt as she wanted to induce some kind of revenge, but, of course, she never would; nor could. Exhausted from his own story, Max sat back and just thought it all though with his wife. They sat, together for some time. Every few seconds, Max would wipe away another tear or so. She kissed him. He looked at her and he tried to smile back; it didn't work.

After a few minutes, he offered, "He was so cheated. History, today, all over the world is different because of a miss-communiqué. How could he lose?

Honey, the world was put back together wrongly because of that. They didn't have telegrams, or cell-phones, or anything except foot soldiers or soldiers on horseback, all too slow. "And," he said, "I didn't go into this, but the rotten weather played out helping Wellesley and greatly hindering Napoléon! I was all so unfair."

Her Napoléon looked deeply into her eyes, "It all went well for Wellesley, and it all went amuck for Napoléon! Ney lost the chance to gain control of Quatre-Bras, why? Why, because he waited for orders that never came! Why? Slow communications, that's why! How does that make any sense? It doesn't I tell you, it doesn't. Additionally, I believe if Ney had taken the initiative instead of sitting on his horse, waiting, and charged forward, we wouldn't even be having this conversation." He wiped away another tear, and offered, "Bastard!"

Nabulio then went on and railed about everything that went wrong: procedures or controls, secondary leaders of Napoléon should have taken care of those mishaps. Maximilian seethed. "Everything was against Napoléon from the beginning, but he still should have won!" Nabulio then asked Constance the question, the question of all questions, "Do you agree with me that Wellesley never did enough to be honored by announcing to the world that he was now— as a reward—given the status as The Duke of Wellington." He didn't give her a chance to respond; he said it, himself, "NO! God, NO! The idea makes me want to vomit." She agreed, wholeheartedly, but wisely, she decided to remain silent. "Would you do something about it if you could?"

"Oh, yes, Max, definitely yes!" she answered almost before Max ended his question.

"Well, you are right!" Max, exploded, "The end of Napoléon's hundred-day reign ended with the Battle of Waterloo, Constance. Napoléon was banished St. Helena, an island where he died in 1821."

"Constance offered, "Bastards!"

"Here! Here! Bastards, indeed," Nabulio offered back even more than just provoked. He was exercised beyond imagination, as was she. "We need to go to go to London now that you know this history, and then we can go back home." He said. She asked why. "I'll tell you when we are there." was all he said.

They went England, to the place where Samantha's head had arrived just a few weeks, before. Constance mentioned that, immediately. Max told her he would tell her a great deal about that within a few days, but today he wanted her to see a statue.

The next day, she stood before the statue, and she read, just as Nabulio had read, "The gift of a grateful nation in 1816." She openly burst into tears. "What a slap in the face to the greatest man, Max, to the greatest man of all, and you are heir to this legacy too. You should tear it down!"

"I have a better, a stronger, idea, but not here, and not today!"

"Soon, I hope, Max, soon! I want to know!" As they walked away, and not fast enough for her, either, he said, "Everything about Arthur Wellesley drives me, Maximilian Napoléon de Beauharnais crazy; but to see that that statue, that prize, that trophy illuminating to the world of a conquest of evil is beyond anything I can stand."

He looked at her, "Honey, there must be one last Waterloo, and this time—Wellington—must meet his Waterloo, not Bonaparte, and not de Beauharnais, either."

Though she didn't know what he meant by that, but she found herself, saying, "Amen!" to it all!

CHAPTER 49—NINETEEN DAYS AFTER THE LAST PAIR OF KILLINGS
GIVE IT UP, POOR JASON A. IRELAND

"He had been sitting in the interrogation room for nearly twenty minutes, already. Walsh and Wellesley sat quietly chattering about each other's fiancés, just to kill time, and to let Jason Ireland stew, of course. Walsh didn't have any problem with the Lieutenant conducting the interview. Yes, they were on Walsh's turf, but it was Wellesley's case. The Lieutenant walked in first, and introduced himself with his full Norfolk, Virginia title; just to be sure Ireland knew what he was facing. Yet, Wellsy knew the poor guy was scared to death. It didn't matter; it was time to scare him a lot more. People open up faster that way.

Walsh walked in a minute later. Wellsy introduce Walsh, and then told Ireland that Walsh was the good cop in this scenario of good cop, bad cop routine. "That makes me the bad, cop buckaroo, so if you cooperate right this minute, you won't even have to see my bad side." He cleared his throat, smiled, or rather smirked and then asked Ireland if he would like something to drink.

"I'm not going to be here, that long, am I? I mean to have a drink; I mean I just did a guy a favor, nothing more, right?"

"You do know that you have committed a felony, don't you!" Whether Jason Ireland thought about it or not, he was certainly considering it now. He sat mute, trembling! Wellesley continued, "When you falsified your signature on that Federal Post Office Document, you deliberately committed a felony! You know that don't you?" He offered the smirk, again. "Fess up; you've already admitted it by merely answering our TV prompt. When you picked up that phone to dial, you as much as admitted it! And we thank you for that, but clamming up now will not go well for you. You are already looking at six to ten years; you know that, so being honest now may save you a lot of aggravation, later. So," the bad cop continued, "Do you want to cooperate, now, or would you like to sit here and think some more?"

"No, I mean, no, I want to cooperate, that is why I am here." Fifty-seven minutes after he answered that first question, he was still in the same room waiting to visit with the sketch artist! Wellesley had left the room. Welsh stayed in the room just to keep Ireland on a short leash. "Am I arrested?"

"You feel you should be, do you?"

"No. I didn't know I broke the law."

"Yes, you did, you just weren't thinking it through, like, maybe you could end up here!" That sound about right?"

"I guess."

"You don't guess. You know."

"What is going to happen to me?"

"That is up to the Lieutenant, but you know, he's dealing with seven murders, and one guy named Parker who probably will never be a man again. Not to mention the poor girl, April who, for whatever reason he left basically alone and alive, but she is still a total basked case, today. So, do you think the Lieutenant cares much about you? I'll tell you what he cares about, he cares about getting his superiors off his ass, and the Mayor, and his Section Chief, and a few hundred thousand citizens in the greater Norfolk, Virginia area, and all the women in that area, and all their mothers and fathers who live within a hundred miles of Norfolk. You think the Lieutenant is giving any thought to poor little you? He's after a monster! Look, buster, you have an opportunity to do the world a favor. You are the only one—as far as we know—that actually knows—that has actually cast eyes upon him. Yes, you—my boy—you are a direct witnessed of this monster. Your memory for the sketch artist is everything to the Lieutenant, and to this case, and to tens of thousands of scared people out there. What, you had to go to bed last night with this on your mind, worried? Is that about right?" He didn't wait for an answer. "This cop, he lives it every second of every day." He looked deep into the kid's eyes, "Jason Arnold Ireland, it's time to just give it up!"

"I—I just didn't know!"

"And you still don't know!" Get your crap together, kid, study in your mind right now that that guy looked like! See him in your mind!"

"Will it help me with the felony?"

"You are *not* going to be charged, dip-shit, just do what you have to do now, and do it well. Screw up, or mess with me or the Lieutenant and you'll never see the light of day, except the light glistening off the iron bars on your lockup."

With that, Welsh walked out of the room! As he entered the main room off the interrogation room, Lieutenant nodded to him. Welsh nodded, back, and offered, "He's primed, Lieutenant. Give him five more minutes and he'll describe things he saw when he was three years old. He'll be relaxed more. Give him that time. He knows he's only going to jail if he screws up!"

"Good job, Sergeant."

Fifteen minutes later Ireland was with the artist. When she came out, she handed the sketch to Wellesley. Wellsy opened his folder of the sketches he had. He handed them to her. She said, "You didn't have much to go on there, LT. Looks like we agree on the mouth, but not the nose. You want me to show him these and ask him if this helps?"

"You would know better than I, officer."

She went back to the room. Twenty-two minutes later, she came out and said, "Here is another sketch." She handed it to him, and continued, "Quite frankly, I think the waters are muddier now. I'd go with his first sketch, Lieutenant, over the second one I just did and over the ones you brought me. This guy saw him the longest and from many different angles. Anyway you've got what you've got." She sighed, "It's your call," she then added, "or you could use them all, but you will get more leads then you know what to do with. Your choice."

"Thanks," Was all he said!

"No need, it's what I do, but you're welcome. It's up to you, now. No offense intended. Good luck!"

"None taken," he replied. She left.

"Shall we go back in LT and talk to him about the vehicle, AK's accent, if any, mannerisms, excreta?"

"You do it, Sergeant, and then fax me and call me. I'm going to get back! I've been away too long. You're good to work with."

"Ditto, Lieutenant, Ditto!"

"Wait a second, Sergeant, give me the sketch, I'm going back in there for just a minutes or two."

"Want me to come with you?"

"Sure, come on, I just want to try something with the guy; just one last time."

"I'm with you, let's go."

Inside the room, Wellsy said, "Have you been totally honest with us?"

"Yes sir, I have been so, and in every way, too, Sir."

The Lieutenant spun about and slammed the sketch down hard on the table in front of the witness. "Ireland, is this man that took you to the Post Office?"

Jason Ireland looked hard, he answered with a simple, "Yes."

Wellsy snapped back. "You better hope the hell we find him, Ireland. I hope you enjoyed the money he gave you. Now, one last question; what would you change on this sketch to make the sketch perfect?"

"His whiskers weren't so messy. His appearance was more like, well more like he just hadn't shaved his stubble for a day or two; I don't think that it was permanent look; just that maybe he hadn't shaved for a couple of days, and he's more handsome, then this sketch. I'd say."

"Anything else strike you?"

"Maybe his forehead wasn't so long; other than that…" Ireland just shook his head. Wellsy turned to the other cop, "Get this sketched cleaned up, and then let this felon, go. Get this sketch out everywhere; fax it to my office in Virginia; and when it's done, download it to my cell phone." He turned to the kid, "Keep your nose clean or I'll have your ass! Cops have a long memory for idiots like you. He turned to the Walsh one last time, and offered, "Book his ass, or let him go, I'm out of here!"

Two hours later Nabulio's sketch was entered into Wellsy's cell phone. He looked at the updated sketch. *Yeah, I thought you were a looker after all. The women probably thought you were cute right up until you sliced their throats; bastard!*

CHAPTER 50—TWENTY-ONE DAYS AFTER THE LAST PAIR OF KILLINGS
HOME COMING—MORE PREPARING

"Constance's indoctrination was way ahead of schedule, for the present, anyway. From Europe they flew into LaGuardia Airport, New York City. From there they waited almost two hours before taking their connecting flight to Norfolk. However, upon deplaning, and walking to their next terminal, they passed by four blown up sketches. Constance looked at the first, and looked harder at the second, and nearly stopped at the third. Max was oblivious to it all. She read: Have you seen the AK Killer, call 1-888-AK-KILLS! *Hmmm*, she thought!

They had a snack at one of the lounges. He had a beer and a chicken sandwich. She had water and a chicken salad croissant. The food was awful, but filling and expensive. He was watching a football game on the restaurant's television. She excused herself to use the restroom. She walked directly back to the 3rd poster. She definitely saw Max. *Not possible*, she thought, not even the remotest of the remotest possibility. Nevertheless, she was dumfounded at the possibility, the look-a-like of him.

She returned. After a half hour he realized that she seemed distant. *Hmmm*, perhaps the football game, he thought. "You, okay," he asked. She didn't respond. He asked, again.

She barely heard his voice, but said, "Huh?"

"I asked if you are okay."

"Come with me," she demanded, and got out of her seat and walked away. He followed toting his carryon bag. They walked directly to the poster. "Look, who do you see, Max."

He seemed unfazed, turned up his nose and said, "Huh, I see me, sort of, whom do you see?"

"The very same." He walked away. She chased after him, "Max, don't you have more to say?"

He stopped, and turned. She nearly bumped into him. "Is that the sketch of the AK?"

"Yes, Max, I guess so."

"Me, too, then, I guess so, too."

"Have you seen him, before?"

"No!"

"Case settled then. Come on, let's go to our gate."

"Well, it's kind of eerie, isn't it?"

"Even more now that my wife has found him." He paused. Stopped, and turned to her. "Shall I turn myself in, now, woman?"

Woman. You call me *woman*! "Is that who I am now? Woman?"

"Well, apparently I'm the Angel Killer, now! Which is worse to be called, woman or Angel Killer?"

"Point taken, I'm sorry."

He sighed, "Sorry, me too! But, that was rather shocking to see, and more so to be accused."

"I did not accuse you!"

"Didn't you? Max asked. "What, do you think I go around killing women? I do not, but there is a time to kill." Grisham's book flashed into her mind, *The Broker,* and then just as suddenly, *A Time To Kill!* She couldn't help but to think how odd that was. She remembered their conversation days, ago, about there being a time to kill. She wondered, why it flashed back to her now.

He walked, away. She followed sheepishly, but still kept thinking, *a time to kill!* They sat in silence until it was time to board the plane, even then they didn't talk. Half way home, from the seat next to him, she offered, "I'm sorry!"

All he said in return was, "Don't be!" She wondered what that was supposed to mean, but she let it pass.

As the plane touched down, she offered, "Is this our first argument?"

He answered with but three words, "No, our last!" He didn't explain and she didn't ask. They scurried to a taxi stand. Within the hour they were home. He was so quiet. She knew he was angry, but she had never witnessed this mood before, so she wasn't sure how to react. They both walked to the bedroom. She was going to unpack, later. She stepped though the doorway. He said, "Stop!" She did. "Turn and look at me." She did. "Take your clothing off." She did. "Take mine off." She did. "Have your way with me." She did. Their tiff was over, but he knew it would be a longer road, ahead, to even get where they were before the three giant sketches of the AK Killer, him, jumped up and bit him!

They slept in each other's arms, peacefully?

CHAPTER 51—TWENTY-TWO DAYS AFTER THE LAST PAIR OF KILLINGS OR SIXTY-EIGHT DAYS AFTER THE FIRST PAIR OF KILLINGS
AK SNOCKERED BY LOCAL CARPENTER

"Besides the incoming calls that were screened, and being fielded in rotation with Captain Rodgers, Captain Herrington, Detective Strange, and Lieutenant Wellesley, nothing much else on the case was happening. Rodgers was paring up with Second Lieutenant Harold Holcomb, a new transfer in from Detroit, Michigan. Herrington had Ted Castle, Strange with Lieutenant Joshua Caruthers, Crimes Against Persons Unit, Homicide Section, and Wellesley chose Jessica House from Campus Security at Old Dominion to be his assistant. That required Rodger's authorization. He had alternative motives; he wanted her on the force, and he wanted to help her get the job. She was so bright and savvy.

On the first day of calling, 239 calls were screened, with 132 actually being forwarded to one of the four teams. Of the 132, 42 were asked to come in to meet with a pair of the team. Day two netted 38 actual interviews, and today, by 2:30, p.m. 31 interviews were conducted. All were tired, but thought that they were averaging out okay.

* * * * *

Max told Constance that he needed some time, alone for the day. He had to do some serious thinking. He asked if she minded. She said it was fine, as she wanted to do laundry, clean the house and figure out why there was a cold draft coming out of the fireplace. She asked if he would at least tell her where he was going, and when he would be back.

He didn't mind. He said, "My dad's home is still here in Norfolk. I've decided to sell it, or find out what I can get out of it as a rental. I also want to hire someone to ready the house, for either renting it out, or selling it. It needed interior painting. The basement needed drywall put up, and both toilets need to be replaced. And," he added, "I think the garbage disposal was on the fritz."

"Where is his house located? Is it in Norfolk?" He rattled off the address, and said, "I'll be home by six, okay?"

"Okay, I love you, Max. You want supper ready when you get home?"

"Love you, too, and yes on the supper. However," he added, "Keep it light, I ate too much the last three weeks." She laughed, but agreed. "See you at six."

He left and took a standby flight to Raleigh, North Carolina. He was on his way 32 minutes later. From the airport he took a cab to Chapel Hill, North Carolina, and then another cab to Fayetteville, N.C. In downtown Fayetteville, he got out of the cab, and walked two blocks to a shopping area, and went inside the phone booth put on her plastic gloves, and called 1-800AK-KILLS. That line was answered with, "AK-KILLS, Norfolk Police, your name and number."

He groveled his speaking. "I know who AK is, and where he lives. I am scared to death for my life. I will talk to Captain Wellesley, only. I will answer no questions from you, at all."

"May I ask, sir…"

Max hung up the telephone. He hailed another cab that took him to Goldsboro, N.C. He called again, knowing he be put straight through. He recognized the same voice. "No questions, I'm too scared, Wellesley, now or I hang up and never call back."

"Lieutenant Wellesley, here."

"I know where he lives. I can give him to you, but I'm sacred. I will call you one week from today. I want money! I want two-hundred thousand dollars." He hung up! He took a cab back to Raleigh. It took a little longer but he was home by 4:45, his father's home, anyway.

He picked up his dads phone and called her and asked what she made for dinner. She told him. How long before it will be done. She told him anytime after five. "Good, put it in a box or something and have a cab bring you and the food to this address. He gave her the address! "I'll be waiting." He called for a carpenter using the yellow pages. Russell Crown had just arrived at his home when Max called. Max told him what he wanted done.

"Look," Crown, said, "I'm just three miles from you. I'll come right now, okay?" Nabulio, agreed.

The smart businessman suggested he have the house painted inside, indeed, but also the outside as well, that that would bring him a lot more money at the sale. He suggested new windows for the upstairs, and a new mantel for the fireplace. He also suggested a few other things, and then gave him a quote, knowing he'd eventually reduce it to 75% of the original quote. Max was too sly for this guy; he offered him 80% of the full amount.

The guy said, "You are tough mister, tell you what, you give 85% on the dollar quote and you got a deal for the whole deal." Nabulio, agreed at 83% of his asking price. He was pleased with himself, he had outsmarted the guy, the guy was happier yet. As Crown was getting into his car to leave, Constance, arrived. She noted the CROWN & CROWN REMODELING on the truck as it drove off. *Cute house*, she thought.

Crown smiled from ear to ear. With the extra 8% he made he could hire two subs and have the job done much quicker and keep his percentages. Life was good. Come spring he'd have that swimming pool put in for his wife Amanda, and for little Billy and Sharon.

Nabulio showed her the quote. She said it looked high. "Just the opposite, I snookered him, he wanted more."

"Well, show me our second home!" He did after they ate! Two hours later, she asked, "What was it you wanted to talk about? "

He said, "Tomorrow would be soon enough. He suggested they run up to the video store and rent a movie with the fireplace burning, real wood and all.

"I love that smell." She said. He added that he did, too. They rented two movies, one with Kevin Cosner in it and an old musical, *Paint Your Wagon* with Clint Eastwood. Clint Eastwood, singing; now that in of itself was a sight to behold; they enjoyed beholding it. When character Lee Marvin took his bride into the tent, and all the men folk cheered, Max scooped up his bride and he cheered all the way to the bedroom. The movie could wait. It did, they didn't!

CHAPTER 52—THIRTEEN DAYS AFTER NABULIO'S CALL TO WELLESLEY—EIGHTY-ONE DAYS AFTER THE FIRST SET OF KILLINGS, AND TWENTY DAYS AWAY FROM JUSTICE
REASONING A TIME TO KILL

Morning sickness was driving Alexandria crazy. She felt like it would go on forever. She was sick of being sick, and sick and tired of being sick and tired. Tired wasn't exactly the right word; exhausted was more like it. She never had any energy, and the toilet bowl was her closes friend. But, the doctor gave her the good news. All her symptoms were normal for this early stage of pregnancy. *Oh lucky me* she thought!

Additionally, Wellsy was stewing and stirring more and more every day. None of the phone calls bore any weight, and the team was also exhausted at the effort. Fortunately or unfortunately, whichever the case may be, the calls were tapering down to trickle. DetectiveStrange was handling most of them. It was tedious, boring, and non profitable; another great idea had grown sour. The only person that recognized the AK killer was his wife, but she didn't accept the thought. How could she, after all, the mind reject any possibility?

Nevertheless, Alex was mostly concerned with Wellsy's attitude and demeanor. He was irritable, and anxious and felt like a total failure. He was irritable because he felt he was a total failure, believing the case would never be solved. After all, seven people were dead, and he had—to date—accomplished nothing, expect to say, that there wasn't anything to say.

He was however excited over the call he had received nearly two weeks, ago. He couldn't wait for the follow-up call, which was scheduled to come, tomorrow. It was the only thing in the case that he felt was real, except for the several grieving families that were not getting any disclosure at all. He had received more than one angry phone call regarding this very issue. In despair, he went to the Captain and asked be taken, removed from the case. He was told to grow up. Just what he needed! He hated life at the moment!

* * * * *

Morning sickness was a joy to Constance, though it was ending, so it wasn't so bad, after all. Over the last couple of weeks or so, she had many conversations with Max; conversations that she was labeling as *time to kill discussions*. She couldn't help but wonder where all his talk was going. He hadn't necessarily changed, but she was seeing sides of him that she couldn't really comprehend. She knew he was leading up to something, but she didn't know what. She did, however notice that he was noticeably excited, or jittery lately, even anxious. He had a habit of marking days off the calendar. She asked him why. He merely told here he couldn't keep track of time. He admitted that he needed something more to do with his time.

His comments made little sense to her, so she decided to put things on the line and find out what was really going on. And that, for sure was going to happen either today, or tonight.

However, it was Nabulio who would make the first bold move that would either put her on his side, or alienate the two of them, altogether. Tonight would be the discussion of discussions with her, and tomorrow would be a brief but intriguing conversation with W. All the pieces would be in place by tomorrow that this time; according to Nabulio's timeline. The Lieutenant had 21 days to live! It was now a count down, twenty days to Emperor, again.

* * * * *

Wellsy sat in his office, with hands on his head. *I'm truly going crazy*, he thought. *I should just quit, and find a new line of work. That would make Alex wonderfully happy.* All it would take is to rise up out of his chair and walk into the Captain's office and drop a piece of paper on his desk. The paper would be written with flowery words, merely stating, *I Quit!*

However, that was the coward's way out. The killings had stopped, there was only one more left? Alex was sure it would be in 20 days, when the killer would celebrate the 100 days of superiority over Wellington, and on that day, it would end. Arthur was sure it would not happen. No matter what, he would—as he had promised Alexandria—be the last man standing in the end.

He rubbed his eyes. It was 2:30 in the afternoon. He decided he would go home. He wanted to lie on the bed with her with his head on her tummy that held his child, but she wouldn't be home for another two hours; school. Never in his life did he need that wonderful woman, more. Her love would keep him alive. He knew it, and she wanted to believe it, too! He scooped up his stuff and went for a ride. *The phone call is coming tomorrow; will it come, or was that guy just a big liar?*

* * * * *

"Dad's house is looking good. I'm getting it appraised, tomorrow," he said as they ate at the kitchen counter. It was an evening of left over food dug out of the refrigerator, BBQ chicken, potato salad, one pork chop, pea soup, and half of a pizza. She nibbled at the chicken and some of the potato salad. He ate the pork chop and sipped the pea soup from a coffee cup. When they were done, the left over food found its way to the garbage. "Come sit on the bed," he asked. She nodded, *ok*! He sat with his back against the bed board. She lay across the bed with her head on his pap. That wasn't comfortable, so—with some effort—she sat up and placed a pillow beside his hip so she was more at an incline. She reclined back down and found that far more comfortable. He twirled her hair with his fingers as they talked. "I love you, you know!"

"I know, Max, and I adore you!"

"We need to talk."

"Yes, we need to talk!"

"Should we make love, first?"

"Is that what you want?"

"No, well, yes, but only if you want to."

"I'd rather not. Is that okay with you?"

"Yup, always. I want you to know, you are the center of my universe." She didn't respond. "You believe that, don't you, Constance?" Again, she didn't answer. "Well, something is obviously wrong. What is it?" She said she wanted to be as honest as she could with him, but that if she was that honest, she feared it would cause both of them some pain. He asked her to go on.

She started with a strong sentence to find out exactly where they were. "No, Max, I do not believe I am the center of your universe. I do believe that you would do anything for me if I asked, so in that sense, yes, I am your center, but there is something else that is part of your life that is not only your center, but it does not include me, at all. Therefore, I am an appendage of that center. She took a breath. "Do not misunderstand what I am about to say, Max, because this could easily be misconstrued, so pay close attention so you do not misunderstand."

She felt tears swelling up inside her wanting to rush out. She fought it, bravely. "There is some secret in you, that I believe you want to let out. It is obviously something you want to tell me, probably share with me, but you don't know how too, because it could either bind us together forever, or drive us apart, forever." He started to speak. She immediately sat up and spun around to address him, and to shush him. She was immediately dizzy, *pregnancy*!

He reached out and steadied her. "Just don't move for a second, it will pass. It's the pregnancy." She bobbed his head in agreement with her own words. That made her dizzier. She got out enough to ask for help. He ushered her to the toilet just in time. He held her hair out of her face, and gently slid his hand back and forth over her back. A few minutes later she was sitting on the edge of the bed, again. He continued to steady her. She motioned that she wanted out. He walked her to the sitting room. He eased her into the lazy boy chair. He moved the other chair around slightly beside her and facing her so she could relax, and talk, and they could hold hands. Neither spoke until she was ready. At her request, he got her a glass of ice chips, no water.

She just started again without any prompting. "Max, you are afraid, because whatever it is could endanger our marriage, and all that we have." She took a deep breath and let it out loudly. She was as scared as she had ever been in her life, but she let it fly, "I do not believe there is another woman in your heart, Max, but there is something equally as bad, or perhaps, worse, though I don't know how that could be possible. It is so bad that it is stronger than you, or me, or most importantly, *us*! So—in a way—yes, you have a mistress, but it is not a she, nor a he, it is something much bigger, larger than the two of us. And," she added, "it will always be first in our life, today, tomorrow and forever, and," she continued, "I believe it has to do with our unborn child and Napoléon Bonaparte!"

With that, she let out a deep sigh, and then added a last thought. "Maximilian, I think whatever it is, it came up several times before, but it all started in St. Lucia with an ending statement to me, when you said something like, 'yes,' and then you stated my name, and then said, 'yes, there is a time to kill.' Max, look me in the eye. Have you killed?"

He was paralyzed with fear. *How could she know?* It took him, over five minutes to respond. He began by asking, "May I answer with a question?"

"You may answer anyway you would like, it is your answer, not mine, but I warn you, do not lie to me, for the second you do that we are finished. Am I clear?"

"Yes, and I will not lie." Now it was his turn to take a large breath of air. "I don't know how to make this make sense to you," he stumbled. "I have to begin with a question."

"Oh dear, Max, just do it and be done with it. I am feeling sickly enough. Just do it, whatever it is you have to do! I am near to being ill, again anyway." She began to tremble. "I," she stuttered, "I fear what you will tell me will cause me to lose this child. I am all twisted up inside with nerves, apprehension, and horrific fear. I am losing control over my body right now, Max. I need you to just hold me for a moment until it passes! Max," she said disparately needing his help, "I am falling apart her, I cannot control myself. Help... I..." She fainted dead, away.

He got out of his chair, lifted her out of hers and carried her lifeless body to the bedroom. He laid her on one side and undid the covers on the other side. He undressed her down to her underclothing and got her under the covers. She was perspiring profusely. He didn't know what to do. He called her doctor's office, and only got a recording, saying that the caller should call back in the morning, or call the emergency room at the hospital, now if necessary. He decided to just sit with her. She woke up at 1:15 a.m.; he was asleep sitting on the floor holding her hand with both of his.

She looked down at him. He was so cute, so loving. She whispered, "Max." He looked up. She was smiling.

His heart soared with joy. "I love you so."

"Max, that was never in question."

"What can I do for you?"

"Come to the other side of the bed, get under the covers and hold me, and yes, you can cup my breast." He did as instructed. They fell back to sleep. At six thirty-seven she woke up. He was in the exact same position he was when he crawled into the bed next to her. "I see you still have your hand full, big guy."

He let go, and sat up. "Are you okay?" She nodded in the affirmative. "In a half hour, though, I want you to call in sick for me."

"I won't do that!"

"Why?"

"Because you don't work. You're an ex-hooker remember?

"No! I have forgotten that part of my life."

"Some juice?"

"Later."

"What do you want?"

"We have no choice, we have to finish last night," she said.

"Are you up to it?"

"No!"

"Then not now."

"Max, we have no choice. I don't know what it is, but whatever it is it's going to take the wind out of me, and I fear it will take all the happiness of my life away, and our joy, our love, our oneness, will be swept away in anguish and sorrow."

"Oh, sweetheart."

"Max, who have you killed?"

"I have killed in battle."

"You have been in war? When, certainly not recently? I am confused, Max, when?"

"For this to make sense, I have to go back in time. I must."

"Do what you must, but don't drag it out!"

"Okay, but you must let me do it my way."

"Just do it, Max!"

"How do you feel about Napoléon?"

"You mean our son, if this baby is a boy?"

"No, not him, Napoleon, the real Napoléon, how do you feel about him."

"I am like you. I, too, think he is, or rather was a great man, and I feel—just like you—that he was cheater of his greatness at Waterloo."

"And, W?"

"W? Who is W, or do you mean Wellesley?"

"Exactly, yes, I mean, no, well yes and no, I mean Wellington."

"What do you mean, that is over, and there isn't anything I can do about that. I'm not sure what you mean, Max, what are you asking, me?"

"Do you wish Napoléon would have killed W, so Napoléon would have conquered, and continued as Emperor, and the world would be so much the better for that act?"

"If I was Napoléon or one of his soldiers, yes, yes, indeed, I would have."

"Then you do agree that there is a time to kill?"

"Well, we're back to that, again. Okay, yes! Under such circumstances, I can say, yes."

"Would you kill today to save his legacy?"

"What? You have lost me, Max!"

"What if you, personally could save the legacy of Napoléon, would you kill to do that?"

"I understand what you are asking, Max, but I don't see the correlation between today and 200 years, or so, ago!"

"Of all the things you learned, and you saw when be were abroad, what struck you more than anything?"

"You already know, Max, you already know that! We are one on that. I would rip that Statue of Napoléon out of the hands of the Wellingtons, or Wellesley' or whatever they are called today, and I would proudly put that Statue in our front yard, for the world to see, and make it a grand monument to his great cause, even in his defeat." She was on a roll now, and he didn't want to stop her, so he nodded, encouraging her to rail on. "I would present him, his statue to the world. I'd turn this very home into a museum, honoring him, Max; you know, Napoléon!"

"And what of the Duke of Wellington?"

She was a little tired, now, and a bit out of wind. "What about him?"

"Would you do away with him to rejuvenate the honor of Napoléon?"

"You mean would I kill him? Do you mean would I kill the 8ᵗʰ Duke of Wellington, the one that is alive now, today living somewhere in England I guess; is that what you mean?" She paused, "Why, kill him? What would that serve?"

He didn't answer her, he merely asked another question. "No, I don't mean him. I mean if there were a warrior, a Wellington warrior today that stood between Napoléon's legacies of extending his rule as Emperor past the one hundred days that Wellesley took from him at Waterloo; reversing history, I guess, would you do that?"

"No! I could not do that?"

"What about another person, a warrior, his son, or his son's son."

She looked at him, dead panned. "I would have to think about that. Part of me wants to say yes, and part says, defiantly, no; Max!

"But if it were part of a battle, a battle against a cunning, ruthless, Wellesley, and a bright young soldier who is protecting, and honoring the great general of generals, a protégée, or—better yet—a son of Napoléon Bonaparte?"

"Yes, maybe then." She thought for a second. "Would this be in war?"

He smiled, "Absolutely, yes, absolutely, in a battle, a war, when it is a time to kill?" It was Nabulio, who then paused for a few second, "Would it not be fitting to kill under such circumstances. Doesn't one country go to battle with another country if another country had wronged them? Is this not so, and are not soldiers killed in such wars, as sacrificial lambs if you will, but all part of the battle?"

She had to admit, that to agree with him, made sense, but she offered, "So few would understand such a war, Max, I fear that only the two sides engaged in the war would fully understand! The soldiers, those that would die would have to understand the cause, wouldn't they?"

"By all means, yes!" He said, and then added, "But even soldiers are not always understanding of the entire operation, because they are soldiers, and soldiers just must obey, and some die, some are wounded, and some are just in the wrong place at the wrong time. And some have to have their throats cut, but," he added, "there are always those that sit on the sidelines and judge, wrongly."

She let out the deepest sets of sighs, "Oh, Max, you are avenging our Napoléon, aren't you?"

He looked deeply into her eyes. "I have. I did. There are only two that are left standing, today!"

She bowed her head, "Yes, you and Lieutenant Arthur Wellesley, who is an heir, a direct heir to Arthur Wellesley, the 1st Duke of Wellington. I am right, aren't I, Max? "She burst into tears."

"It has to be done, it is a time to kill."

"The soldiers, Max, she said through a flood of tears, repeating herself, "are the seven girls, aren't they?" Tears fell from his face as well. His heart was pounding. She felt as though her heart had stopped ticking! You killed them all, haven't you, Nabulio? It is your time for killing, isn't it, Max?"

He didn't answer!

CHAPTER 53—EIGHTEEN DAYS TO JUSTICE
THE PHONE CALL

It was early evening. Max had driven around the stupid parking lot for nearly two hours, waiting. Finally, a lady he had been watching for five or six minutes pushed the button on her cell phone and tossed the phone—in disgust—on the bucket seat beside her. June Kennedy collected her purse, opened the door, flung it closed and walked toward the grocery store. Nabulio drove up beside her car, and waited for her to disappear into the store. *If you remain patient, sometimes things just work out well,* he considered.

Max then put on plastic gloves, and got out of his car. He looked around. Nobody was in insight. He opened her passenger side door and took her cell phone. He stepped back inside his running car and drove to the northwest corner of the jumbo-sized parking lot.

$$* * * * *$$

Morning slipped quickly into afternoon and afternoon into early evening. At 7:10 Wellsy left the office. The phone call never came. He had sat in his office the whole day. Three times he called the switchboard, making sure that some how he had not missed an incoming call. He was assured all three times that he had not received one call the entire day. At seven twenty-two he decided the call wasn't going to come. He arose from his seat, preparing to leave. His cell phone went off.

He answered it on the 3rd ring, "Wellesley, here."

Still holding the ladies cell phone with his plastic cover gloved hand, to his left ear, Nabulio held the well thought out text in front of him. He had already placed a once folded handkerchief over the cell phone, to collect spittle, or any other possible DNA secretions. He spoke, actually reading from his text; "You'll have to excuse me Lieutenant, but I am still scared, so I cheated, and I lied. I called your home number and got your cell number from the misses. Don't be made at her, I told her I was Detective Sergeant Emerson Walsh from Baltimore and I needed to talk to you immediately, because we thought we had the AK in custody, but I couldn't get through to the switchboard at the Norfolk police department, so she gave me your cell number. I'm sorry I lied."

Wellesley was furious, "It's okay. You know the AK, is that right?"

"Yes, for many years!"

"How do you know him?"

"The wrong person is in charge of this call. I am meek, but it must be my way. Write this all down, I will only say it once, don't talk. You must come to me. I will not come to you. In Warrenton, Virginia, go out toward the mountains on two eleven, that's two, one, one. Turn right when you get to six eighty-eight, also known as Leeds Manor Road. When you get to route six thirteen, that's six, one, three, turn to the left, and go toward the bridge. Drive over the bridge. When you get there, to the other side;" Nabulio hung the phone up.

He let the Lieutenant stew for nearly seven minutes. Nabulio, redialed. "Wellesley."

"When you get there…"

Wesley interrupted, "Look…"

"Say another word I will hang up and you'll never know." He paused for 30 seconds it seemed like a lifetime to both men. "Like I said when you get there, to the other side of the bridge, turn your car around, and drive back up to the opening of the bridge on that end. Be sure to park your car so no one from that side can drive around your car and enter onto the bridge. It is a very narrow bridge, however." He took a deep breath. "Turn you lights off, and put your parking lights on, and put your dome light on, too, and then walk to the middle of the bridge."

Nabulio then had a fake sickly coughing spell. "After you are in the center of the bridge, sit down and face your car. Do not look over your shoulder. I will be walking toward you. When I am behind you, I will tell you to turn around. At that point, I want you to stand up, and turn around. Come alone, Lieutenant, don't be foolish! I will be scared to death as it is. The last thing you want is to have me clam up; you know that! You will never catch him without me. I have my escape planned, so don't think you can catch me. You may bring your gun if you want, because I know you think I might be the AK. I understand that. So, you may bring your gun. You won't be needing it, but feel free to bring it, though guns scare me!"

He was quite for a moment. "Do you have any questions about directions? If you ask a question about any thing other than the directions, I will end it all now, but I can give you proof that I know the killer. If you have a DIRECTIONS question, ask, now, but only direction questions."

Wellsy wanted to ask a zillion questions, but angrily, he listened to the dead sounding connection. "Be at the bridge at 11:50 p.m., no sooner, no later, and be there exactly 18 days from today, so make that 18 days plus about 4 hours from now. Here is my proof that I know him. I don't need to tell you which one, you already know, but neither the press nor anyone but you and your small circle of detectives knows this. AK bit the nipple off one of the girls." He quickly added, "Don't say a word, or I'm gone forever."

He waited about three more minutes "I know you will try anyway, but I'm trying to save you time. It is impossible for you to trace this call, but, like I say, I know you will try." Again he paused for well over two minutes. "This is your only chance to ask a question, now, you may ask two questions, and only two questions. If I think your question or questions are a trick, I will hang up the telephone. You may ask, now!"

"How do you know the killer?"

"I am his doctor."

"That's it, that's all I get?"

"Yes, and that was your second question, you did not choose wisely." He took his last long pause, about 45 seconds. "On the night in question, I will give you his address, and a short history of him." Wellsy's cell phone went dead. He quickly called his number to again listen to his conversation. It didn't work. He tried three more times, nothing. There was nothing recorded, *How is that possible*, Wellsy, questioned, himself.

Max drove back to where the woman's car was still resting. He reversed the process. He drove away with the woman's cell phone lying on her bucket seat, pretty close to where she had tossed it. He stuffed the paper he had read from in his shirt pocket, and jammed the handkerchief into his jeans front pocket.

Thirteen minutes later, the woman returned and put her groceries into her trunk. She got in the car and called Claudia and when Claudia answered, Beverly Sing, said, "Claudia, I'm sorry." Beverly told her it was not a big deal. Claudia drove home in peace. Her tiff with Claudia ate away at her as she collected her groceries.

Four hours later the police arrived at her apartment. They wanted some tough questions answered about the usage of her cell phone earlier in the evening. She didn't have a clue. They took, confiscated her phone, and gave her a receipt. The phone would be returned to miss Kennedy when the police were finished with it! While at her home, they dusted her car for prints. All of there work would end in folly. When they left; June was in a tiff, all over, again!

CHAPTER 54—ELEVEN DAYS TO JUSTICE
INNOCENT FIND, GRAVE REPERCUSSIONS

"The house is finished," the caller, said. Constance, told him that she'd be right over. She arrived and handed the man a certified check that Max had left her to give to the carpenter. Over the past three days, Max had worked hard cleaning all the stuff out of the house. Most of it went directly to the dump. Only four boxes had been taken home. Most furniture and stuff went to good will, along with clothing, and stuff. He had called in Ace Company to clean the carpets and stuff. So, Constance spent the day doing easy clean-up jobs.

By the time she got to the house, most of her morning sickness had worn off. She was actually feeling quite well, to the degree she was singing as she worked. It felt good to be doing something constructive.

At 11:30 the Realtor came and put the FOR SALE sign in the front yard. Ten minutes later the guy who was hired to put up a new ceiling fan in the kitchen, arrived. He was there all of twenty-five minutes. At 4 o'clock the realtor came back with the Applebee's, a family of three. They wanted to see the house. Constance said she was almost done, and let them into the house.

She took her last large plastic bag into the bathroom and emptied the small amount of tissue that was in the wastepaper basket. She then checked each room. There wasn't any trash. In the kitchen there was a small amount of papers and such in the wastebasket. She lifted the bag, and emptied it into the large plastic bag she had been toting around the house. The bottom contents that were dumped into her bag nearly filled to the top of her bag. She reached in and her hand found a blue sheet of paper, somewhat crumpled up. She picked it up and looked at. It alarmed her. She stuffed that paper into her pocket, tied the bag up and took it to her car, and placed it into her trunk.

She went back into the house, gather up a couple of things and returned to her car. Just over a half hour later she arrived home. Max was in their indoor pool doing laps. She sat at poolside, and waited. When he saw her he swam to her. "Hi, where have you been?"

"I got word the house was finished, so I went over, and gave that guy the check and then did some final clean up."

"You didn't over do it, did you?" She shook her head, *no.* "How does it look?"

"Fantastic. Just as I was leaving the realtor showed up with a family to look at the house." She paused, "Are you sure you want to sell it?"

"Yes, why?

"Sentimental reasons I guess." "

He climbed out of the pool. She handed him a towel. He sat. "No, let the dead bury the dead."

"I've never understood what that meant."

"When it is over, it is over, let it go."

"Is that what you think when you think of those seven women?"

He didn't like the insinuation. He quipped, back, "Victims of a battle of war!"

"Isn't the war you talk about one sided?"

"No. Do not underestimate W, he is a most worthy foe."

"He doesn't have to be. Please, let it go!" She was still unsure of her feelings. She decided to change the topic. "I'm too tired to cook tonight, can we go out, or order in?" They decided to go out to the Blue Hippo!

Later, while getting ready to leave for the restaurant she found the crumpled paper that she had stuffed into her pocket. *Why was that there at the old house?* She opened her top dresser drawer and placed the blue paper inside her pink bra, the one she seldom wore. She put the other cup inside the first, concealing the paper. She couldn't figure out why she just didn't toss it away.

As they were leaving the house the telephone rang. She answered the telephone, and then yelled for Max. He took the phone and accepted the offer on the house. Ten minutes later, while they were on their way to the restaurant he said, "The house is sold."

"For the whole amount?"

"Close, one thousand, less."

"Congratulations."

"To us."

"It's not my house."

"You are my wife, what is mine is yours."

"Can I keep the money?" She laughed.

"Yes! What are you going to do with it?"

"Use it for Christmas money."

"On me?"

"Who, else?"

He laughed, as did she! "Can I have some of it?"

"Yes, how much," she asked?

"Ten dollars?"

"What on earth do you need ten dollars for?"

"I want to get you a Christmas present for you, too!" They laughed together and continued to the restaurant."

The war, and the battles were taboo topics. They ignored them, but it had to be readdressed, soon, very soon!

Chapter 55—Seven Days to Justice
DECEPTION FOR THE SAKE OF LOVE

He told her that the Captain was forcing him to go on a seminar in Charlotte, North Carolina. She asked when and for how long. "For just two days, I leave in four days.

"What's the seminar on?"

"It's on Computer and Digital Forensics, dealing with crimes that leave digital trace evidence."

"Why you?"

"Good question, I use it when I need something from the computer, Alexandria. I guess I'll just go and find out!" He added, "Rodgers says it's a high-demand field right now and we are way behind in technology. I guess that is true, I have to come back and give a report to a combined department's meeting, and then the brass will decided where we go from there."

"You know, you will get back on the day that is the 100th day."

"I said that to the Captain. He suggested that that might be good to get me out of town."

"How do you feel about that?"

"I don't know. It's all a maze. Nothing seems to fit. There isn't anything to investigate anymore. We found nothing on the cell phone."

"What cell phone, you didn't tell me anything about a cell phone."

Damn, he was caught and he knew it. He freewheeled it. "AK, or I guess I should say, we think it was the AK that called the department a few days ago and actually talked to the Captain. The whole conversation—for whatever reason—didn't get recorded; really, the whole thing, but the cell phone had been stolen from some lady at the Willows Shopping Mall. Detective Strange and two other patrol officers went over to her house, but she knew nothing at all. We didn't get any prints, nothing. We figured he stole the phone, used it and returned it back to the owner, somehow. I don't know!"

"Why didn't you tell me?"

"Well, from what you just heard, there isn't or wasn't much to tell." She agreed. "How are you feeling?"

"Okay." He felt guilty as sin. This was the first time he ever deliberately mislead her. He hated himself for doing it. And, now he was telling lie after lie. It was all deception, but—on the other hand—he couldn't tell her where he was going, to confront someone—probably AK, himself—at near midnight as some lonely bridge over 200 miles away near Culpepper, Virginia. He was hurting inside. How could a marriage survive if he was telling lies over something that could well get him killed? He just couldn't do it. He knew that one day this would all come back on him, and rightfully so, *but what else am I to do?* Some Secrets are for the best. This was one of them.

He was dead wrong!

Chapter 56—Three Days to Justice— Really Just Two!
THE FINAL DISCUSSION

It was the shank of the evening. It was now or never, Nabulio, decided. There really wasn't any other choice. He knew that in a smidgen's time—just over two days—it would all be over. He knew that, and she knew it too, but he needed confirmation from her, her acceptance. Actually, he wanted more. He wanted her to offer appreciation of what he was doing for Napoléon Bonaparte, the absolved Emperor, and for himself, and for her, and certainly for the speck of little Napoléon she carried. That acceptance was paramount. How could they continue to live as a family without her endorsement? So, at 9:30 at night, just three days from justice he looked at her. Immediately she knew the topic from that singular look. Yes, it was thee topic of topics, and she knew exactly where he was going with this discussion. She quivered inside.

He began with a lie. He knew he was lying, obviously, and so did she, obviously. "I have to go out of town for a couple of days," he began. Well, that wasn't actually a lie, but the lie was where he was going with this whole conversation.

"Do you, Max?"

Already he knew it was going to go badly. He had thought of this moment for days, and weeks. "Darling…"

She knew this moment was going to come, too. She had thought about it long and hard. She was reluctantly ready for this moment. He could not have guessed! "No, Max, don't, not this time. This conversation is not going to happen." She stood up, and walked away from him, but only about five feet. She turned around and commenced to remove her clothing, first her blouse, and then her skirt, and then her slip, then bra and panties. She stood before him, naked. "Come here, and stand in front of me, but do not touch me!" He offered a most unwelcome look, but obeyed. "Stop!" He did. He smiled; she shook her head, no! His smile disappeared. "Look deeply into my eyes, and tell me what you see."

He did as she offered. "I see the heart of my heart."

"Max, do you? Do you really?" He didn't answer, he merely nodded, yes. She spoke, "I am going to ask you to do some things." She paused, and then added, "Please, Max, do exactly what I say, nothing more, nothing less. Do not speak unless I say you can. Will you do that, Max?"

"Yes!"

"Walk towards me until I say stop." He did. He came within a foot of her. She ordered him to stop, and then told him to take a single step backwards. He did. "Look at my entire body, Max. She put her arms straight out to her sides, parallel with the floor and ceiling. She then parted her legs about two feet. Finally, she moved her arm upward so hat her legs and arms created reversed V's. She knew that raising her arms upward would cause her breasts to rise just a little. She knew his infatuation of the breasts and she wanted them to be most inviting. Max thought it was purely a welcoming picture. "Now, Max, point at the part of my body you cherish the most. He took his right hand and placed his index finger on her forehead, and then slid the finger to her temple. "So you cherish my mind, more than anything, correct?"

"Yes!"

"What part of me do you hunger for the most?" He wasn't sure where to point with regards to this question. Again, he pointed to her mind. "What part of me do you hunger for the most, Max, and be honest?" Again, he pointed to her mind. "You are either very clever, Max, or you are being sly, and perhaps, honest as well." He offered nothing back. Max, what part of me do you most often think about?" He pointed at her abdomen. "The child?" He offered a meek and lovely *yes*. "Thank you, this is also where my thoughts lie as well." She stepped toward him, bringing her arms toward his face. She cupped his face with her hands, leaned forward and kissed him lovingly, passionately with all the love and devoted admiration she could muster.

She then took a step back. "Napoléon," she said, "is who you are, now. Somewhere, somehow, you have lost Maximilian. You have been Nabulio for so long, and Napoléon for so long that you no longer think or see straight. Your reality is askew. You see through their combined eyes, not your own, and no, Max, they are not one in the same. However, there are parts of that that I love, and there are more parts that I loathe. I need you to think back to the first two women you killed. Are you doing that?

"Yes!"

"Tell me what you know about them."

"Not very much."

"Who were they?"

"His soldiers."

"No, no they were not, Max, they were two young college students, who had a rich life ahead of them." He turned away. She grabbed him by the arm and jerked him back toward her. She grabbed his wrist of his right hand and drew it hard and fast and pushed it into her groin. It hurt her deeply as she felt something tug inside. She had used too much force in her violent action. She screeched in pain, but continued though it. "Do you feel that? Do you?" Before he could answer, she said, "Through this door you discharged part of you and of that event, this is the results," she said as she took his other hand and placed it where the fetus was inside of her surrounded by her protective body.

She took a deep breath, "In this womb, is a child developing, growing, a real person. And what, twenty years from now some lunatic snuffs him or her out because he has some twisted fanatical drive; abhorrent agenda!" More tears swelled.

"On that day, Nabulio over three months ago, you believed you were killing two of his—Wellesley's—soldiers. That is pure nonsense, Max! That is your lunacy Max, and I will tell you why." Her body began to tremble. "They, those two co-eds were two young women and I would venture to guess that probably neither of them could tell you two single words about who Napoléon Bonaparte was, let alone who Arthur Wellesley was. They probably never in their lives even heard of the name, Wellesley, let alone be soldiers of his." Did you hear what I said?" He nodded.

"Nevertheless and notwithstanding that, Max, you snuffed them out as if they were sacrificial lambs of your great cause, and then you did killings five more times, to five more totally innocent women." Tears streamed down her cheeks. She took a cleansing breath; "Let me ask you, Max, if some lunatic takes your child—this child—" she replaced his hand to her abdomen, again, "and destroys his or her life because of some concocted fantasy this madman is living. Max, as the grieving father of that poor innocent child whose life has been taken, what do you do?" She didn't wait for an answer; no, not one second. She continued, "We—you and I—would want some kind of understanding that we might at least comprehend, how and why this killer, this monster slaughtered our child. And then, later, Max, later, you learn that the killer said, that the child he killed—OUR CHILD MAX, that she, or he was a soldier.' Oh, God, Max, can you not see the psychosis of this all?"

She removed his hand from her body, and turned away. She lowered her voice. That voice had a scary calmness to it, as she stated, "The day you destroy the living Arthur Wellesley of today, your—would be Duke of Wellington—on that day," she paused, and turned toward him, and repeated, herself, placing his and, and her hand over their child, "On that day, this child dies. Your Napoléon—this child—dies with your Wellington," and that ends Napoléon's dream of redemption as Emperor, Max. It is your choice."

That said, she nearly fell apart, but mustered enough to say, "Your choice is simple, you can have me forever and this child, or you can kill the Wellington in your life, and lose us! Which is it going to be, Max?" He opened his mouth, but she wasn't finished. "There aren't any other alternatives. I will somehow find a way to overlook the killings of those seven children, somehow, and we can move forward with our unborn son, Napoléon, or it all ends now. It is your choice." She then added, "Max, you are the kindest and most loving man in the universe, but you cannot continue to be a double minded man. Cleave into this child, and me or make your transition to an empty throne as the final Emperor status you seek for a dead man, whom the world has—for the most part—long sense forgotten." She was quivering, but she took a breath and finished, or tried to. "I love you with every portion of my being, but…" She could not finish.

Neither spoke for the next five minutes. In the stillness, she put her clothing on. The pain in her groin had subsided, so she assumed she would be all right. She was the first to speak, "Tomorrow, I'm booking a plane for the West Coast, I'm leaving for a few days to visit my parents. I assume you too are leaving for a few days, too, I suppose."

For the first time in his life, Max had nothing to say. To say he was taken aback would be an understatement. Everything was wrong! He didn't know who he was, anymore, if he ever knew. *Where do we go from here? You are everything to me Constance, without you, I am nothing. I thought we thought the same.* He thought all this, but couldn't utter a word to her. He was dumbstruck, shackled by her persona.

She left the room wanting to die.

CHAPTER 57—THE DAY BEFORE JUSTICE—OR ONE SECOND AFTER MIDNIGHT!
THE LAST MEETING—DEATH

Nabulio did not slept with his wife neither last night nor the night before. They were not talking, except when it was necessary. "I have to leave in a couple of hours, I will not be home until tomorrow night!" he flatly stated.

"I'm leaving for the airport, now." She said, adding, "I'll get my ticket at the counter and leave on whatever flight gets me out of here the soonest."

"Tell your parents I said, hi." He paused, "When will you be back?"

"When will you be back?"

"Will you be back within the week?"

"Max, that depends on you! Will you be back tomorrow?"

"Yes, tomorrow."

"When you arrive back here, will you have blood on your hands, Max?"

"When I return, will my wife and my child be here?"

"If she is, he will be here, too, but she is leaving now, as is he!"

"And if there is blood on my hands? Nabulio, asked."

"Then I guess there will be blood on my hands, too!"

"You will not kill your own child."

"I wish I could say the same about you!" With that, she walked to her suitcase, which was already packed. She picked it up and walked out of the bedroom. In the hallway, she stopped, and turned to him. "Max, I love you with all my heart. Don't kill us all!" She set down her suitcase, crossed back to him, closed her eyes and kissed him—maybe—farewell." She quickly departed. She didn't want him to see her tears." As she walked away, she remember a book her dad had once told her about when she was a young, girl. She thought it was titled, *When All The Laughter Died Away In Sorrow*. At the time, she had asked her dad, what the title meant. Lewis responded with "A football player wrote it Turnip.

He did some bad things in his life that he thought was humorous at the time. Later in life he learned that they were not funny, but sad. He lost a lot from making the wrong decisions in life, and it cost him dearly. She asked her dad if she could read the book. He said, "no," but if she got one of her books, he would read it to her. *Choices*, she thought. *What would the night bring in?*

Two and a half hours later, Constance's plane took off, with her on board. In her luggage, and for whatever reason, she had placed the note that had tucked away in the cup of her bra into the suitcase. She would try to figure it all out, later.

About the time Constance was boarding her plane, Nabulio was driving his rented car to the bridge up north west of Culpeper, Virginia where the expanse crossed Rappahannock River. He had a work to do that would be completed just after midnight, and then he would board a plane and fly to his wife in California. He was getting used to flying to the coast after a night's work. He decided they would live on the West Coast, after all. He loved her parents, and wanted them to be near Napoléon, his son.

He smiled; very soon his work would be complete. Out of that work, he would write a book, and have it published at his death. The book's title would be simply, *Napoléon's Revenge!* The author of the book would be no one less than a direct descendant to thee Napoléon.

CHAPTER 58—TODAY
DAY OF RETRIBUTION

Nabulio arrived at 8:15 p.m. He drove his car about 20 yards into the woods, and parked it facing towards the road. He put his keys under the drivers side rear tire, behind the tire. It was already dark. That was fine with him. He walked the perimeter of the river on the south side, from water's edge, up and over the bridge to water's edge on the other side of the bridge. He did it on north side as well, though he felt it a waste of time. He was sure that Wellesley would come, and he was equally sure that he would come, alone. Nabulio knew what Wellesley knew; this was totally personal; dating back over 250 years; neither would use additional soldiers. There wasn't any need for such silliness.

Next, Nabulio set the trap, that should anything go wrong he was free to escape. The small remote control would do the trick. It took him all of ten minutes to set it up. He would let Wellesley know before hand that it wasn't personal. He looked around for another fifteen minutes or so, and then returned to his car.

At 11:35 Wellsy arrived. He stopped just before he got on the bridge. He looked around, seeing nothing, he proceeded forward, across the bridge as per his instructions. At the other end he followed his directions by turning the car around. He proceeded to drive up to the opening of the bridge. He looked around to be sure there wasn't enough room for anyone to get around his car if they came up from behind. He turned off his headlights and then put the parking lights on. He then reached up and put the dome light on. He withdrew his Glock G37, and put it into his heavy lined jacket. He rubbed his fingers over his sweatshirt. He felt the bullet-proof-vest underneath. His heart was pounding. He could actually hear it; beat after living beat. So far, everything he did was as he had been instructed. He had practiced twice, earlier, in the day. He got out of his car, looked about, and walked in front of his car, and began his walk down the center of the bridge. He walked slowly but surely to the middle of the bridge—its center—he turned around and sat facing his car and waited for the bullet to slam into the back of his head.

The Lieutenant heard the sound of Nabulio walking toward him. It was a casual, steady sound. He listened carefully, memorizing what he heard. The footsteps ceased their noise, "Slowly stand up and turn around." Wellsy, did.

The two men glared at one another. "You are shorter than I guessed." Again the cop stood silently. "I am scared to death. Are you, Wellesley?" Wellsy stood mute. "Do you have your gun?"

"Yes, two of them."

"Ah, yes, cops always have two guns. Which one is in your coat pocked?"

"My Glock."

"Nine millimeter?"

"No!" Wellsy, sighed.

"You are impatient?"

"Do you have a name for me, or are you him?"

Nabulio laughed, "No I am not he, not hardly. Not by a long shot."

"Why is he doing what he is doing?"

"Revenge?" is all Nabulio offered.

"Yes, revenge, Napoléon's revenge."

"Explain!" Nabulio, demanded.

"He is a direct descendant to thee Napoléon."

"And what then is his revenge? Nabulio, paused, "You toy with me, master *Wellesley*, you toy with me!"

"Ah, Wellesley, as in The Duke of Wellington."

"Indeed!"

"No, not at all, the 1st Duke of Wellington is the hero in this story, the 2nd through the present 8th Duke are his legacy. I am only a shallow figure of any one of them."

"To the contraire, you are a fighter, a warrior, a soldier, you are his only nemesis, the true heir to the 1st Duke of Wellington." He paused. "Just as he is the only true heir to Napoléon."

"Is that what this is about, he wants to kill me to have Napoléon's revenge, then?"

"Exactly so! Exactly!"

"And why do you want to help me?"

"Let's just say I don't want any more nipples bitten off."

"That may make some sense to you, but not to me!"

"Yes it does. It does indeed!"

"Well, it's cold out here, and I've enjoyed our quid pro quo, but…"

Nabulio interrupted, "I'd prefer tit for tat under the circumstances."

"Clever!"

"Clever, indeed!" He paused, well, I have to take care of some business if you don't mind?" Wellsy was definitely on the alert, now! *Watch his eyes, the window of his soul. Watch everything, he is the amateur, not you!* "I'm sure you are on the defense this very second. You may take your gun out and point it at me if you wish. I will hold still." Wellsy complied, gladly. Nabulio reached into his pocket and withdrew the small electronic device. "This is just to secure my getaway. Please, allow me. He pushed the button. Wellsy jumped as two small quick explosions erupted by both of his front tires. The car bounced up and lifted up off the ground and then came down on deflating tires. "Sorry, no offense intended.

"None taken."

"Well, it's one minute to midnight. Take notes."

"I'll remember."

Suite yourself. He lives in Hopewell."

"Northeast of Petersburg, correct?"

Nabulio nodded. "He drives a green jeep Wrangler. His address is 1522 Eiffel Street. That is all you need to know."

"You are a doctor, what are you treating him for?"

"Let's just say that he has—at most—a year to live, though he can be as active as he likes, today."

"Why are you doing this?"

"Why, the reward, of course. After you catch him, I will call you for the money. With it I can retire. I'm only 35 but I have mutual funds, galore, but those combined with the reward will set me free. I'm leaving now. He turned to leave, and then turned back around, "Be careful, he is very clever, and most tricky. Don't trust him at all. If you talk to him, don't believe a word he says. And remember, he is stalking you. He will probably kill your wife, first."

Wellesley ignored the last comment; it was for effect, only! "What else can you tell me?"

"Actually, I'm not sure. It would be all speculation, anyway." He paused, "But I believe he will kill your wife first." He was pissed that Wellesley didn't respond, again, to the threat on his fiancé. They looked at each other for another moment, almost as if each was waiting for the other to draw his weapon and shoot, though Wellesley's was already drawn. "Okay, Lieutenant, turn around, sit down and face your car until I am off the bridge. I will yell to you when I'm off." Wellsy complied. Again, he waited for a bullet to slam into the back of his head. He listened to the footsteps; they were not walking down the middle of the bridge—mussel memory told him that—but rather the footsteps were walking off to the left side, he thought. *Think! What is he up to?* Suddenly he heard the clanging of metal on metal.

Wellsy made a quick push off and rolled to the right, and then jumped up just as the gun blasted from behind him. His body swirled and then slumped to the ground as the slug slammed into the fleshy part of his left arm just above the elbow, grazing the bone, causing the hot lead to veer upward and tore a piece of meat from his left ear. Less than a second and a half later, a second shot rang out. The bullet slammed home, dead center to the mark this time, nothing more could be done. It was over; the body fell to the pavement. The young Lieutenant never got off a single shot, and his bulletproof vest was useless.

Chapter 59—Today, 5:52 a.m., Five Hours, Fifty-One Minutes After the Firing of the Second Shot That Found Its Mark
REVERSAL OF FORTUNE

Alexandria tossed and turned all night. She knew Arthur wasn't at any convention, or training seminar, anywhere. She—better than anyone—knew that today was the one hundredth and first day since, the first two killings. She knew that today would be the day that Wellesley would meet Bonaparte, and if it wasn't Bonaparte, then it was Napoléon, and if not Napoléon, then certainly it was Nabulio. They were all one to her, anyway, so it didn't matter.

She had been up since one thirty, pacing back and forth, worried, scared out of wit's end. At one or two minutes after midnight, she woke up with a start. She felt something was very, very wrong. She was a nervous wreck. She fell back to sleep, but awoke again about one thirty one. That was it. She had been up, since. She was near hysterical. Nothing seemed right. She kept wishing he would call. She knew better. She paced. She cried. She fretted. Often she had trouble breathing. It was a living nightmare. Helpless!

Presently, she was sitting in his favorite recliner. She was startled when she saw the lights flash through the front window. For a few seconds, the lights danced on the wall, and then the ceiling, and then back on the wall, and then disappeared altogether. She stood and peered out the window from behind the partially drawn curtains. A car had pulled into her driveway. She snuck a peek around the curtain. A woman was slowly approaching the door. Alexandria's heart was pounding; after all, it was just before six a.m.

She wanted to douse the lights and run to the bedroom where she knew Arthur kept a spare revolver. She nearly jumped when the doorbell sounded its chimes. With great caution, she approached the door. "Who is it?" she offered with a meek and trembling voice.

"I have important information, please let me in." The voice was weak, morose and frail sounding. There was alarm and resignation about the voice on the outside. Alex opened the door to the extent the goal chain would allow, about three inches. "Please," the voice offered, "Please let me in. I mean you no harm, please!" The woman was dressed in black, all black. She was beautiful. Alex tried to look past her. "Please," the woman begged.

"What do you want; it is six o'clock in the morning? This is no time for calling on someone! Please leave, I am not well."

"Nor am I, Mam, nor am I, well." The weak voice hesitated, and then responded, again, "I wish to speak to Mrs. Wellesley, on an urgent matter."

"I'm afraid you have the wrong address; there isn't any Mrs. Wellesley here. Please go away."

"There isn't any Alexandria Wellesley here?" she pleaded.

"I'm the only woman of this house. I'm the only one here, and my husband is sleeping, and my last name is Southerland." She paused, "Please leave!"

"This is the home of Lieutenant Wellesley isn't it?"

She let out a deep and forlorn sigh. "Yes!"

"And you are not his wife?"

"I am his fiancé; we are engaged to be married. Please leave, I am not well tonight, or, I guess it is morning!"

"I understand that, fully, completely. Please let me in, it is most urgent for your welfare."

Against her better judgment she let the woman in and invited her to sit on the sofa. The woman dressed in black looked awful. She wore no jewelry, no make-up, and her hair was a mess, nevertheless, she was beautiful, breathtaking beautiful. "Are you cold, can I get you a blanket? The stranger was nervous, jittery, looking almost unbalanced. Alex also noticed that she was grasping tightly to a small satchel. "Are you okay, Mam, you don't look at all well."

She brushed off Alex's comment and reached into the paisley satchel, and with a severe shaking hand, she extended a two-inch stack of papers bound together at the top to Alex. "Please take this and read it later, was all she would offer." Alex took the stack and laid it aside. Again, Alex was concerned at the woman's appearance; there was obviously something very, very wrong. She was obviously young, but she looked so old and haggard. Alex offered her something to drink. She declined. She reached into the satchel, again, and withdrew two pieces of blue paper. These papers, too, she offered to Alex. Alex reached out and took them. "Please, just read them out loud, now!"

"Why?"

"Mam, please, we need to hurry with this, please!" The poor woman seemed to be weakening as she spoke."

"I think you need to lie down. Can I get…" she didn't finish.

"Just read, Mam, please, just read." She was having trouble breathing, so her voice shook, dreadfully. "Read them, now, out loud to me so that I too can hear."

Alex was most confused, but she read aloud. Her voice was also shaky, just as the woman in black's voice had been. He own voice sounded hollow to her. She was still scared. She read, "You will have to excuse me Lieutenant, but I am still scared," she stopped and looked at the woman.

"Please read, I do not have much time. The letter is from my husband to yours, or rather your fiancé. Continue, please. I haven't much time," she said as her body continued to quake.

Alex started from where she had left off, "so I cheated, and I lied. I called your home number and got your cell number from the misses. Don't be mad at her, I told her I was Detective Sergeant Emerson Walsh from Baltimore and I needed to talk to you immediately, because we thought we had the AK in custody, but I couldn't get through to the switchboard at the Norfolk police department, so she gave me your cell number. I'm sorry I lied." Alex stopped reading; she remembered this call that came to her home. She looked up at the intruder, and continued reading, "I am meek, but it must be my way. Write this all down, I will only say it once, don't talk. You must come to me. I will not come to you. In Warrenton, Virginia, go out toward the mountains on two eleven, that's two, one, and another one. Turn right when you get to six eighty-eight, also known as Leeds Manor Road. When you get to route six thirteen, that's six, one, three, turn to the left, and go toward the bridge. Drive over the bridge. When you get there, to the other side… (*HANG THE PHONE UP HERE. WAIT, AND THEN CALL BACK. CALL BACK AND CONTINUE*)," She stopped reading, I don't understand."

The woman in black, responded, "I had to figure that out too, the capital letters were notes to himself—my husband—not something to be read to your husband. Sorry, your mate. Please, continue."

Alex, continued, "Turn your car around, and drive back up to the opening of the bridge on that end. Be sure to park your car so no one from that side can drive around your car and enter onto the bridge. Turn you lights off, and put your parking lights on, and put your dome light on, too, and then walk to the middle of the bridge.' (OFFER A FAKE COUGHING SPELL, AND THEN CONTINUE)." Alex looked up. Constance acknowledged that those, again, were for her husband.

"After you are in the center of the bridge, sit down and face your car. Do not look over your shoulder. I will be walking toward you. When I am behind you, I will tell you to turn around. At that point, I want you to stand up, and turn around. Come alone, Lieutenant, don't be foolish! I will be scared to death as it is. The last thing you want is to have me clam up; you know that! You will never catch him without me. I have my escape planned, so don't think you can catch me. You may bring your gun if you want; because I know you think I might be the AK. I understand that. So, you may bring your gun. You won't need it, but feel free to bring it, though guns scare me!' (BE QUIET FOR A MOMENT)"

The voice continued, "Do you have any questions about directions? If you ask a question about any thing other than the directions, I will end it all now, but I can give you proof that I know the killer. If you have a DIRECTIONS question, ask, now, but only direction questions.' (LET HIM RESPOND)

Be at the bridge at 11:50 p.m., no sooner, no later, and be there exactly 18 days from today, so make that 18 days plus about 4 hours from now. Here is my proof that I know him. I don't need to tell you which one, you already know, but neither the press nor anyone but you and your small circle of detectives knows this. AK bit the nipple off one of the girls." Alex stopped reading, how clearly she remembered. She continued, "Don't say a word, or I'm gone forever. (WAIT THREE MINUTES)'

'I know you will try anyway, but I'm trying to save you time. It is impossible for you to trace this call, but, like I say, I know you will try. (PAUSE FOR TWO MINUTES) This is your only chance to ask a question; you may ask two questions, and only two questions. If I think your question or questions are a trick, I will hang up the telephone. You may ask, now. (ANSWER HIS TWO QUESTIONS AND HAND UP!)"

Alex looked up, as Constance spoke, "I am the wife of the AK killer."

"Oh my Go…"

"Be at ease, I offer you no harm." Now, Alex wondered what else was in the satchel, perhaps a loaded gun that the woman had come to kill her. She stared at the satchel. Constance looked down at the satchel, too, and then pointed at it. "Pay it no mind. I will get to it. My husband, the AK wrote that which you have just read as a text for him to say to Lieutenant Wellesley over their telephone conversation. I don't know why he so carelessly discarded it at our second home. He wrote it as a lure to get your husband their late last night, or the wee early minutes of today, the…"

Alex interrupted, and finished the woman's thoughts, "The one hundred and fist day, yes, I know!"

"You know?"

"Yes, I know. Did they meet tonight?"

"Yes!"

Alex's heart, sunk, she asked the obvious, that wouldn't make much sense to this woman in black, "Was one of them left standing?"

What an odd question. "Yes! Well, yes and no!"

Alexandria's entire being was trembling. Tears flowed. She could scarcely breathe. "Who, who was left standing?" The woman reached down to the satchel. Alex gave up, she knew she was about to be killed." *Maybe it is for the best! Never had she been so scared. I hope it doesn't hurt, let me die quickly.* Then, then she only thought of one person, *my baby, oh God, no; not my baby.*

Constance withdrew a revolver from the satchel. "Mam, my husband had an old army rifle hidden behind one of the steel girders off to the side of the bridge."

"They were on a bridge?"

"Yes, the Waterloo Bridge north of Culpeper here in Virginia." Alex's heart leaped. *Waterloo!* Constance, continued, "Nabulio, my husband shot him with that hidden rifle."

"And," Alex offered trembling, and dying inside. She felt her own life beginning to trickle out of her. She repeated, herself, "And, Nabulio was left standing?"

"He was, but your husband, was only wounded."

"What?" Alexandria said hoping for the best.

"Nabulio took dead aim at him, again, but it was this gun that went off." She held up the revolver that she had in her satchel. I fired the shot that killed him." Alexandria couldn't believe here ears. He heart seemed to have stopped. She looked at the gun that was pointed at her heart. Somehow she mustered, "You killed my husband? You did it, you killed, him? How could you, why, to protect that animal, your husband?" Alex crumbled to the floor. Her body was quivering out of control, "and, now you come here to kill me, too. Do it, do, it quickly! Oh my Lord, do it quickly; my baby; my poor baby!" He voice tailed off, nevertheless she mumbled over and over again, "My poor baby…"

"No," Constance scrambled to the floor, and cradled this poor woman, this stranger, "No," she said, lifting Alexandria, head and face up to her own face. Tears flooded from both women, "Oh, no, not you, I'm not going to kill you, poor child" She waited a couple of seconds, it was going to be so hard to say it, "I, I, I, killed my husband Max, or Nabulio. I discharged this weapon and killed the AK killer." She fell on top of Alex, and continued, panting, gulping for air, and refuge. Her voice was shaking miserably, so badly that Alexandria could hardly make out what she was saying. "I could not let him kill anymore, seven was enough? Your husband was only doing his job. But, I cannot live with this. I hold within me his child, Napoléon's child. I cannot let him grow up to this legacy. He must never know his father and I cannot live with this pain." She too was uncontrollable now. She quivered! She shook and she reeled.

Alex put her hand on the hysterical woman. He body wreathed, rocked, back and forth, to and fro. Alex tried to talk, but Constance didn't let her. "Shush, poor woman," Constance babbled though a flood of her own tears, "your husband is alive, he was only slightly wounded. I rushed him to the hospital, and then I quickly slipped away and came directly here. Peace to you and your husband, and to your child, I bid, farewell." She then said but one last sentence, "But I must kill two more times to protect my child from his horrible history, his legacy." With that, she then ran from the house, and out on to their frozen grass. She then pushed the revolver to her temple and pulled the trigger, firing but one shot that killed her and her baby instantly. The fetus was far too small to survive; he stayed within the mother to his grave and her grave.

The noise took Alex's breath away. The blood bath was over. Justice had been served, or had it? Alexandria held her body. She felt something churn within her. Something was going very wrong. She heaved. It was living hell.

CHAPTER 60—TODAY AND THE FUTURE
THE PAPERS. THE AWARD. HIS NAME.

Constance had given Alexandria her hand written last Will and Testament. Of the multi millions they—Max and Constance—had, each of the seven women slaughtered: Carolyn Ann Nowicki, Jessica June Andersen, Yan Bi, Whisper Katharine Ulrich, Labella Lucille Litchfield, Sissy Sue Isaacs and her cousin Samantha Overhang, each—well, their parents, anyway—were each to received one tenth of the total sum, after taxes, if any. She left Erick Parker and April Pinkerton a trust fund to take care of all their medical bills for the rest of his life. They also were to receive one half of an equal amount of cash that of each of the butchered women's relatives were to receive.

Arthur and Alexandria, Wellesley also received one tenth, combined. Constance also left to her parents a half million dollars, and the remainder of the money went to a profilers association to study tendencies of Serial Killers. It was a rather well thought out Last Will and Testament from a woman who was about to commit double suicide at the time.

The document held up in court. There wasn't any heir to either of the deceased, except Constance's parents, and they had no reason to challenge it. Thirteen months after Constance's death, Mr. and Mrs. Arthur Wellesley received a check, for $2,299,521.82. By that time, Arthur had already left the police department, and was enrolled in Forensic Science at Old Dominion. The Wellesley's had been living on Alexandria's school paycheck. Together they had twelve thousand in the bank, so once baby Ashley was born, Alex took leave, and they were surviving on the paltry twelve thousand, and it was dwindling, fast. So when the check for 2 million arrived, life was bliss.

Arthur finished school, and became a teacher of Forensic Science at the University of Maine, at Presque Isle, Maine (U.M.P.I). Alexandria gave up her teaching and dedicated her life to her husband and their three children, Ashley Sue, Colleen Shay, and Arthur Blake.

Nabulio was never spoken of in their household; Constance was, often spoken of, and most fondly thought of. She, too, was a victim. They thought of her as a woman of great courage. She held honor in the Wellesley household.

Arthur and Alex retired on a small farm in Aroostook County, Maine. They were a quite people! A good, people! Until he died, Arthur had dreams—off and on—of slaughtered women, and what that monster had done to them. He felt guilty. He wrote a book about it. He called it *Napoléon's Revenge*!

At sixty-six he told his wife he wanted to take her out to dinner. He said "Grab some clothing for a couple of days. He grabbed their passports, too. They drove to Norfolk, Virginia and had dinner at the Blue Hippo! From there they traveled to Europe, England. They went to the place of his heritage, and he wept when he saw the statue of Napoléon Bonaparte; Wellington's pride and joy of honor; a statue that in such a strange way caused the death of seven people and one fetus by the hand of the statue's ancestry.

A caretaker of the facility stepped up to Arthur. "Are you all right, Sir?" Aged, Arthur nodded, yes. They chatted for a bit. At length, the caretaker asked for his name, Wellsy beamed with great pride, saying, "I am heir to the Duke of Wellington, my name is Arthur Wellington Wellesley!" No man in all of history had ever been so humble and so proud to state his name in this facility which he considered almost sacred. That was his legacy! He was, after all, of Royal English decent!

Alex spoke up. "My husband has brought a gift to leave at this wonderful place. She handed the small suitcase to the caretaker. They happily accepted the Wellington family bible.

* * * * *

On his death bed, Arthur offered to his devoted wife, "Soon I will know if God blames me fore those five lost women killed so many years, ago."

"No, good husband," she returned, "You have carried the weight of that burden for too long, already; God will soon release you from that burden." She then cried a woman's tears. He passed a moment, later.